DENYS JOHNSON-DAVIES

The Anchor Book of Modern Arabic Fiction

Denys Johnson-Davies, "the leading Arabic-English translator of our time" according to Edward Said, has translated
more than twenty-five volumes of short stories, novels,
plays, and poetry, and was the first to translate the work
of Nobel laureate Naguib Mahfouz. He is also interested
in Islamic studies and is co-translator of three volumes of
Prophetic Hadith. Recently he has written a number of
children's books adapted from traditional Arabic sources,
and a collection of his own short stories, *Fate of a Prisoner*,
was published in 1999. Born in Canada, he grew up in
Sudan and East Africa and now divides his time between
Marrakesh and Cairo.

The Anchor Book of
Modern
Arabic Fiction

Edited by

DENYS JOHNSON-DAVIES

ANCHOR BOOKS
A Division of Random House, Inc.
New York

AN ANCHOR BOOKS ORIGINAL, OCTOBER 2006

Copyright © 2006 by The American University in Cairo Press

All rights reserved. Published in the United States by
Anchor Books, a division of Random House, Inc., New York,
and in Canada by Random House of Canada Limited, Toronto.
Published simultaneously in hardcover in Egypt by
The American University in Cairo Press,
Cairo and New York.

Library of Congress Cataloging-in-Publication Data
The Anchor book of modern Arabic fiction / edited by
Denys Johnson-Davies.
p. cm.
1. Arabic fiction—Translations into English.
I. Johnson-Davies, Denys.
PJ7694.E8A53   2006
892.7'3608—dc22   2006043980

Anchor ISBN-10: 1-4000-7976-4
Anchor ISBN-13: 978-1-4000-7976-6

Book design by Rebecca Aidlin

www.anchorbooks.com

Printed in the United States of America
10 9 8 7 6 5 4 3

Contents

v

Introduction

This anthology of modern Arabic novel-writing and short stories in English translation includes the work of seventy-nine writers from fourteen countries, from Morocco in the west to Iraq in the east.

Readers may be surprised to find the work of a writer from Yemen, for example, alongside that of one from Tunisia. Can it be that both writers are employing the same language? How is it that classical Arabic has remained virtually unchanged over the years and continues to be the language of short stories and novels and newspapers throughout the Arab world? How is it that Arabic did not follow the way of Latin and give birth to a whole litter of different yet related languages? The answer is that classical Arabic as written is the language in which the Holy Qur'an was revealed, and Muslims have therefore been reluctant to allow changes to it. The advantages are obvious: with a knowledge of the written language you can read the daily paper in Casablanca or Baghdad, and hold a conversation with an educated Arab no matter how distant his native country happens to be. It is only the hapless illiterate peasant of Morocco who, finding himself suddenly transported to Iraq, would be as much at sea as he would be in the streets of London.

For the writer, the natural choice is to employ only the written language. Some writers—the Egyptian Yusuf Idris, for example—use the written language for the narrative parts of their writing and the colloquial for the dialogue. This can sometimes create difficulties for the reader who is not familiar with the particular colloquial dialect. I recently started to read a novel by an Iraqi writer I admire and found myself faced with whole sections of dialogue whose meaning I had to guess at. In rare cases, both short stories and entire novels have been written wholly in the spoken language, and recently—perhaps to show that the spoken language possesses such potential—a translation of Shakespeare's *Othello* in colloquial Egyptian Arabic was published.

Most writers, however, avoid the colloquial altogether. I recollect arguing many years ago the written/spoken case with the Egyptian Nobel laureate Naguib Mahfouz, who writes his dialogue in a simplified form of the written language. He pointed out the advantages of a text that could be read from one end of the Arab world to the other, and ended up suggesting that when reading such dialogue, Egyptian readers would automatically perform in their minds the necessary minor changes to render it into the colloquial. At least for the moment, as the instrument for the writing of literature, the classical language reigns supreme.

In the West, modern fiction was a natural extension of a literature that already existed. The situation in the Arab world was different: after the great flowering of classical Arabic literature between the seventh and fifteenth centuries, there followed a long period of cultural sterility. It thus happened that modern Arabic fiction emerged, not through the development of a literature that already existed, but as a result of Arabs coming into cultural contact with the West for the first time some hundred or more years ago.

From reading the literatures of the West, it was but a step to translating them, and the next step was to produce original creative works. The birth of the Arabic novel is dated to 1929, with the second (and more successful) printing of *Zaynab* by Muhammad Husayn Haykal.

But many were the prejudices that had to be overcome. The idea of an author creating characters and making them inhabit worlds of his creation not only was foreign to the Muslim Arab mind but was even regarded as almost unacceptable. Take, for example, the ever-entertaining stories of *The Thousand and One Nights*. This anonymous work, so esteemed throughout the world as a masterpiece of imaginative literature, remains for most Arabs a work unworthy of serious consideration. Arab men of letters have long looked askance at the extravagances of *The Arabian Nights*, as the book is better known in the West, finding them suitable only for minds incapable of appreciating other forms of literature, and grudgingly admitting that the stories might have some merit only when the outside world lavished praise on them. Had *The Arabian Nights* been held in higher regard by the Arabs themselves, it might well have given rise to a modern Arabic literature before Western literature made its mark.

I remember in the very early days reading the work of a young writer of short stories and feeling that he possessed talent. To my mind, nobody was in a better position to help him get published than Mahmoud Teymour, regarded as the pioneer of the Arabic short story. On one of the occasions when I met up with Mahmoud Teymour at his favorite café, I handed him one of the stories. I was taken aback at a subsequent meeting when he handed the story back to me rather brusquely, observing that certain subjects were not suitable for literature—in this case the description of a donkey urinating as it made its way along a dusty track. Although Arabic literature has come a long way since then, much that is readily acceptable in the West can still sometimes find fault with the religious authorities. In the West our sacred cows have long been slaughtered.

Even so, it has taken a long time for the West to begin to acknowledge the new Arabic literature. Sir Hamilton Gibb, professor of Arabic at Oxford University and one of the few orientalists to have taken an interest in the modern literary renaissance, summed up his views in the 1963 revised edition of his *Arabic Literature*: "All of these productions, however, short stories, novels and plays, remain bounded by the horizons and conventions of the Arab World; when translated into other languages they are often more interesting as social documents than as literary achievements." It was not an altogether fair judgment, resulting perhaps from inadequate reading of the literature available or from the wholly academic approach that had for so long been brought to the study of oriental languages. It should be appreciated that up until very recently Arabic was studied in the West as a dead language, much like Latin and Greek. The small band of Arabists were happier surrounded by piles of dictionaries, dealing with a poem written in pre-Islamic times, than they were with a modern short story.

It was in Egypt in particular that the foundations were laid for a renaissance of Arabic literature. In the middle years of the twentieth century, the country was fortunate in having a small group of talented men of letters who were open to trying their hands at the new genres of writing that had been introduced. Among them were the Teymour brothers, who were pioneers in the realm of the short story. Also noteworthy as a writer of short stories, and more important as the author of the seminal novella *The Lamp of Umm Hashim*, was Yahya Hakki, a diplomat and lawyer who had lived abroad and knew several foreign languages; he also contributed to a new movement through his imaginative editing of a magazine that encouraged young writers. Tawfik al-Hakim was a figure of great influence. He had studied law in Paris but decided to devote his talents to literature. Almost single-handedly he brought into being an Egyptian theater, not to mention contributing at least one masterpiece in the area of the novel. Another writer, primarily of short stories, was Yusuf Idris, a doctor who abandoned medicine for writing and who, like no one before him, wrote from deep within the Egyptian ethos. Yusuf Idris also showed that the rich spoken language of Egypt was not to be despised and could be employed as an effective tool in the armory of the modern Arab writer of fiction.

Over much of this formative period there presided the figure of that remarkable man of letters, Taha Hussein, who, blind from early childhood, occupied various official positions in Egypt, including that of minister of culture. He founded and edited an influential magazine that introduced its readers to the writings of such literary figures of the time as T. S. Eliot, William Faulkner, Samuel Beckett, and Albert Camus. He also contributed to the Arab literary renaissance with several of his own writings, including critical works that shed fresh light on the literature of the past and an autobiography of rare accomplishment.

This renaissance in Arabic literature was not confined to Egypt. In such countries as Syria, Iraq, and Lebanon, the new genres of writing were being practiced with success. In the countries of North

Africa, where Arabic was having to compete in literature, as in the affairs of daily life, with the language of the occupying power, an Arabic renaissance was being slowly achieved. Sudan, too, was soon to give to the modern movement a writer of singular talent in Tayeb Salih.

It might be said that the achievements of modern Arabic literature were properly recognized only as recently as 1988, when Naguib Mahfouz became the first Arab writer to be awarded the Nobel Prize in literature. That the Nobel committee could come to such a decision was made possible by the existence at that date of a fair representation of modern Arabic literature in English and French translations, languages familiar to the members of the committee.

The various translations of volumes of short stories and the occasional novel invariably came out from small, specialized publishers, often under a university imprint, and were aimed in the main at students of Arabic. I myself, back in 1947, had published—at my own expense in Cairo—the first book of short stories translated from Arabic, *Tales from Egyptian Life*, by Mahmoud Teymour. Around this time I had read Naguib Mahfouz's first realistic novel, *Midaq Alley*, and felt that it deserved to be translated. Having completed half of the translation, I recognized the futility of trying to find a publisher for a translation from a literature that was still unknown, and I consigned my efforts to a bottom drawer. Some years later Trevor Le Gassick translated the novel and found a publisher for it in Beirut—and *Midaq Alley* still holds its place among Mahfouz's favorite works.

While still teaching at Fuad al-Awwal University (now Cairo University) in the 1940s, I decided to collect material for a volume of short stories intended to give a picture of what had been achieved by the modern literary movement in the Arab world, and I was determined to find a London publisher. This proved more difficult than I had foreseen. It was only by one of those strange strokes of fortune that on one of my visits to London I happened to meet somebody who knew somebody at Oxford University Press. I was naturally delighted when the volume was accepted for publication by such a prestigious publisher, though I was surprised that it was accepted as a work of scholarship rather than for the literary merit of the stories. Its acceptance was also conditional upon the book having an introduction by a leading Arabist. Professor A. J. Arberry, at the time in ill health, and admittedly not an expert on the modern literary movement, kindly agreed to write it. The publication in 1967 of *Modern Arabic Short Stories*, though not in itself a success, nevertheless led to some sort of recognition. (The Naguib Mahfouz story that was included in the volume remained for some time the only example of modern Arabic writing to be included in the *Norton Anthology of World Masterpieces*.)

It was also through Oxford University Press that I met the editor of Heinemann's African Writers series, where several of my translations were published. The question came up about translations of Arab authors who were not African, giving rise to the Arab Authors series, in which more than twenty books were published. Failing to gain the support of the Arab world, Arab Authors was closed down, and mere months before Naguib Mahfouz was awarded the Nobel Prize, the American University in Cairo Press, which already had nine translations of Mahfouz's novels in print, bought the rights to the titles in the series. With the appointment of Mark Linz as director of the AUC Press, I suggested that the Press institute a yearly prize in Mahfouz's name for the best novel written in Arabic and that the prize include the translation of the work into English and its publication in Egypt and the United States. Mark Linz and I paid a visit to Naguib Mahfouz, who received the idea of a prize in his name with enthusiasm. The prize was set up in 1996 and is open not just to Egyptians but also to writers from all over the Arab world. Soon it was felt that, apart from the prizewinning book, there were other Arabic novels that deserved to be translated, and for the first time a fund was set up to finance the translation of such works. Until this time, modern Arabic literature had had to rely on the enthusiasm of a few competent translators to undertake translations of works they admired in the hope of finding favor with one of the few specialist publishers of Arabic fiction in translation. Not surprisingly, many worthwhile works, particularly if they were of daunting length or difficulty, had remained neglected. One sign that this new literature is at last poking its head out of the academic cupboard is the recent inclusion of Tayeb Salih's novel *Season of Migration to the North* in the Penguin Modern Classics series.

For the reader coming to Arabic literature for the first time, several hurdles present themselves. No doubt in the same way as early readers of the masterpieces of Russian literature boggled at characters with names like Raskolnikov, so too with Arabic literature one must accustom oneself to unpronounceable names. More important, though, is the unfamiliar social background: the foreign reader of fiction that has been written in Arabic is, as it were, eavesdropping on another culture. The Arab world is of course largely Muslim, and so the subject matter of Arabic fiction, not merely the setting, will inevitably differ from what the American or European reader is used to. Sex and love, for example, are handled differently in Arabic fiction than in Western fiction, for it should be remembered that Arab society is by and large conservative and conventional, with most marriages arranged, and sex outside of marriage regarded as sinful. When a writer oversteps the bounds as set by society, the work is often banned. This happened with Tayeb Salih's *Season of Migration to the North*. The Moroccan writer Mohamed Choukri's autobiographical *For Bread Alone*, translated by Paul Bowles, was banned in Egypt. And yet the recent novel *The Yacoubian Building*, by the previously unknown dentist Alaa Al Aswany, has escaped unscathed, even though it paints an unflattering picture of downtown Cairo, with at least one explicit gay sex scene. It quickly went into a second edition, unusual for an Arabic novel, and was immediately translated into English. It now has been made into a film.

Many Arab writers have no experience of the outside world or of a foreign language, and their reading of world literature is confined to works translated into Arabic. Thus a reader of Mohamed El-Bisatie's *A Last Glass of Tea* will find that every one of its twenty-four stories takes place in villages around Lake Manzala in the Nile Delta. But readers in the West have shown themselves capable of relating to cultures that they come across for the first time in fiction, especially when captured by a master's hand. The works of Naguib

Mahfouz, for example, have sold very well in the United States; they feature Egyptian characters who never venture beyond the boundaries of their native country (in the same way that Mahfouz himself has chosen to live between the cities of Cairo and Alexandria). Tayeb Salih's novella *The Wedding of Zein*, whose characters all inhabit the same Sudanese village, is a work of singular charm and appeal—Kingsley Amis admired the urbane technique that was brought to bear on such outwardly primitive material. The Libyan writer Ibrahim al-Koni, whose substantial body of work has only recently attracted the attention of translators, also focuses to good effect on a narrow and virtually unknown area of the Arab world—that of the Tuaregs of North Africa. It is a testament to the talents of these Arab writers that they are able to make the unfamiliar universally appealing.

After publishing an anthology of Egyptian short stories in 1978, I was interviewed about it by a woman from the BBC. She expressed surprise and disappointment that it contained not a single story by a woman, and that women hardly featured—except in a casual way—in the stories themselves. Of course she was right—and it is one of the West's criticisms of the Arab world today that women do not feature sufficiently in public life; it is also true that it has taken time for women to participate in the renaissance in Arabic literature. Today it is interesting to note that, after Mahfouz, the two Arab writers most widely read in the West are women: the Egyptian Nawal El Saadawi and the Lebanese Hanan al-Shaykh.

I've arranged the writers in this anthology not according to country—I prefer to treat the Arab world as the one cultural unit that it is—but in alphabetical order by family name (ignoring the definite article "al" or "el"). The names appear as the writers themselves have chosen to write them, rather than in accordance with academic rules of transliteration. A short introduction about each writer precedes one or more examples of his or her writing, either a complete short story or an excerpt from a novel.

—*Denys Johnson-Davies*

The Anchor Book of Modern Arabic Fiction

Ibrahim Abdel Meguid
(b. 1946)
EGYPT

Ibrahim Abdel Meguid has combined critical and creative writing throughout his literary career. His novel *The Other Place* was awarded the Naguib Mahfouz Medal for Literature and was published in translation by the American University in Cairo Press in 1997. His latest novel, also about Alexandria, is entitled *Birds of Amber*. He is a consultant for cultural matters at the Popular Culture Council. *No One Sleeps in Alexandria*, from which the extract below has been taken, describes how the Second World War affects the lives of an assortment of Egyptians who settled in Alexandria, Egypt's second city. Two of the main characters are a devout Muslim with peasant roots and a Copt; the novel looks at their unusual friendship and explores the delicate question of religious differences.

FROM *No One Sleeps in Alexandria*

During the past few weeks, the city of Alexandria had built a number of open shelters in the poorer neighborhoods, but the inhabitants use them to relieve themselves. That forced the municipality to assign policemen to guard the shelters, and stopped the building process. The military court in Alexandria, under the emergency law, held a session to try a poor girl who was practicing prostitution without a license. She was fined three Egyptian pounds. A house in Karmuz was raided for being an unlicensed brothel. When the police surrounded the house, the owner shouted, "Where's

Goebbels? Where's the Gestapo? I am Hitler!" But the valiant policemen were not fooled. They arrested him and gave him a sound
beating on the back of his neck. The newspapers received a great
number of letters asking about the beautiful Hollywood actress
Norma Shearer and whether she would remarry after the death of
her husband. The answer was in the affirmative, that the prospec-
tive husband was the actor George Raft, with whom she had a close
relationship while her husband was still alive. People were also wary
and cautious, as the Italians were a stone's throw away from Alexandria. That was why, when the air-raid sirens were heard several
times in the daytime, they realized immediately that these were no
longer drills, and when they saw anti-aircraft guns blasting away,
they were certain that the time of drills was gone.

Strict orders were given to drivers to paint their headlights dark
blue, after it was noticed that they had become lax about it in the
past few months. People were instructed to paint their windows
and to apply adhesive gauze strips vertically and horizontally to the
glass from inside so that it would not fly around if shattered. People
were also warned not to assemble on the streets during raids, and
that all vehicles must come to a stop and passengers get out of the
cars. Landlords were instructed to vacate the ground floors of their
buildings and to convert them to shelters for people without access
to the public shelters. People whose property was damaged as a result of the air raids were told to apply as soon as possible to the city
of Alexandria to get new building materials—wood, steel, and
cement—to repair the damage or to reinforce old buildings.

That night when Magd al-Din awoke, people heard the intermittent sound of the sirens and felt it was different from earlier
ones. It was accompanied by unusual scurrying about and panic;
there was more worry in their hearts. The daytime air raids the previous week had been shorter and had not caused any obvious casualties or damage. Tonight it seemed that real war would come to the
sky over Alexandria.

It was midnight and very hot. A few people walking on Ban
Street quickly went into the nearby houses and stood in the entrances. Two taxis stopped; one of the drivers did not leave his cab.

One of those standing in the entrance of a nearby house looked at him and invited him to come in to be safe, but he said, "If the house falls on top of me, will I live?" It seemed to make sense. Those standing in the entrance looked at each other, but they could not violate the civil defense regulations. Standing in the entrance of a house was safer than being out on the street in the open.

Even though the moon was not full that night, it was bigger than a crescent, and it lit up the streets and betrayed everyone.

Khawaga Dimitri, his wife, and his two daughters had gone downstairs to Bahi's empty room and turned off the light. Lula had also joined them. In the confusion, she did not think to wear something to cover her shoulders and arms. Her husband did not join her there. He was the solitary type. Besides, he lived on the first floor, so what good would it do him to move to another room? The truth was slightly different. As soon as the air-raid sirens sounded and the guns began blasting away, Lula shook with fear and moved closer to her husband, who hugged her tight and reached to take off her panties. She heard the footsteps and voices of Dimitri and his family and tried to break away from her husband, who held on and wanted to have sex right then and there. He thought that was the best way to overcome fear. She resisted him and also resisted her own desire, which lit up as soon as he touched her. She was thinking of what would happen if the sounds of their lovemaking were to reach the ears of Dimitri and his daughters. That was why as soon as she was able to break away from her husband, she dashed out and joined them in her long, white nightgown, her shoulders and arms lighting up the eyes of those standing in the dark.

Magd al-Din was guided in the dark by Dimitri's voice and did not let go of the hand of Zahra, who screamed as soon as she got in the room, "My God! Shawqiya is upstairs!" Magd al-Din had to go up to bring the little girl while Zahra stood with the others in Bahi's room.

The guns fell silent but the all-clear was not sounded. The silence lasted for a long time, and so did the people's patience. They all pricked up their ears to hear a slow, calm droning sound like rains coming from far away. The buzz grew in volume, as if swarms of killer bees were coming to the city, like a storm gathering on the horizon to overrun the desert, or armies of locusts homing in on green plants: *ZZZZZZZ*. That was sound of the German and Italian planes coming in for their targets in large formations, coming in close to the city and close to the ground. The sounds of bombs and explosions and the flashes of lightning passed quickly in front of the closed windows, penetrating the shutters and the glass.

"Open the windows so we'll know what's happening," Dimitri exclaimed. Magd al-Din was close to the window so he opened it. In front of them the night looked like daylight, white and red, and engulfed in a river of blue smoke. The sky was burning to the north and people on the opposite side of the street screamed as they saw the smoke. Magd al-Din, Dimitri, and the women watched the light come in from the north and burn bright into the south, like a sword brandished by a celestial warrior. Magd al-Din began to recite the beginning of Sura 36.

"*Yasin, By the Wise Quran, verily you are among those sent on a straight path, a revelation of the Mighty, the Merciful, to warn a people whose forefathers had not been warned, so they are heedless. Already the word has proved true of most of them, for they are not believers. Verily We have placed yokes around their necks to their chins so that their heads are forced up. And we have put a bar before them and a bar behind them and so We have covered them up so that they cannot see.* God Almighty has spoken the truth." Then he repeated, "*And We have put a bar before them and a bar behind them and so We have covered them up so that they cannot see.*" He repeated the verse, his voice growing louder, and as he swayed the moonlight revealed him to everyone, though he was completely oblivious.

"*And We have put a bar before them and a bar behind them and so We have covered them up so that they cannot see.*" Zahra began to repeat after him, and his voice kept getting louder. Sitt Maryam kept repeating, "We ask you God, the Father, lead us not into temptation but deliver us from evil," while Dimitri repeated with her, "We ask you God, Our Lord, lead us not into temptation, which we cannot endure because of our weakness. Give us help to avoid temptation, so that we might extinguish Satan's fiery arrows." His voice and Sitt Maryam's voice grew louder, "And deliver us from evil Satan by Jesus Christ, our Lord. Amen." Magd al-Din raised his voice even louder, "O God I ask you to lift every veil, to remove every barrier, to bring down every obstacle, to make easy every difficulty, and to open every door. O God, to whom I appeal and resort in hard times and in easy times, have mercy on me in my exile. Amen, Lord of All Creation." Magd al-Din, still swaying, began reciting the Quran again after his prayer. Dimitri continued his own prayers. The words intermingled in such a way that one could only make out that they were the prayers of sincere souls devoting every bit of their being to God, the Savior:

"By the wise Quran, . . ."

"O God, our Lord, . . ."

". . . on a straight path . . ."

". . . lead us not into temptation . . ."

". . . a revelation of the Mighty . . ."

". . . deliver us from evil . . ."

". . . whose forefathers had not been warned . . ."

". . . because of our weakness . . ."

". . . true of most of them, for they are not believers . . ."

". . . us from evil . . ."

". . . and we have put a bar before them . . ."

". . . that are Satan's . . ."

". . . that they cannot see."

Amen. Amen.

Voices come from the street, men, youths, frightened women, and crying children.

"Where's it coming from?"

"The searchlights or the bombs?"

"The bombs."

"From Mina al-Basal, Bab Sidra, and Karmuz."

"All the bombing is in Karmuz—the houses are shaking."

"The searchlights are not stopping. The guns in Kom al-Nadura, Kom al-Dikka, Maks, Qabbari, and Sidi Bishr are all going at the same time. More than a hundred planes!"

"The sky is full of the blue flies of Death!"

"Where has all of this been hiding, so that it appears all at once?"

"Khawaga Dimitri, get out, the houses are going to collapse," a voice came from outside.

"Who's that?"

"Ghaffara."

The voice was nearby and muffled. Ghaffara looked in on them from the window. The women had gathered in a corner close to each other. As soon as Camilla and Yvonne saw him, they screamed, "Mama!" They heard a muffled voice coming from behind the fez-mask that he had tied on his face.

"Have no fear, ladies. This is Ghaffara's anti-air-raid mask. Khawaga Dimitri, Sheikh Magd al-Din, please forgive me. I know you, and I was friends with the late Bahi. The houses in Karmuz are falling down and they are shaking here. You'd be better off coming out and standing in the street."

He was looking from behind his glass eye-pieces at Lula's arms and shoulders gleaming in the dark as if they had black covering in the daytime. Dimitri and Magd al-Din came out but the women did not.

Translated by Farouk Abdel Wahab

Mohammad Abdul-Wali
(1940–73)
YEMEN

Mohammad Abdul-Wali, one of the few Yemeni writers to have made a name for himself, was born in Ethiopia. His mother was Ethiopian and his father an emigré from North Yemen. In 1955 Abdul-Wali began studies in Cairo and developed Marxist sympathies. Expelled from Egypt, he returned to Yemen and then went to Moscow, where he learned Russian and attended a course in literature at the Gorki Institute. Having joined the diplomatic service of the newly created Yemen Arab Republic, he served in Moscow and later in Berlin. Back in Yemen, he was briefly director-general of aviation before falling out with the government and being imprisoned. He died in a plane crash. A collection of his stories, *They Die Strangers*, has been published in English translation.

Ya Khabiir

I was on my way back from Hayfan after spending two days on a law case at the governor's office. As usual, I didn't get any results. The legal procedures would continue, but nothing would be resolved.

It was late in the day. I was walking alone, many worries gnawing at me. I had already chewed more than two bundles of sharari qat, which tossed and turned in my stomach. Although I usually don't like walking alone at night, especially for long distances, I had quelled my fear this time and hit the road with my stick while continuing to chew qat. I felt zeal and hate building up inside me. The cool evening breeze, water flowing into small ponds by the side of the mountain, and the vision of the valley in the distance were combining to create sad and revolutionary tunes in my mind.

"Ya Khabiir! Ya Khabiir!"[1]

I turned and cursed the voice that broke my solitary thoughts. Then I trembled slightly when I saw a man. He ran after me barefooted, wearing a short sarong and carrying a gun. His eyes were red from chewing qat.

"Where are you going, Ya Khabiir?"

"To Qutabah," I answered, a sense of loathing filling me. As much as I hated death, I detested soldiers even more.

"Then we're on our way together!"

I continued on my way, followed by the soldier. All the thoughts in my head vanished; only the sound of the soldier's footsteps remained as they forcefully hit the earth. I turned back from time to time to look at him. Adrenaline began to rush through my blood. I

---

[1] An address of respect for a learned professional.

hate soldiers. I fear them and have never walked with any of them. Common stories that spread throughout our village about their savage and brutal violence now led me to believe that this man intended to kill me. What would prevent him from doing so? He might think that I had a lot of money. What would stop him from doing away with me? There was no one here to see us. The road was deserted. We had reached the middle of the mountain, and the nearest houses were far away at the bottom of the valley or at the top of the mountain. He had a gun while I had nothing but a thin stick.

The idea began to grow in my thoughts so much that I imagined seeing the soldier take his gun off his shoulder; I imagined the sound of his footsteps to be the sound his gun made as he cocked it to shoot. I stopped by the side of the road, pretending to pull out a thorn in my foot so that he would go ahead of me, but he stopped after a step or two and looked at me. I wished he would just go on, but he waited.

"Do you have a thorn?"

Then, as he looked up at the evening sky, he said thoughtfully, "It's a bit dark. You won't be able to see."

I nodded my head in agreement.

He walked ahead of me this time and I could hear him breathe, letting out a pained sigh from time to time. He tried to hum a sad Sanaa tune, but soon he stopped and, instead, resumed sighing.

He was tall and broad-shouldered, with a tribal manliness about him. He looked as though he could carry the mountain on those shoulders. He swung the gun as if it were a feather. The thud of his feet on the ground was so strong that I imagined the earth to cry painfully.

"Why don't you talk?"

"What do you want me to say?"

I was still afraid of him. I saw his head move as he put more qat in his mouth. From behind the clouds, the light of the moon crept softly. I heard the man's voice; it was simple and deep, with some harshness of the northern accent.

"Ya Khabiir, did you have a law case? My God, what's it with you people from Hujariyyah, that makes you love going to court? Any one of you who has two coins in his pocket files a lawsuit. Why can't you live in peace like the rest of God's creatures without such headaches?"

As he was talking, he scratched his head as if he were contemplating a very difficult problem, then continued. "Or do you think that there's justice only through the regional governor, and not through the local officials? Justice is dead; it was eaten by those with fat bellies. As for you, you civilians, you take a hundred or two hundred riyals and pour them right into the mouth of these fat bellies like bottomless pits. While *our* stomachs are empty, right?"

I couldn't answer him, for the last thing I expected him to talk about was justice, courts, and fat bellies. We civilians had come to see the soldiers as a force for repression and injustice. They were the ones who carried out the governor's orders. We Yemenis could never forget how the soldiers abused us.

But the soldier didn't wait for my answer. He sucked on the qat in his mouth and said, "You live here in Qutabah and I live in Hashid. There I have a home, a family, a wife and children, thank God. But we have no money, no land. The sheiks took our land from us, and we became soldiers trying to get an income. They said there was gold in Hujariyyah. We came here. But, I swear to God, there is nothing here but greed, looting, and envy. Everybody here wants to rob his brother, his friend. Yes, you may have money, but you have no honesty, no morals, no love or care; I swear if I died back home it would be much better. At least then I would be near my wife and children. True, we would still be looking for work and be hungry. But we wouldn't be filing lawsuits against each other. Those fat bellies only got fat with your money."

As I neared him I asked, "Okay, but why do you loot and steal from people?"

He sighed deeply and said, "Loot and rob people? Not all soldiers loot and steal, Ya Khabiir. But, I say that whoever does loot and steal is no worse than the governor. You give the governor one hundred riyals under the table, but if you give a soldier one riyal, you say the soldiers looted and robbed you. Look, the soldier is no different from you; another governor steals from him in his own hometown, both justly and unjustly."

He stopped and looked at the sky; then he unloaded his gun from his shoulder and turned to me. He said, "It's evening, time for the evening prayer. Will you be the imam and lead the prayer?"

"No, you lead the prayer."

Translated by Abubaker Bagader and Deborah Akers

Yahya Taher Abdullah
(1942–81)
EGYPT

Yahya Taher Abdullah was born in Karnak near Luxor in Upper Egypt. He had little formal education but came to be regarded early on as one of the most promising of the younger generation of writers. He published three collections of short stories and one novella. His collection *The Mountain of Green Tea* has been published in English translation. Abdullah died in a car crash.

Rhythms in Slow Time

Coiling up his little body, the child passed through an opening in the wall of the central courtyard and reached the enclosed space that was connected with the house on its east side.

A while ago the crazy north wind had blown, carrying away sesame and cotton twigs from the roofs of the houses and gathering up the dead leaves from the branches of mulberry, tamarisk and *lebbek* trees, and now, under the walls, the leaves and dried twigs had come to rest. A dust-coloured donkey and two black goats, and over there at the far end was a small hutch, the chicken house.

The child was content, nobody was watching him. Squatting on all fours, he put his small hand through the narrow aperture.

Inside the hutch, the small hand was fumbling about in the darkness and a small body was dodging the hand: the squawks were uninterrupted though stifled, then came the desperate beating of the two wings of a living body.

Suddenly, there burst out from the aperture a white hen; with a leap it slipped out of the boy's hand, quickly crossed the floor of the enclosed space and made towards the east side; with three thrusts of its white wings it leapt upwards, jumping from the wall opening to the spacious central courtyard.

Over there lay the filled water jars on the mud roof, and a large jar for storing water sat on a three-legged stand: the outer surface of the storage jar was green, the colour of the grasses that grow on the verges of waterways.

The white hen had spread its white wings, carrying its feet quickly, wildly, from the ground into the air, from the air to the ground, scattering dust behind it—and suddenly it disappeared.

A white aeroplane ran along the ground of the small airport, behind it a white ribbon of smoke, and suddenly the aeroplane flew off to some unknown land.

In the wide open space were discs of dough on wooden boards awaiting the sun veiled behind the mist of the wintry day, and the mother was looking at her two daughters and the discs of dough.

A moment ago the dust was asleep on the surface of the central courtyard because of the water sprinkled by the youngest of the girls, and now five handfuls of dust lay on the discs of dough, scooped up by the palm of a child from the quantity of dust that lay on the surface of the central courtyard.

The mother grasped hold of the small boy and angrily set about beating him with her hand on his backside.

The cat, which had arched its back and jumped onto a wooden box without a lid when the white hen had run off, still had its back arched, fearful, ready for an approaching enemy, its eyes ablaze, their colour deeply black, deeply gleaming. The cat still stood on the edge of the box.

The child was still weeping; he had screwed up his face and had blown his nose so that a skein of snot hung down from it. "Dirty," said the mother. The child replied, frowning, still crying: "I'll kill it." Said the mother in a resolute tone of voice that did not frighten the child: "I'll kill *you*." The child grasped the sleeve of his shirt and, gathering it up in his small hand, wiped the snot from his nose.

On the rope fastened by two nails to the east and west walls, a shirt that the child had taken off that morning dangled by its two sleeves; traces of dried, mud-coloured snot were visible on it.

The mother looked at his sparkling black eyes (the well is black, hollow, deep and full of secrets and terror) while the boy moved away from the courtyard, again crying. He said: "O Lord, give me peace of you." Said the mother: "Don't go over there."

The cat leapt down from the box to the ground of the central courtyard. Bereft of its misgivings, it felt ashamed of its sensation of danger as it introduced its head into the opening in the wooden box: the two small black cats were awaiting it, also its grand-daughter, the grey cat. Resting its supple body, it turned over onto its right side, shook its nipples and presented them to its little ones to suck at.

In front of the house lay a black dog. The child, still crying, picked up a large stone and struck the dog. The dog jumped up and barked. The child stopped crying and looked at the vast expanse in front of the house. The branches of the nearby *nabk* tree looked like an uneasily suspended mist. So did it appear in the sparse light of day, while the white hen under the trunk seemed very small, coming and going in confusion as it went on looking for somewhere safe to lay, and he would get hold of the egg and boil it and eat it or he might go to the mill and swop the egg for three pieces of sugar-cane.

The youngest of the girls attended to sprinkling the courtyard with water so that the dust would again abate. She was wearing a dress of coarse printed cotton with large red and yellow flowers. The elder girl lit the kerosene lamp and hung it up in an aperture in the east wall.

The darkness thickened where the stars had disappeared from sight behind the black, tightly knit mist, and a savage silence had taken hold. (The frogs, retaining their right to be refractory, then set up a continuous croaking; the dogs too barked intermittently;

the female cats proclaimed to their toms their right to procreation.) The houses, the lanes, the date-palms and trees had merged, forming an intensely black mass.

In the riverside room, the mother's arm remained on the small child's chest, her palm exactly where his heart lay; alongside them lay the two girls, their breasts rising and falling in regular movement. The lamplight winked with the cool draught of air that penetrated through the solitary blocked-up aperture. On the bed opposite, the old man who was head of the household coughed and spat. From underneath the bed he took a water skin made of a rabbit's pelt filled with warm water; he drank a couple of mouthfuls, then, wrapping round his body a woolen waistband, he went back to sleep and to snore.

The fire had died down and its smoke was thick on the ceiling, which was supported by the trunks of date-palms. The air that penetrated through the aperture in the wall grew cooler; the aperture was blocked up with the cover of a wall diary. The diary had writing on it and pictures of people in military uniforms, also congratulation to the Egyptian people on their glorious army from the owner of the sweet factories who had sponsored the calendar.

The weather was steadily moving towards the coldness of morning. On top of the minaret of the large mosque there was someone watching the mist that had formed an arc, blanketing the houses and reaching to the cloud-covered horizon. Expanding his chest and blowing out ringlets of white vapour, he prepared to give the call to dawn prayers.

Translated by Denys Johnson-Davies

Leila Abouzeid
(b. 1950)
MOROCCO

Leila Abouzeid is one of the few Moroccan writers to have gained recognition in the English-speaking world. Her

works include the novel *The Last Chapter* and her autobiographical *Return to Childhood*. She has written about
women's struggle for justice and independence and, unlike
many of her compatriots, she writes in Arabic rather than in
French. The short story "The Discontented" is from *The
Year of the Elephant*, which includes the title novella and several short stories.

The Discontented

The official left the meeting room. In the hall one of the custodi-
ans walked toward him and stopped. The official stared at the familiar face before him. The two men embraced, each asking how
the other was and blaming one another for first breaking off the ties
of kinship.

"Let's go to your house," the official said. They quickly departed
in his luxury sedan. The official again inquired about his cousin's
news.

"My pay is very low," he replied. "The children are endlessly in
need of things, costs keep rising, and no one gives a damn about us."

"If only you hadn't left school," the official said, a note of cen-
sure in his voice.

"It was bad luck," the custodian answered bitterly. He scowled.
A long silence ensued. The official realized his mistake and regret-
ted his sharp words. The custodian, staring straight ahead through
the car's windshield, muttered to himself. "Fortune, my cousin,
lifted you to high office and dragged me to the ground, though you
were once as wretched as the rest of us."

They came to the outskirts of town where the government had
built housing for poor families. Directed by the custodian, the official stopped his car in front of a small house.

Inside, the official sat cross-legged in silence while the custodian
surreptitiously observed him. Despite his fine suit, he seemed at
home in the house. He looked down, where through holes in the

worn mat, the cement floor appeared. He was perspiring in the heat and sluggish air.

Outside, beyond the open door, lay a large vacant lot full of trash and the remnants of ruined shacks.

Children ran in, one after another. Swarming about him, they seemed to the official to be more numerous than they actually were. The small room spun around him in confusion.

"I wish the house were more suitable to your higher station," the official heard his cousin say after another long silence. He did not know how to respond for he knew the poorer man was comparing their two lives. The custodian busied himself with pouring tea into inexpensive glasses.

"Some people are doomed to menial work," he said as he finished.

"All work is honorable and never menial," the official replied, feeling uncomfortable.

The custodian pulled nervously on his thick mustache with his thumb and index finger, then pursed his lips.

"I'll find you a better job," the official said in a conciliatory tone.

He stood up to leave. Outside more children surrounded his car, and scurried away at his approach. As he opened the car door, he saw that they had scratched "Long live Morocco" on it with a sharp tool. Before leaving he gave his address to his cousin and suggested he contact him again.

Urged on by his wife, the custodian finally arranged to visit the official. But when he arrived at the latter's house, he felt intimidated by its grandeur. A European-style edifice in the middle of a green lawn, it was surrounded by rose beds and slender willow trees. He hesitated, then pressed the doorbell, and for a moment heard nothing in the deep silence but his own breathing. A servant opened the door and showed him into a spacious parlor containing an unimaginable assortment of furniture and objects. Dazzled, he gazed around the room, that first impression settling permanently in his mind. He wondered what sort of wood was on the walls, where the rugs and housewares had come from, and how much it had all cost.

Realizing that the roses in the glass vases were the only things with which he was familiar, he sneered inwardly at his own incredible ignorance.

The official greeted him and invited him to take a seat. He had found his cousin a job as a supervisor on a government farm outside Casablanca.

A supervisor? A government farm? Casablanca?

"But I know nothing about farming," he stammered.

"You have only to oversee operations and distribute wages," the official said. "You'll make twice what you're earning now, plus free housing, water, electricity, and all other living expenses. And you'll be surrounded by water, greenery, and fresh air. What do you think?"

The custodian did not answer. He tried to imagine himself supervising peasants from Doukkala and Chaouia. He rose to leave, saying he had a train to catch. His cousin said the new job would start on the first of the following month. At that, the custodian's anxiety grew. He forced a smile and hurried out of the house.

The first of the month came and the custodian drove off as usual on his motorcycle, roaring into the traffic, which soon swallowed him.

That same day, the official received a cable from his cousin. "I cannot accept your offer," it read, "as it would create difficulties in the children's education. Thank you anyway."

The official exploded in anger. "It's useless trying to help the man! He'll die as miserable as he lived!" His voice lowered. "And these are the men who blame the government for their wretched lives!"

"Some people are born to follow orders and others to give them," his assistant said, unaware that the two men were related.

The official wadded the telegram into a tight ball, then with a flick of his thumb tossed it into a wastebasket.

Translated by Barbara Parmenter

Yusuf Abu Rayya

(b. 1955)

EGYPT

Yusuf Abu Rayya was born in the town of Hihya in the Nile Delta. He studied journalism at Cairo University and has published several volumes of short stories. His novel *Wedding Night* was awarded the 2005 Naguib Mahfouz Medal for Literature.

Dreams Seen by a Blind Boy

It's a Friday and the blind boy is in the company of his mother on the road to the graveyards. In the graveyards are mourning women with grandfathers and fathers and mothers and husbands and sons in the earth.

In the Qur'an, which the blind boy has learnt, there is compassion for all.

His mother sits him down where the women want and he recites: "Say: He, Allah is One, Allah the Everlasting Refuge . . ." Then he recites: "Say: I take refuge with the Lord of mankind, the King of mankind . . ."

He receives bread, leavened and unleavened, and his mother doesn't take him back to the house until her baskets are filled. On other days his mother would take him in the mornings to the Sheikh, where he would recite, with the rest of the boys, verses from the Qur'an; he would hear too about the life of the Prophet and would learn that the Prophet was born a child like every other child and that he was poor and an orphan. When, though, he became a man he had said to his people: "Your gods are of stone, but Allah is the Light of the heavens and the earth," and he said to the slaves: "Men are equal like the teeth of a comb." He rode a strong horse, in

his hand a sword of fire, and he led them to where he killed ignorance and built for people a shining city.

The Sheikh, though, would strike him with the wide piece of
wood when he made a mistake in repeating things about the
Prophet's life. They were not in his mind as the Sheikh would have
liked but were down in the depths of his heart, aglow with soft and
joyous light. They would glow too during his night of dreams when
he would see the Prophet in his white robe riding on his white
horse, in his hand the green standard and the gleaming sword. And
he, the young blind child, would see, between the horse's legs, the
light and the horse's shadow on the yellow sand, and he would
stretch out his little hand wanting to grasp the standard with the
three stars, or the sword that sparkled in the sunlight.

At other times he would see himself wearing a flowing robe, on
his head a red tarboosh with a black tassel, standing on the high
pulpit, the people wide-eyed in front of him, saying things to them
that illuminated their hearts, that shed green light for them on their
paths.

Then he is standing in the prayer niche, decorated with designs
and Qur'anic verses, with the people behind him, rising to their feet
as he rises, bowing in prayer as he bows. He says: "Not of those You
are angry against, nor of those that are astray." And with the voice
of a single strong man they reply: "Amen."

At last he awakes, opens his eyes and finds that they are still looking at everlasting darkness.

Benumbed by the night's dream, he gets up and performs his
ablutions. Feeling with his stick along the ground, he makes his way
to the nearby mosque, where he stands behind the Imam and in-
tones with the people: "Amen." When the sun shines and the
people are moving about in the streets, his mother takes him to the
Sheikh, where he slips in between the other boys, recites verses from
the Qur'an and listens to the life of the Prophet. On Fridays he recites to the dead so that the baskets may be filled with leavened and
unleavened bread.

Translated by Denys Johnson-Davies

Idris Ali
(b. 1940)

EGYPT

Idris Ali is a Nubian from southern Egypt who studied at al-Azhar University in Cairo. He is the author of three collections of short stories and five novels, one of which, *Dongola*, was published in English translation in 1998. It tells of the tragedy of the flooding of great parts of Nubia to make way for the Aswan Dam. The main characters are Awad Shalali, who, like many Nubian men, has left his native land to make a living elsewhere; his mother; and his young wife, Halima, who, in the extract that follows, desperately awaits his return.

FROM *Dongola*

By January first, three years after Awad Shalali had left, she had received no further letter nor any telegram giving the date of his arrival, and yet she waited for him, as if his arrival were a certainty. The Temperature of her readiness rose. She incensed the house and perfumed the water jug, swept the whole house, and prepared some fowl and sacrificial animals. She dyed herself with henna, put on perfume, and dressed in her most expensive silk, so that she looked like a fabulous bride. She got to the station before everyone else, with a tray of popcorn and dates. A question ran through the village: Who was Halima waiting for? Hushia al-Nur thought this over in her mistrustful mind, and thought, *God help us.* Everyone had the same thought, and questioned her sanity. Otherwise, what could explain all this fevered activity to meet a man who was still far away? The train had whistled and arrived, let off its passengers, and taken its dreams on to Aswan, and Halima still stood there dazed, until a woman spoke to her.

"The train is gone, Halima."

"Train?"

"He'll arrive safe and sound tomorrow."

"Tomorrow?"

"God give you patience."

"Patience?"

She left the station in despair, utterly shattered, and went to the telegraph office.

"Yazid Effendi, is there any news?"

"Bless you, Cousin."

"Any telegram from the man?"

"Who's the man?"

"The effendi, Hushia's son."

"What, aren't I the only man?"

"All you do is joke."

"You should greet me first, Halima."

"I swear by the Prophet's tomb, you are stupid."

"It is a duty to greet people, by God."

His hand, offered through the little window, was an open invitation to friendship and innocent affection, but his welcoming smile did not hide predator's fangs like those of Hamad Tawfiq. He was just a shy teenager. She was not afraid of him, even though he was one of her pursuers, because his amorous efforts never made it farther than the telegraph office. But a question perplexed her: did he do this with all the women who came in here, or was she the only one? Whatever the case, she would never respond to his overtures while she was married to another man. He might be the one she wanted, though, if she became free through a divorce. There was nothing wrong with keeping him ready for the day he was needed. She smiled and gave him her hand. He clasped it between his two hot, trembling palms. She loved his heat, and her body quivered slightly. She felt uncomfortable and withdrew her hand. She left, adjusting her clothing. She almost fell; her heart pounded with joy and fear.

Translated by Peter Theroux

Daisy Al-Amir
(b. 1935)
IRAQ

Daisy Al-Amir is a well-known Iraqi writer of short stories. She lived for many years outside Iraq, notably for a long period of time in Lebanon as a member of Iraq's diplomatic mission in Beirut, and, more recently, in the United States. She now lives in Beirut. Her stories are bleakly economical. "The Doctor's Prescription" is from her collection *The Waiting List*.

The Doctor's Prescription

She asked the pharmacist for some tranquilizers, and he wanted to know whether she had a doctor's prescription. The question surprised her, since she wasn't requesting sleeping pills. He understood her request, he replied, but a prescription was also necessary for tranquilizers.

She pleaded with him: the tranquilizers could do no harm, she said, and she had gotten used to them. He responded that it wasn't a question of what she was used to, there were dangers involved.

"Do you mean suicide?" she interrupted.

"Not exactly," he replied, "but there are dangers."

She asked him what types of tranquilizers he had in stock. He said he had only one kind and mentioned its name. It was a tranquilizer with a very limited effect, perhaps not even enough to help calm her hypertension, yet he worried that people might use it to kill themselves.

Do you realize, she asked, that if someone wanted to commit suicide with this tranquilizer, he would have to swallow hundreds of pills? That means dozens of bottles. It would take hours to swallow them, and an enormous amount of water. All that liquid would upset the stomach, and the long time needed to take the pills would provide an opportunity to reconsider the death wish. The person would have to be determined in this matter, since the pills would require even more time to take effect, and while that was happening the person might begin to despair of rushing too quickly to depart this life. One could go out like this any time, but one wouldn't be able to bring back life. Thinking over the reasons that compelled attempting suicide, one would see that they weren't as important as thought, and one might consider another chance and seeing if one could cope with the problems.

As this person began to feel drowsy, the instinct for self-preservation would take hold and she would think that she'd made a mistake, that life is more powerful. She'd try to call for help and drag herself to the nearest window or door to shout, so people would hear . . . One would open her eyes in the hospital, stomach having been pumped, an intravenous feeder attached to an arm, and friends all around. One would repent, and life would seem beautiful after nearly being lost.

So you see, such mild tranquilizers are hardly appropriate for suicide.

"With an intelligent woman like yourself," the pharmacist says, "who thinks through all these stages, I suppose there's no concern about . . ."

"About any of the dangers you're thinking about," she answered. He gave her one bottle of pills. She thanked him and left.

At the second pharmacy she needed to repeat the story.

At the third pharmacy she was given a bottle before finishing the story.

At the fourth, a few sentences sufficed, and so on at the fifth, sixth, and all the others.

The newspapers reported that a woman was found dead in her bed. On the table next to her were a number of empty sleeping pill bottles and a note. "I came into this life without anyone consulting me," the note read, "but life never understood me, so I've decided to end it after sufficiently convincing myself that I can no longer endure this lack of understanding between us. This decision to end my life is mine alone."

As people read the news and looked at the smiling face in the photograph they shook their heads in sorrow. "Poor thing. She killed herself in a moment of despair," said some. "It seems that the one she loved wasn't faithful to her," said others. Psychiatrists contended that she was in full control of her senses when she made the decision to commit suicide. The pharmacists, after recognizing her picture in the papers, told no one of her conversations with them.

"We all tried to help her," her mother kept repeating between tears.

She did not take her secret with her, and yet no one said, "How much she loved life!"

Translated by Barbara Parmenter

Radwa Ashour
(b. 1946)
EGYPT

Radwa Ashour is an Egyptian novelist, critic, and professor of English literature at Ain Shams University in Cairo. In 2003 her novel *Granada*, the first in a trilogy, was published in English translation. It tells the story of a Muslim family living in Granada in 1492 at the time of the city's fall to Spain's Christian rulers. "I Saw the Date-Palms" is from the anthology *My Grandmother's Cactus: Stories by Egyptian Women*, edited and translated by Marilyn Booth.

I Saw the Date-Palms

It had been a long winter and I could make myself wait no longer. I put on my old overcoat, wound my woollen scarf round my head and went outside. After passing through several streets I reached the trees. I looked them over, checking each one closely. When my eyes found nothing on the dry boughs, I reached out to run my hand along the branches, probing them with care. Sometimes my hands would stop and my heartbeat would quicken; then I would discover that what I felt was not what I was looking for but just a knot on a dried-out branch. I was confident, though, that I would find them—the stiff, tiny, globular buds.

The colour deceives you at first. You think it is nothing, but if you look carefully you will find that it is a bud. Its greyness is not really grey, nor is its dry touch really dryness. If you go on watching it, and if you wait, it will enlarge and open, revealing its hidden greenness to you.

I was searching for just such a bud when one of my colleagues caught sight of me.

"Fawzia," he called, "what are you doing out in the street in this accursed cold, when everyone else is indoors at home?"

"I'm searching for buds," I replied.

"God, Fawzia, you're mad!"

He was joking. I remember clearly the laughing tone in his voice and the warm, friendly look in his eyes.

And at the end of a day spent searching I returned home unsuccessful, asking myself, "How long will it be?" It was then that I remembered the cactus plant which my aunt Fatima had brought me from our home town. I had set it next to the front door and forgotten all about it. When I remembered it, I told myself that it must have died, for I had not watered it in several months. I went to have a look at it anyway. The soil had dried out completely, cracking and becoming the colour of blond coffee beans. The stem was dry and yellowish, although it showed new growth. The needle-edged blades were unchanged: rising broadly where they separated from the trunk, they became thin and pointed as they opened and arched downwards. My aunt's cactus stood straight and green on its stalk. I watered it.

I came to love planting and I began to plant things—in a clay pot, in an empty tin, in a glass. Anything that would do for planting I filled with earth. At the proper depth, I'd implant a fruit stone or infix a green shoot, and then I would water the soil.

In those days no one said I was insane. But later they said so—on the day they brought me news of my cousin's death.

"Your cousin has died, Fawzia."

"Died?"

I asked them to wait so that I could accompany them to offer my condolences. They saw me squat before them, fill an empty tin with soil and fix a sweet basil shoot within. I steadied it by pressing my fist down repeatedly on the dirt so that it would hold the shoot fast, embracing it until soil and shoot were intertwined. I inundated it with water.

"Now we can go," I said.

I saw them slapping their palms together in pity, they found my behaviour so strange—and I heard them saying, "Fawzia has gone mad—may God compensate us for her madness!" I didn't understand why they had said this, and I was even more surprised when I heard one of them whisper, "Fawzia is imitating rich folk who decorate their homes with plants!"

I was surprised because the speaker is from our village, and he knows. We are peasants. It is true that the women of our Upper Egyptian family do not go out into the fields to till the soil, but farming is their life. They open their eyes upon farming, and—at the moment of death—close their eyes upon it too. And I remember that our house in the village had a mint plant on its roof; inside there was a cactus and at the door a date-palm. I remember that my father—God rest his soul—used to say that the date-palm is a blessed tree; with it the Lord graced His servants, and by mentioning it in the Qur'an He bestowed honour upon it. And my father said that the Prophet—God's blessings be upon him—said: "Honour your paternal aunts the date-palms." And that he called them our "paternal aunts" because they were created from the extra clay left over after the creation of Adam, and that they resemble human beings. They were created male and female, tall and straight of stature, palm cores growing on their tops like the brain of a human being in his head. Should evil afflict that core, the date-palm would perish.

My father used to entrust the date-palms to my brother's care, just as my mother charged me every dawn (as she gave me her daily instructions for sweeping the house and feeding the chickens) with watering the mint plant. Whenever I forgot—and I was always in a hurry, since I did these daily chores before leaving for school—she got angry, and would raise her voice and scold me.

"Shame on you, my girl, this is a bad omen! May the Lord give your father long life and give our home prosperity."

But God did not extend either his life or hers. Even my two brothers departed, and I became—after moving to Cairo and settling here—like an orphaned branch severed from its tree. And it seemed I had forgotten the mint, the cactus, the date-palm and everything.

Then my aunt Fatima, my father's sister, came to visit me. She pressed me to her bosom, weeping over the ruination of our House, whose light had gone out and whose cactus plant had dried up. She restrained her tears and sat down cross-legged on the Assiuti rug to open the basket that she had brought with her.

"I brought you some bread I've baked and dates from your papa's palm-tree, and I broke off a branch from the cactus in our home so that you could have it."

As my aunt passed the cactus cutting across to me, she went on speaking, tears still in her eyes.

"The cactus in our house was a cutting that my mother broke off from her own plant the day I got married and moved to my husband's house. So this is from your grandmother's cactus, from your grandmother's grandmother's cactus. God bless you, Fawzia, my daughter, and make your home prosperous."

My aunt had reminded me. And when I remembered, I began to plant things. And people said I was insane.

At work, too, they whisper together behind my back. Once a colleague said to me, "Fawzia, look at your hands."

I understood that she was referring to the black lines under my fingernails. "This isn't filth," I said. "It's mud left over from my planting."

She patted me on the shoulder. "It isn't proper, not at all proper for a government employee."

I don't understand what offends my colleagues when I grow plants. The place where we work is gloomy and ancient. Bits of paint are always falling off the walls, spiders have woven their webs in the corners and insects have made their nests. And I am certain that rats have their lairs here. At evening they leave their dens, roaming all night among the offices with nothing to restrain them. Every day I thank God that they haven't yet chewed up any of the papers in the files in my custody (those old grey files ranged on wooden shelves that are worn half away, their original colour hard to fathom). And even the long rectangular space that extends along the façade of the building—we call this space the garden—is flooded by the overflow from the sewers. We can't even enter or leave the building without walking very cautiously along five adjacent stones that form a bridge to the doorstep.

I was not remiss with my colleagues. When I realized what the conditions were like where I work, I planted three shrubs of Indian jasmine at home and tended them carefully. When they had grown and the leaves were thick on their branches, I carried them to the office and placed them side by side on the building's only balcony. But my colleagues paid no attention to the jasmine's beauty, even when the bushes produced blossoms, although they did pay attention to the dirt under my fingernails.

At work they don't understand me, and in my neighbourhood, too, I heard them with my own ears talking about "mad Fawzia who throws herself on date stones as if they are golden guineas." My behaviour astonishes them, and theirs amazes me. When any of them eats a date and spits out the stone, he'll spit it so that it falls at a distance, or he spits it into his hand first and then tosses it away with a full swing of his arm so that it lands even further away. I run to pick it up and I hide it in my deep pocket. When I get home, I place it on a piece of dampened cotton and leave it for four or five days, tending it each day and following its progress as it swells and grows soft, until I can touch its freshness and I know that the time is near. Soon after, I bury it in soil and saturate it with water. And then I wait.

I have wished that my home had a lot of space; I have wished it were surrounded by ground that I could cultivate. It saddens me that my home consists of only one room and a single balcony which is so small and narrow that it doesn't even provide enough space for everything I grow. I used to put my flowerpots on the balcony wall but I stopped doing that because the children on my street kept throwing stones at them. The first time I found a flowerpot shattered and the shoot planted within broken, its leaves wilted, I thought of them, but I repeated to myself the proverb that says: "To think even a little evil of someone is a sin."

When the incident recurred my suspicions were confirmed, and even more so when the children began bothering me as I was coming home carrying a tin or two—large ones of the kind used to preserve white cheese or olives. Amm Mitwalli the grocer used to give them to me so that I could use them as planters. But when he realized that I wasn't buying perfumed soap or imported cheese in silver and gold wrappers he became irritated and would no longer give me the tins, despite my assurances to him that I can't buy these items from him, or from anyone else either, because they are expensive and my salary is meager.

Whenever Amm Mitwalli gave me the tins, the boys would walk behind me, chanting a processional for me, their voices like solemn chimes:

> *The madwoman's coming back*
> *Clutching a tin in her hands*
> *She's got no mind*
> *She's got no brains*
> *A* falso *brain and a mind of tin!*

Their behaviour grieved me; I felt a tightening in my throat and I wanted to cry. Instead, I leant over to pick up the first stone in my path and I hurled it in their direction, all the while swearing at them out loud.

On one of these occasions, Umm Sulayman—that heavy woman with the gold tooth—materialized suddenly before me. Hands on her ample hips, she blocked my way.

"I am sorry, Sitt Umm Sulayman, I didn't intend any harm, but your son Sulayman and the other boys were swearing at me and insulting me," I said to her in my own defence. "Also, Sitt Umm Sulayman, yesterday they broke the planter that I had put next to the front door."

Her laugh startled me but I went on, "Umm Sulayman, you consider yourself responsible for watching over Sulayman and protecting him, isn't that so? Consider me a mother too—I'm a mother of plants!"

Umm Sulayman wiggled her eyebrows and a raspy voice came scraping from her throat: "Congratulations on the birth of your *zar*', your plants, Umm Zar! May you have a long life and bear many more!"

She turned her back on me and walked away, resuming her fearful, high laughter.

I found no one to whom I could complain except Papa Muhammad, who is a hired hand at the plant nursery and lives in a wooden shack right at his workplace. When we first got to know each other, I called him Amm Muhammad and he called me Sitt Fawzia, and when we became friends, I began to call him Papa Muhammad and he named me Umm Ahmad, after my father, God rest his soul, whose name was Ahmad. When the world starts closing in on me, I go to him and talk. This time I complained about Umm Sulayman and he advised me to insult her just as she had insulted me.

"I'll try," I told him, and I returned home. But I wasn't sure that I could do it, because Umm Sulayman has scared me so much that I see her in my dreams, laughing until her teeth show, long and frightening, especially that gleaming gold tooth. I see her laughing and the dream becomes a nightmare.

But not all my dreams are nightmares. When I am untroubled, I see the fields and then my dreams are beautiful, like dreams should be . . . and they're in colour. When I see a field of wheat, it looks to

me like pure gold, the ears of wheat undulating, bending and bil-
lowing in a sea of saffron.

When I see a field of maize, the cobs are already mature on their
stalks, their tufts a winey red. The field, although green, looks
brownish red like the waters of the Nile in the ninth month, heavy
with silt, before the coming of the floods.

And when it is an orange grove that appears, I see the trees looking small and rotund and weighted down with fruit, like the women
of our village. Against the green of the branches the oranges show
off their colour, and in the blue heights the sun mirrors them.

When the plants are still concealed, I see the earth between
moisture and dryness stretching out free and black, the seeds hiding
within, except for a few which have split their shells and sent out
their shoots of green.

Once only I saw the date-palms, a grove in the early morning.
The sun had not yet risen but was about to, and was already dyeing
the violet horizon with the colour of henna. I saw the date-palms,
lots of them, straight and towering. In them I saw the faces of my
family, my father and mother and aunt and cousin. Their faces were
green, pale with the hue of the palm leaves. But I could not tell for
sure whether they were standing behind the trunks or whether the
trunks were behind them. I heard a mellow, warm voice. It sounded
like the voice of a Qur'an-reciter chanting holy verses before the
dawn call to prayer, or like something else, I really don't know. But
the voice rang out, echoing across the date-palm grove in the moments before dawn, and I told myself, "Fawzia, you are at the gates,
so prepare yourself."

But then I awoke. I opened my eyes and found only the picture
which hung on the old wall, and I knew it had been a dream. A tear
rolled from my eye, then I pulled myself together and got up.

Today a woman who lives on my street came to see me. She said
she had seen the flowerpots on my balcony and she told me they were
pretty. She asked me shyly if I could teach her. So I showed her how,
I gave her a mint sprig that I had planted, and then we sat and talked.

Translated by Marilyn Booth

Ibrahim Aslan
(b. 1939)
EGYPT

Ibrahim Aslan was born in the Nile Delta. The Cairo correspondent for the Lebanese daily *al-Hayat*, he has published
several collections of short stories, and his novel *The Heron*
was made into one of the most successful Egyptian films.
His most recent work of fiction, *Nile Sparrows*, from which
the second extract is taken, shares the Nileside setting of his
best-known work.

The Little Girl in Green

Mohammed Effendi Rasheedi went up onto the roof of the house
and looked down at his son's car parked in front of the door and at
Umm Husein the grocer who was busy selling bread.

Raising his pate with its scanty hair, Mohammed Effendi saw the
roofs of the houses, empty except for the lines of washing hung out,
and he told himself that that ass of a woman Umm Husein had
blocked the whole street with baskets and that if there was a car
wanting to pass through and go to the *souk* she'd have to get up and
drag the baskets right along to the shop's doorway. He inclined his
head till he was able to see Fadlallah Othman Lane from where it
began. When he found it empty, with no car approaching, he felt
annoyed. He left where he was and stood in front of the dusty
prickly pear in the roof-top corner. He saw that its earth had grown
dry and cracked in its round clay jar. He thought of going to the
bathroom and filling a large glass from the tap to water it with. He
went down the stairs at his own pace, without turning to the open
door of his flat. Arriving at the ground floor, he stood before the

partly open entrance and stretched out his finger and tapped on the closed glass panel.

"Come in, whoever's knocking."

Mohammed Effendi put the palm of his hand on the door and gently pushed it, listening to its slow creaking. He remained standing there till his eyes grew accustomed to the darkness and he saw the sofa to the right and the old lady sitting on the edge of it to this side, then he went forward and seated himself on the other sofa. He arranged the folds of his *galabia* in his lap and said: "Good evening, Mrs. Umm Abduh."

"Greetings, Mr. Mohammed. Welcome." She looked with her tiny eyes at the chain of the metal watch fixed to the buttonhole and hanging on to his chest and said that none of the children was there. "Otherwise they'd have made you a glass of tea."

"It's not necessary. Just a couple of words and the reply to go with them."

"All's well, I hope."

Mohammed Effendi raised his face to the picture of the late Mohammed Effendi Othman hanging on the old wall, then he looked at his feet and asked her if she knew that they had bought a 128 car, to which Mrs. Umm Abduh said: "Why, of course," and she informed him that she had met Umm Islah[2] in the skylight area when she was giving water to the chickens and she'd congratulated her, "the very next day."

Mohammed Effendi said he'd heard of that: "But I was very annoyed when I found that your son was letting out the air from the tyre."

"My son?"

"Every blessed day."

"I wonder which one of them it could be: Abdul Raheem, Husein or Muhsin?"

"Whichever one of them."

However, Mrs. Umm Abduh said: "How can that be, seeing

---

[2] Mohammed Effendi Rasheedi's wife. Literally "the mother of Islah."

that each one of them lives in his own house with his wife and children?"

"But they visit you."

"Even so, Abu Islah,[3] they're grown-up men."

Mohammed Effendi said: "Abdul Raheem, Husein and Muhsin are like our own children and if it was a question of a day or two, I'd say, 'So what?—let them play as they like.'" Then he added: "It's been going on too long, because it's a 128 car and its motor is set crossways. It's actually a private car and anyone seeing it in front of the door would say it was a private car, but we're intending to turn it into a taxi and get it done up, and that's something that'll need a lot of money. It might take a month or a year, or God knows how long. And naturally it's quite disgraceful of them to go on all this time letting the air out of the tyre and our pumping it up, and they letting it out and our pumping it up."

Mrs. Umm Abduh got up from the sofa, saying that such talk was quite wrong and that he'd gone too far, and she hurried out of the living-room. Standing in the skylight area, she raised her head and kept calling: "Umm Islah. Hey, Umm Islah."

Mohammed Effendi left her still calling and went out of the flat. He descended the few steps and stood in the doorway by the back of the parked car and saw the young girl in her green silk *galabia* sitting alongside the front wheel. She had in her hand a wooden matchstick which she was pressing into the inside of the valve. The compressed air was gushing out and causing her to close her eyes and making her soft hair blow out. He set about crossing the street slowly. He stood in front of Umm Husein the grocer who was putting some money down the front of her dress.

"Good morning, Mrs. Umm Husein."

Umm Husein took hold of the nearest loaf and threw it to the other side of the basket. "Welcome."

"The girl is your son Husein's daughter—every blessed day she lets the air out of the tyre."

---

[3] "Father of Islah," i.e., Mohammed Effendi Rasheedi.

Umm Husein looked in the direction of the girl and said: "Hit her."

"No, Mrs. Umm Husein, before doing any such thing there are grown-up people one should refer to, and you're now the main person in charge of the shop."

"And if I'm the main person in charge of the shop, should I leave the buying and selling and go running off after a little girl?"

"That's all very well, Mrs. Umm Husein, but what's to be done?"

"I'm telling you but you don't want to know: when you find her at it, get hold of her and wring her neck." Then she called out: "Get out from where you are, girl—I really don't know what you find so fascinating about that old wreck."

The little girl got to her feet and ran off laughing. Mohammed Effendi said that if it were a question of a day or two he'd let her play around as much as she liked but that it had been going on for a long time: "Mrs. Umm Abduh is completely in the picture." He turned towards the other direction of Fadlallah Othman Lane and said: "Has there been the call to noon prayers yet?"

Umm Husein said she hadn't heard it: "It's enough to turn your brain inside out."

Mohammed Effendi turned round and entered the house. Gently he stretched out his hand and pushed the wooden door that was still slightly open, listening to its slow creaking. He saw Mrs. Umm Abduh sitting on the edge of this side of the sofa and the border of the frame of the picture of the late Mohammed Effendi Othman; then, raising his *galabia*, he made his way up the stairs till he reached the roof. The son of his daughter Islah had raised his *galabia* above his small, extended stomach and was standing peeing on the prickly pear. "Ah, you little wretch!" The boy ran off laughing, without lowering the *galabia* or ceasing to pee. Mohammed Effendi continued to watch him in silence, then once again moved towards the roof wall. He looked down at Fadlallah Othman Lane and saw the car parked in front of the door and Umm Husein the grocer, and he spotted the young girl coming over there. He immediately drew back and hid himself out of sight. He thought he'd let her be until she felt secure and started playing about with the tyre, then he'd go to the bathroom and fill the large glass from the tap and pour it down on top of her. He gazed at the dusty prickly pear and saw the marks of urine spattered on the plump leaves so that their colour showed up. He told himself that she was now sitting on the ground in her green silk *galabia* holding a matchstick and the compressed air would be gushing out and making her soft hair blow out. He nodded his head in confirmation and approached on tiptoe until he was against the roof wall. Mohammed Effendi Rasheedi leaned over all of a sudden, but he was quite unable to see her.

Translated by Denys Johnson-Davies

FROM **Nile Sparrows**

Dalal would leave them to go to sleep. When Abd al-Reheem came home early, she would fix them tea before turning in. No matter what time Abd al-Reheem returned, Hanem would hear his movements as he unfastened the package and put its contents on a plate, calling out to her, "Get up, Ma." She sat with him at the front of the courtyard with Fadlallah Uthman stretched out before them. Every once in a while, she picked up a crumb of the food he always brought: a small bit of feta or Kasseri cheese or a piece of halvah, in addition to a few olives, sometimes black and sometimes green. She spent the evening chewing thimble-sized pieces of bread or cheese, and if she tried to chew an olive with her toothless gums, she swallowed it with the pit by mistake. So she stayed away from olives despite her fondness for them. When he brought a new kind of cheese such as cream cheese, cheddar or Roquefort, he would draw her attention to it until reassured that she noticed the difference in taste. They talked all night about their village or its chief Abd al-Rahman, their land, or Nargis, or anything at all until the peep of dawn rose over Fadlallah Uthman.

When Abd al-Reheem died, Hanem's grandson Mr. Abdalla ibn al-Bahey Uthman bought her the same kinds of food and gave it to Dalal to arrange in the plate and put in the front of the courtyard, because his grandmother still left her room at night and sat at her usual place. Time would pass and she would laugh and say, "That boy Abd al-Reheem is late," and Dalal, trying to keep an eye on her as sleep overtook her, would reply, "He'll be here soon." Sometimes Hanem would touch her inside pocket to make sure the two ten-pound notes were still there, the money she had put away years ago to finance her funeral: the money for the car that would transport her from Cairo to the village; the shroud for her body; the under-taker's fee; the female mourners' fee; the fee for the stentorian-voiced Shaykh Mustafa al-Safti, the well-known Qur'an reciter (who had died thirty-four years ago); and also the dinner that Nar-gis would prepare for their neighbors from Fadlallah Uthman. Even though this pouch where she kept the money was fastened onto her inner slip with a safety pin, a few years ago Abd al-Reheem man-aged to unhook the pin and take out the banknotes, replacing them with folded lined notebook paper. Dalal knew because when she did laundry he asked her not to tell his mother about the folded notebook paper in the pouch.

For her part, Dalal wasn't shocked by anything he did after she saw him tie his ailing tooth to a thread attached to a nail in the wall. He lit a cigarette to distract himself and asked her to talk to him about anything. "What do you want me to talk to you about?" she asked him. "You're so stubborn. I told you . . ." he said, and jerked his head back suddenly. At the end of the thread hung his long, dark tooth.

Translated by Mona al-Ghobashy

Alaa Al Aswany
(b. 1957)
EGYPT

Alaa Al Aswany is a dentist who has written prolifically across the political spectrum on literature, politics, and so-cial issues for Egyptian newspapers. His second novel, *The Yacoubian Building*, describes—through the lives of various denizens of a building in Cairo—several facets that make up the capital's society. It caused a stir in Egypt when it was published in 2002 because of its frankness about aspects of contemporary Egyptian life. It was recently made into a film.

FROM *The Yacoubian Building*

During that year Busayna learned a lot. She discovered for example that her beautiful and provocative body, her wide, dark-brown eyes and full lips, her voluptuous breasts and tremulous, rounded backside with its soft buttocks, all had an important role to play in her dealings with people. It became clear to her that all men, however respectable in appearance and however elevated their position in society, were utter weaklings in front of a beautiful woman. This drove her to try out some wicked but entertaining tests. Thus, if she met a respectable old man whom she thought it would be fun to test, she would put on a girlish voice and bend over and stick out her voluptuous breasts, then immediately enjoy the sight of the sober-sided gentleman going soft and trembly, his eyes clouding over with desire. The way men panted after her gave her a gloating pleasure similar to that of revenge. It also became clear to her during that year that her mother had changed completely, for whenever Busayna left a job because of the men's importunities, her mother would greet the news with a silence akin to exasperation and on one occasion, after it had happened several times, she told Busayna as she got up to leave the room, "Your brother and sisters need every penny you earn. A clever girl can look after herself and keep her job." This sentence saddened and puzzled Busayna, who asked herself, "How can I look after myself when faced with a boss who opens his fly?"

She remained in the same state of puzzlement for many long weeks, until Fifi, the daughter of Sabir the laundryman, who was a neighbor of theirs on the roof, appeared. She had heard that Busayna was looking for work and had come to tell her about a job as a salesgirl at the Shanan clothing store. When Busayna told her about her problem with earlier bosses, Fifi let out a great sigh, struck her on her chest, and shouted in her face in disbelief, "Don't be a fool, girl!" Fifi explained to her that more than ninety percent of bosses did that with the girls who worked for them and that any girl who refused was thrown out and a hundred other girls who didn't object could be found to take her place. When Busayna started to object, Fifi asked her sarcastically, "So Your Ladyship has an MBA from the American University? Why, the beggars in the street have commercial diplomas the same as you!"

Fifi explained to her that going along with the boss "up to a point" was just being smart and that the world was one thing and what she saw in Egyptian movies was another. She explained to her that she knew lots of girls who had worked for years at the Shanan store and given Mr. Talal, the owner of the store, what he wanted "up to a point" and were now happily married with kids, homes, and husbands who loved them lots. "But why go so far afield?" Fifi asked, citing herself as an example. She had worked in the store for two years and her salary was a hundred pounds but she earned at least three times that much by "being smart," not to mention the presents. And all the same, she had been able to look after herself, she was a virgin, and she'd scratch out the eyes of anyone who said anything against her reputation. There were a hundred men who wanted to marry her, especially now that she was earning and putting her money into saving co-ops and setting money aside to pay for her trousseau.

The next day Busayna went with Fifi to Mr. Talal at the store. He turned out to be over forty, fair-complexioned, blue-eyed, balding, and stout. He was snub-nosed and had a huge black mustache that hung down on either side of his mouth. Mr. Talal was not at all handsome, and Busayna found out that he was the only son, among a bunch of girls, of Hagg Shanan, a Syrian, who had come from Syria during the Union and settled in Egypt and opened this store. Once he started getting on, he had handed his business over to his only son. She learned too that he was married and that his wife was Egyptian and pretty and had borne him two sons, though despite all that his predations on women never stopped. Talal shook

Busayna's hand (giving it a squeeze) and never raised his eyes from her chest and body while he spoke. After a few minutes, she started her new job.

In just a few weeks, Fifi had taught her all she had to do: how she had to take care of her appearance, paint her fingernails and her toenails, open the neck of her dress a little, and take her dresses in a bit at the waist to show off her backside. It was her job to open the store in the morning and mop it out along with her colleagues, then set her clothes straight and stand at the door (a way of attracting customers familiar to all the clothing stores). When she had a customer, she had to talk to him nicely, comply with his requests, and persuade him to buy as much as possible (she got a half of one percent of the value of all sales). Naturally, she had to put up with the customers' flirting, however obnoxious.

That was the job. As for "the other thing," Mr. Talal started in on it the third day after she came. It was the time of the afternoon prayer and the store was empty of customers. Talal asked her to go with him to the storeroom so that he could explain to her the different items they had in stock. Busayna followed him without a word, noting the shadow of an ironic smile on the faces of Fifi and the other girls.

The storeroom consisted of a large apartment on the ground floor in the building next to the À l'Américaine café on Suleiman Basha. Talal entered and locked the door from the inside. She looked about her. The place was damp and badly lit and ventilated and was stacked to the ceiling with boxes. She knew what was coming and had readied herself on the way to the storeroom, repeating to herself in her head her mother's words, "Your brother and sisters need every penny you earn. A clever girl can look after herself and keep her job." When Mr. Talal came close to her, she was struck by strong and conflicting feelings—determination to make the best of the opportunity and the fear which despite everything still wracked her and made her fight for breath and feel as though she was about to be sick. There was also a sneaking, covert curiosity that urged her to find out what Mr. Talal would do to her. Would he woo her and tell her, "I love you," for example, or try to kiss her right away? She

found out quickly enough because Talal pounced on her from behind, flung his arms around her hard enough to hurt her and
started rubbing up against her and playing with her body without
uttering a single word. He was violent and in a hurry to get his
pleasure and the whole business was over in about two minutes.
Her dress was soiled and he whispered to her, panting, "The bathroom's at the end of the corridor on the right."

As she washed her dress in the water, she thought to herself that
the whole thing was easier than she'd imagined, like some man rubbing up against her in the bus (something that happened a lot) and
she remembered what Fifi had told her to do after the encounter.
She went back to Talal and said to him in a voice she made as
smooth and seductive as she could, "I need twenty pounds from
you, sir." Talal looked at her for a moment, then quickly thrust his
hand into his pocket as though he had been expecting the request
and said in an ordinary voice as he took out a folded banknote,
"Nah. Ten's enough. Come back to the store after me as soon as
your dress is dry." Then he went out, closing the door behind him.

Ten pounds a time, and Mr. Talal would ask for her twice, sometimes three times a week, and Fifi had taught her how from time to
time to show her liking for a dress in the shop and keep on at Talal
until he made her a present of it. She started making money and
wearing nice clothes and her mother was pleased with her and was
comforted by the money that she took from her and tucked into the
front of her dress, uttering warm blessings for her after doing so.
Listening to these, Busayna was overwhelmed with a mysterious,
malign desire to start giving her mother clear hints about her relationship with Talal, but her mother would ignore any such messages. Busayna would then go to such lengths with her hints that
the mother's refusal to acknowledge them became obvious and extremely fragile, at which point Busayna would feel some relief, as
though she had snatched away her mother's mask of false innocence
and confirmed her complicity in the crime.

As time passed her rendezvous with Talal in the storeroom had an impact on her that she would never have imagined. She found herself no longer able to perform the morning prayer (the only one of the required prayers that she had performed) because inwardly she was ashamed to face "Our Lord," because she felt herself unclean, however much she performed the ablutions. She started having nightmares and would start up from her sleep terrified. She would go for days depressed and melancholy and one day when she went with her mother to visit the tomb of El Hussein, no sooner had she entered the sanctuary and found herself surrounded by the incense and lights and felt that deeply-rooted hidden presence that fills the heart than she burst into a long, unexpected bout of weeping.

On the other hand since retreat was not an option and she could not stand her feelings of sin, she started to resist the latter fiercely. She took to thinking of her mother's face as she told her that she was working as a servant in people's houses. She would repeat to herself what Fifi had said about the world and how it worked and often she would contemplate the shop's rich, chic women customers and ask herself with spiteful passion, "I wonder how many times that woman surrendered her body to get to where she is now?"

This violent resistance to her feelings of guilt left a legacy of bitterness and cruelty. She stopped trusting people or making excuses for them. She would often think (and then seek forgiveness) that God had wanted her to fall. If He had wanted otherwise, He would have created her a rich woman or delayed her father's death a few years (and what could have been easier for Him?). Little by little, her resentment extended to include her sweetheart Taha himself. A strange feeling that she was stronger than he was by far would creep over her—a feeling that she was mature and understood the world, while he was just a dreamy, naive boy. She started to get annoyed at his optimism about the future and speak sharply to him, mocking him by saying, "You think you're Abd el Halim Hafez? The poor, hardworking boy whose dreams will come true if he struggles?"

At first, Taha didn't understand the reason for this bitterness.

Then her sarcasm at his expense started to provoke him and they would quarrel, and when he asked her once to stop working for Talal because he had a bad reputation, she looked at him challengingly and said, "At your service, sir. Give me the two hundred and fifty pounds that I earn from Talal and you'll have the right to stop me showing my face to anyone but you." He stared at her for a moment as though he did not understand and then his anger erupted and he shoved her on the shoulder. She screamed insults at him and threw at him a silver outfit he'd bought for her. In the depths of her heart, she craved to rip her relationship with him to pieces so that she might be freed of that painful feeling of sin that tortured her as soon as she set eyes on him, yet it was not in her power to leave him completely. She loved him and they had a long history full of beautiful moments. The instant she saw him sad or anxious, she would forget everything and envelop him in genuine, overflowing tenderness as though she was his mother. However bad the quarrels between them got, she would make up with him and go back to him, and their affair was not without rare and wonderful times. Very soon, however, the gloom would return.

Translated by Humphrey Davies

Liana Badr
(b. 1950)
PALESTINE

Liana Badr was born in Jerusalem and spent her childhood in Jericho when it was occupied by the Israelis. Since then she has lived in Beirut, Damascus, and Tunis. Her works in English translation include the collection of novellas *A Balcony over the Fakihani* and the novels *A Compass for the Sunflower* and *The Eye of the Mirror*. She now works for the Palestinian Ministry of Culture.

FROM **A Land of Stone and Thyme**

THE PHOTOGRAPH

Last night I dreamt that we walked together. He always visits me in my dreams. We were walking near the martyrs' cemetery. No sooner had I seen him than he left me and went under. Just leapt down and went among the graves. He tore his photo off one of the tombs, and went off I don't know where. I looked around. I saw the graves with their white tombstones, with wreaths of dry flowers on them and, around them, spring grass, green and soft. I looked for him but didn't know where he'd gone.

The photo is on my mind. I couldn't believe it till the photographer developed it. I thought I'd go and place it on his grave in the martyrs' cemetery. But the situation is tense and the fighting is on. Who these days would dare to go down to the martyrs' burial ground? I discussed it for a long time with my sister, Jamila. But she took the enlarged photo from me, stuck it in a cupboard and locked it up. She said that I was pregnant, that I was due to deliver by the end of the month, and that it would be difficult for me to run if I got caught in the shooting. What am I to do then? Wait? Life has been nothing but waiting upon waiting, even though I never did expect one day to marry a man who loves me, longs for me and waits with me and who then goes away for ever and never returns.

They used to call him "the Indian" in al-Damoor Camp. When I first set eyes on his dark features and black eyes, I really took him for an Indian. The first time we spoke with one another, I asked him, "Are you an Indian?" He laughed so long he almost fell flat on his face.

"Me? Indian? Yusra, I come from the village of Jamaeen on the outskirts of Nables."

Later on, he loved to remind me of how I'd fallen for the joke and had really taken him for an Indian.

AL-DAMOOR

After our exodus from Tel al-Za'tar, we lived for nearly a year in al-Damoor. Our house, situated on the roadside, was dismal: no windows, or doors, or tiles, or sanitation. It was a big house, burnt from the inside, and, like the rest of the al-Damoor houses, its tiles were ripped out and its floors were sand and gravel. The first thing we did was clean it. We spent about a week cleaning it. My mother had a go at whitewashing it with lime, but it was thick with soot and grime. We got some empty ammunition boxes, the wood of which my brother used to make a front door. The windows we covered up with plastic sheets.

At night the wind would blow. We were near the sea facing it. Mother would stay up all night, too frightened to sleep. The wind would beat against the plastic sheets and would bang against the transparent oilcloths, making sounds like the bombing. She went on feeling jittery and frightened. She was afraid in the winter and afraid in the summer. Only Mother alone was afraid.

When the Israeli planes started bombarding us, my mother's nerves got so frayed that we could no longer stay in al-Damoor. Life was so hard and harsh there. The distances between houses were too great for us who had been used to living among many neighbours. The shop was far away and the vegetable market was further still. There was no running water in the house. Eventually we managed to stretch an electric wire from the main street lamp, on which we hung a bulb inside the house. But Mother was always frightened and we did not like al-Damoor. We left, and moved into one of the flats in Beirut abandoned by those who had fled the fighting.

AND WATER HAS MEMORY

During the last attack on the refugee camp, I was out getting water. At the last stronghold they attacked and took from us, there was a water tap. Throughout the siege, Jamila and I used to go daily to the bottom of the alley leading to al-Dikwana. The most we could ever get were two large cans of water. The water would be cut off from early morning till the afternoon or evening. We would spend eight or ten hours waiting for our turn at the tap. Sometimes we managed to get our turn; at other times the attack would begin. Bombs would shower down upon us and the water would be cut off before anyone could fill a thing.

In the beginning—the beginning of the siege—we used to fill up at the Djanin School, near the George Matta metalworks. We used to sleep in the wide vault that was the George Matta factory. The place would fill up with more than seven hundred people who shared it with pieces of metal and huge machines. We would spread the bedding between the closely stacked bars and the cutting, smelting and plumbing equipment. There was hardly any room for us amidst the heaps of chairs, beds and metal swings, all piled one on top of the other. We couldn't get any sleep for the metal and its stink. Whenever we tried to sleep, the smell of metal would get up our noses and stifle our breath.

In George Matta we remained for nearly a month. It was a dangerous site because of its proximity to the Monastery of the Good Shepherd. Every day the women swept and sprinkled water on the floor of the factory. They did their baking on a tin tray placed on a kerosene primus. People baked and kneaded and slept and rose inside the shelter. During the first days we were able to go out sometimes to fill sandbags and to put up fortifications inside the camp. Even my mother, who had just had a baby, went out with the other women, a month after her delivery, to fill up the sandbags the comrades had distributed. Each one of us did what he could.

Every now and then some *fedaiyin* would pass through the camp. They would console us and lift our spirits saying, "Don't be afraid. There's no danger." During the last ten days of the month, their visits stopped. And after that none of us dared peep out of the door of the shelter.

They were near us, very near. If any one of us so much as peeped out, we were shot at immediately. They came so near that only a street separated us, with us at the top and them at the bottom. Five people were shot dead, although during our early days as refugees there had been no casualties, except for the time when the bomb landed near the door of the shelter.

One day, a girl was peeping through the door when she saw them sneaking up towards the camp. We never heard a sound. But we knew that the next attack would be on our camp. We knew that the fascists had penetrated the camp next door to George Matta's factory and that they had killed a hundred and twenty people. Seventeen from the Shoqair family died in the other shelter. When the snipers gained control of the main entrance, our people posted guards and dug another door in the back wall. People fled, seeking shelter elsewhere.

At five in the afternoon, we got out with only the clothes on our backs, leaving all our belongings behind. The next day, before the militia had completed its occupation of the area, I went back with a group of people to collect whatever we could carry of the supplies that had been left behind in the camp. I had to fetch the milk bottle for my baby brother because my mother's breasts had dried up and no longer had any milk for nursing him.

After we came out, a lot of people were shot. The shooting took place as if the people were standing right in front of the barrel. The sniper would shoot and the people would fall down one after the other. Lucky the ones who could escape by the skin of their teeth.

Translated by Sahar Hamouda

Hala El Badry
(b. 1954)
EGYPT

Hala El Badry was born in Cairo and took a degree from Cairo University. Her fourth novel, *A Certain Woman*, was awarded the prize for the best novel of 2001 at the Cairo International Book Fair. Its frank treatment of sex, coming from the pen of a woman writer, has shocked some Egyptian readers.

FROM **A Certain Woman**

Nahid said, "I want you as you are, the whole truth, no matter what the price."

Omar replied, "The truth is painful. You might imagine that knowledge is more important than pain, but you are not ready for that."

"I don't accept that others share something with you without me. I don't want to deal with a picture in my imagination, but with reality, which I love without falsehood."

"Listen then: there is another woman in my life. I don't love her, she is nothing to me."

"Since when?"

"Three months. She invited me to dinner at her house. I was lonely and confused and you were away. I confess I enjoyed being with her and she with me. But I thought about what being with her meant and I knew that our relationship was in danger and that it wouldn't have happened if our relationship had not been going through a crisis."

"You are one half of the relationship, so why didn't you try to save it?"

"I didn't know we had a crisis until I found myself with her and I realized what I had not been aware of."

"Why didn't you tell me at the time?"

"I feared for you. I thought I could get over it, then talk to you. Then I traveled and decided to stay there and start working for a London newspaper. And before the conference was over, I got tired and bored. I couldn't stay. I came back because I want you."

She didn't know how the conversation went, nor where the little fires burning her skin at that moment came from. She shooed them away with a calmness that did not fit the event and painted a smile that soon faded away from her face. His words turned and moved in a different direction that she saw on his face before he said another word. He suddenly looked like someone who had fallen into a trap even though she hadn't said anything.

She heard him describing his fear for their love and she took note of things that seemed strange to her: he feared the consequences of what happened in our story, he feared that our relationship might collapse because of a passing moment which would not have taken place at ordinary times.

"Why do you imagine that our relationship is so fragile? Of course it will endure in the face of all risks it is exposed to. I am your friend. Who would you confide in then?" she asked.

"I cannot separate my friend from my lover. I do not see the line between the two women who would trade places in no time at all. One moment you won't be able to bear it."

"If your lover broke down, your friend will embrace you. Have no fear; we'll get over the crisis."

Three days passed. They meet without mentioning the forbidden subject. They have short, quick dates during which each treats the other gently as if it were the last time they will see each other. He showers her with warmth and she showers him with affection then they part, each looking at the other with pleading eyes, begging for hope in tomorrow's meeting. She mulls over the minutes and takes her time, no sleep and nothing much to do except trying to reconstruct what happened over the past three months. She sees him in her embrace asking if she is tired of his advances. She imagines Salma Abed in his arms and she burns. She staunchly refuses to cry when in fact she wants to scream. She plunges into the sea of the moments they spent together and recalls them drop by drop: "He goes through a crisis about which he complains and moves away sadly. I stay patient until the problem is solved. I protect him from knowing about my problems so that I can meet him smiling and calm, and he runs away to another woman."

He immerses himself in his work to run away from his thoughts. Unsure of her reaction, he wants her to feel secure by any means and he pursues her by phone everywhere she goes, telling her the details of his day without her asking him. He receives telephone calls from Salma and notices the amount of empty chatter that he hadn't noticed before. Time kills him. He stays away from Maggie, determining the distance between them, and is comfortable with the silence which prevents her from starting quarrels. He stays in front of the computer until the morning and gets into bed when Sharif's alarm clock goes off. As he begins to doze off he hears Maggie's instructions to Sharif before he goes to school.

The explosion came on the fourth day after she had stayed up all night telling herself, "He tells me 'I love you' and says that Salma was not a sudden desire for a woman, but the result of the collapse of our relationship. How?"

She asked him, shaking, "Do you feel lukewarm towards me?"

He dodged the question, looking at her like a child who wanted to run away from his mother at that moment, but later come back to find out that she had forgotten what he had done. But at that moment, Nahid was the lover, not the friend or the mother. She was prepared to understand his lust and his weakness for a lonely beautiful woman who desired him. But she was not ready for him to blame what happened on their relationship.

"You have an evil strain in you that I close my eyes to and often forget, but it surprises me despite myself, in its depth and virulence."

"You wanted me as I am."

"How cruel! How did your heart go along? How could you? Didn't you remember me at the time?"

"If I remembered you, it wouldn't have happened. It was a moment between a woman and a man alone. This won't happen again. We will preserve our love and forget what happened."

He ran his fingers through her hair as his hand pulled her head to his chest. She melted the moment her lips touched his shoulder. She began to hallucinate as thoughts swirled around in her head haunting her with the image of him embracing Salma. She felt lost and small in a world that was too big for her to cope with.

"If your love is dwindling, tell me now and I'll be able to take it. But I will not be able to live with you and see it dying. Tell me that your feelings for me are no longer what they used to be and I will leave without remonstrance, but don't let me tend its death."

He hugged her hard, their words overlapped and intertwined

without either one of them waiting for the other. Each was talking to himself.

Omar whispered, "Don't ever say that. Our responsibility is to recapture and keep what we have."

"It's not the beginning of the end."

"No, it's the crossroad, we either go together or love will be lost. Hold on to me, please; don't leave me. I need you now more than any other time in the past."

"I love you but I want to understand, just understand: how can you love me and run away from me? How were you able to embrace her?"

"Sex for men is not the same as sex for women. I told you that and we've discussed it together many times."

"It is the same. I still say it is the same; the differences depend on the individual."

"I have known women and dealt with them without loving them, just for pleasure. But you can do that only for one man. Believe me. It's a passing matter and will not affect us. I am over it and I know that you will be over it too."

On going their separate ways as she crossed the isthmus to her other world, she asked herself, "Why don't I hate him? Is my love for him a sickness?"

Translated by Farouk Abdel Wahab

Salwa Bakr
(b. 1949)
EGYPT

Salwa Bakr, born in Cairo, made her name with her first book of short stories, which she published at her own expense. A selection of her stories, *The Wiles of Men*, has been published in English. Her novel, *The Golden Chariot*, is also available in English. The incidents of *The Golden Chariot* take place in a women's prison, where one of the prisoners dreams of having a golden chariot to take her and her

friends up to heaven. The stories of the criminal and sometimes insane inmates reflect in miniature aspects of a society
that, in the author's view, has lost its way. The second extract below is from *The Golden Chariot* and tells the story of
one of the inmates.

Dotty Noona

Apart from her father and the officer, his wife and son, almost no
one, when the question was asked at the office of the public attorney, knew Noona. The only exceptions were: Hasanein the seller of
bread; Futeih the grocer; Salim the man who did the ironing; and
the garbage man. The latter, on being questioned, said he had no
idea at all about her features, because he was always concerned with
looking at the rubbish bin when she used to hand it over to him for
emptying into his basket each morning.

Everyone's statements conflicted on the question of her features,
for while the officer was certain she was snub-nosed and that her
upper jaw protruded slightly, his wife answered at the office of the
public attorney, "Did she have any features?" then added, "She was
a very dotty girl, very weird." As for her father, he contented himself by saying, as he dried his tears, "She would have been a lovely
bride, a girl in a million"—and to prove to the government the
truth of his statement, he produced from the inner pocket of his
galabia a small golden earring with a blue bead, which was the total
bridal gift presented by the future husband, whom she had never
seen.

Even Noona herself didn't know her own features well. The most
she knew was that the officer's son had beautiful black hair like his
mother and a vast nose like that of his father, except that the latter's
nose had small black specks scattered around on it. She had noticed
them any number of times when he got excited and wrinkled it up
as he exclaimed "Check" in a voice hoarse and strangled with laughter to his opponent at chess.

In any case, the girl Noona was not concerned about her looks, which she often saw reflected on the surface of mirrors, either in the bedroom of the officer and his wife, or in their son's room, when she would enter to clean and tidy—quickly lest time flew and the school hours came to an end. She would snatch hurried moments in which to search yet again for "the pupil of the eye," that being she never believed existed although the teacher had confirmed it over and over again. Each time, standing on tiptoe, she would crane forward with her short body and get as near as she could to the mirror, then would pull down her lower lids with her swollen fingers, which were covered with burn marks and small cuts, and in bewildered astonishment, get her eyes to bulge out, two black circles, while she peered around in search of two arms or two feet, or a nose or a neck, or any of the human parts of the body of that person, "the pupil of the eye." When, bored, tired and feeling that the tips of her feet had begun to ache because of her stance, she would lower herself, screw up her lips in rage, fill up her mouth with air, or put out her tongue and move it around in continuous circular movements, then go back quickly and start making the beds, hanging up the clothes and putting things in their proper places.

It is impossible to deny that the girl Noona had a secret desire to be pretty and charming, not like the officer's wife, who owned all sorts and kinds of clothes, something short and something long, and something with sleeves and something without sleeves, but pretty, like the teacher whom she used to imagine in the likeness of the fairy-tale princess whenever there came to her from beyond the window, while Noona stood in the kitchen, her beautiful voice asking the girls to repeat after her the hemistich, "Flanks of antelope, legs of ostrich."

"Flanks" used to puzzle Noona greatly, so when she began to repeat it with the girls and listen to the effect of her high-pitched solo voice declaiming "flanks of antelope," she would stop for a while scouring the dish she was washing in the sink, or stirring what was cooking in its saucepan on the stove, and would rest her right leg against her left for a time and start sucking her thumb with relish as she thought about the real meaning of this "flanks" and asking herself, Is it clover? Or candy with chickpeas? Or a young donkey?

The images burst forth in her imagination as she searched for the truth. When the questions defeated her and she discovered that water was beginning a trickle over the top of the sink, or that the cooking had boiled enough, she would apply herself again to her work, while rage and perplexity built up, a huge force within her body, and she would rub and scour the dishes till they were sparkling, or rearrange the spoons and forks in their places more neatly, while muttering the words "legs of ostrich" and looking out of the window enclosed by the iron bars through which she could see the school building opposite, and the open blue sky sheltering it. There traveled up to her the voices of the girls in one strong harmonious sound, and she would feel that she was on the brink of madness, and she would shout, along with them, with all the strength of her throat, "He lopes like a wolf, leaps like a fox."

She yearned to know the secrets of many other things, things she had heard from this magical world hidden from her behind the window, just as she longed to know the true meaning of "flanks," that word on which, through the girls' school, she had made raids from time to time, and which had made her learn by heart strange words she didn't understand and made her wish she would find someone to assuage her heart's fire and explain their meanings to her. She had in fact attempted to get to know the meaning of these words by asking Hasanein the bread-seller about "flanks," but he had just winked at her and raised his eyebrows obscenely and made a movement with his thumb that reminded her of the village women. Though she cursed him and reviled his father and his scoundrelly ancestors, she was frightened after that to make another attempt with Futeih the grocer. She would have made the decision to ask the officer's son, if it hadn't been for what occurred on the day of the square root, which caused her never to think of it again. Surprised one day by her mistress when stirring the onions and scrutinizing them in her search for hydrogen sulphate, which the teacher had said was to be found in them, Noona adamantly refused to tell her the truth of the matter when she asked her in surprise what she was doing. She contented herself by saying that she was looking for something strange in the onions, which caused the officer's wife to say in reference to this occasion—and numerous other occasions—that Noona was dotty and weird and that her behaviour wasn't natural, particularly when she saw her jumping around in the kitchen, raising her legs up high and extending them forwards, in exactly the same way she had seen the girls do when they wore their long black trousers in the spacious school courtyard.

The lady used to say this about Noona and would add, whenever she sat among her women friends of an evening in the gilt reception room the like of which Noona reckoned the headman of her village himself couldn't possibly have seen, that the girl was a real work-horse and had the strength to demolish a mountain, despite the fact she wasn't more than thirteen years of age. She said she'd never throw her out of the house, despite her being mad, specially as maids were very few and far between these days and hard to come by.

Although this opinion didn't please Noona at all, and although the lady once slapped her on the face because of her having sworn at her young son and called him an idiot, she didn't dislike the officer's wife, for she knew that the slap had been a spontaneous reaction, just as Noona's swearing had been.

The boy had been sitting in the living room with the teacher, with his mother seated opposite them knitting and making cracking noises with her chewing-gum, when Noona came in carrying the tea-tray just as the teacher was asking the boy about the square root of twenty-five and the good-for-nothing was picking his nose and looking at his mother stupidly and giving no answer. As Noona had heard a lot from the schoolmistress about square roots, she couldn't help herself, when suddenly the boy brazenly answered four, from shouting in excitement, just as the schoolmistress used to do, "Five, you idiot," which almost caused the tray to fall from her hands. The teacher guffawed in amazement, and the boy ran towards her trying to hit her. The mother, however, got there first, for she had been concerned about the crystal glasses breaking, and had slapped Noona: the one and only slap she had given her during the three years she had been in the house. And whereas the lady didn't lie when she said to the teacher that Noona had no doubt heard that from the schoolmistress, one window looking right on to the other, Noona learnt never to talk about such things with anyone in the house lest the lady might think of dismissing her, for she wished to remain forever where the schoolmistress and the girls were, that beautiful world whose sounds she heard every day through the kitchen window, a world she never saw.

Despite all this there was a fire of longing that burned night and day in her breast for her mother and her brothers and sisters, and a desire to run about with the children in the fields, to breathe in the odour of greenness and the dewy morning, to see the blazing sun when she went out each morning, to hear the voice of her mother calling to her, when she was angry and out of sorts, "Na'ima, Na'ouma, come along and eat, my darling, light of your mother's eyes."

She used to love her real name Na'ima, also her pet name Na'ouma, but found nothing nice about the name Noona which had been given to her by the lady and by which everyone called her from the time of her arrival at the house from the country up until the time she left it forever on that day after which nothing more was known of Noona. Before that her life had been going along in its usual routine: she had woken as was her habit, had brought the bread, had made breakfast for the officer, his wife and son, had handed over the tin container to the garbage man and had entered the kitchen after they had all gone out. It wasn't until about four o'clock that her life began to change when there was a knock at the door and Abu Sarie, her father, put in an appearance in order to drop his bombshell. After saying hello and having lunch and tea, and assuring her about her mother, and about her brothers and sisters one by one, and chewing the cud with her for a while, her father had said, as he eyed her breasts and body and smiled happily so that his black teeth showed, that he had come to take her back because she was going to be married. He showed her the gold earring that had been bought for her by the husband-to-be, who had returned from the land of the Prophet bearing with him enough money to furnish the whole of a room in his mother's house, and more besides. At that moment Noona's heart had sunk down to her heels and she had been on the point of bursting into tears. Smiling as he saw the blood drain out of her face and her colour become like that of a white turnip, Abu Sarie told her not to be frightened, for this was something that happened to all girls and that there was no harm in it. He asked her to make herself ready because they would be going off together next morning. Then he decided to make her happy with the same news that had made him happy, so he informed her that the lady would give her an additional month's wages as a bonus, also two pieces of cloth untouched by scissors, and that her younger sister would take her place in the job, if God so willed it.

"And everything was normal that night"—so said the officer's wife at the public attorney's office. Her husband and son both agreed with her, and even Abu Sarie himself. Noona had prepared supper, had washed up the dishes, had given the boy tea while he was studying in his room—"and there was nothing about her to arouse one's suspicions," she added—and this was in fact so. What happened was that Noona spent the night in her bed in the kitchen without having a wink of sleep, staring up at the dark ceiling and from time to time gazing towards the window, behind which stood towering the school building, with above it a piece of pure sky in which stars danced. She was in utter misery, for she did not want to return to the village and to live amidst dirt and fleas and mosquitoes; she also did not want to marry, to become—like her sisters— rooted in suffering. The tears flowed that night from her eyes in rivers, and she remained sleepless till dawn broke. She saw with her two eyes the white colour of the sky and the black iron of the window, but by the time the lady called out to her to get up and go to the market to buy the bread, sleep had overcome her. She dreamed of the schoolmistress and the girls, and of the officer's son who, in her dream, she was slapping hard because he didn't know the square root of twenty-five. She also saw "flanks," and it was something of extreme beauty; she didn't know whether it was a human or a *djinn*, for it seemed to be of a white colour, the white of teased cotton, with two wings of beautiful colours of a rainbow. Noona seized hold of them and "flanks" flew with her far away, far from the kitchen and from the village and from people, until she was in the sky and she saw the golden stars close to, in fact she almost touched them.

Those who had seen Noona on the morning of that day mentioned that her face had borne a strange expression. Both the officer and his wife said so, confirming that the look in her eyes was not at all normal when she had handed her master his packet of cigarettes as he was about to go out and when her mistress had asked her to straighten her kerchief before going to buy the bread.

The officer's wife was heard to say, with many laughs, to her women friends, after having told them the story of Noona, as she sat with them in the large living room, "Didn't I tell you—she was crazy and altogether dotty? But as for her sister, I can't as yet make her out."

Translated by Denys Johnson-Davies

FROM **The Golden Chariot**

As time dragged by in prison, Safiyya became increasingly exasperated and angry with the Government which she saw as the cause of all her problems and unhappiness and her separation from her family. She didn't understand, and nor would she ever understand, why someone like her should suffer all this unhappiness. She was aware that the Government intervened in matters relating to picking pockets, stealing and murder, but drugs . . . why drugs? People bought drugs willingly and taking them made them feel better and revived their spirits. Safiyya decided that what people said on television about drugs was nothing but stupid exaggeration because even food could be very harmful if people did not control how much they ate. She was equally convinced that everything in the papers was a pack of lies because those who pontificate in them about drugs were the very same people who told lies about everything else in the country. As the circumstances of her life had become confused, perhaps she could not be blamed for consistently defending and glorifying evils of this kind. The feelings of injustice which she believed were inflicted by the Government were directed towards the Faculty of Law which she cursed vehemently, invoking God to curse it after each call to prayer, especially the dawn and the evening prayers, because she believed that her curses at these times would be more effective. Her favourite curse was "May a goddess destroy the Faculty of Law," because, in her opinion, it was from the Faculty of Law that the oppressive judge, who had passed the unjust and abominable sentence on her which decreed that she would be separated from her boys for twenty-five years, had graduated. For this reason she continued to hurl abuse in every possible direction, including the Leadership of the Republic and the Council of Ministers, on the basis that the sentence handed down under their law was inappropriate and unnecessary. These complaints were also one of the threads which tied Safiyya to Mahrousa because Mahrousa, who was friendly with Safiyya's family, oversaw writing and sending the complaints for her. There was also a bond because of their close proximity in age and the common experience of bearing children but it was Safiyya's overwhelming generosity which was at the heart of the solid relationship between the two women. Safiyya gave generously to Mahrousa from gifts that her boys brought her on their visits to prison. This might be food, clothes and shoes—even medicines—which Safiyya shared with Mahrousa, especially medicines for rheumatism and colds. These were always in short supply at the pharmacies, especially during the winter months when there was a run on them, for reasons best known to the senior managers in the companies of the public sector. On top of this, Mahrousa considered Safiyya her private bank, often borrowing money from her from resources outside the prison. Inside prison the only currency which circulated was cigarettes. These were in such demand that you could get anything in exchange for them; the proportion of prisoners who smoked had reached at least ninety-nine percent and the number of packets consumed depended on the individual prisoner's financial situation and the extent of her addiction. Naturally the amount consumed by those who were hooked on drugs, and by the prostitutes, was more than the other prisoners. Mahrousa was in the habit of taking interest-free loans from Safiyya's sons when they came to visit their mother in prison or when she went to see them at home. No cloud hung over the relationship between the two "sisters"; Safiyya's husband even began to work in the video shop which Mahrousa's daughter, who now had a diploma in commerce, allowed him to run in return for a reasonable monthly income. He also became a conciliator in disputes which broke out over the car mechanic the girl wanted to marry. The mother flatly refused his proposal of marriage, swearing that none of her daughters would marry as long as she was alive. She considered men evil, created from the devil's rib, and her remaining daughters were in total agreement with this view perhaps because they were, both in looks and speech, exact replicas of their mother. The only exception was this youngest daughter, who had soft fair hair, made even finer by the force of gravity since it stretched down to the middle of her back. Her hair opened new prospects for her as regards men when the car mechanic, who had been bald since he was twenty-four, fell madly in love with her. She also used all kinds of beauty preparations on her face—red, blue and green—in order to stimulate his desire and encourage him to propose to her.

In deference to Safiyya's beloved husband who had intervened in this matter, Mahrousa finally agreed to the marriage after making over a large down payment for the bridal dower. She hoped that the marriage would end quickly and that her straying daughter would return to the pen, secure from Satan's rib, and would rejoin her daughters' squad which was hostile to men.

For many years, Aziza watched the relationship between Mahrousa and Safiyya grow stronger and observed every minute aspect of the rope of love which stretched between them. As she spent long nights thinking about these women, she became obsessed with the desire to achieve justice and mercy on earth. She sipped her imaginary wine, inhaling deeply on the cigarettes which she smoked incessantly and which mingled with the smoke already in her chest. Her deep experience acquired in the women's prison had taught her that whenever she came across a true, caring relationship based on love and sincere devotion, like that which had sprung up and grown between Mahrousa and Safiyya, this kind of relationship was what really counted in deciding who to include amongst the passengers of the golden chariot ascending to heaven. She came to this conclusion despite the fact that she had never liked nor respected Safiyya because, as far as she was concerned, she was a tramp with a criminal nature and time had shown that, even if she were to live for a hundred years, she would be incapable of mending her ways. However, she would take her to heaven for the sake of Mahrousa, the warden with the angelic soul and devilish face who had shed so many tears of pain and torment and whose pure spirit and body was that of a true saint who could only be venerated in heaven. Aziza did not want to separate her from Safiyya's caring heart since she was the only person she had ever loved. She would give Safiyya one more chance and perhaps, if she ascended to this celestial world amongst angels which would be awaiting her and all the other women on the golden chariot, all the evil she had been tainted with in her earthly life would be erased. In any case, as her experience with Mahrousa had confirmed, she was not wholly devoid of good and her heart was not all black; there were some patches where light shone through which, given the chance, might spread and dispel all the darkness inside her. However, time was to extinguish any such hope. About two weeks after the day when Mahrousa's face was covered in honey, she found Safiyya lying in her bed one morning, in the final repose of death. Her glass eye stared ahead, in a way which made all the prisoners who had gathered around the motionless body feel as if it was a real eye expressing sorrow and unhappiness as it fixed on the piece of blue sky which could be seen through the bars of the cell window nearby. Her expert hands, which had stolen for so long with ease and dexterity, now firmly gripped a photo of her two sons, resting on her chest. They smiled happily without fear for the future.

Translated by Dinah Manisty

Hoda Barakat
(b. 1952)

LEBANON

Hoda Barakat was born in Beirut and took a degree in French literature from Beirut University. In 1976 she left for Paris, where she continued her studies and worked for a time in journalism. Two of her novels, *The Stone of Laughter* and *The Tiller of Waters*, have been published in English translation. *The Tiller of Waters*, from which the following extract has been taken, won the Naguib Mahfouz Medal for Literature in 2000. It is set in devastated Beirut, and its main character and his father are textile merchants who see the world through the code of cloth.

FROM The Tiller of Waters

In all of the stories of silk you will find betrayal, evil, and abundant covetousness. It was not simply the bounties of the Nile that Julius Caesar sought as he waged war against Cleopatra. For the army commanders had informed him in their reports that this queen possessed "fabrics made of the breeze." When Caesar returned to Rome with the chests of the defeated Cleopatra, Rome saw silk for the very first time. The city's senators hurried to warn Caesar that wearing these "breezes" would be detrimental to the morals of the city: it would be the beginning of the end, the hazardous prelude to decline and decadence. And sure enough, later in the Senate and the senatorial residences, their wives and their concubines found themselves ensnared in silken filaments, struggling uselessly in their gummy resin.

Rome drowned in its own silk, submerging itself ever deeper until it sank under barbarian siege. To loosen his hold, the audacious and bold Visigoth Alaric's primary demand was five thousand garments of crimson silk, in addition to gold and spices. Although they gave him all that he wanted it was not enough, for when he opened the chests of silk, that unbounded desire swept over him and he pierced Rome like a sword stabbing water.

The sacred books of the Jews warned against amalgams and prohibited the plowing of a field with a team composed of an ox and a mule. But this was not in fear of uniting what God had separated, honoring boundaries between species whose violation would signal malediction and the victory of evil and its folk. Rather, the sacred word aimed to avoid combining the respective perfections of two pure kinds, that is, two species brought to consummate perfection through a single passion.

The earliest Muslims understood as much, as soon as they saw the silk of the Persians and the Byzantines. *Haraam!* they said. It is forbidden, they proclaimed, to fuse two such perfect temptations, the summits of desire: the body of a woman and the fabric of silk. So passionate was their longing for that female body that its encasement in silk beyond the walls of home must be prohibited. It is forbidden, they said; for it yields a perilous cupidity. An awful torture, and a test too taxing for human endurance, for the human eye that sees the forbidden. A source of chaos in the streets that brooks no laws of mercy and compassion, takes no account of where the modest abilities of people to control the call of their desires end. Thus the multitudes of Crusader soldiers, the wearers of hemp and wool, saw no silk in the cities they entered—except in the princely courts. The army generals wrote their dispatches, announcing to their capitals, so chilled and remote, that in the East they had seen lights emanating from coffers. They described the emirs' thrones as more splendidly fiery than the sun in these countries, even though it was unblemished by clouds. And so, they said, they must press on, fighting the battles; those at home must pluck the very last rural farmer from his muddy plot of land to arm him with a sword. The ships laden with coffers that burst with bewitching suns would not float but on seas of blood through which they must row on their homeward route to Europe.

But through long and slowly passing eons, silk's discoverers managed to preserve themselves from its evils . . . in great measure, at least.

An ancient Chinese legend relates that in the beginning the worm that becomes a moth was a princess, murdered by her father's wife, jealous of her loveliness and filled with envy. Her killing, or her burial alive, transformed her into filaments or eggs. This filament, then, was not offered in peace or as the blessing of bounty, and as we approach it we must remember this. As expiation before the deed, recognition of an evil inherent in its discovery and production—and to repel the consequences of its temptation— the Chinese sowed the ancient silk road with sacred sketches offered up to the Buddha in more than nine hundred and ninety grottoes dotted along a distance of eight thousand kilometers. A merchant would stop at each shrine to offer his devotions and supplications.

The Taoist Chinese silk weavers revered a text entitled *The Book of Changes*, composed in the distant past, the seventh century before Christ. It comprised sixty-four secret linguistic orders, and only each wise Grand Master of the silk weavers' brotherhood learned how to read its ideograms. Each formula is composed of connected lines that represent the male principle and interrupted lines that signify the female principle. Each represents the Tao, the cosmic principle that orders the world—indeed, the entire universe. The loom's warp is the yang and its weft is the yin. The closeness of the weave and the decrees that govern it represent the measure of our relation to the world and a calculation of our place within it, balanced between past and future. And how can secrets of this import be given to anyone but the knowledgeable and the wise? How can we entrust to the ignorant, the irresponsible, or the fickle the weaving of a silk like polished atlas, for example? The weave structure of this silk must be carefully calculated according to the number of points where it is warped onto the loom—whatever type of loom it is—to repeat a pattern, structurally and visually, that is known as "satanic squares." Actually called "magic squares," their

chessboard-like arrangement in black and white signals at once op-
position and concord, and brings into harmony all of the contradictions: between femininity and masculinity, night and day, yang and
yin. They become "satanic" if they manifest any flaws, no matter
how slight or innocent these may seem. Thus, any blurring of un-
ambiguous boundaries, drawn strictly between the ultimate examples of two pure categories, brings ruin down upon the order of
things in the world, and evil's curses prevail.

My father taught me many other things, bringing to a close my
last lessons in silk . . . the lessons he imparted before his death, as if
to free his conscience and uphold the obligatory formalities.

Translated by Marilyn Booth

Mohammed Barrada
(b. 1938)
MOROCCO

Mohammed Barrada was born in Rabat, Morocco. He earned
a degree in Arabic at Cairo University and a doctorate in
modern literary criticism in Paris and is presently a professor of Arabic at the University of Rabat. He has published a
number of critical works and has translated books from
French. Two of his novels are available in English translation: *The Game of Forgetting* and *Fugitive Light*.

Life by Installments

We woke late, yawning as we lay on the bed, our bones feeling as
though they'd fall apart. It seemed to us that this day would proceed
on its way like its predecessors. We leaned our head against the
wooden headboard. Our sight was bleared and no doubt a dark yel-
lowness overspread our face. Having previously visited the doctor,
we had submitted our state of health to him and he had shaken his
head knowingly:

"You're not alone—all those who think and dream and aren't content with reality are afflicted with your condition."

We remembered the same answer having been given by a doctor—perhaps by our own doctor himself—to a friend when he complained of indigestion and heartburn.

"Is there a cure, doctor?"

"I shall give you some pills that will do you good, but I don't advise you to be too optimistic. Every morning, on opening your eyes, search around in your mind for some amusing story or event, grin from ear to ear, then leap out of bed and lift up your voice in song—in these circumstances an unpleasant voice is acceptable."

We wanted to try out the doctor's advice so we searched round in the crevices of our memory for some story that would set us off laughing first thing. Ah yes, we had found it: the story of the foreign neighbour who from time to time amused herself by taking a taxi, despite the fact that she was a car-owner. When the cab arrived at the door of the building she would claim she had forgotten her money at home and that she would go upstairs to bring the man the fare. She would then go up and not return, and the poor man would continue to hoot away and everyone in the building would look down without understanding what he was up to. Of course he wouldn't know the building and would make off in despair, while she would go on laughing her head off inside her room. Ha ha ha! We had our fill of laughing and secretly gave thanks to our clever neighbour, then we jumped out of bed and began a new day in the long holiday.

For a long time we wandered aimlessly round our well-stocked library. We noticed that most of its contents were books we had put off reading and which we had decided to return to when there was sufficient time. Our hand stretched out to a red volume whose author had lived forty years ago in the red city of Marrakesh. It was Mohammed ibn Abdullah al-Mu'aqqat's *The Marrakesh Journey or the Temporal Mirror of Vile Deeds*, also called *The Sword Unsheathed against Him Who Renounces the Prophet's Sunna*.

". . . then after that Sheikh Abdul Hadi ṣaid: 'And this person asking and the person asked were from among the people of the tenth century, so how much more so in this time of ours which has become like the unbelieving night? As for its leaders, they have brought tyranny to their subjects. They have eaten flesh and drunk blood; they have sucked the marrow from the bone and have swallowed up the brains, leaving people neither the world nor yet religion. As for the things of the world, they have made away with them; and as for religion, they have enticed them from it. This is something we have witnessed, not something we have thought up . . .'"

Abu Zeid asked: "May Allah give you strength, is it permissible for one to remain in such a place when one is incapable of changing that which is objectionable?"

The mind finds no relaxation in reading: the old appears new, the new old, and the brain shrieks out at the impossibility of this being so, does not accept that "the sun is blind." We have told ourselves that the source of all that was perhaps boredom, the length of the association, the unearthing of hidden depth, the exposing of illusions, the scattering of one's dreams, clinging to what is to come and being oblivious of that which exists. Let us then train the soul to patience and let us live the detailed and elaborate present, the daily routine that is repeated.

Our guest at lunch was a relative who was getting on for sixty. He had learnt the Qur'an by heart when young, knowing its every letter, and had eventually become a *muezzin*. When his wife had died a year ago he had chosen a relative of his to get married to, it not being permissible for a *muezzin* to remain unmarried, but he had preferred that the marriage should take place after his return from the Pilgrimage. During his absence busybodies had intervened and the woman had got married to someone else, leaving him with nobody. He is nevertheless still searching for a wife.

"Please Allah, you are well. In all circumstances we give thanks to Him. And how's the health and the work? Fine. May we always be in your prayers. And how is this young lad getting on: Is he making a bit of an effort? Ask him and he'll answer you. For myself I see him as a slacker. Shame on you, my boy. If only you'd model yourself on your uncle Abdurrahman."

As though his words had awakened some clouded-over memory, we said:

"The one who died of drowning?"

"Yes—and as a martyr too. The Prophetic Tradition singles out three categories of people to be considered martyrs: those who die by fire, those who die by drowning, and those who die by having a wall collapse on top of them."

He now directed his conversation at the young lad, who showed no annoyance, so used was he to listening to advice and instructions in a variety of shapes and forms.

"Your uncle Abdurrahman had a thorough grasp of all the sciences when he was eighteen years old . . ."

Smiling, the boy interrupted him:

"I'm still no more than seventeen."

"Your head is emptier than the skull of a donkey. You should put to good account what we are saying to you. The future is yours, and you are the loser if you don't follow our advice. Do you think it's easy to make a living? Some wear decorations round their necks, others a headstall."

The Hajj continued what he had to say:

"Abdurrahman, may Allah continue to bestow His blessings upon him, was proficient in all the sciences. His handwriting was exceedingly beautiful. He was employed at the Finance Department and donned the *kaftan* and turban when he was still young. He was a great swimmer and an accomplished horseman. One day a jurisprudent who came to visit us from Sousse saw him and was taken by his intelligence and knowledge, especially when he found that he had learnt al-Dumyati by heart. Afraid for him from the envious eyes of man and djinn, he wrote him a charm to wear called 'the amulet of the sea and the nullification of hindrances,' which he ordered him to hang on his *kaftan* so that no harm might come to him."

In order to exhibit our interest in the subject, be it only outwardly, we said:

"And despite this amulet he was drowned in the sea?"

"Everything is by divine decree. He was returning from Rabat to Sale and crossed the *wadi* of Abu Raqraq in a boat. He then took off his turban, made his ablutions and performed the midday prayer. He later left the place and hadn't gone twenty paces when the idea of having a swim came to him. So, going back to the same place, he took off his clothes and went in to have a swim."

In the same way, with the same smile, the boy interrupted him: "Used they to swim in the nude in those days?"

Though we found the question a reasonable one, the situation demanded a different reaction. We therefore looked daggers at him, clapped our hands together in a gesture of despair and made every effort not to burst out laughing.

"No, they used to swim in a loincloth. It happened that day that he had left the amulet in his other *kaftan*. His skill in swimming helped him not and the sea has kept him swallowed up until now."

Thus did Abdurrahman die and, where the sciences of this world and the next are concerned, it is we who were the losers.

The conversation petered out with the lunch not yet over. We looked at the man as he chewed away leisurely. Was there any other subject we could engage him in? We recollected some of the stories and bits of news he had on numerous occasions recounted to us. It would be sufficient for us to make reference to one of them for him to burst forth in a repetition of what we had already heard. We could for example say: "By Allah, the people of that time used to do it with real feeling when they called out to their king: 'Glory and gold be to Moulay Abdul Aziz,'" for him to tell us again of the battles and skirmishes that took place between Sultan Moulay Abdul Aziz and certain tribes, and he would continue on till he arrived at the time of Bu Hmara and the entry of the French. However, finding that this would be tedious, we thought instead to ask him about his private life: What did he do with himself after giving the call to prayers and performing his prayers? The smoking of hashish he had given up after his return from the Holy Places and the new wife hadn't yet put in an appearance, so how did he pass his time? Did he regard himself as being dead? It seemed that his relationship with the world surrounding him was extremely limited. He would pick up various bits of news, corroborate them and conclude his words with: "Allah gives a choice and He chooses."

The boy eats greedily; perhaps he's not thinking about anything. He is drawn to what is taking place around him, be it only in a mechanical manner. He has discovered the pleasure of smoking, chasing after the neighbours' daughters, also the football craze. After some thought he announces his desire to travel to Europe during the summer vacation, even if he has to walk (which would multiply the cost of his pilgrimage).

And we? We think about the old man and the boy, and we make guesses about what may perhaps be filling their minds and about their relationships with what is around them. And after that? The siesta. And then? Wandering around and getting a breath of fresh air. And then? We'll telephone our girlfriend. We'll meet up, we'll chatter away, our temperature will rise, our instincts burst forth. Boredom will take over again. We'll part. We'll meet up with some friends. We'll talk about everything. We'll criticize. We'll commend. We'll show displeasure. Enthusiasm will vanish when we see the extent of our impotence. We'll set off anew into the street. We'll feel lust renewing itself through the vibrations of the rounded and curved portions of women's bodies. Always we used to ask our married friends: "Does it mean that your wife acts as a representative for her sex?" We get the answer: "Not all, there is no one who desires other women more than married men, even though we love our wives." We try to comprehend the question, to rationalize it. No doubt it's due to the mixing of the sexes, to provocative advertising, to make-up, to high heels and . . . and what else?

We told him that and he interrupted us sharply:

"That's rubbish. With love we can overcome the infatuation of sex."

"And where is love?"

"Ah, you're one of those pessimistic types. I'll tell you my story." Of course his story is run-of-the-mill: they wanted to marry her off to an old man, so she threatened to commit suicide and the two of them pledged themselves to love each other until death etc.

He won't understand us then—no point in repeating to him what Freud said: "I am accustoming myself to the idea of regarding every sexual act as a process in which four persons are involved."

We exaggerate and the moment grips and imprisons us. It is not the infatuation of sex alone that threatens or tempts us. There is the infatuation of crime, of suicide, of drink, of revolt. The other categories do greatly tempt us because they do not destroy the familiar. And writing?

"And I was silent and no answer was seen from him and he started to tell his beads. Abdul Basit said to him: 'Master, I have always known about you that you possess a tongue that renders the most eloquent speechless and dazzles their minds . . . You embolden us morning and eve with those treatises that captivate the heart, leaving in our souls its delectable mark. It is thus that I used to know you, so howabout you now?'"

In the evening we were conscious of the same feeling of disintegration in our bones, also an even gloomier melancholy. We thought of ridding ourselves of it through the same famous medical prescription, but we hesitated because the doctor was precise about determining the time it should be taken: in the morning, not the evening. We shall wander round the streets, we shall scrutinize people's facial expressions that perchance we may hit upon the remedy. We walked for a long time: the cafés are full, the bottles of beer are emptied in a flash, laughter rings out, the never-slackening rattle of fruit machines. Even so our melancholy persists, will not let up. The cars fly past, the buses are slow, jam-packed, the cinemas advertise their heroes. It appeared to us that everyone around us was running away, and it occurred to us to stop them, to shout at them: "You're running away." But the idea seemed fatuous, unsupported by any basis.

Translated by Denys Johnson-Davies

Mohamed El-Bisatie

(b. 1938)

EGYPT

Mohamed El-Bisatie was born in a Nile Delta village over-looking Lake Manzala. Although he has lived most of his life in Cairo and also spent time in Saudi Arabia, his fiction is set almost exclusively in the region where he was born and raised. According to the critic and translator Roger Allen, "the inhabitants of this rural microcosm all live, work and die in a social atmosphere akin to a fishbowl." A representative volume of El-Bisatie's short stories was published under the title *A Last Glass of Tea*, from which the story below is taken. His short novel *Houses Behind the Trees* has been made into a film and is available in English translation, as are his novels *Over the Bridge* and *Clamor of the Lake*, from which the second extract below is taken.

Drought

Date-palms stood thick around the village, stretching far into the open country. The two men left the darkness of the date-palms and walked into the open country. The tall man left first, wearing a black shirt and light shoes. Turning around, he saw the other man approaching. After that he didn't turn around. The other man was wearing a dark-colored gallabia and had a dirty white shawl around his head. The distance between them remained constant.

It was an extensive area of wasteland covered with numerous crevices and dried-up water channels, along the sides of which were scattered thorns and thin leafless trees, their branches looking like sticks for firewood. The sun's glare was fierce and there was a hot wind that carried with it powdery dust.

They crossed over the wasteland heading toward a green patch that showed up from afar. They walked deliberately, as though the wind was impeding their progress; the man in front leaned forward, the other had placed his shawl about his mouth and nose. The air was colored a pale yellow, the sun covered over with a turbid coating.

The green patch rose slightly above the ground and the man disappeared into it. The other was still striding behind him in the dust storm, his gallabia wrapped tightly around his body.

The man walked along a narrow watercourse, on the sides of which were dark green thornbushes tipped with yellow flowers. Thickly branched trees began to shake in the wind. The canal ended in a cement barrier, after which the land sloped down toward open country. He turned at the sound of faint footsteps and appeared to have been caught unawares by the other man at the side of the watercourse. In silence they exchanged glances.

The whirlwinds were chasing each other beyond the trees, sweeping away the dried thornbushes with them as they went. The man in the gallabia bent over and washed his face, drying it with the end of his scarf. Then he crossed the watercourse. He was short and had the face of an old man, with a thick black mustache and small eyes. The other, the man with the black shirt, was clean-shaven, with the face of a child; he smoothed back his hair from his eyes as he breathed heavily, his back against the trunk of a tree.

The wind increased in violence, the sound of it echoing emptily among the trees. The glare of the sun disappeared; its weak light still penetrated through from time to time, the air smelling of the dark-colored dust.

The short man placed his hands into the side openings of his gallabia: he appeared to be smoothing out his waistcoat. He took a step forward and the young man's hands shook slightly, then remained in repose by his sides. His face was moist with sweat and dust.

The man rushed at him quickly, lunging at the young man's stomach, turning his hand from left to right. For an instant the young man looked as though he had been taken by surprise; his hands took hold of the man's fist and he leaned over noiselessly. He was slowly slipping down, his head falling onto the man's shoulder;

as he made a further effort, his head remained where it was. The man withdrew his fist and the young man's body twitched; the man grasped him under the arms and gently lowered him. The young man collapsed in a heap, turning over on his back, then crawled forward a little until he was up against the trunk of the tree. He let out a gasp, then became limp and silent.

Dry leaves covered the place, clinging to the tips of the thornbushes and floating on the surface of the watercourse. Removing some with his hand, the man washed his knife and returned it to his pocket, then set off back.

The violence of the wind had lessened, though the air remained redolent with the smell of dust.

Translated by Denys Johnson-Davies

FROM *Clamor of the Lake*

Gomaa's wife used to go to the shore on the days of the gale. In early youth she had found a silver bracelet among the debris spewed up by the sea. She wore it on her wrist and never took it off, and though more than twenty years had passed since that day, she would still go out to the shore, never missing a gale. Her small house near the lake was stacked with fantastic objects picked from the shore: shells, hollow and flat; hard, colorful stones; bottles of different shapes and hues; empty cans; spoons; plates; knives; broken bits of chairs; deflated dinghies.

She would leave her house in the midst of the gale, slipping out unnoticed, into the gloom of the somber dawn, with an empty sack slung over her shoulders. When the catch was abundant the sack was quickly filled. Paddling home, she towed the sack in the water. Her husband, sensing her return, would be standing on the threshold, wrapped in an old quilt. He would take hold of one end of the sack. Preceding him into the courtyard, she would stand by the fire, wringing her wet gallabiya while he emptied the sack. Then she would return to the shore. But when the gale was niggardly, she could remain on the shore until midday and return with a sack only a quarter full.

Women neighbors saw her days after the gale wearing new things. Once she wore leather slippers adorned with roses. Although the leather was cracked and the petals were broken, the slippers looked dazzling on her feet, which she had rubbed with a pumice stone. Another time, they who had never seen anything but black veils saw her in a soft, colorful, transparent one. They touched it in amazement, with its delicate colorful prints—red, yellow, green. True, they spotted its frayed edges and the tiny holes mended with thread similar to the thread they used. But all these defects became invisible once it was on her head and began to wave in the light breeze above her hair, which she had washed, parted in the middle, and braided for the occasion. She smiled at their glances and pulled the veil, holding it with her lips. And on her chest they saw beads of all shapes and colors, and also hairpins the like of which they had never seen, sometimes in the shape of a leaf, or a boat and a fish.

One day she went out to the town market with her husband. She wore a yellow knee-length silk dress with brown diagonal stripes and a zipper in the back. She also wore black boots. Her husband, riding the donkey, was in front of her. The women accompanied her for a little while. Her bare knees were dark and her calves had green bulging veins. They told her that the boots looked like a soldier's, but she paid no attention.

They said they were far too big, but she had inserted some stuffing in the toes, and so it did not bother her.

They said that the dress was frayed around the zipper and torn under the arms, that her stitches were obvious for all eyes to see. She quickened her step and caught up with her husband.

She took them to her house one day when Gomaa was in town. They had shown admiration for a green and yellow woolen waistcoat that she wore over her gallabiya. It was too tight for her, but it was lovely. On the right side of the chest it had a tiny pocket with a bead. The women gathered in the room and she pushed the door shut.

A small window close to the ceiling gave off a little light. They

saw an old sheet draped over one part of the wall, apparently covering hanging objects, their prominence visible from underneath.
They lifted the corner of the sheet to take a look but she pushed
them away, saying that these were Gomaa's things that he did not
like anyone to see. They moved toward a heap of things piled in
a corner of the room, rummaging through the empty bottles and
the shells. One of the women picked a red shoe with a high heel.
She was examining it when Gomaa's wife took it and tossed it on
the pile, saying, "There's only one . . . until I find its twin."

Gazing at them and laughing, she hitched up the gallabiya to her
waist. They saw her panties, as small as the palm of a hand, barely
covering anything at all. They squealed in wonder. The panties were
soft to the touch and had a bright print. Pulled taut above her
thighs, they made her curves look beautiful. They had strings forming two bows at the sides. She said that as soon as she pulls the
strings, the panties fall of their own accord, then she pulled the
string on either side and they saw the panties loosen in front and in
the back. She said she had found two pairs in the last gale. Then she
spun around and let down the gallabiya. Leading the way to the
door, she said that not once did she pass beside Gomaa without his
stripping her, and then she laughed.

They saw Gomaa, too, come out in new things after the gale.
Once he wore shoes, and because he had never before worn shoes
he walked sluggishly, lifting his feet more than necessary. Another
time he wore brown sunglasses, and went on about the scorching
sun that harms one's eyesight. In his hand was a rosary, the round-
ness of its beads and their color unlike any they had seen, and a
small penknife sheathed in ivory that he would open to scrape a
reed stalk or a stick. One day he went out with his sleeves rolled up,
with a watch on his wrist that was full of water that shook under the
glass—but then that would only take a few days to evaporate. And
they saw plates made of a metal that does not rust. There was also a
small rocking chair fit for a boy, which Gomaa's wife placed on the
threshold of the house, saying it was for decoration, and a year later
they saw the small table beside it.

They also saw a lantern with a slightly rusty net of thin wire encircling its round glass. Gomaa's wife hung it on a nail above the entrance to the house. Gomaa took it along whenever he went out at night to buy tobacco or stay up in the café. It had a knob on the side to turn down its flame. He would sit relaxed, the lantern by his feet, all eyes on him. Gusts of wind blew and the flame did not flicker. Gomaa spoke of the dark night, of the ditches and the animal dung and human feces that fill the alleyways. You smell them but can't make out where they are in the dark. You sense them when your foot sinks into them and they stick to it and move with it, and the moon doesn't help, because the moon doesn't come out when you need it, and it doesn't come out in lands that have incurred God's wrath.

Translated by Hala Halim

Mohamed Choukri
(1935–2003)
MOROCCO

Mohamed Choukri was born in northern Morocco and spent most of his life in Tangier. The American novelist Paul Bowles translated a number of his writings, including *Jean Genet in Tangier* and the well-known autobiography *For Bread Alone*. Choukri was remarkable for being self-taught; he did not know how to read or write until the age of twenty-one. His autobiography is banned in much of the Arab world because of its frank homosexual content.

Flower Crazy

Outside in the lane the children are yelling.

She wakes and sits up. With legs dangling over the side of the bed, she bends her head forward. The two of them are eating bread dipped in oil and drinking cold green tea left by their mother in the pot. They look at her as they chew. Lost in thought, dizzy, she takes her head in her hands and presses down on it. Rising unsteadily, a hand over her mouth, she goes to the lavatory. Its loathsome smell helps her to be violently sick: viscid, yellow vomit. The sound of her vomiting is choked like that of an animal being slaughtered. Her elder brother brings her a plastic bucket containing some water. She drops back exhausted on the bed. She is sobbing. The younger brother goes out, the other is sitting silently in front of her. She sits up and they exchange glances sadly. Her lusterless eyes water with tears. She smiles. They both smile. With a movement of head and hands she invites him over, seats him alongside her, hugs him to her breast, smiling; smiling, she takes his small face in her hand; smiling, she wipes away the trickle of his tears.

The children outside are playing ball and yelling. She gives him a coin. He smiles. He kisses her cheek and goes out.

Outside in the lane misery is more friendly to young and old. There beauty looks out curiously from small, gloomy doorways. It is the same beauty as is sold on the streets of the new city.

The crippled poet of the quarter is a witness to what has happened ever since all the people of this lane were living in shacks. He teaches the young and the old, for a fee or for thanks; he reads and writes lovers' letters; he gives support to the ailing by reciting the Qur'an, to love through poetry; he plays with the children and sits of an evening with the old men.

A child eats bread and chocolate. She is sitting on the doorstep of her house looking out at the goings-on of the lane. She savours what she is eating. A little boy in front of her has a red flower in his hand. Its stalk dances between his thin, dirty fingers. The hunger in his eyes woos the bread. She stops eating, the chunk of bread close to her mouth. He is looking at the flower, smelling it, while he smiles at her enticingly. The dance of hunger lies in his eyes, his legs, his hands, his whole body. Her dreamy eyes ask for his dancing flower. His hand is stretched towards his mouth, hers towards her nose.

She gets up and drains the pot into one of the two greasy glasses and sips at the dregs. She rubs her eyes and takes from her handbag a packet of Virginian cigarettes. Sitting on the bed, she lights one. She looks at the picture of her father in a small dilapidated frame on the oozing wall. She smokes, looking at the picture of her father. She coughs violently. She remembers her father's cough and the threads of blood he would spit out. Again she feels dizzy and gets up, coughing and throwing away half of her cigarette, to go to the lavatory. Straining, she vomits a thin thread of spittle. She is reminded of the spittle of drunks, their senseless chatter and their violence amidst the clamour of the singing and fog of smoke. She looks into a small mirror hanging near her head. Her night face has the colour of oil; it is puffy, the eyes bleary. She clasps her hands in front of her, then presses down on her shoulder muscles with repeated movements, her chest shaking and thrust forward. She feels her breasts and finds them firm. Sighing, seated on the bed, she opens her legs, then scratches at the bush of hair that she has not shaved for a long time. She loves to see her nakedness through her own eyes, much more than through the eyes of men.

Flower Crazy. This is how the people of the quarter have called him. The crippled poet is a witness. Flower Crazy lives with his mother in a hut. Every morning they go together to the city, only returning at evening. She begs and he distributes his flowers amongst the beautiful women and girls. He asks nothing of them. He buys his flowers with his mother's money or he steals them. He has been arrested and sent to court many times but, through pity for his madness for flowers, he is let off. His last flower he always throws to the woman living on the ground floor. Once, out of sympathy for his madness for flowers, she threw him her handkerchief. That night he dreamed of gardens of flowers that he would pick with mad joy and of handkerchiefs that fell upon him from the window of the handkerchief woman. The day of the handkerchief is better than a thousand days. Peace she is, the woman, after the day of the handkerchief. So did he start talking to those he knew. He began to date his life as from the day of the handkerchief: this happened before the day of the handkerchief, this after the day of the handkerchief. Even women before the handkerchief were not the same as after the handkerchief. No longer did he give his flowers to all women. The bunch that had been bought or stolen was for the woman of the handkerchief. His coming with the flowers and her presence at the window was the promise of a rendezvous between them. When the husband was cured of his cold, he smelt Flower Crazy's smell on his wife's body. When the husband was cured of his eye ailment, he saw Flower Crazy leaping from the window and his wife nimbly going out of the door and running after Flower Crazy. He was too fat to run after them.

She made up her night face, putting blue drops into her eyes; she exuded an aroma of costly perfume. From her small wardrobe she took out an expensive dress, more diaphanous, sleek, and clinging than all her other dresses, and a pair of beautiful, silver-coloured shoes with high heels which she wrapped up in the pages of a foreign magazine she had bought both for her new and her old shoes. She put on an old pair of shoes and carried the new under her arm. Before going out she cast a glance at her large, beautifully dressed doll she had bought with her own money when she had grown up and begun to earn.

Her younger brother is sitting by the doorstep playing with a kitten and a paper ball tied to a string, while in front of him is an emaciated dog lying in the shade overcome by sleep and fatigue. Leaving the kitten, he comes to say goodbye to her. She gives him a small coin and kisses him. He asks her to come back early in the evening, before he goes to sleep. Her other brother is far away, playing football with the team of youngsters from the lane. Women and children are drawing water amidst curses and clamour at the hydrant for the lane. A child excretes near the hedge, then scratches at the excrement with a small stick and smells it. A lank dog hovers around; its eyes widen, its tail wags. Two young girls insult one another where their buckets lie in a row. One of them has lifted her dress, exposing her naked bottom, and says to her rival in the queue around the hydrant:

"You're no more than that to me."

The other exposes her front to her, then they both start slapping each other, pulling at each other, shouting insults. Some young men seated on the ground, leaning against the wall, and listlessly smoking, look on derisively at what is happening. One of the young men whistles at her in mock flirtation and two children beg money from her. She gives them two coins and goes on her way through the mud, distressed and miserable. Some of the looks she gets are of admiration, some of hate and envy.

Near the entrance to the muddy lane she hides the worn-out shoes and puts on the new ones, then walks along the asphalt road to the new town.

The crippled poet of the lane writes about these things that go on in the lane, also about things in the town, things he hasn't lived through or seen but has heard of from those who have seen them or related them. These are some of his memoirs:

Yesterday I thought anew about my life through zeros. From the right to the left I thought of the value of zeros. I thought of everything through nothing. "He will not be questioned about what He does but they will be questioned." What befalls you from the right is from Allah and what befalls you from the left is from yourself. Allah divides and you multiply but you do not act equitably and Allah is best at acting equitably in computation. To destroy all idols—that is what you know. But Allah does not plot against you if you should do away with what you built for yourselves.

Sex! Sex! Sex! This is your misfortune, so seek the happiness of the Promise if you are steadfast believers. I am angry at this human hunger that does not cease till death. I no longer remember my pride which used to prevent me from loving. Sweet distance was my sole solace. The debauchery that is stronger within me than the chastity always gets the better of me. Never did she who at the time I desired come to me. That one you grieve at parting from and are wearied by her staying on. Beauty! Oh for the beauty that tears at me and is possessed by someone else, someone who mocks me. I have not understood a single woman other than in spurts of imagination: in sips, not at one gulp. Maybe I have thought about them all. My desires were divided amongst them. The life I thought about I haven't lived. Ask that one who has lived it, not thought about it.

It is the confession of the final glass, the final friend to leave me. Ask that one who is separated from his homeland. I have a friend who, like me, is overwhelmed by beauty; he hates me in the eyes of his wife and loves me in the eyes of those women who pass through my life. Ask that one who has wearied of the familiar face. Under compulsion I circumambulated the Kaaba, trailing a woman for three whole days, and after her I no longer circumambulated for more than a day of its sun or its moon. The contract of consummation is the whole token of esteem of that friend, while for me it was a subject of talk at the end of the night, the final glass, the final insolvency. Ever averse to performing the obligatory prayers, who can blame me or judge me about the additional ones? We are brothers in the exercise of the power of choice, enemies in compulsion.

Like me the bachelors of this town have become addicted to the night and to the glass of wine, or to merit in the Hereafter or to emigrating before reaching thirty, fleeing from madness, ignorance, and death. Today I am alone with my glass, like those who escape to the bars or the brothels in the hope of retrieving some of their bachelorhood. They glorify drink in the evening, curse it in the morning. Every soul will taste of its sweetness and splendour and of its curse. But in all the brothels I have found my sisters and my friends' sisters. I have seen the delirium of night melting away their make-up and ripping off their masks, while, in the prime of youth, their teeth are being eaten away with decay. I have heard them recalling the purity of their childhood in school songs that have been truncated in their recollection, have been reenacted in romantic novels, films of love, and old and recent memories.

In the main street she enters the bank. She takes out a cheque from her beautiful and expensive leather bag and with difficulty, her hand trembling, signs her name. The cashier looks with curiosity at the cheque and at her. She draws out two hundred dirhams and leaves in confusion. At a shop she buys an illustrated women's magazine and a packet of gold-tipped cigarettes.

In the tea salon of Madame Porte the beautiful waitress comes to her and stands waiting politely. She knows how generous she is with her. In a voice flawed by the hoarseness of the night's fatigue, she says:

"Bring me an orange juice, cold milk, and toast with butter and jam."

In the Grand Socco her mother calls out, her eyes on the security guard who chases away women peddlers like herself:

"Onions! Radishes! Oranges!"

In the lane her footballer brother shouts:

"Goal!"

The younger brother is playing with the kitten near the crippled poet of the lane, and the emaciated dog slumbers in front of them, while a child with a dying sparrow in his hand deliberately pees on the shoes she has left in the hedge.

Translated by Denys Johnson-Davies

Rashid al-Daif
(b. 1945)
LEBANON

Rashid al-Daif was born in Lebanon to a Maronite family. He is a lecturer in Arabic at the Lebanese University in Beirut, as well as a well-known novelist and poet. His novel *Dear Mr. Kawabata* has been translated into a number of European languages, and Margaret Drabble has written an introduction to the English translation. The novel is a lyrical account of life and death in the Lebanese civil war; the passage below comes near the end of the book, when the narrator, in one of his imaginary letters to the Japanese novelist of the title, describes how he was wounded and left for dead.

FROM *Dear Mr. Kawabata*

Mr. Kawabata,

When I was hit, hit very seriously indeed, in my neck and shoulder, in every part of my being, I remained lying on the ground for a long time, bleeding. No one dared to approach me because the position was still being shelled. Meanwhile, I was hovering between life and death. I opened my eyes after my return from death as if opening them, not for the first time in my life, but for the first time in history.

I say: I was opening my eyes after returning to life, as if I was opening them for the first time in history. My gaze fell on things that were clear and bright, as if they were just emerging from the prehistoric gloom.

Mr. Kawabata,

Today you know well what death is, so you are better able than anyone else to understand what I am saying: after every lapse into unconsciousness, I would open my eyes for the first time in history. Perhaps the same thing didn't happen to you, since I believe you closed your eyelids once only. And remained like that.

The film of my life didn't pass before my eyes quick as a flash during those moments, as people say it does. This film passed by on other, more difficult occasions.

When I returned to consciousness, I was seeing for the first time in history.

Seeing, nothing else!

That repeated itself several times before the pain—pain, not death—began to shoot right through me.

Mr. Kawabata,

During that period, death was what I wished for. I was not

feeling pain. It was absolute rest. *It seems that this last expression might be about to run away with me!*

Death is nothingness!

Oh!

Sir, either language is not helping me, or else I can no longer master it, but my consolation is that you understand me. This is a great consolation.

It gives me great pleasure, Mr. Kawabata, that you understand the difficulty—perhaps the impossibility—of a man describing a death he has experienced, a death that only lasted for a few moments, but was repeated several times in the space of a few minutes.

For a moment I was dead. I felt no pain, I could not see, I could not think, I was not worried, I was not afraid. When I returned to life, I felt a deep yearning for the preceding moment.

Sir, I want to tell you something I have never told anyone before. My friends have forgotten, especially *him*, that one day in the past I was wounded.

Indeed, when I remind any of them today that I was wounded, they seem surprised. How can I permanently impress on their consciousness that my neck is bent to the right, not naturally, but as a result of a shell. It seems as if they hear what I am saying and understand what it means, but in fact they are simply waiting to take the opportunity when a moment presents itself—it might be a breath I take to enable me to go on talking—to take the floor from me immediately and proceed to talk about their own circumstances. I wish one of them would talk about something worth paying attention to. It is pure garbage, trivial, worthless chatter, enough to make you lose any pleasure in conversation; enough to make you lose everything, like confidence for example . . .

Translated by Paul Starkey

Zayd Mutee' Dammaj

(1943–98)

YEMEN

Zayd Mutee' Dammaj is Yemen's foremost writer of fiction. He has published several collections of short stories. *The Hostage* was the first Yemeni novel to be translated into English. A short novel, it tells of a young man who has been taken hostage by the ruling imam to guarantee his father's continued support.

FROM *The Hostage*

That night, after carefully arranging the bed of my sick friend, the *duwaydar,* and getting him everything he needed, I lay awake all night long, because I'd drunk some wine to try and forget Sharifa Hafsa. I couldn't get her out of my mind for an instant. What was she doing at that moment? Was she lying in her soft bed, in all the beauty of her plump young body, her charms revealed clearly through her transparent clothes? I could hear her husky voice, filling my ears like the hissing of a snake!

From time to time my friend would sleep for a few minutes between his fits of coughing, and I'd take advantage of this to drink another glass of wine and smoke another of his famous cigarettes.

The wine made me feel I was in a different world, and, without thinking too clearly about it, I decided to go to Sharifa Hafsa's house. Drinking another glass of wine, I went out into the courtyard, walked up to the house and knocked at the door. It was opened by a servant girl who knew me and let me in, and I climbed the stairs to Sharifa Hafsa's room. Then I stood at her door, hesitating. What could I possibly say to her at this time of night? Had she heard the knock at the door, and was she getting ready to see who it was coming so late to her house?

I decided to go back, and hurried towards the main door. Then, all at once, I heard her husky voice asking her servant who it was. The girl replied that it was the hostage.

I felt her breath suddenly caressing my neck.

"To what do I owe the privilege of this visit from the servant of our Master the Governor?"

I made no answer, wildly regretting my stupid adventure. She now stood completely facing me.

"What does the servant of my Master the Governor want from me?"

"Nothing," I replied—I had to say something!

She reacted with astonishment.

"Nothing?"

"No, nothing."

"Then what exactly are you doing in my house?"

"I was looking for something I left here. But perhaps I'm wrong. I must have left it somewhere else."

"How very odd! Is it something that's important to you?"

"It used to be."

"How very odd! If it wasn't important, surely you could have waited till morning and let the servants help you find it?"

"I'm deeply sorry, Sharifa, for intruding. I'm very glad, at any rate, that I haven't disturbed your sleep."

"How polite you are! So very polite! But might not one of my servant girls have the thing you're looking for?"

"No."

"Do none of them appeal to you?"

I leapt angrily towards the door, but she took me by the shoulders and pulled me towards her till our bodies were pressed against one another, and I felt her panting. She kissed me till I felt ready to faint, then took me by the hand towards her favorite room. There she locked the door, then embraced me, and I melted beneath her second kiss, like molten metal in a goldsmith or black-smith's furnace.

I plucked the sweetest of kisses from her lips, and my hands wan-

dered everywhere over the soft body I'd dreamed of for so long. Together we floated in pleasures till the roosters of morning crowed.

Translated by May Jayyusi and Christopher Tingley

Brahim Dargouthi
(b. 1955)
TUNISIA

Brahim Dargouthi was born in southern Tunisia and graduated from the Teachers' College in Tunis. He has worked as
a teacher and is now a headmaster. He has published four
novels and four collections of short stories. Three of his novels have been translated into French and one into German.

Apples of Paradise

Don't concern yourselves with me overmuch, for I am a woman
who has had more than what I'm entitled to. I lived for forty years
after my husband's death. I awaited death's knife and bared my
jugular vein to it without fear or dread. I have said to Azrael on cold
winter's nights as I laid my head on my arm, "When you set foot in
my room, don't tread on tiptoe, for I am not afraid of you. Set in
motion a bell above your head or let off a bomb. I want to see you
when you seize hold of my soul and put it in a small cage and fly off
with it to I know not where. I want to see that small sparrow that
they say comes from my nose as I depart this life."

Then I cover myself up and go to sleep.

I have stayed waiting and baring my jugular vein every night.

Yet he hasn't come.

I told you not to concern yourselves with me overmuch, friends,
for it is not worth your while following my story. Thus, basically, I recount it to myself. Only to myself. Perhaps "Mr. Know-All" will tell
you words that are nearer to the truth than what I have said. That is
up to you, for I shall not judge you and shall not ask of you to take my

side. I merely hope you won't say that I'm a feeble-minded woman, for, by God, I am unjustly treated and do not deserve all the suffering that my son and my daughter-in-law Munjiya have heaped upon me.

Do not call me a mad old woman before listening to the whole story, then be fair to me in respect of my son and call down mercy upon me, may God have mercy upon you.

A Gazelle in the Trap

When my mother Maryam gets angry with me, she curses the moment I sprouted inside of her. She used to do that when I was young; when I grew up she stopped cursing me openly but perhaps continued to do so inwardly.

Once when I asked her about my father she said, "Your father died before leaving you a picture of him in your memory."

He left me on my own and went his way.

My mother Maryam used to go to the market at a time when a woman who looked out from behind the door would have her throat cut. She bought cheap pieces of cloth and would trade with them, selling them to women inside their houses.

"I swear to you, by the Omnipotent Lord, that this is a piece of Indian silk."

"But its price is very dear, Maryam."

"Take it and pay for it by installments."

"No, I can't do that, even by installments, for you know how stingy my husband is."

My mother would say to her, "Don't worry—I'll fix it."

I knew what she meant by "I'll fix it," but that used not to concern me greatly. I would go to Uncle al-Jilani and say to him, "My mother says the gazelle has fallen into the trap. Our appointment is for tonight after the evening prayer, in the paddock of Beni Kilab." Uncle al-Jilani pays the woman the price of the cloth and the woman pays it to my mother and my mother pays me the price of some Syrian halva. Once again she goes off on her own to the souk, the men's souk, and she buys some bottles of cheap perfume, incense and paper screws of nuts, chewing gum and sticks for cleaning the teeth. She knocks at doors and the veiled women open up to my mother and trade with her for goods with "I'll fix it." Uncle al-Jilani isn't stingy with his money, and I enjoy myself with Syrian halva. This went on until I reached the age of manhood, when she ceased to entrust me with conveying the news of the gazelle who had fallen into the trap to Uncle al-Jilani for passing on to the men who paid and went to the paddocks after the evening prayer.

Maryam Restores Virginity

"How much will you pay, O mother of the bride?"

"A hundred francs, Auntie."

"A hundred in advance and a hundred when the guns boom out."

I take the hundred and shove it in the box and ask the visitor to return at night with her daughter.

How lovely she is! She's worth her weight in gold!

I open her legs for her and put the middle finger into the opening and measure it. "Who deflowered you, my girl?"

Her cheeks redden and she cries, "I beg you to keep my secret, Auntie. My father's no longer alive and the man promised to marry me and he broke his promise."

I move my finger about in the wide opening. "Why did you let him do these things to you?"

"He promised to marry me, Auntie."

Her mother hits her on her mouth, her face, her stomach, and tears out some of her hair and wails, "You've ruined your life, you good-for-nothing. Tongues will be wagging about you."

She pictures to herself the scene in the lanes of the village: her daughter riding on a donkey, her face spattered with black and the children screaming behind her and the women throwing stones at her from behind doors until at evening she reaches the house she left to the sound of drums and pipes.

"Have pity on me, Mother Maryam. Guard my secret, don't give away my condition."

"Don't be afraid, my girl—I'll fix it."

I bid her farewell with her mother and go off on my own to bring the medicine for maidens whose virginity has been taken. Then I enter with her into her new home and I sit down on the rug. We look at the bridegroom who's being made a fool of—poor fellow! Generally he is more frightened than the girl. I let out a trilling cry of joy as he steps across the threshold, and another one when, as agreed, the bride lets out a cry when the bogus blood flows down between her thighs, and yet another trilling cry of joy as he throws us the "gown of chastity" and the women gathered in front of the door begin to dance. They grab hold of the gown drenched in blood and dance in the courtyard of the house, and the bride's mother cries with joy and guns boom out from the rooftops. I take hold of the other hundred francs and shove them into the box.

LIVE COALS IN MY PANTS

We were young. At night we'd collect in an open space in the middle of the street. We'd get some firewood and make a fire, a large one, and we'd dance around it and sing. Then when the flames had died down we'd gather around in a circle, boys and girls. Ezzeddin would tell us stories about ghouls and the sons of sultans, and about weddings that went on for seven days and seven nights. Aisha would go into a dark corner and Yasmeena would join her there and prepare her for the bridegroom. She'd comb her hair and plait her pigtail and spread under her a heap of earth. I would join them there to sleep with her. Yasmeena would open my trouser button and I'd lie on top of Aisha on the heap of earth and Yasmeena would look at us and let out trilling cries of joy and would smack me on the bottom, and she would call out to Ezzeddin for him to sleep with the bride. Ezzeddin would still be telling stories about ghouls—"And had not your welcome preceded your words, I would have eaten up your flesh together with your bones!"—and about the sultan's son who was still looking for "the fragrant apple" that restores youth to an old man. Aisha refuses to sleep with Ezzeddin and Yasmeena threatens to give us away. The young bride gives in to the lying threat of the girl, and Ezzeddin lies on top of her so that she can smack him on his bottom. Aisha's mother arrives, blows on the fire, and takes up a large live coal to put inside my trousers and burn my flesh. "Please forgive me, Auntie," I say to her, "I shan't sleep with your daughter again!" She forbids her daughter to play with us and Yasmeena complains to her mother, who threatens that she'll tell her father. She cries and says to her, "Speak to Mother Maryam to look around for a husband for me! Everyone of my age has married and I only find children to play at bride and groom with." We children grow up and we can't get hold of women. In the brothels they want payment in advance, which we can't manage, so we have to look around for stray female donkeys with which to have sex!

No, Not Now, Azrael!

They told me that my son had married a she-donkey; so, at my wit's end, I bought him a wife and asked him to fill the house with boys and girls.

The first girl came, then the second, and so on until the fifth, and not a single boy survived. When the first boy came he died of measles. As for the second one, he died of a flux of the stomach. The girls came and they filled the courtyard of the house. Their mother was like a locust. By the time the boy finally came I hated life: I had reached the stage where I couldn't stand up or collect my wits together. I had been looking forward to rejoicing at a circumcision party the like of which the village had never seen. But it came when I was baring my neck to Azrael every night.

His mother had given presents to all the women of the village on the occasion of circumcision celebrations: eggs and milk, tea and sugar, and lots of money. Every night she would calculate how much money she had coming to her from the women, and what she would purchase with these dirhams when she came to lay her hands on them on the day of the circumcision. She was dreaming of gold around her neck and on her hands, of the color television, the fridge and the electric fan she would be buying by installments.

But Azrael, whom I'd waited for all this long time, didn't come. He came only when I didn't want him! He came the night of the child's circumcision and took possession of my soul. I saw him taking out the small sparrow from my nose and about to place it in the cage. I asked him to delay it for a day and a night, just for twenty-four hours. I said to him, "The body doesn't matter. Take my soul but leave the cage hanging from the ceiling. I want to see how the family will mourn me." I embarrassed him when I kissed his hand and wept like a mother bereaved of her child, so he agreed to return the following day.

My daughter-in-law Munjiya came in to see how the joints of lamb in the large pot in a corner of the house were doing. Then it occurred to her to talk to me. She called to me but I didn't answer her—of course not, for I was dead. She placed her hand on my forehead, which she found to be cold. She saw my staring eyes, my rigid body. She wrung her hands, scratched her cheeks and bit her fingers. I was happy. "The poor thing," I told myself, "is going to weep tears at my death." Then I hear her saying, "The bitch! She couldn't find any other time to die! What shall I do? I'm ruined and have lost my money. Everything I gave to the women on the occasions of the circumcision of their sons is lost. You're ruined, Munjiya, ruined by that bitch!"

My body grew even more rigid as I heard her. My soul was frightened and clung closer to the bars of the cage. The same thoughts came to me as when I was in the transient world. The whore! The daughter of a whore! You woman who had lost your virginity! I restored it for her with my own hands and married her to my son! I shielded her from scandal, telling myself it was better for him to marry her than running after stray she-asses! I repaired things for her more than once after evenings in the paddock, and I didn't say a word to that idiot son of mine. I know that most of the daughters are hers alone and that my son played no part in producing them. I clothed her and clothed her whelps from the money of the men who paid up after the evening prayer. And here she is now all distressed because I've died before she was able to collect back the whoring monies I'd earned all these past years and distributed to the rest of the harlots as presents for the circumcision of their sons!

She began wandering around the house not knowing what to do. The loud sounds of the drums and the pipes came to her, and the drumming of the dancing women's feet on the ground agitated her, increasing her fury.

She crouched above me, telling herself that perhaps I was having a nap. She called to me in brassy tones, then shook me violently by the shoulder until my head banged against the dirt floor. When she was sure I was dead she wagged her middle finger in my face and said, "Confound you, you old woman! I shan't spoil my son's festivities for a monkey that's going to hell!" Then she shut the door of the house behind her and went off to join the great circle of dancers.

APPLES OF PARADISE

I learned of my mother's death only at night. When I asked Munjiya to give me my supper she said, "Your mother has died."

"What?" I said. "My mother's died! When?

"Why didn't you tell me?" I said.

"Do you want me to spoil things for my son because of the death of your mother!" I couldn't believe her.

I went to her house. I saw her lying on her back, her eyes open. I called to her, "Mother! Mother!" She didn't answer my call. I went down on my knees and placed my ear over her chest to hear the sound of her heartbeats, but I heard nothing. I raised her hand and let it fall, and it fell back like a piece of wood. I crouched down like a dog that's been beaten and my heart blew up until it became like a wet ball, and I burst into tears. I cried as I did when, for the first time, I saw a man greedily taking his fill of her! I called to her and wept. I struck out at the man crouched on top of her and wept. I sank my teeth into his shoulder as I wept. He screamed, rose to his feet and began kicking me. I fell against my mother's outspread thighs. She quickly got up and pushed the man out of the house, then came back to me. "Why are you crying, now?" she said. "Be quiet—I've turned the man out." But I went on crying, both awake and in my dreams. I continued to have spells of weeping whenever I saw my mother's friend entering our house, right up until the time he bought my silence one night with a toy train.

As I grew up I would leave the house and meet up with Aisha and Ezzeddin, who told us stories about the sultan's son and the fragrant apple and the ghoul who was never satisfied however much human flesh he ate. Aisha would undo my trouser buttons and say, "Leave Ali the sultan's son looking for the apple, for here on my breast are all the apples you could want!" So I would eat the apples and drink pure milk and honey and would stamp on the viper's head and refuse to humble myself. And I'd eat again the apples from Aisha's bosom. I would drink mellowed wine from Aisha's mouth and have no shame about my private parts, becoming boisterously drunk as I danced with her, while Ali, the sultan's son, went on roaming about in the deserts and saying hello to the ghouls—his greetings always preceding what he had to say! Why, mother, do you die now? Why? And what shall I do with the Quranic injunction that one should not say harsh words to one's parents and with the Prophet's saying that paradise is at the feet of mothers? And Uncle al-Jilani, will he enter paradise? I don't know what to do.

But the solution has come to me! I shall go out to them all: the men and the women, the dancing women and the drunken men, with my wife among them. I'll say to them, "Good people, may your joy be everlasting. We who have extended the invitation thank you for coming. Now goodbye to you. Give our regards to your families. Leave us—and thanks!"

But the drunken men may become troublesome and the women dancers may refuse to leave the dancing area, and my wife will be displeased at my interference in her affairs. So what shall I do?

Or shall I ask them politely, talk to my wife on her own and say to her, "My mother has died, dear wife of mine. By the Almighty, she's dead, so don't make a worse scandal for me in the village!" Yes, I know she's stupid and stubborn and doesn't easily understand anything, and that she's a bitch, the daughter of a thousand dogs, so what shall I do if she refuses to go along with me?

Shall I complain about her to the police?

But the police will say it's a family matter and has nothing to do with them.

Yes, by God—I'll complain about her to her mother. But her mother hates my mother and will agree with her daughter that we'll lose all the dirhams we've paid in the past to the village women if the celebration is turned into a funeral.

Why didn't the idea occur to me before? Just to say to the revelers, "My mother's died. Goodbye!"

But the wretched woman might tell the people I was drunk and didn't know what I was saying, and order me to be shut up in one of the houses.

"What shall I do, mother? Tell me what to do, I'm really at a loss."

When I raised my head toward the ceiling I saw a cage hanging there. Inside the cage was a small bird, the like of which I had never seen. I stood up and stretched out my hand to take it, but it was no longer there! I again sat down on the floor and the door opened and Uncle al-Jilani entered—Uncle al-Jilani who had died long ago. He was just as I'd known him before: tall and broad, with a beard dyed red with henna. He came closer to me, and with every step my life was reduced by ten years until I had become a child playing with a train. He patted my hair and said to me, "Get up, boy! Go and play with your friends in the street." I put the train under my arm and went out. When I turned around I saw him stretching out his hand to the cage hanging from the ceiling and taking from it the bird whose like I'd never seen. Taking it in his hand, he pressed it into my mother's nose as he kissed her. I slammed the door behind me and found my wife right there in front of me.

"What shall we do now with your mother?" she said to me.

When I didn't reply she went on: "You'll say nothing until we've finished the celebration—it's winter and her body won't decompose!"

"When will you finish collecting the money from the women?"

"Tomorrow morning," she said.

"I'll go tonight and dig the grave. I'll dig it by myself."

I went to the cemetery.

Translated by Denys Johnson-Davies

Ahmad Faqih
(b. 1942)
LIBYA

Ahmad Faqih is a prolific writer who has published novels, collections of stories, plays, and essays. He is widely traveled and has lived in both London and Cairo for long periods. His best-known work is his trilogy, *Gardens of the Night*, which contains echoes of *The Arabian Nights* (the hero in the first volume is working on a study of the Arabic masterpiece). The following extract is taken from the second volume. In it, the hero tells of the unusual place called Coral City.

FROM *Gardens of the Night*

I had learnt, during my stay in Coral City, that the people here did not know what a lie was. As far as they were concerned, it was something that had not yet been invented and they could not be anything but truthful, for they had no reason whatsoever to tell lies. I was the only exception. Due to the fact that I came from a different time, I could not be honest with them and, therefore, I did not speak candidly about myself. I put on my disguise and wondered what it was in man that made him adept in the game of lost chances, which deflects the diagram of the development of civilization, causes wars, disputes and pollution and invents weapons of mass destruction, and how it was that human society, within the space of a thousand years, could have forgotten the simple formula which made Coral City such a perfect place. Here, they left the citizen to his own spontaneity outside the frameworks, the regimes and the rules and regulations of government and state; it was man's innate nature and intellectual faculties alone which guided him to a sense of his responsibilities. Man had built the city of his dreams

without the guardianship of any institutions to run his life for him
and without the need for an external corpus of legislation to impose
a system of behaviour upon him. Guided by an education which
taught him that his original homeland was among the stars, and he
was part of a greater whole, man managed to stay in contact with
the elements of nature and live in a tightly knit community, making his life on earth a reflection of the harmonious movement of existence itself and sharing with his fellow men in the creation of a
utopian dream which renewed itself daily. Even matters of love and
sexual relations were an expression of a life free from any oppressive
morality. When they reached adulthood they married out of love
and free will. There was no class distinction to interfere with marriage. Two people got married because they were in love with each
other, and if their love waned, they simply separated. They even
planned their families by calculating when the women were at their
most fertile. In that town I saw only lovers, old and young, who
gave free vent to their emotions, sincerely and spontaneously. They
were completely unaware of what we call adultery, infidelity and
dishonour.

I do not know why, in a moment of frankness, I found myself revealing to Narjis al-Qulub the secrets of the trip which had led me
to their city. Perhaps I was influenced by all the candour around me
and could no longer hide the truth about myself, or perhaps I said
it in order to unburden myself, indifferent to the consequences. I
was sitting with her one night on a balcony overlooking the garden,
watching the moon and the stars weaving their lattice-pattern
of light on the surface of the pools and brooks. I told her that I
sneaked into their time to escape another time, almost a thousand
years ahead of theirs, and that the inventions I had described to her
were not things from the kingdom of the jinn or something I had
read about in books of legends, but real things which people like us
had achieved. I came from a time which had not yet come. I myself
had used those inventions, flown through the air, owned a car and
lived in a house illuminated by electricity in which I kept my tape
recorder, camera, radios, television and telephone. She asked me if
I was joking. I replied that I was speaking of things I knew about

and had witnessed, that I had decided to reveal the truth about myself so that my relationship with her would not be based on deceit or fraud. She burst out crying, thinking that I had caught a fever and had become delirious. I remained silent, and in spite of her crying, I felt somehow relaxed and lucid. She prepared a herbal infusion to calm me down and led me by the hand to the bed to sleep it off. She treated me like a capricious child who was speaking gibberish; I neither objected nor resisted.

In the morning, she called for Jalaladin, who came early and woke me up. He took me on a walk around the palace gardens and told me that he had visited many countries as an emissary of the princes of Coral City. He had been so far east that he felt he had visited the place where the sun rose. He had crossed deserts and seas to reach kingdoms so far in the west that he had come to the very edge of the world. He had seen countries of giants and dwarves, and yellow, red and black races. He had seen people who rode elephants and carts pulled by dogs, as well as people who built houses out of ice and huts on the water. All in all, he had seen all manner of inventions and creatures, but what I had told Narjis al-Qulub was something beyond all imagining, something of which no one had ever dreamt. It occurred to me that I could take the easy way out and avoid entering into conversation about things which this man would not be able to grasp, however great his wisdom and understanding, by claiming not to remember anything and stating that I must have seen these things in my sleep. My spirit, however, would not obey me. I had been cleansed by the air of their city and I could not bring myself to lie. I told him everything about the accomplishments of twentieth-century science and technology and the achievements of man in the fields of medicine, industry, agriculture, printing, education, transport and communications. I also told him about the progress which had been made in space exploration and warfare. I ended by telling him that, despite it all, science had not succeeded in creating its promised city, and that it had not managed to provide more favourable living conditions for man than those in Coral City, and that man in the twentieth century lived under the threat of annihilation at any moment, for even a

small part of the munitions stored up by governments could destroy the world in an instant. I had been carried from that world to
their city by a miracle. I had no regrets about that journey. In fact,
I was delighted by the thrilling, enjoyable experience I was living,
for now I was meeting the people I had always wished to meet, and
was living with them to see for myself through first-hand experience how man could be free from fear, how he had discovered his
latent possibilities, awoken the god sleeping within himself and
achieved spiritual communion with the greater soul of the universe
which saved him from the social ills which afflicted societies that
still crept on the earth in spite of their machines spinning in space,
and in spite of the fact that they were a thousand years more advanced. I did not know why the world had developed in a way
which was contrary to the essence of god in man, and I told Jalaladin that, if it were left to me, I would bring the whole world back
to their city to learn the true meaning of life and the ideal way of
exalting and celebrating it. After listening with great interest to
what I said, the old man asked me how I had been able to travel
across time and bring them my knowledge. I related the incident
with Sheikh Sadiq, told him how he had had access to secret powers and used his spiritual expertise to grant me this favour. Sheikh
Sadiq had seen how distressed I had been by my life there among
those people, how much I despaired at what was going on in the
world and how overcome I was by ennui and a pervasive sense of estrangement and gloom which weighed upon my body and soul. I
had become obsessed by the blissful world I had read about in the
legends which we called *The Thousand and One Nights*, and so the
sheikh had revealed the hidden to me and folded back the earth beneath my feet and, by the miracle of inspiration and his spiritual
powers, had managed to transport me through a chink in the wall
of time from one age to another and from one place to a better one.
He had chosen to send me back to a city where man was at his most
perfect and where his life was a daily wedding renewed at every
sunrise.

Translated by Russell Harris, Amin al-'Ayouti,
and Suraya 'Allam

Fathy Ghanem
(1924–98)

EGYPT

Fathy Ghanem was a prolific writer who is today best known for his novel *The Man Who Lost His Shadow*, which was published in a translation by the English Arabist and writer Desmond Stewart in 1966. In it, Ghanem narrates the story of Yusif Abdul Hamid, an ambitious and unscrupulous newspaperman willing to sacrifice people and principles for the achievement of his goals. The novel is narrated in four parts, each with a separate character's voice—a technique new to Arabic writing at the time. The following short story is representative of Ghanem's work.

Sunset

Sea water washes away sins. In the late afternoon she plunged into the sea. She felt the water purging her clean, dripping from her hair and face, the waves coming at her, while she rose and fell so easily, so lightly.

On the beach stood Uncle Ali the lifeguard, composedly watching her. He knew her, she used often to come at this time; alone, unaccompanied, she would swim in the water like a fish.

Uncle Ali used to like the late afternoon best. It was then that the beach was free of the thousands of human beings with which it teemed in the morning. All of them, men and women, appeared identical to him as he stood there, his whistle in his mouth, his eyes ever moving from place to place. In the early afternoons there was no one but the maidservants—Zeinab and Hanem and Umm Saad—who would squat in the water in their *galabias* and whenever a wave came along they'd jump up in terror and scream, their wet clothes clinging to their bodies, revealing the colour of flesh under the cloth, while Uncle Ali looked on with an intent gaze that seemed almost to touch their bodies from afar.

On the corniche a child pointed out to his mother:

"The girl's alone in the sea."

"Yes."

"Why is she alone in the sea?"

"Because most people go to the sea in the morning."

"And why doesn't the girl go to the sea in the morning?"

"Because she was busy."

"Was she doing the cooking at home?"

"Yes."

Darwish Bey the archaeologist leant against the iron railing. In a deep, husky voice he said to his friend: "It's a wonderful view, the sun before it sets and the girl in the sea."

Darwish Bey gazed out at the horizon. He had lived his life with the ancient Egyptians, the frontiers of his world the end of the Empire. His joys had been with Mena and Cheops, his desires and ambitions with Thutmosis and Ramses, his sorrows with Hophra, Psamtik and Cambyses's invasion of Egypt.

It was as if the girl swimming in the sea were some Pharaonic princess. Feelings of nostalgic sadness rose up within Darwish Bey as he quoted to himself the words of an anonymous poet:

> *"My beloved lies on the other shore*
> *Between him and me the river's arm,*
> *The river's crocodiles.*
> *But I have gone down to cross it.*
> *Alike are land and water under my feet*
> *When love grants me strength and purpose."*

On the other shore of the sea road Mitchou stood in front of the empty tables. He had finished laying them in preparation for the people who would be coming. Mitchou looked at his watch, then at the sun. The sun had almost set. The shore and the sea were empty, and no one came.

The water felt warm. She rolled over in it. This is what I want: sea, air, and to be alone and far from people. I feel that what clings to me can be washed away only by the sea. Beside him in bed, the room dark, his breath filling my nostrils, his forehead and disheveled hair moist with sweat, I suddenly felt as though I were in a garbage bin. My nose was filled with a repulsive stench and my body revolted. Rising, I quickly dressed and went out as he watched me with doltish incomprehension. Till when would I stay with him? He wasn't going to marry me and I didn't want a husband like him. He's repellent, worthless, filthy, yet always I return to him, like a moth that hovers round a flame. My father's an old broken man, incapable of movement, though in the past he had been strong. He was an eccentric person, and had bred huge dogs; one day one of them had bitten him and he had attacked it, breaking its jaw and strangling it with his bare hands. My mother plays poker and coon-can and has a red or green feather sticking out of her hat. When she sees me she gives me a lot of money to spend but she won't kiss me in case she spoils her make-up. When I'm going out to meet him my father says: "Where are you going?"

And I answer him coldly: "To my girl-friend's house."

Shall I tell him the truth? Shall I talk to him of the bed, the room, the darkness? Even if I were to tell him he wouldn't do anything, for he is old and broken. Though he would hear things that would anger and degrade him, he would be helpless and would keep quiet. Those hands that had killed the dog now shake, are weak and wasted.

Uncle Ali fidgeted as he stood there. Should I blow my whistle? She is enjoying the sea and she swims well. I must, though, perform the afternoon prayer—the sun has almost set.

The child said to his mother:

"The sun will fall into the sea."

The mother was occupied with her own thoughts.

"Why will the sun fall into the sea?" asked the child.

The mother wavered before the momentous question. He wasn't asking about his father who had died or about what his future life would be, he asked only about what he saw.

"Why does the sun fall into the sea?" the child persisted.

"It sleeps there."

Darwish Bey closed his eyes and opened them, as though not believing what he was seeing. He was floating about in his Pharaonic world, his heart filled with humility and awe: the sun is setting, it is the ship that carries the dead to the other shore. The burial grounds are over there in the west and burial should not take place after sunset, for the sun will have departed from our own to the other world. This moment is decisive, it separates two worlds.

Mitchou seated himself on one of the chairs. I must not be seized by despair. In '32 I was on the point of committing suicide because my mother was ill and I didn't have the money to buy medicine. All night long not a soul had come to the café to pay me a single piastre, then suddenly the fat gentleman came in with some women dancers; they drank in a corner and got drunk and gave me five pounds, five whole pounds.

I hate him, I hate him—and she struck out in the water. He'll get up from the bed and he'll open the window and the light will enter. In the bath he'll rub himself over with Yardley cologne; he'll put on his blue shirt and get into his red car and speed along the sea road to meet up with Carmen and Juliana and they'll go to the cinema and to Rippas and Boudreau and Ilyonka and drink tea and eat cakes and meringues and the band will be playing waltzes and the Fire Dance. I've swallowed water, the waves are so high, I'm far from the shore and my arms feel so heavy. Shall I stay or return? The beach looks empty, there's no one about. No one awaits me. The current's preventing me from returning. Why am I so eager to return? I'll wait awhile. Underneath me, though, the water is moving. My hatred for him runs through my body like poison. Salt water is filling my stomach. My father loves no one; he hates me because I'm his daughter. My mother dresses as though she were a mannequin. At the hairdresser's she's cropped her hair like a young girl of twenty. If only someone would come along to marry me, I'd avenge myself on him; on the wedding night I'd relate to him all I'd done with that despicable person, I'd tell him about the room and the darkness and the Yardley cologne in the bathroom. I'd avenge myself when I saw him. I've gone far from the shore. Where am I going? But I don't want to return, I'm in need of the sea.

Peace be upon you and the mercy of Allah, peace be upon you and the mercy of Allah. Having greeted the two angels who stood to his right and to his left, Uncle Ali passed his hand over his face, his eyes filled with a radiant light as his gaze took in the water's surface. The sea was empty of people, Umm Saad and Zeinab and Hanim having gone back to their mistress. The disc of the sun was touching the water; in a few moments the time of departure would draw near.

Mitchou got up and was on the point of raising his head to the sky. Sunset had come but where were the people? No one was seated at the tables. Were there no more people on the face of the earth? Had they all drowned in the sea?

Darwish Bey gazed fixedly at the sun. Here was the ship disappearing into the middle of the sea. He murmured to his friend:

"The ship has set off to transport today's dead to where Osiris will meet them at the head of forty-two judges and in his hand Osiris holds the feather of truth and justice. Those arriving will present their hearts to him and Osiris will weigh them: the heart in one scale, the feather in the other. Over there is the higher wisdom that decides upon the fates of men."

"Why is the sky red?"

The mother gave a sigh and the child again asked:

"Why is the sky red?"

Translated by Denys Johnson-Davies

Gamal al-Ghitani
(b. 1945)
EGYPT

Gamal al-Ghitani was born in Upper Egypt and grew up in
the Gamaliya district of Old Cairo, an area depicted in
Naguib Mahfouz's *Cairo Trilogy*. Like many Egyptian intellectuals, he spent time in detention for his political activities. He worked as a war correspondent and since 1985 has
been the editor of *Akhbar al-adab*, Egypt's sole weekly journal devoted to literature. His novel *Incidents in Zafrani Alley*
was published in English translation in 1986, but al-Ghitani
is best known for his novel *Zayni Barakat*, which was published by Penguin with an introduction by Edward Said.
The novel, through various narrators, tells the story of the
rise to power of Zayni Barakat, the ruthless governor of
Cairo in medieval Egypt. The well-known Arabist Robert
Irwin says of it, "Whether read as a colorful evocation of
past times or as a bleak political parable, *Zayni Barakat* suc-
ceeds brilliantly."

FROM *Zayni Barakat*

Zakariyya ibn Radi thinks that his meeting with Zayni had taken
place on the same night. Usually nobody disturbs him during the
last hours of the night, except for something very serious. That
night he listened to Wasila telling him about her country. He likes
to listen to descriptions of people's customs, habits and different
kinds of food. He asked her why the slave merchant hadn't deflowered her after her abduction. She has got used to the strange questions and no longer feels ashamed. She said that he coveted her as
everyone who saw her did. "It happened near Aleppo that . . ."

Zakariyya reached out and placed the tips of his fingers on her
lips. "Tell me about Aleppo."

She was not perturbed; she has got used to his changing the subject suddenly. She began to recall the city, the roads leading into it, the postmen in the small buildings that stood by themselves in the middle of nowhere, the eyes of the Syrian women as they watched the caravan and how they hurried to lock their doors. She remembered how the guards greeted the caravan. Mansur, the merchant, knew them all and paid them a certain amount of gold regularly, and they not only never bothered him but guarded him as well. Zakariyya is holding a polygonal glass. He never drinks wine. He doesn't like his consciousness to be affected for one moment. It happened two hundred years ago that wine was responsible for the downfall of one of the best spies that Egypt had known, during the reign of al-Zahir Baybars. Ibn al-Kazaroni became an alcoholic and started to babble in private and in public about all he knew of the affairs of the State and people. This resulted in his disgrace and later the loss of his life. He had perfected a new wine concoction, which, it was said, got a person very drunk if he as much as smelt it. The new wine was later named after him: the "Kazaroni wine." The Sultan Nasir ibn Qalawun was later to ban it and dump what had already been made. Zakariyya loved fruit juices and had imported a device from Tlemsen to squeeze the toughest kind of fruit and remove the seeds.

Zakariyya was sipping grape juice, passing his hand very softly over Wasila's neck as she kept on talking. Her words suddenly trembled as his hand went up and down and as his fingers got close to her ear. His hot breath at the back of her neck made her whole body tremble; he felt that as he followed the tremor on her lips. Suddenly he took her little ear into his mouth, sucking it. She gasped, her limbs convulsing and her hands reaching to cup her breasts. She closed her eyes and felt transported far away. Suddenly, with one stroke he tore up her dress; he didn't unbutton it; he just ripped it and listened to the sound of the cloth being torn. The beginnings of the soft world appeared to him. A movement of her eye betrayed how young she was, opening up from a bud into a flower, a girl at the threshold of her feminine life, surprised as she was brought to the edge of the world. Did such pleasure really exist?

At that moment, at exactly that very moment, Shihab al-Halabi struck the brass shield that hung in the lower courtyard. Zakariyya went down to him. Zayni Barakat had sent a messenger requesting that Zakariyya come right away for a matter of great gravity. Zakariyya made a gesture with his head, went up to the wardrobe and selected an Azhar shaykh's garb. Since his confirmation as Deputy *Muhtasib*, Zayni has not sent for him; the only contact between them has been in the form of a daily report sent by Zakariyya to Zayni. Naturally it is a specially prepared report. Only a few times did Zayni send inquiries about matters of "general interest," as he said. Zakariyya responded, amazed at how petty the requests sometimes were: for instance, the names of the slave girls that Emir Bashtak had purchased in 907 AH; how much wine Emir Qusun drank every night; the name of the mother of a pickle vendor in Husayniyya; favourite dishes of Chief Justice Abd al-Barr; the number of meters of fabric needed to make an embroidered cloak for Khond Zaynab, Tashtamur's wife; how many Mamluks had six fingers on each hand and how many of those were in each garrison.

Zakariyya received these requests in disbelief at first, but he quickly changed his attitude; there should be no room for derision here. A man like Zayni wouldn't make these requests unless they were really important. When he met him the first time at Birkat al-Ratli, he realized what a rare kind of man he was. Each of us was born to meet the other, he thought. He went downstairs quickly. When he gets close to Zayni's house, he will not show his surprise but will talk calmly to him. Nothing comes as a surprise to Zakariyya. He will suggest to him that he had anticipated Zayni's intention to summon him. He went out to the big courtyard; the leaves on the trees rustled audibly. How wonderful it would be to go back to Wasila; he hasn't had his fill of her yet. His eyes wandered, looked for Mabruk. Mabruk is the only one who would always spot him, even if he were disguised as a jinnee. To strangers he is a mute, but he does speak a little. Sometimes he takes Zakariyya to task and upbraids him. Zakariyya accepts that and listens to it and does what Mabruk tells him to do. Zakariyya asked, "Where is Zayni's messenger?" Mabruk led the way. Zakariyya whispered, "If

I am not back by tomorrow noon, tell the Head Spy of Cairo to take his orders from Shihab al-Din, the Private Secretary. Understood?"

Zakariyya entered the sitting-room in the hall. A veiled Bedouin got up. "Welcome to the Supreme Shihab Zakariyya." Zakariyya looked at the veiled face, the wide leather belt studded with metal spikes. He examined his outfit. These little details helped him get rid of his surprise when he saw that the messenger was none other than Zayni himself. Zayni got to the point right away, with no beating about the bush. "Very briefly, I want to know exactly where Ali ibn Abi al-Jud has hidden his money."

Zakariyya leaned his forehead on two fingers of his right hand. Briefly, as if in an official document, he said, "Don't know." A strange bird made a strange sound in the sky; the night was getting old.

Zayni got up in one movement and slowly came close to Zakariyya. "You, Zakariyya, know exactly where Ali ibn Abi al-Jud's belongings are. Nothing is hidden from you. If anything were, I wouldn't have risked my reputation and confirmed you as Deputy *Muhtasib*. You know, not because you were Ali ibn Abi al-Jud's deputy, but because you are Zakariyya. Do you understand me? Because you are Zakariyya ibn Radi, the ablest man to assume the post of Chief Spy of Egypt."

Translated by Farouk Abdel Wahab

Nabil Gorgy
(b. 1944)
EGYPT

Nabil Gorgy was born in Cairo. He studied civil engineering at Cairo University and later worked as an engineer in the United States. Upon returning to Cairo, he began writing short stories under the influence of such writers as Kawabata and Borges, as well as the Sufis. He presently lives in Paris. A selection of his stories was published in English translation under the title *The Slave's Dream*, from which the following story is taken.

Cairo Is a Small City

On the balcony of his luxury flat Engineer Adil Salim stood watching some workmen putting up a new building across the wide street along the center of which was a spacious garden. The building was at the foundations stage, only the concrete foundations and some of the first floor columns having been completed. A young ironworker with long hair was engaged on bending iron rods of various dimensions. Adil noticed that the young man had carefully leant his Jawa motorcycle against a giant crane that crouched at rest awaiting its future tasks. "How the scene has changed!" Adil could still remember the picture of old-time master craftsmen, and of the workers who used to carry large bowls of mixed cement on their calloused shoulders.

The sun was about to set and the concrete columns of a number of new constructions showed up as dark frameworks against the light in this quiet district at the end of Heliopolis.

As on every day at this time there came down into the garden dividing the street a flock of sheep and goats that grazed on its grass, with behind them two Bedouin women, one of whom rode a donkey, while the younger one walked beside her. As was his habit each day, Adil fixed his gaze on the woman walking in her black gown that not so much hid as emphasized the attractions of her body, her waist being tied round with a red band. It could be seen that she wore green plastic slippers on her feet. He wished that she would catch sight of him on the balcony of his luxurious flat; even if she did so, Adil was thinking, those Bedouin had a special code of behaviour that differed greatly from what he was used to and rendered it difficult to make contact with them. What, then, was the reason, the motive, for wanting to think up some way of talking to her? It was thus that he was thinking.

The situation so held Adil's attention that he was unaware of

Salma except when she passed from one tent to another in the direction he was looking and he caught sight of her gazing towards him.

The man who was sitting in a squatting position among the three others spoke. Adil heard him talking about the desert, water and sheep, about the roads that went between the oases and the *wadi*, the towns and the springs of water, about the Bedouin tribes and blood ties; he heard him talking about the importance of protecting these roads and springs, and the palm trees and the dates, the goats and the milk upon which the suckling child would be fed; he also heard him talk about how small the *wadi* was in comparison to this desert that stretched out endlessly.

In the same way as Adil had previously built the seven-storey building that represented the seven months, each month containing twenty-eight days, till he would see Salma's face whenever it was full moon, he likewise sensed that this was the tribunal which had been set up to make an enquiry with him into the killing of the man whom he had one day come across on the tracks between the oases of Kharga and Farshout. It had been shortly after sunset when he and a friend, having visited the iron ore mines in the oases of Kharga, had, instead of taking the asphalt road to Assiout, proceeded along a rough track that took them down towards Farshout near to Kena, as his friend had to make a report about the possibility of repairing the road and of extending the railway line to the oases. Going down from the high land towards the *wadi*, the land at a distance showing up green, two armed men had appeared before them. Adil remembered how, in a spasm of fear and astonishment, of belief and disbelief, and with a speed that at the time he thought was imposed upon him, a shot had been fired as he pressed his finger on the trigger of the revolver which he was using for the first time. A man had fallen to the ground in front of him and, as happens in films, the other had fled. As for him and his friend, they had rushed off to their car in order to put an end to the memory of the incident by reaching the *wadi*. It was perhaps because Adil had once killed a man that he had found the courage to accept Salma's father's invitation.

"That day," Adil heard the man address him, "with a friend in a car, you killed Mubarak bin Rabia when he went out to you, Ziyad al-Mihrab being with him."

This was the manner in which Engineer Adil Salim was executed in the desert northwest of the city of Cairo: one of the men held back his head across a marble-like piece of stone, then another man plunged the point of a tapered dagger into the spot that lies at the bottom of the neck between the two bones of the clavicle.

Translated by Denys Johnson-Davies

Abdou Gubeir
(b. 1950)
EGYPT

Abdou Gubeir was born in Upper Egypt to a religious family. Destined for a career as a muezzin or a preacher in a mosque, he escaped to Cairo at an early age and has worked on various literary magazines and as a freelance writer. Recently he spent several years in Kuwait and has now settled in a village outside of Cairo, where he devotes himself to writing. He has published several volumes of short stories and four novels.

Have You Seen Alexandria Station?

As they stood under the wooden awning on the platform he said to her, "Do you know"—and she didn't—"some years ago I wrote a story called 'Have You Seen Alexandria Station?'"

She turned with a smile and said, "Really?"

"Yes," he said.

Then he began glancing around at the milling passengers leaving and boarding the trains. But she—because she loved him, and he her, so much so that he would never forget her walking in front of him along the seashore in a bathing costume as he observed her from behind, nor the way she walked afterward in the lights of the city as she shivered with cold, and as he approached her and hugged her to him—because of this, she said, "What's this story about?"

And as he had not in fact written any such story, he said, "It's about two people who are standing on the station platform and talking about their pain, because they're leaving Alexandria and would have liked to stay longer, for they loved the sea, and she liked swimming, though he didn't, because he'd once nearly drowned. But he used to like the way she walked along the seashore beside him, or for them to sit together under the faint light of night and talk as they watched the waves."

"And what about the station?" she said. "Is there a station in this story?"

"Of course there's a station," he said, "because they were standing on the platform and talking about the sea, and about the streets, and about that strange atmosphere that Alexandria leaves in one on leaving it before one's had one's fill of it."

"He definitely loved Alexandria?" she said.

"He loved it all right—and who doesn't love this city?" he said.

"She loves the seashores," she said, "but she's not interested in the city."

"Because she hadn't lived there in winter," he said. "If she had, she would certainly have loved it when she returned."

"Perhaps," she said, "but there must be another reason, because one can't love a city just because it's a city. There must be another reason."

"Naturally, had she wanted to know, there's a love story, but it's between the lines and not easy to make out, because it's extremely complicated."

"Why is it extremely complicated?" she said.

"Because the girl he loved," he said, keeping his eyes on the passengers, "was his wife's sister. He hadn't seen her before, but when he did see her he fell in love with her—and that was of course difficult."

"But why did you make such a hero, someone who seems to love life, who loves the sea, why do you make him have such feelings?"

"He didn't want to and he was sorry about it, but it happened, and there was nothing he could do but record it, which he did."

"Oh," she said.

Then she began to watch the passengers, as he observed her, and they stayed silent for a while, during which she moved restlessly. His wife came back from buying him cigarettes—he was tired and out of sorts and had not been able to go off to buy them himself.

"All you have to do is to read the story and you'll like it," he said to her.

"What story?" interposed the wife.

"The one called 'Have You Seen Alexandria Station?'" he said.

"Did you write a story with that title?" she said.

"Yes," he said. "A long time ago."

"I thought I knew all your stories," she said with a shrug of her shoulders, "but it seems there are stories I don't know of. Are you writing secretly?"

"Yes, sometimes," he said. "But look, the train's coming. Let's go."

But as he was tired and out of sorts, he hung back, as he watched them entering the carriage door. Ill at ease, he cast a final glance at the station, the platform, the people, and that bell.

Translated by Denys Johnson-Davies

Emile Habiby
(1921–96)
PALESTINE

Emile Habiby was a leading Palestinian writer, particularly known for his outstanding novel *The Secret Life of Saeed, the Ill-Fated Pessoptimist*, an innovative work steeped in irony that gives a realistic picture of the life of the Palestinians who remained in their land after the breakup of Palestine in 1948. Habiby was politically active beginning in the early 1940s and was a member of the Communist Party. He was also a member of the Knesset from 1953 to 1972 and was awarded the State of Israel Prize for Literature in 1992.

At Last the Almond Blossomed

Spring, take me back to my homeland
Even as a flower

—*a song sung by Fairuz*

"In the romantic years of my youth, I read Dickens's novel *A Tale of Two Cities*. I idolized Sidney Carton as the hero who gave his life to save the husband of the woman he loved by putting on the husband's clothes and taking his place in the Bastille, beneath the blade of the guillotine.

"But like everyone else, none of my heroes have been able to resist the trials of adversity. Rather, they have risen and fallen as life itself, until now there remains only Hugo's philosopher Gringoire, that miserable rogue in *The Hunchback of Notre Dame*, who was also asked to sacrifice himself (in order to rescue Esmeralda, the beautiful gypsy) but refused. When questioned as to what made him so attached to life, he replied, 'My greatest joy is spending every day from morning till night with the genius who is me. It's wonderful.'"

"And Arabism?"

"Are you going to tell me off and be sarcastic after we've been apart for twenty years?"

That was exactly what I had in mind when I reminded Mister M of Arabism. His unexpected night visit had astonished me, and raised my doubts. He had asked me to listen to him patiently.

We had been close friends at preparatory and secondary school. Together we had set up the first secret society in our school to fight the British. Its membership consisted only of the two founding members, and its sole effect was to leave us with a deep-rooted habit of smoking which we considered one of the prerequisites of undercover work. We wore sunglasses too to hide our manly tears when we celebrated the end of secondary school and made our farewells and promises to one another.

We each went our own way after that. He moved to Jerusalem to complete his studies at the Arab College. He then came back to our town and got a job as an English teacher in the local secondary school, where he still works to this day. Since the establishment of the State of Israel, I have had no contact with him whatsoever. He would even avoid saying hello if ever we happened to meet in the street. This estrangement pained me at first, till I got used to it and I put him out of my life altogether as soon as I realized that he was that kind of person; just like a woman before she gets married, she never puts down a novel until she finds another, but when she finds a husband she never reads anything again, not even the newspaper clippings in the lavatory.

Our friend, with whom I would exalt the conquests of Khalid Ibn al-Walid, the elegies of al-Mutanabbi, the atheistics of Abu al-Alaa and Arabism, had married his job. What else could he do if he were to keep hold of it under Israel? For it is necessary that one cuts all ties with any friend or relative, even if it is one's own brother, the son of one's own mother and father, if he is an agitator against the state.

Then, one night after the Six Day War, he suddenly knocked on my door, sat down with me after an estrangement of twenty years and said, "Listen till the end . . ."

What was it that had put this lion into his heart and made him dare to visit me? Mister M continued where he had left off.

"With the hairs that fell to my first razor blade, Sidney Carton vanished from my album of heroes, but the title of Dickens's novel, *A Tale of Two Cities*, has continued to haunt and enchant me and colour my taste all these long years. Its influence appeared in ways which confused me at first, but then I succumbed to it. I even began to carry it around, harbouring some affection for it, treasuring it like a person with a charm which his mother hung around his neck when he was a child.

"It was not long after these strange effects began that I started to write *A Tale of Two Cities* of my own, about two cities from our country, Haifa and Nazareth. As soon as I wrote the first chapter, the story ended; so I put it aside. Then I decided to specialize in two subjects, English and Law, but nothing came of it. I took up writing poetry in English and Arabic but I managed to write nothing in either language. It saddens me that I only had one son when I really wanted two. Just ask your own boy whom I teach in the secondary school and he'll tell you how I always set them two books to read, two poets to memorize, two literatures to compare and two hours for the exam. And there are other things in my life, no need to mention them now, that confirm the hold of that duality, that bewitching title *A Tale of Two Cities*, over my taste and my mind. But surely you must have noticed that when we were friends in our youth. Have you forgotten how you gave me the nickname 'the man with two chins'?"

"You were huge, with really chubby cheeks . . ."

"No. I was just like you with one chin. You called me that because I loved to repeat the phrase, 'I do not mind a bearded chin or a powdered chin.' Two chins, a man's chin and a woman's chin, two, *A Tale of Two Cities*. This is the duality, the charm I have worn around my neck since I was a child."

This old friend of mine is a tidy person, in attire and in speech. He is extravagant in his conversation but without affectation, so I let him ramble on as I used to in the past, especially since I was so amazed by his sudden appearance. In my case I wanted to ascertain the purpose of his visit. I believe that I had begun to understand and I said to myself that one of two things had happened: either the wars had stirred something in his conscience and made him, after twenty years, come and explain the break in relations by this duality; or someone had sent him to me for something or other, and he wanted to revive our friendship by talking about this enchanting duality. I was on my guard and I looked forward to the end of his monologue.

He said, "That's why I wasn't too surprised when we drove up the winding road of al-Laban Heights for the first time after the June War, on our way from Nablus to Ramallah.

"I let out a great grasp as we took the first bend and my tongue shook as I held the steering wheel. I shouted to my colleagues who were with me in the car. For twenty years I've been dreaming of this winding road. This hill hasn't been out of my mind for a single day. I can remember every bend. There are four; count them. And those mountains, stretching up, guarding the green plain. There are ten; count them. This pure air. This fragrance I know. I'm breathing in an aroma that's been with me all my life. This place is my place!"

I understood . . . at last I understood why the poor man had come to me after a break of twenty years. My childhood friend! How cruel time had been to us! I'm sorry I ever doubted you. I almost stood up to embrace him but he didn't give me a chance.

Mister M did not pause in his monologue. "My friends agreed, after I had insisted, to let me stop the car at the last bend, the fourth. They got out with me so that we could inhale that air and feast our eyes on the view of the mountains and the sheltered plain. Almond trees covered the plain and the hillsides. They really should have called the place Almond Bends. Something inside me told me to prostrate myself; something in my eyes was melting into tears. I felt like someone beholding a wonderful spectacle unfolding right in front of his eyes, as if I were reliving the years of my youth, in the haunts of my youth, not just seeing them but living them, breathing their air, feeling the blood of youthfulness, with the smell of fresh bread and dried figs, coursing through my veins.

"But my colleagues did not give me enough time and they soon brought me down from the heights of those winding roads to the lowliness of my reality. One of them wanted us to continue on our way immediately because our permits did not allow us to stop at al-Laban Heights, while another mocked my memories of the place by reminding me how, twenty years before, I had stopped to relieve myself on one of the bends. There was other banter too of the kind we teachers indulge in when we are away from our students and our wives.

"I kept on brooding upon this astonishing incident all the way to Ramallah, on to Jerusalem and then Bethlehem and during the return journey. I pleaded with my memory to retrieve what it was that happened to me during my youth, in that same spot, that had made me stand there, spellbound, never wanting to leave it, ever.

"But it was no use and when we reached the place on the way back we drove by without stopping. One of my colleagues noticed my distress. He put his hand on my shoulder to console me and said, 'It looks like the heights at al-'Abhariya on the road from Nazareth to Haifa. Maybe you've got them mixed up.'

"His words lifted a huge weight off my mind. For about twenty years I have been going to Haifa twice a week to give extra lessons in a secondary school and I used to pass by al-'Abhariya Heights on the way there and back. My collegue had convinced me with his simple explanation, even though I knew the two places bore no resemblance to one another whatsoever, because I am well aware of my own secret and my weak spot for *A Tale of Two Cities*. There was no doubt that al-'Abhariya Heights had always been linked in my imagination with al-Laban Heights. I accepted the explanation and felt much relieved."

How strange man is! Does he really slaughter in his memory those things which he cannot bear to recollect? I used to think that people with no consciences developed hearts of stone so that they wouldn't feel guilt. But that's not the case. If a person is unable to kill his conscience he kills his memory! So, why had he come to tell me this story!

My old friend went on, "You may recall that I had a number of friends and acquaintances in the West Bank, from schooldays and from later on: teachers, lawyers, doctors, businessmen, politicians, one minister and would-be ministers. I have visited them all and we have rekindled former memories and renewed former friendships. They have become once again, as they were twenty years ago, a very dear part of my life. Not a week goes by without me visiting one of them or one of them visiting me. I thought in the past that they had forgotten me or were ashamed of me and had cut me off the tree of their lives as one prunes a dead branch so that the tree can grow and burst into leaf."

"But we are a branch that life has sprouted . . ."

"Right. At first I would visit them hesitatingly, unsure of how they would receive me, but then I would find an unexpected nostalgia for old friendship and a pride in it. I found that they had kept up-to-date with our news; they had picked it up from the beaks of birds. And I found also that they hold us in greater esteem than we hold ourselves. I had wanted to hide from them my twenty-year withdrawal into my shell; but it turned out that they knew and understood perfectly. They saw me differently than I saw myself. They thought highly of me, and I lived up to it. They lifted me up and I stood tall, and my head rose above the blows.

"That's why I told you that they had become such a valuable part of my life . . . the life you used to know twenty years ago."

"Did you visit me openly tonight, with you so tall?"

"Is there any way I can visit you other than openly?"

"But is that why you visited me?"

"No. There is something worrying me, keeps me awake at night. I've told you already that the feeling of surprise engendered by the winding road of al-Laban Heights was short-lived. I had put it down to the charm which had clung to me all my life, to the duality of my thought process and my logic and to my constant exposure to a similar group of hills at al-'Abhariya.

"I've driven up and down the winding road at al-Laban dozens of times since then and if ever that strange painful longing comes over me, I have an immediate explanation to relieve my conscience. That was until one day last February. I was with my wife and son on our way back from visiting some friends in Old Jerusalem. It was noon as we began to wind our way down the road at al-Laban. The almond blossoms were opening, red and white embracing in spring rapture, and all ten hills were dancing."

"What language did you compose this ode in?"

"The language of my eyes and my heart. And you will listen to me until I finish speaking.

"My wife insisted we stop the car to pick some sprigs from an ancient almond tree which I believe had been there also in the old days. We got out and picked four sprigs. They smiled at us and we smiled back at them.

"And when my wife asked, 'Is it true that if you plant an almond

sprig in the soil a tree grows?' my heart sank and I began to remember.

"Do you remember, when we were still young, we had a friend.
He fell in love with a girl from Jerusalem or Bethlehem, somewhere
like that, and we loved this love."

"We all fell in love, and we loved his love."

"In fact our friend's love was more beautiful than ours. There
was a story to it. We were on a trip. We stopped by that tree at the
bottom of al-Laban Heights. There was a house there with chickens
and cows. The house is still standing but I no longer see any chickens or cows. We asked the occupants for water. Then all of a sudden
a group of girls turned up, on a trip from Jerusalem. They picked
branches of almond blossom. Our friend's girlfriend was one of
them. They met and she gave him a sprig full of blossoms. Were
you with us?"

"What happened next?"

"I remember a beautiful story about it. I don't know how I came
to hear about it, but his girlfriend broke off two sprigs from the
branch. One she gave to him, the other she kept for herself. They
made a pact that each one would keep their sprig and that they
would meet again the following spring, when the almond trees
blossom, and he would come with his family to ask her hand in
marriage. What was the end of their beautiful story?"

"Why are you so interested in them?"

"I don't know. I just feel a really strong impulse pushing me to
revive all my old friendships. It is as if I want to bind my present to
my past so that they will never again become undone. It was past
overflowing with hope. It embraced the world and all that was in it
and it was pure and open like a child's eyes. I feel today as if I want
to grab its threads and extricate myself from this present. Do you
think that I am actually drowning, holding on to threads of air?"

"Search me!"

"Ever since the June War I've been making my troubled rounds
in search of old friends and every time I meet one of them I get an
even greater desire to meet others. You see, since I remembered the
story of that friend of ours I've been searching for him, always on

the lookout. None of my old friends recalls his story. It's an obsession that has got me in trouble more than once for I can hardly meet one of those old friends without insisting he tell me how he met his wife.

"And now there is no one left from the days of our youth except you to ask about this friend of ours. That's why I came. Do you remember him? It would put my mind at rest."

"You were always a strange one, my friend, but tonight you're stranger than ever. Why are you so obsessed with a side issue?"

"You say a side issue! I realize now that I had never withdrawn into my shell, or curled up except when I cut my links with the past. What is this past? The past isn't a time. The past is you and so-and-so and so-and-so and all the friends. It's like we drew the picture of this past and each one of us coloured it with his own special colour until it emerged, an image of shining youth, to embrace everything in the whole world. I will never regain my links with this past until the parts of the picture are complete with all their colours. I see this friend of ours, with his beautiful love, I see him as the smile in this picture. What past remains without him? What would remain of La Gioconda if her smile were wiped away? It is his story; whether it ended joyfully in the return of the lover to his beloved or sadly in everlasting separation, his story I see as the most truthful expression of the springtime of our past. I want this past to return like the spring returns after every winter."

"I see you've returned to the tale of the two cities, the two sprigs, the lover and his beloved, the happy ending and the sad ending. But life is not lines moving along independently of one another. It is lines intertwining. Why couldn't it be that your imagination, awakened by a spring-like nostalgia for lofty mountains, conceived the whole story?"

"Certainly my imagination has awakened and I never want it to sleep again. That's why I am looking for our friend. Am I to presume that you don't remember him?"

"Let me think about it. If I do remember him, I'll let you know."

Mister M left more troubled than I had ever seen him in my life, and I remained where I was, more troubled than I had ever been in mine. For a few minutes after his departure I had to restrain myself forcibly from running after him and shaking his memory back to life.

But, can I bring back the dead?

How could I not remember the beautiful love story whose hero Mister M was so anxious to remember? And how many times had I asked myself: How can a person kill in his heart a love like that?

After the June War, I had visited the good and loyal woman in Jerusalem or Bethlehem—or somewhere like that, as Mister M would say. She showed me the withered almond branch which she still kept and which almost kindled red and white as she told me its story. She told me that he had visited her with some of his teaching colleagues. He was in an excellent mood and had talked all the time. She took them into her office to look at the books and artifacts she had collected and he noticed the withered almond branch. He asked her about it and she told him that the almond blossoms in February. He changed the subjects to apricots and his apricot harvest. She was extremely surprised. But now, after Mister M has visited me and told me his tale, I understand everything.

I am convinced that Mister M is sincere in his forgetfulness and is sincere in his anxiety to remember. By some strange subconscious desire he has truly forgotten that he himself is the hero of the beautiful love story, and that it was his smile that shone on our youth.

Is it my duty to remind him, to put his mind at rest as he asked? And why should I put his mind at rest? And anyway, am I really going to put his mind at rest?

If he has really stood tall, like he told me, then he should manage to get hold of this story and read it. I wonder if then he will remember, re-establish ties with his past and extricate himself from his present?

At last the almond blossomed and we met. Spring was smiling and fate absolutely roaring with laughter.

Translated by Anthony Calderbank

Tawfik al-Hakim
(1898–1987)

EGYPT

Tawfik al-Hakim was the leading playwright of his time in Egypt and the founder of a vibrant dramatic movement that sadly has not been maintained. In all, he wrote approximately seventy plays. He was sent to France to complete his studies in law, but—as he amusingly recounts in his autobiographical work dealing with his early years—he returned from his stay in Paris with the selfsame bag he had traveled with, the selfsame clothes, and crates filled with books, but without the one thing he had gone there for—a doctorate in law. During the following years he wrote copiously. In addition to his plays, he has two major novels to his name: *The Return of the Spirit*, which was published in 1933, and the better-known *Diary of a Country Prosecutor*, which came out three years later. *Diary of a Country Prosecutor* is a fast-moving satirical novel about peasant life—the primitive conditions under which the peasants live and the abuse they suffer from those in power. In his introduction to the novel, P. H. Newby observes: "Tawfik al-Hakim's comedy is blacker than anything Gogol or Dickens wrote because life for the Egyptian peasantry, the fellahin, was blacker than for the nineteenth-century Russian serf or English pauper. It must also be said that the first readers of Gogol or Dickens would not have been prepared to look at unwelcome facts with the honesty Tawfik al-Hakim expected of his readers." Tawfik al-Hakim's novel *Bird of the East*, the forerunner to several other novels about individuals from the East experiencing life in the West (most notably Yahya Hakki's *The Lamp of Umm Hashim* and Tayeb Salih's *Season of Migration to the North*), is also available in English translation.

FROM *Diary of a Country Prosecutor*

When we got back, it was time for the session to begin. Our car approached the court, where we saw people crowded like flies at the entrance. My assistant had slumped down at my side completely prostrate and I took no further notice of him. It did not occur to me to summon him in that state of fatigue to sit through a court session with me after attending an investigation. He was not yet accustomed to a twenty-four-hour day and the instructive night which he had just spent was quite enough for him.

So I decided to deal gently with him in the early period of his service; and as soon as we came to the court, I made the driver stop and ordered him to take my assistant home.

I bade farewell to the ma'mur and alighted from the car, clearing a path between the serried ranks of men, women and children. When I entered the conference room the judge was already sitting. As soon as I saw him, my spirits dropped. There are two judges in this court and they work on alternate days. One of them lives in Cairo and travels up for the session by the first train. He always hears his cases with the utmost speed in order to catch the eleven o'clock train returning to Cairo. No matter how great the number of cases for hearing—this judge has never yet missed his train. The other judge is an excessively conscientious man who lives with his family in the district office. He is very slow in dealing with cases, for he is afraid of making mistakes through haste; and perhaps, too, he is eager to fill in time and enliven his boredom in this provincial outpost. Moreover he has no train to catch. So from early morning he sits at his desk as though he were inseparably nailed to it; and he never leaves it till just before noon. He generally resumes the session in the evening too. These sessions have always been a nightmare to me; they are a veritable sentence of imprisonment—as though I were condemned to be tied to my desk and remain immobile the whole day long. The red and green sash placed around my neck and under my armpit seemed like a yoke. Was it divine vengeance for all the innocent people whom I had inadvertently sent to prison? Or is it that the consequences of our professional mistakes recoil upon us, so that we pay for them some time in our life without knowing when?

I said nothing when I saw the judge. It was clear to me that I was in for a merciless session after a night of continuous toil. I don't know what can have blurred my memory and made me imagine that it was the turn of the brisk judge to preside this morning . . .

I entered the court. First of all I glanced at the list and saw that we had to deal with seventy misdemeanours and forty felonies—quite sufficient to ensure an endless session with this particular judge. There were always more cases for him than for his colleagues; and the reason was quite simple. The conscientious judge never imposed a higher fine than twenty piastres for a misdemeanour, whereas his colleague raised the fine to as much as fifty piastres. People charged with misdemeanours had got to know this, and always took special care to escape from the expensive judge and patronize his more reasonably priced colleague. Today's judge had often complained and grumbled about the way his work increased in volume from one day to the next, and had never discovered the cause. I used to say to myself, "Raise your price and you'll have a pleasant surprise."

The usher began calling out the names of the accused from a paper which he was holding. Kuzman Effendi, the usher, was an old man with white hair and a white moustache, endowed with a presence and bearing fit for a Justice of the Supreme Court. Whenever he called anyone to the box, he was extremely majestic in his movements, gestures and voice. He would turn to the court attendant with an air of supreme authority, and that worthy fellow would echo the name outside the chamber just as he had heard it from the usher, except that he would introduce a long-drawn-out chant and an intonation like that of a street-hawker. A certain judge had once noticed this resemblance, and said to him, "Come Sha'ban, are you calling out the names of defendants in crime cases or selling potatoes and black dates?"

And the man replied, "Crime cases, potatoes, dates, it's all the same; it's all to make a living."

The first defendant took his place. The judge, who had plunged into his papers, now raised his head, adjusted a pair of thick spectacles on his nose and said to the man before him, "You have contravened the Slaughter of Animals Regulations by killing a sheep outside the slaughter-house."

"Your honour, we slaughtered the sheep—saving your presence—on a very special evening (may you be granted one like it)—it was the circumcision of our little son and . . ."

"Twenty piastres fine! Next case!"

The usher called out a name. And so it went on—name after name—a whole succession of cases exactly similar to the first on which sentence had been pronounced. I left the judge to his verdicts and began to amuse myself by observing the people in the court . . . They filled all the seats and benches and overflowed onto the floor and gangways, where they sat on their haunches like cattle gazing up humbly at the judge, while he pronounced sentence like a shepherd with a staff. The judge grew weary of the succession of identical cases and shouted, "What is all this about? Is there nothing in this court except sheep outside slaughter-houses?"

He glared at the crowd with eyes like little peas behind his spectacles, which bobbed up and down his nose. Nobody, not even himself, caught the implication of what he had said. The usher went on calling out names. The type of charge had begun to vary and we were entering a different world, for the judge was now saying to the accused, "You are charged with having washed your clothes in the canal!"

"Your honour—may God exalt your station—are you going to fine me just because I washed my clothes?"

"It's for washing them in the canal."

"Well, where else could I wash them?"

The judge hesitated, deep in thought, and could give no answer. He knew very well that these poor wretches had no wash basins in their village, filled with fresh flowing water from the tap. They were left to live like cattle all their lives and were yet required to submit to a modern legal system imported from abroad.

The judge turned to me and said, "The Legal Officer! Opinion, please."

"The state is not concerned to inquire where this man should wash his clothes. Its only interest is the application of the law."

The judge turned his glance away from me, lowered his head, shook it and then spoke swiftly like a man rolling a weight off his shoulders: "Fined twenty piastres. Next case."

A woman's name was called. It was the village prostitute. She had blackened her eyelashes with the point of a match and smeared her cheeks with the glaring crimson colour which can be seen painted on boxes of Samson cigarettes. On her bare arm was tattooed the picture of a heart pierced by an arrow. She was wearing on her wrist several bracelets and armlets made of metal and coloured glass.

The judge looked at her and said, "You are charged with having stood at the entrance of your house . . ."

She put her hand on her hip and shouted, "Well, darling, is it a crime for someone to stand in front of his house?"

"You were doing it to seduce the public."

"What a pity! By your honour's beard, I've never seen this Public—he's never called in at my place."

"Twenty piastres. Next case."

Kuzman Effendi summoned the next defendant. He was a middle-aged farmer of some prosperity, to judge from his blue turban, his Kashmir galabieh, his cloak of "imperial" pattern and his elastic boots of screaming yellow tint. As soon as he appeared, the judge sprang the accusation upon him: "You, sir, are charged with not having registered your dog within the statutory period."

The accused coughed, shook his head and mumbled as though reciting a religious formula, "A fine age we're living in—dogs have to be 'registered' like plots of land, and a great fuss is made over them!"

"Twenty piastres fine. Next case . . ."

The hearing of the misdemeanours continued, all in the same

vein. Not a single one of the defendants showed any sign of believing in the real iniquity of whatever he had done. It was merely that fines had fallen upon them from heaven, whence all disasters proceed; they had to be paid, for so the law required. I had often tried to convince myself of the purpose of these sessions. Could one claim that these judgments had a deterrent effect when the delinquent had not the least idea of what fault he had committed?

We got through the misdemeanours and the usher called out, "Cases of Felony." He glanced at the list and shouted, "Umm as-Sa'ad, daughter of Ibrahim al-Jarf."

An old peasant woman walked slowly down the center of the room until she reached the dais, where she stood in front of Kuzman Effendi the usher. He directed her towards the judge, at whom she gazed weakly for a while. Soon she turned away from him and stood once more with her eyes fixed on the aged usher.

The judge buried his face in the papers and asked, "Your name?"

"Umm Sa'ad, sir."

She appeared to address this reply to the usher, who made a sign directing her once more to face the dais. The judge questioned her: "Your profession?"

"Woman, your honour!"

"You are charged with biting the finger of Shaikh Hasan Imara.'"

She left the dais and addressed the usher again: "I swear to you, by the honour of your white hair, that I haven't done any wrong— I swore, I gave a sacred oath that my daughter wouldn't be married for a dowry of less than twenty gold pieces."

The judge raised his head, adjusted his spectacles, looked at her and said sharply, "Now then, speak to me. I'm the judge here. Did you bite him? Answer yes or no!"

"Bite him? God forbid! I've got a temper, I admit—but I don't go as far as biting people!"

"Call the witness," the judge said to the usher.

The victim appeared—his finger bound in a sheath. The judge asked him his name and occupation, made him swear that he would tell nothing but the truth and asked him to elucidate what had happened.

"Your honour, I wasn't on one side nor on the other, and the matter arose because I generously offered to mediate."

He relapsed into silence, as though he had completely clarified the whole matter.

The judge glared at him in repressed anger, and then upbraided him and ordered him to recount in detail what had happened. The man made a full statement to this effect:

The accused woman had a daughter called Sitt Abuha; she was wooed by a peasant named Horaisha, who offered a dowry of fifteen gold pieces. The mother refused and demanded twenty. The matter stood there until one day the suitor's brother, a young boy called Ginger, came along on his own accord and informed the bride's family, quite falsely, that the suitor had accepted their terms. He then went back to his brother and told him that the girl's family had agreed to reduce the dowry and to accept his offer. As a result of this cunning joke played on both parties, a day was appointed for reciting the Fatiha at the bride's house, and the bridegroom deputed Shaikh Hasan and Shaikh Faraj to be his witnesses.

Everybody came together and the girl's mother killed a goose. Scarcely had the meal been made ready and served to the guests when the dowry was mentioned and the trick was revealed. It was evident that the deadlock had not been solved and a quarrel flared up between the two parties. The girl's mother began to shout and wail in the yard: "What a dreadful calamity! How our enemies would rejoice. By the life of the Prophet, I will not let my daughter go for less than twenty gold pieces." The woman, half-crazed, rushed in amongst the menfolk to defend her daughter's interests, fearing that the men would settle the matter in an unsatisfactory way. Shaikh Hasan was moved by the spirit of devoted zeal and did not touch the food. He began to argue with the woman, vainly trying to convince her, while his colleague, Shaikh Faraj, stretched out his hand towards the goose and began to guzzle it avidly, without entering into the impassioned dispute. It appears that the enthusiasm on each side went beyond the limits of verbal discussion, and soon Shaikh Hasan saw that his hand was not in the plate of goose but in the woman's mouth. He let forth a resounding shriek and soon the whole house was turned upside down in chaotic confusion. Shaikh Hasan grabbed his companion, pulled him violently away from the goose and went out, gnashing his teeth with rage. His companion, who had not said a single word, had been rewarded with an excellent meal; whereas he, after all his zeal, had left the banquet hungry, with his finger bitten by the old woman . . .

The plaintiff went on at great length. Suddenly the judge was seized with agitation. His conscientious scruples had come to life, and he interrupted the witness, saying, as though in a soliloquy, "I wonder if I made the witness take the oath!"

He turned to me and inquired, "Prosecuting Counsel, did I make the witness take the oath?"

I tried hard to remember, but the judge could not banish his doubts. He shouted at the witness, "Take the oath, sir. Say: 'By almighty God, I swear to speak the truth!'"

The man swore the oath—whereupon the judge called out, "Begin your evidence from the beginning!"

I saw that we would never finish the session. I was utterly bored and sank, yawning, into my seat. Sleep began to play with my eyelids and there elapsed an interval the length of which I cannot surmise. Suddenly I heard the judge's voice calling to me: "Prosecution! What is the request of Prosecuting Counsel?"

I opened a pair of bloodshot eyes which requested nothing but sleep and was informed by the judge that he had just studied the medical report, which said that the injury had left a permanent infirmity—the loss of the medial parallax of the third finger. I sat up in my seat and immediately demanded a ruling of *ultra vires*. The judge turned to the old woman and said, "The case has become a felony and within the jurisdiction of the Criminal Court."

The old lady showed no sign of understanding this subtle distinction. In her view, a bite was a bite. How could it suddenly be transformed from a misdemeanour into a felony? (What an accursed law it is—far beyond the comprehension of these simple folk!)

The next case was called. It dealt with a violent quarrel, leading to blows, which had broken out between the father of Sitt Abuha and the family of the husband, Sayyid Horaisha—for eventually the marriage had taken place. The bridegroom had sent some of his relations with a camel to take the bride from her father's house, but her father had received them with sharp abuse, shouting in their faces, "What? A camel? My daughter leave here on a camel? Not likely! There must be a Toumbeel [an automobile]."

The two parties began to argue about who was to pay for this newfangled device provided by modern scientific development. The argument led to the raising of sticks and the effusion of a few drops of blood—quite inevitable in a situation of this kind. Finally, a well-intentioned person produced a banknote from his pocket and hired one of the taxis which plied on the country roads.

The judge gave his ruling on the dispute, and remarked, "Thank heavens, we've finished with the joys of matrimony. Next case."

Translated by Abba Eban

Yahya Hakki
(1905–92)
EGYPT

Yahya Hakki began his career as a lawyer and then served in various parts of the world as a diplomat. After resigning from the diplomatic service, he devoted himself fully to writing. Together with such figures as the scholar Taha Hussein, the playwright Tawfik al-Hakim, the short story writer Mahmoud Teymour, and of course Naguib Mahfouz, he belongs to a small group of exceptionally talented men who laid the foundations for the literary renaissance in Egypt midway through the twentieth century. He is best known for his novella *The Lamp of Umm Hashim*, which recounts the difficulties faced by a young man who is sent abroad to complete his studies in medicine. It was the first of several works in Arabic dealing with the way in which an individual tries to come to terms with two divergent cultures. The short scene that follows is set in England.

FROM *The Lamp of Umm Hashim*

The extraordinary thing I could not explain was that Ismail recovered from his love for Mary to find himself a prey to a new love. Is it that the heart cannot live untenanted? Or was it that Mary had inadvertently caused his heart to wake up and come to new life?

Ismail used to have only the vaguest of feelings for Egypt. He was like a grain of sand that has been merged into other sands and has become so assimilated among them that he could not be distinguished from them even when separated from all the other grains. Now, however, he felt himself to be a ring in a long chain that tightly bound him to his mother country. In his mind Egypt was like the forest bride touched by the wand of a wicked witch that had sent her to sleep. She was dressed in all her jewelry and finery for the night of consummation. Cursed by God is the eye that cannot see her beauty and the nostril that cannot smell her perfume. When will she wake up? When? The stronger his love for Egypt grew, the greater his irritation with Egyptians. None the less they were his flesh and blood, and the fault was not theirs. They were the victims of ignorance, poverty, disease, and chronically long oppression. Many a time he had stared into the eyes of death, had handled leprosy, had put his mouth close to the mouth of someone in fever. Could it be that he would now flinch from touching this human mass when his flesh was part of theirs, his blood from theirs? He had pledged to himself, in his love for Egypt, that whatever objectionable thing he set his eyes on he would remove it. Mary had taught him to be self-dependent, and woe after that to whoever sought to feed him with their superstitions, fantasies, and customs. Not in vain had he lived in Europe and taken part in its prayers to science and logic. He knew that between him and those with whom he would come into contact there would be a long struggle, though his youth made him underrate the fight and its difficulties. In fact, he was already ardently yearning for the first battle. He let his mind wander and saw himself as a journalist writing in the newspapers or as an orator at a meeting expounding his views and beliefs to the masses.

The train moved off and he had not sent his telegram. He did not know why he shrank from meeting them at the station amid the clamor and bustle, the confusion of luggage, and under the gaze of other people. He wanted to meet his dear ones in their own home, far out of the sight of strangers. He did, however, appreciate the shock this would have on his father and his aged mother. When he thought of them his heart trembled: was he able to pay back some part of the debt he owed them? He was returning home equipped with the very weapon his father had wanted for him, and he was determined that with this weapon he would carve for himself a path to the front ranks. He would stay away from government service and would open his own clinic in the best district of Cairo. First of all, he would astonish the Cairenes, then the Egyptians in their entirety, with his skill and the breadth of his experience. When the money came pouring in, he would see to it that his old father would no longer have to work and he would buy him some land in their village so that he would be able to live in comfort. Ismail then brought himself up with a start as he remembered that he had brought no gifts with him from Europe for the family.

He consoled himself with the thought: "What is there in the whole of Europe that is good enough for my father and mother?"

And Fatima al-Nabawiya? The memory of her brought a certain feeling of discomfort. He was still bound by his promise: having returned a free man, he had no excuse to call it off. But this was a complex matter and was best left to the future.

He looked out of the window and saw a moving landscape that appeared to have been coated by a sandstorm, a landscape dilapidated, begrimed, and devastated. The vendors at the stations were in tattered clothes, pouring with sweat and panting like hunted animals.

When the horse-carriage he took from the station entered narrow Khalig Street, which was not wide enough for the tram to pass through, the sight that met his eyes was uglier than anything he had imagined: dirt and flies, poverty, and buildings in a state of ruin. He was overcome by depression. Struck dumb by what he saw. The flame of revolt grew stronger within him, and he became more determined than ever to gird himself for action.

Standing before the house, he took hold of the knocker and let it fall back. Its knock mingled with the beatings of his heart. He heard a gentle voice calling in the tone used by the women of Cairo: "Who?"

"It's me—Ismail! Open the door, Fatima!"

Translated by Denys Johnson-Davies

A Story from Prison

The fact that it was a duty many times repeated did away with any feelings the sergeant might have had as he shoved those under arrest into the cell. But with this particular man he was annoyed; with his mouth screwed up and his grip cruelly tight, he enjoyed cursing him and striking him on the back of the neck. It was not because his eyes had alighted on legs that were sore and chapped, or that his nose was assailed by a disgusting smell emanating from a dirty blue gallabiya patched in numerous places with pieces of darker colors, for he was accustomed to such things in the peasants who crossed his path. Rather, it was because, ever since learning that the accused was one of the band of gypsies the police had been after, he had regarded him with an eye of repugnance. It was not the look one man gives to another, but the scrutiny accorded by a superior species to an inferior one. His hand had no sooner fallen on the other man's shoulder than he was seized with a feeling of disgust that was close to nausea. Gypsies! Were they human beings?

The gypsy entered the cell with a smile on his mouth brought about by embarrassment, a smile that was cold and doltish and became wider and more idiotic when his gaze alighted on a young man sitting in a corner, who he saw was also smiling. Turning his face away and squatting down in another corner, he proceeded to ruminate and so pass the time. His inactivity did not last long. After a while he again glanced furtively at the young man, gradually arousing in the latter a desire to enter into conversation. He began by asking the young man his name, what village he came from and what he was charged with, and from there the conversation branched out. The name of a famous criminal came up and he mentioned that he knew him, that they were in fact distantly related.

"You're both from the same village?" the young man asked.

"Yes, he and I are from one and the same part of the village."

"I heard the policeman calling you a gypsy. How was it you got mixed up with the gypsies, then, if you're a peasant?"

The noise in the police station courtyard grew louder as the sound of rifles being put into racks was heard, with here and there the crash of policemen's boots. A three-sentry patrol came along and sat down to chat alongside the prison cell. Their words reached the two men clearly, as well as their bursts of laughter. The gypsy drew closer to the young man until he was sitting beside him—he had not been friendly with a peasant for a long time. In the dreariness of prison and amid the unusual hubbub, there was kindled in his heart a sympathy and affection for his companion. It may have been as a result of all these circumstances that he began to talk, neither evasively nor aggressively. He was not so much recounting his story as reliving his past.

"I had rented fourteen qirats of land—just over half an acre—from the umda's brother, and I had a few head of sheep that I let loose in the fields in spring. When the Nile flood came I had no work, so the fellow with the land said to me: 'Ellewi, seeing as you've nothing to do, why don't you go up to Minya with my sheep and take them to a merchant I know there. I can assure you, my friend, I'll make it worth your while.' I said to him: 'The journey's too difficult for me.' He replied: 'You're experienced with sheep, and I've chosen you—you're my man. The journey isn't as difficult as you think. Just keep along the Ibrahimiya Canal, going north-ward all the way, and you'll find yourself at Minya.' And the man went off, bought me a fine knife, gave me a donkey, and handed over sixty-five head of sheep. I went out of the village with them, with the floodwater lying a foot high on the fields, and continued driving the sheep ahead of me along the embankment of the Ibrahimiya Canal."

Sheep, though not timid animals, are not easily driven. They move slowly, and if not continually urged on, come to a stop, and only a vigilant stick will bring them together once they get scattered. Sometimes Ellewi would have to gather them together with his long cudgel to allow passage to approaching cars, while at other times he would have to descend into the fields behind some stray ram. The whole day might well pass without him uttering more than a drawn-out, whistled, shushing sound. With his long cudgel he would give sharp taps to the sheep's backs to bring them together into a single, easily managed flock, while their short, delicate feet stirred up clouds of dust. Their cries of *ma . . . ma . . .* were continuous, some short and staccato, others almost a form of speech, in which there was an unmistakable call for help. Some calls were harsh and husky, issuing from throats that had desiccated with the years, whereas others were like the twanging of the thin string of a musical instrument and emanated from small lambs, full of vivacity and exuberance, whose bellies were not yet distinguishable from their backs and whose mode of progression was by sideways leaps and playful buttings. A flock of sheep also bears within its fold the chain that binds life with death.

Ellewi, fearing that a young lamb would lose its way, raised it up by its legs, at which it set up a loud, continuous bleating. He walked along with it, cleaving a way amid the sheep, every now and again lowering his hand so that it fell on a wave of wool set ablaze by the sun; the collected dust, mixed with the animals' sweat, had become hot and sticky above scalding bodies that bore their suffering with patience. When he reached the donkey, he opened a bag and placed the lamb inside. A skinny ewe, cleaving its way with an effort even greater than his own, had followed after him with a will that spoke of its determination not to be diverted by anything, and which replied to each *ma* with an answer containing a tenderness that expressed the loving concern of a mother.

Ellewi's appearance gave no indication that he was capable of bearing the burden of looking after a flock of sheep, for he was in his early youth. While one's eyes might not notice the signs of his pharaonic ancestry—his tall stature and broad chest—they would not miss his obvious thinness and the lack of proportion between his large, splayed feet and his spindly legs. Under his collarbone was a hollow, possibly the result of hunger; the exposed hair of his chest ended at the two protruding bones. His face consisted of taut skin and muscle; whatever happened, no spare flesh quivered there. When he moved his jaw, the surface of his temple was broken up into hollows and bumps. He was nevertheless ever on the go, his energy renewed by some mysterious power that flowed in the Valley and was no less forceful than the Nile itself, a power that had not been crushed by the building of a pagan monument like the Pyramids or by being entombed by the passage of thousands of years.

Ellewi would cover great distances with nothing remaining in his mind of the journey other than the names of the villages or the small, white memorial domes set up to various holy men; some of these would lie high up on the canal embankment so that the village could bury its dead around them, while others would be down in the agricultural land flooded by the Nile so that the crops might benefit from their blessing. Ellewi, like the peasant he was, and because he was making the journey for the first time, had little contact with the places he passed, nothing attracting his attention unless it affected him personally. Thus he was not at all impressed by the Ibrahimiya Canal embankment, which looked ugly under the burning sun of Upper Egypt, screened by a thick cloud of dirt stretching out before him like a vast ribbon of piled-up, jagged-edged earth; continually rising and falling, its uneven surface was ever changing its mind as to whether to be narrow or broad. It was rendered even uglier by the fact that it was much higher than the canal itself, so that nothing could be seen of the trees planted at the water's edge except for short branches that blocked the view, branches that the person walking along the embankment could touch with his hand. What would Ellewi say if someone were to tell

him that much of the height of the embankment was not made up
of earth, that deep within it were also many skeletons of peasants,
among them perhaps some of his own forebears, who had dug the
canal across four provinces with their primitive picks, perhaps even
with their nails? When a peasant died, the earth was piled on top of
him, just as he was, with his basket, his pick, and his one blue gallabiya. The canal had eaten up their bodies, wiping away their flesh
and the lash marks on their skin.

"On the fourth day, just after the call to afternoon prayer, I
reached Nazali Ganub. I was intending to walk straight on and
spend the night with the sheep in Sanabu, but I don't know what it
was that made me bring the sheep to a halt in front of this village.
I'd be lying if I said I was tired—perhaps it was because I'd found a
derelict mill on the embankment."

The young man interrupted him in an almost sarcastic tone, like
a man listening to a child. "Or was it just your destiny that it happened like that?"

The young man was still smiling. His eyes never left Ellewi,
whom he regarded as an entertaining spectacle, for since feeling
that Ellewi was treating him like a brother he had despised him.
Whenever he interrupted the other's conversation with his mocking
remarks—which was often—his body shook with pleasure.

"The Lord knows best. I didn't believe it when I found the mill
had a big wall, so I got the sheep arranged and said to myself:
'You're going to have a good night's sleep tonight, with no sheep escaping and you having to run around after them.' So I settled myself down. When the time for evening prayer came, I moved close
to the sheep, took off my gallabiya, and put my head on my arm to
sleep. But my eyes hadn't yet met up with sleep when I found a
group of people making their way toward me from the direction of
the village. In their midst were a couple of donkeys, and some goats
were going in front of them. When they came to where I was, I realized they were a band of gypsies. I said to myself: 'What rotten
bad luck—but maybe, my boy, they'll go straight on.' I got up and
hid myself to see what would happen. They came right alongside

me and stopped, and after a while I found them spreading their things out around me."

Two men went to the donkeys and unloaded some thin screens, which they leaned up against each other—and there, in front of Ellewi, were two small tents. They knocked some pegs into the ground, to which they tied their goats. A woman took out a cooking-pot and sat down to rub it clean with earth, then went to the canal. One of them brought out three pieces of stick tied up in a bundle. He unfolded them, fixing their feet in the ground, and brought a kettle, which he hung in the middle, lighting a fire beneath it and leaning his head forward and blowing at it. After a while there was the smell of tea, and the gypsies became aware of their neighbor.

"One of them said to me: 'Please have a drink of tea with us.' So I got up and went over to them and sat down."

"Had it been a long time since you'd had a drink of tea?" the young man asked him.

"You know that peasants are stupid and won't say 'No' to any invitation. But to tell you the truth, I was frightened, what with all those stories in our village about gypsies being thieves and kidnappers and playing tricks you'd never even think of. I said to myself: 'My boy, keep an eye on these people.' They had a girl with them, who went back and forth in front of me. I only noticed her when I saw the men frowning at her. Not one of them would speak to her in a decent, friendly way, all the time shouting and snapping at her. Sometimes she'd make a reply and sometimes she'd just walk by in silence. I don't know what she'd done to them for them to swear at her without listening to what she had to say, saying such things as: 'You crazy girl, you'll see. We'll show you!' After that, every time she passed in front of me I took a good look at her."

He saw she had a dark brown face, almost completely round, and a thin nose; she had a green dot on her forehead, and a recent tattoo on her chin. She was short and straight-backed, and the way she was constantly moving her head showed a very nervous disposition. She would hide her anger by visibly pressing down on her lips, which made them longer and more pinched. When she came to pass round the glasses, a smell that was alien to his nose was wafted from her to him, a mixture of sweat and dirt and a perfume containing cloves and sandalwood. Before he knew it Ellewi was engaged in conversation with them.

"We went on talking and they went on asking me about the sheep: Where was I taking them? How many had I got? I was frightened they were distracting me because of some plot they were hatching. I said to myself: 'Get up and look to your sheep.' I went back to my place but wasn't able to sleep at first. Then no sooner had my eyes closed, well after midnight, than I was woken by the barking of a dog and found that my sheep were all rushing about in front of three policemen, whose horses' eyes gleamed like sparks in the darkness—I can still recall them even now! I went crazy, running about and falling over. Every time I turned in the direction of the gypsies I saw the policemen knocking down the tents. The fire was out and turned to smoke. I heard them being cursed: 'Thieves! Robbers! Sons of bitches!' Their arms were waving above their heads as they screamed: 'Have mercy, Sergeant.' But it was no good. They rounded them up on a chain, and I went on collecting the sheep until, thanks be to the Lord, I got them all together. I went back to my place and was about to take off my gallabiya and go to sleep when I looked out and found the gypsy girl rolled up in a heap right up against the wall. To tell you the truth, I was trembling from the shock of it. What a business! What sort of mess was I getting into?

"'Hey girl, what are you up to? What brought you here?'

"She motioned to me with her finger. Then, when the police had quite taken themselves off, she flung herself at me and said, 'I'm at your mercy.' She told me, 'Those men wanted to kill me. They thought I gave them away in the Qusiya robbery. They put us all in prison, and as soon as they came out they stole again. I beseech you to take me with you. I'll go wherever you go, just so long as I get away from those people.'"

The gypsy girl stretched out her arms and clasped him round the neck. She was neither trembling nor breathing quickly—the only thing that had changed in her was that the tightness of her lips had disappeared and they now looked swollen and revealed two large teeth. She lowered her eyes. Was it that he was tired, or was it because it was Ellewi's first experience? Perhaps, too, it was because he had never before smelled at close quarters the scent of cloves and sandalwood. Whatever the reason, Ellewi felt his strength melt away between her hands as his arms dropped limply to his side. There came back to his mind the image of this woman passing in front of him as he sat drinking tea with her companions and he remembered the way she had of tossing her head. He had not realized then—though he did now—that these tossings of the head held an extraordinary attraction for him, a powerful fascination. His silence lasted a long time, and he analyzed it as being an effect of his upbringing, which had taught him since he was a boy to stand in awe of gypsies. But he did not repel the woman's arms; in fact after a while he had the sensation that the numbness in his nerves had been replaced by a throbbing in his forehead, a dryness in his throat, and a trembling in his heart. All these things combined to fill his veins with blood that boiled and thundered in his ears. Then his arms were on hers and he was further inflamed when she drew gradually closer to him, impelled toward him by a feeling that was a mixture of joy and defiance. Perhaps her passion was not for the man but resulted from savoring the pleasure of her freedom on this her first night. No sooner had the man returned her embrace than there burst forth from its hiding place a strong desire that had long been suppressed, and in its unloosing a tornado was set free. It was none the less careful not to expend itself too quickly, curbing its impetuosity and veiling its vehemence with a screen of deliberation and poise. Her whole concern was to give the man what he had not previously had, and to take from him as much as she could. As his mouth lay on hers there shone in her eyes—despite the darkness— the image of conquest. Were instinct to have had a body and were it to have looked down upon them, it would have nodded its head in pride and satisfaction, and it would have excused itself for this by saying that while it was not happy about the bashful and timid manner in which most people indulge their instinct, there were, here and there, at different times, a few individuals who realized its full potential, persons who gave up their very souls to it and allowed themselves to be wholly possessed. The kiss did not last long, for the woman came to her senses and became aware of where she was. She therefore rose to her feet and, drawing the man by the hand, entered through a gap in the wall of the mill, where the darkness wrapped them round. This night it was for the dog to guard both the sheep and its master.

"To cut a long story short, she spent the night with me. I said to her, 'My good girl, I'm a God-fearing man and I want to have the blessing of the law.' She said, 'I have given myself to you.' I said to her, 'I accept, and if anyone hears about this I'll say that many peasants marry in country places purely by mutual consent.'"

"But not on the embankment, they don't," said his friend, "—and not with gypsies!"

"At the time I didn't know what I was doing."

He did not know how he had got any sleep as he drove the flock along. When day had come he had found himself not the master of a flock but the slave of a fate whose staff made no distinction in the way it drove both humans and sheep. Despite this, he felt that this woman had bestowed upon him a pleasure that was new to him: like a tired man he had been led to her, finding after his exertions a comfortable bed. Ellewi let himself relax and rely upon her, not caring, in this honeyed state of lethargy, what fetters she bound him with, so long as the stream of vitality that had been awakened in him—and that thereafter he was unable to curb—found no other outlet but her in which to swell and pour forth. Ellewi forgot the days of his past and confined his attention to the moment he was in, and in the morning he walked off, still in a state of bewilderment, behind his flock.

"We went off at dawn, with me in a daze. We made Dayrut—no, no, I'm forgetting. After we'd been walking awhile I looked around for the dog and didn't find it. I went back to look for it and found it near a tree in the throes of death."

The dog was lying with its hindquarters flat on the ground, its head raised on quivering forepaws, its body shaken with convulsions. The dog stared at its master, and in its eyes there shone a momentary gleam of hope, which was quickly extinguished by a deep and silent sadness. He had never before seen eyes weeping like the glassy, staring eyes of the dog, addressing him and saying, "Will this be the last time you'll see me?" It opened its mouth, but death placed his hand over it and the dog was unable to bark. Instead of a yelp came streams of viscid slaver that told of the unknown pain that boiled in the animal's stomach. Ellewi did not understand the reason for what had happened. Perhaps someone had beaten it, for many was the peasant who cruelly beat stray dogs, or perhaps some young boy had thrown a stone at it—this vicious act that the first criminal tendency in a child's head puts into practice. He stretched out his hand to run it across the dog's back and found it undamaged. He felt the gypsy girl by his side.

"She had come to sit beside me and watch. I looked at her and she said to me, 'My people have poisoned it—they wanted to steal your sheep while you were asleep. They weren't given the time, the Devil take them. Don't be angry, tomorrow you'll find another one. And just so you'll feel better I've brought you two of their goats— there in the middle.' I said to her, 'Are they yours, the two goats?' She said, 'No, they're theirs.'"

The young man again interrupted him. "Got yourself a bit of loot for free."

"By Allah, I wasn't happy about taking them but what could I do?"

Just as his dog, lying between the hands of death, had been unable to bark, so he, between the hands of the woman who had stolen his mind, was unable to open his mouth. Nothing was more expressive of the difference between their two natures than the slight smile that played on the gypsy girl's mouth, matched by a perceptible frown on the peasant's brow.

The dog's trembling grew less, little by little, until its movements ceased altogether and the flies dared to settle on its mouth and eyes. As Ellewi rose to return to his flock, grief for the dog he was leaving behind contended within him with a feeling of dread at the two goats that walked in front of him and that embodied the first crime he had ever committed; he who had lived all his years in awe of the police station, who shook before the umda and would greet policemen with respect.

"From the first day I found that the gypsy girl was clever. She would save the milk she drew off and sell it. In the past I hadn't known what to do with it. Also she weaned several lambs for me, having fixed a bag on each of the ewes. I had forgotten about the two goats. I said to myself: 'Tomorrow, my lad, you'll return to your village and you'll raise your own sheep, and if you've got yourself a girl as clever as this one, why not take in other people's sheep and keep them with you and graze them? Tomorrow, my lad, you'll have yourself a better living—your Lord is generous.'

"After several days I reached Mallawi and found some bare land at the entrance to the town. I left the sheep there and went up to the embankment in front of a café and sat down. The girl disappeared below with the sheep. Right from the beginning the night was cursed. I don't know what came over the girl—she had turned completely against me by the morning."

The gypsy girl had gone down to walk slowly among the ewes. There was nothing to keep her with the flock, likewise nothing to prompt her to return to Ellewi.

She had begun to be bored with her new regulated life, which proceeded along a known course, and she yearned again for her old nomadic existence. Her whole pleasure lay in being hounded from one village to another, her link with each place not exceeding a single night. The initial passion had waned and there was now nothing more to Ellewi than a peaceful man whose goodness she could be sure of, and she felt nostalgia for a life that was half love and half hostility. The gypsies are egoists and do not accept strangers in their midst. She had continued to submit to one of their men, not from love but through necessity, and she used to find her pleasure in the continual struggle between her passionate nature and her bitter dislike of him. What greater pleasure was there than refusing to submit until after a flood of desire had risen up to her mouth, almost drowning her and making her forget her dislike, great though it might be? Whenever fulfillment coincides with breaking point the spirit enjoys the most sublime extremes of ecstasy. For the present she submitted, be the flood at her feet or at her knees; she did not know the pleasure of satiety because she had been deprived of the pleasure of being hungry. While she did not hate Ellewi, she would have liked him to have been a gypsy.

The light of a lamp that lit up the embankment where Ellewi was sitting cut through the gypsy girl's thoughts. A café came into view; in the center, under a lamp, was a wooden dais, where a man sat with a two-stringed fiddle, singing. She forgot her thoughts and came up to listen to the story of how Marei, Yahya, and Yunis were imprisoned at the palace of Zanati in Tunis, and the return of Prince Abu Zeid to the ruins. The man let out a succession of shouts at which the murmurings of those seated abated and all gave ear to the story and the poetry. As the night drew on, the breathing of the lamp grew more constricted, choked by a thick circle of mosquitoes that, despite the rising smoke, had congealed like dirt around it. The universe was wrapped in total silence; the sky in its darkness was as though the wing of a bat had alighted on the earth. From time to time it gave a slight shudder, the result of the vibration of those few stars that flicker and then grow still. Neither the lamp with its hissing, nor the singer with his fiddle, was able to disperse any of the sadness that oppressed the universe. Was night the corpse of day and this sadness the hymn of death? Or was the world in mourning because it sensed it was perishing little by little? Or perhaps it was as a result of the thousands of oriental souls created by God sad and sore of heart that wander about this vast expanse? This very same sky, when covering the north, is perhaps the epitome of joy, fulfillment, and ecstasy, and the flickering of its stars a dance.

This atmosphere weighed heavily upon the fiddle, which gave out a monotonously plaintive sound. The whole world stood on one side, the fiddle on the other, and a dialogue took place between them, each giving up its secrets to the other. So affected by the story were the listeners that the singer disappeared from their view and Abu Zeid took shape before them, sitting on the dais and letting out his warlike cries. Times became so mixed up in their minds that they did not know whether it was he who had been brought back to life to recount to them the stories of his battles, or they who had been transported by some magic hand to his distant age. The poet chose an ode he knew from experience would make an impression on his audience, and he ended his evening with it. The last verses he sang were:

> *O woe, my heart, at what happened*
> *When with six fetters separation shackled me.*
> *Outwitted by the worries that came to me,*
> *When will those old days return?*
> *Destiny's voice answered by saying:*
> *Time that has passed will ne'er again return.*
> *Weep, O eye, for the time that has passed,*
> *Your recompense is from God the One, the Adored.*

Did the anonymous poet know, as he described the sufferings of his heroes, that his poetry would be heard by this gypsy girl on the embankment and that she would receive it like a knife-thrust? Perhaps he knew this and more than this, or otherwise how was it that he pronounced what was in her innermost being as though he already knew her, had been associated with her, and had heard her grievance many times? Her eyes watered with copious tears, then her stubbornness and unruliness awoke and she suppressed her worries. She rose to go to sleep, having resolved to act on the idea that had been occupying her mind those last few days.

"I woke up and found her walking along the embankment, her gallabiya hitched up under her arm. She was walking slowly but I realized immediately that she was running away from me. I went after her, caught up with her, and seized her by the arm.

"'Where are you going?'

"'Walking . . .'

"'Where to?'

"'Off west, to the desert—maybe I'll be able to join my people there.'

"'By yourself?'

"'Yes. Let me go my way and you yours.'

"'My dear girl, I've told you, the sheep aren't mine, their owner is in Minya, which is now no more than a stone's throw from us, after which I'm going straight back to the village with you.'

"'Your village and all that's in it can go to hell,' she told me right out."

The young man stared at Ellewi as though expecting the angry outburst of a peasant who accepts everything but the insulting of his kinsfolk. However, Ellewi had been almost completely separated from his family and kinsfolk by that time; the insult did not arouse his sensitivity, and he swallowed it.

"I said to her, 'Let's not go to the village. All right, we'll go anywhere you want.'

"'Come with me.'

"'And the sheep?'

"'Bring them with you.'

"'They're not mine.'

"As though annoyed at what I'd said she sharply averted her face. She walked off again and was nearly out of sight. While all this was happening, the Devil was trying to turn my head."

Ellewi stood there, every vein in him pulsating and alert. Her impetuosity had intoxicated him, had made him lose his head. He cast a glance at the woman, then a glance at the flock of sheep, while the Devil stood in front of him, smiling and holding the balance. The scale came down on the side of the woman.

"'Slow up,' I shouted at her. 'Slow up, I'm coming.'

"I ran to the sheep and drove them from the embankment to another road leading west to the desert, and we walked off without giving the world a thought. I really didn't know where it was all going to end.

"That night I saw her do something extraordinary. We were passing by a farm and saw a hen pecking about in the road. The girl took a long piece of thread out from her pocket with a grain of maize tied on the end. She threw it in front of the hen, which picked it up. It stuck in its throat and the hen began scraping its beak on the ground. It wanted to cry out but couldn't. The girl pulled the hen toward her very gradually and put it under her arm. As soon as we'd put a distance between ourselves and the village she slaughtered it. We got to the desert . . ."

"Wait a bit—who ate the chicken?"

"We ate it together."

"Why was it the girl didn't pull this trick before?"

"How should I know? This food was like poison to me and I prayed to Allah for His protection."

"You're right there—someone who steals sixty-five head of sheep chokes on a chicken!"

Ellewi was silent and sighed loud and long. The moon had disappeared and the glow from a lamp hanging some way off reached the solitary prison cell in the middle of the station courtyard. The loud thumping of horses' hooves on the asphalt rang out and a donkey brayed alongside them. Then the place quietened down again and Ellewi, with broken heart, returned to his story. His affection for his companion had waned, preoccupied as he was with himself as he recounted his adventures in brief: he was not reliving his past so much as remembering with an effort some of what had happened to him.

"In the desert we met up with her group of people. She was alone with their leader for a while. God knows what they were saying about me. I saw her pointing at the sheep and the man looking at them as though he were counting them. I went off with the sheep. Two or three days later I found that one of them had gone missing. I must say my blood really boiled. I got hold of the girl and said to her: 'If someone doesn't want to lose his life he'd better not go near the sheep.'

" 'We're now gypsies together,' she said. 'All our belongings are together.' I said to her, 'Gypsies or not, I don't hold with such talk.' She screwed her mouth up at me and stopped talking to me. After a couple of days I went to her and said, 'My good girl, I've sold my people and my honor for you.' Though she made it up with me, she was really having me on. Every other moment she would say to me: 'Don't be afraid for your sheep, gypsies don't steal from one another.' Even so, every time we came near a market I'd find one or two head of sheep missing. She had lied to me."

"She hadn't lied to you. It was you who'd considered yourself a gypsy, while they didn't consider you one. That's why they were stealing from you. You were booty for them, fair game."

"The sheep ended up at ten, then five. I said to myself, 'What's it all about, lad? Are you going to be left stark naked, or what?' One night I fooled them and got up before dawn and drove away those that were left and went to the market, where I sold them once and for all."

"You fooled them? After all, weren't the sheep yours?"

Ellewi did not reply but continued with his story.

"About a week ago they bundled me off with them and they stole—we stole together—a sack of cotton from a field. Last night we were arrested."

It was inevitable that Ellewi should taste some of the insults and harassment that gypsies experience. The night when the horsemen had attacked, the lashes had fallen, and the handcuffs had been fastened, had come and gone. However, spending time in the company of gypsies had made him able to accept abuse, handcuffs, and the lash with equanimity. A year ago he had been a witness to what had befallen the gypsies, and his terror, as a spectator, had been greater than it was today as, after a beating, he walked in chains to the police station. In the year that had passed it was not so much his life that had been consumed as his morals and habits that had been demolished. He had been a peasant whose concern was with the Nile, the umda, the police station, and the boundaries of the land that he would measure by span of hand and length of finger. As for now, he was a gypsy concerned only with the day he was in: the whole world was before him and it had no boundaries. If he was able to get something from it, then he should grab it, and be happy.

"And the police brought her along with you?" the young man asked him.

"The girl? No, she got away again."

"Let's hope this time around she doesn't find someone else to bring down."

"No, where will she find anyone? As soon as I'm out I'll go off and start looking for her."

This time the young man did not make fun of him. Yawning and stretching, he lay down on the ground. Before going to sleep he recited in a low voice, without singing it, this folk song:

> *Can you leave your beloved*
> *Even if, O the pity, she's done you wrong*
> *Or filled your glass with bitterness,*
> *Stirred it round and given it you to drink?*
> *No, not even if she's raised a stick against you*
> *And, woe betide you, had driven you before her.*
> *Night, O night, thus is my fate.*

> *Translated by Denys Johnson-Davies*

Sherif Hetata
(b. 1923)
EGYPT

Sherif Hetata is a novelist and medical doctor. He is married to the well-known writer Nawal El Saadawi. After graduating from medical school with honors in 1946, he held a number of positions, including eight years with the International Labor Organization, first in Asia and then in Africa. He has written on subjects ranging from travel to politics to health, but since 1968 has devoted himself to novels. He has translated into English two of his own novels, *The Eye with the Iron Lid* and *The Net*; it is from the latter novel that the following extract is taken.

FROM *The Net*

I remembered how it was Amina's voice that first drew my attention to her. I was seated in the suburban train on my way to Helwan. My eyes were closed and a winter sun warmed my face, penetrating my eyelids with an orange glow.

I opened my eyes each time we approached a station, to watch the dense crowds rush over the platform, surge through the doors in a struggling mass of bodies, until they had filled every inch of space in the carriage. They would remain motionless until the train neared the next station, then something like a high tension current of movement would pass through the human mass in preparation for the coming battle.

I heard her speaking to someone. The ring in her voice caught my ear. It radiated with pure optimism, a full and spontaneous joy. Yet beneath it I sensed a seriousness which every now and then was swept aside by small avalanches of delighted laughter. Her voice came to me from somewhere nearby. I kept my eyes closed, enjoying its freshness, letting myself be carried along on its flow, until someone stepped on my foot. I turned round and found myself gazing into two black eyes. Their look was steadfast, almost taunting, and I quickly dropped my eyes as though I had been caught in a shameful act, for I still felt intimidated when faced by a woman. After a while I looked around for her again, but she had disappeared in the crowd. Gone with her was a sudden sensation of "coming alive" that her voice had awakened within me. Once again I was assailed by an obscure feeling of sadness as though I was just hovering on the edge of life—a barely perceptible sadness, a dismal half light, like dusk, and so elusive that at each moment it seemed to be there and yet not there inside me, a dream aborted or a still-born hope. From the moment I walked out of the huge wooden portico into the street, only when I was deeply absorbed in something could I forget.

But now my life entered a new phase. Every day I took the morning train like thousands of others, rushed with them over the platform to catch it in the nick of time, sat at a desk, read files, drank coffee and gradually slipped into the daily, unchanging routine. At the end of the day I would hurry back home with the jostling crowds, eager to take refuge in my room.

I was now an employee. Nothing distinguished me from the others except perhaps for a tiny flame which continued to burn inside. Through the window of the train I watched the houses go by, and wondered whether this was all.

At moments a sudden panic took hold of me. I would jump out of the train before it came to a stop, and rush out of the station, fleeing from a net I could almost see closing around me. The city harried me with short bayonets fixed to automatic rifles, with bottles of Vat 69 and offshore banks, with the roar of endless traffic and the glare of blinding lights, with the beat of disco music and the muezzin's call to prayer in the quietest hour of night, with sewer water in the back streets and gas fumes in my eyes. I could see my city falling apart, its entrails bursting with people, its arteries blocked with cars. And there I was pushing my way through the crowded streets, a stranger searching for the things I had once known and could recognize, for the ring of truth in a voice which would lighten my heart.

The train raced from one station to another. I stood, hemmed in by a mass of bodies. A woman's voice rang out pure and vibrant, over the clatter and thud of wheels. I had been hoping to hear her voice again ever since that morning when I had first heard it. Something within me came to life. My eyes traveled slowly over the people crowded on the seats and thronging the aisles. I found myself contemplating two black eyes that returned my look with a serene confidence. This time I tried not to lose sight of her, but every now and then my increasingly insistent looks were interrupted by the head, the arm or the movement of some passenger. Her hair was rich, falling in dense waves to the shoulders. I kept saying to myself: "don't run away from this encounter." As the train drew near to Helwan I saw her edge slowly towards the door. She was tall and slender; her black hair shone in the sunlight flickering through the windows.

I pushed my way through in her wake, oblivious to the voices muttering in protest. She walked slowly down the platform by the side of her companion, her long limbs moving gracefully, her waist narrowed abruptly above the fullness of her hips. I contemplated her with the emotion of someone embarking on a wonderful experience. My heart beat strongly. I felt fearful, bold, determined and hesitant all at once. My pace quickened when I came up to her, I said: "Good morning," in a firm voice.

She turned her head towards me, but before she had time to answer I continued: "Please excuse me. My name is Khalil Mansour, I work in the Thebes Pharmaceutical Company. I have seen both of you in the train before, and assume you work in Helwan. Do you mind if I accompany you part of the way so we can talk?"

She examined me with a long steady look. Everything around seemed to recede and disappear, except her eyes with their expression of unhurried contemplation, as though I was being carefully weighed; her full lips pouted slightly as she framed the words: "No, of course not. My name is Amina Tewfik," and waving her hand towards her companion, she added, "And this is my friend Aleya Moustapha."

I nodded my head in greeting and was silent, searching for words to continue the conversation. She came to my rescue with a question: "How long have you been working in Helwan?"

"Since last August."

"I saw you in the train only once."

Cautious but confident in herself, I thought. Just once, and she had not forgotten. My heart was beating quietly now.

"The train is always so crowded. Besides, maybe we take it at different hours. I also saw you only once."

I could see she had not missed my point. A quick smile lit up her face. She reacted with a calm, yet immediate spontaneity. "Do you remember when that was?"

"Yes, four and a half months ago. Your voice attracted my attention. You were standing in the aisle talking to Miss Aleya Moustapha."

She looked pleased, but turned the conversation away from herself by remarking: "My friend is married, and has two children."

"She looks like a young university student," I said.

Their laughter rang out over the monotonous sound of hurrying feet. On one of the balconies I glimpsed rows of flowers, their colours vivid under the morning sun.

My mind flew over desert sands. There was an artesian well but its water came up hot, so we dug a reservoir two metres deep, forty metres long and twenty-five metres wide, using a plough drawn by oxen, and shovels. We used to leave the water to cool in the reservoir at night, and run it out through a canal to irrigate the reclaimed land during the day. Around the sides we embedded aquatic plants, and at the end of the day's work sat there looking at the wide expanses of sand, the setting sun, and the colourful flowers.

The vibrant ring of her voice cut through my wanderings: "What are you thinking about?"

I shrugged my shoulders and said: "The flowers," pointing to the balcony.

She eyed me curiously. When we arrived in front of a high wall with a big gate guarded by men in blue uniforms, she turned to me and said: "This is where we work. It's called the International Modern Furniture Company." There was a hint of irony in the way she pronounced the name. "I am head of the designing section and Aleya is responsible for plan execution."

"Then this is where we part?"

"Yes."

I hesitated, reluctant to continue on my way. My heart had started thumping again. If I said nothing, this could be the end. The thought made me bolder than usual: "How can we meet again?"

She answered slowly, as though turning something over in her mind. "We take this train every morning at half-past seven from Dar El Salam."

We shook hands quickly, and they passed through the big gate, disappearing behind the wall. For a moment I felt I was on the verge of losing something very precious. My feet remained rooted to the ground. A few passers-by threw curious glances at me, as I stood there. So I moved along mingling with the early morning crowd.

Translated by Sherif Hetata

Bensalem Himmich
(b. 1949)
MOROCCO

Bensalem Himmich's recent novel *The Theocrat* deals with al-Hakim, the eccentric ruler of Egypt in the eleventh century. His earlier novel *The Polymath*, which has won several prizes, has as its central character the widely traveled philosopher and historian Abd al-Rahman ibn Khaldun, who lived in the fourteenth century. In the two short excerpts from *The Polymath* that follow, we find Ibn Khaldun in Cairo, where he has been appointed a judge. His wife and children have met a tragic death at sea, and he suddenly discovers happiness in a new marriage to a young woman who has been left a widow by the death of her husband, a close friend of Ibn Khaldun's.

FROM *The Polymath*

Six months went by after my marriage to Umm al-Banin. The latter half of that year represented a turning point in my life and my understanding. I came to know my Lord in the beauty of His creation, male and female. More than ever before, I used to yell out, "Life, Our Lord did not create it for nothing." I rediscovered Ibn Qayyim al-Jawziya's work, *Meadow for Lovers*, and delved into it with confidence. My only interest was making the lover happy and placing her between heart and rib.

So I'll say it: Even though I'm almost sixty years old, love and life are two facets of a single blood. Anyone without love is without life. This too: Love and prayer are like conjoined twins; if you don't cloister yourself with the one, you miss the other and lose out on God's favor and welcome.

Ideas like these had definitely occurred to me when I was with my first wife, but their impact and integrity were negatively affected by external distractions and the enticements of rank. Today, however, such thoughts have come to occupy center stage in all their glory.

So many matters and activities that I used previously to ignore or pass by I now find myself paying attention to: food, for example, drink, clothes, walks, and old buildings.

I now know the names of all the food and drink that Umm al-Banin prepares for me. They're all of excellent quality and, because they're beneficial and easily digested, they're much prized by me. When they're brought to me, all I can do is offer my thanks and admiration, since they clearly represent the best of this earth's fruits and a harbinger of those others in the Garden of Eden.

I have always been anxious to wear clothes that were fairly plain in both color and design. But when Umm al-Banin chooses them or sews them herself, the quality is measurably higher. What is more, she uses the nicest powders in scenting them.

We arrived home safely and found Sha'ban anxiously awaiting our return. Removing my cloak and shoes I collapsed on the bench. Umm al-Banin disappeared inside for a moment and came out with a bowl of warm water. She started rubbing my feet in the water, something she had done for me regularly ever since we were married; she paid particular attention to ankles and toes. I had told her previously that, whenever my late wife had been cooking, resting, or taking a cure, she had regaled me with her own spontaneous remarks. So now Umm al-Banin proceeded to do likewise, adding some categories of her own, whose secrets she had learned from women in Fez, including telling jokes—"yarns" as we used to call them.

I asked Sha'ban to prepare lunch for us. He was delighted and took his time over it. I made use of the opportunity to convince Umm al-Banin that she should leave some of the household chores to my aged servant. Then he would not get bored with sitting around with nothing to do; that would make him forget the idea that we did not need him any more. Tyrannical regimes are bad in politics, I told her, and they are just as bad in household management. She relented and supported my position, promising to slow down a bit and take advice, something al-Hakim, the builder of the mosque, had never done.

I had to take a nap, and did so in the bedroom before the time came for afternoon prayers. While I was dozing, a thought occurred to me about incipient old age, the first signs of which I had glimpsed during our morning walk. On the basis of such early symptoms I came to the conclusion that it involved having one foot in the grave and the other in a state of patience; a gradual process of finding movement increasingly trying to the point of impossibility, all that accompanied by a distressing realization that it was actually happening. Death consisted simply in a confirmation of rigidity brought on by a lack of awareness of the body.

In order to keep pace with my wife and make her happy in intimate as well as public matters, I would need, as of today, to keep old age's clutches at bay and thwart all efforts launched by decrepitude and weakness to gain control of my body. I would have to follow the lead of old people who were fit and well, seeking aid and sustenance from Him who is Eternal and Alive. O God, I beseech You not to cover my head with too many gray hairs, nor to weaken whatever strength of mind and body I have left!

Somewhat resentfully, I got up and joined my wife on the roof veranda overlooking the Nile. She was sitting there modestly contemplating, all the while devouring a pomegranate and staring at her stomach. When she realized I had come up, she told me somewhat bashfully that she really wanted some pears and cake. I asked Sha'ban to go to the closest market and get some. Just then she started crying like a baby. I asked her if she wanted some more fruit or sweetmeats, but she hid her face in her hands and seemed surprised that I did not seem to realize why she was having these cravings. For a moment she hesitated, but then stuttered out her wonderful news: "I'm pregnant, Abd al-Rahman, pregnant!" I was so overjoyed that I almost started crying too; I had never seriously thought that this could happen.

"So you're pregnant, Umm al-Banin!" I said, hugging her to me. "Have you made quite sure?"

"The signs are all there. I can tell and so can the midwife."

"*Pray to Me and I will answer you.* All praise and thanks to my Lord!"

The kind of joy that I could now see making my wife cry was something the like of which I had never witnessed before. I can offer it as a definition of life itself. Life requires of us that we be willing to accept it as it is and offer it tokens of generosity and happiness. Joy and energy must win the battle against gloom and restraint.

Sha'ban came back with the things he had been asked to get and a tray of coffee. I stood up and hugged him, whispering the good news in his ear along with instructions to help Umm al-Banin around the house. He was excited and offered me blessings, prayed that she would have a safe delivery, then withdrew. I started sipping my coffee, while my pregnant wife wiped the tears from her face now smudged with kohl and bits of cake.

Translated by Roger Allen

Taha Hussein
(1889–1973)
EGYPT

In the words of the critic Louis Awad, Taha Hussein was "the greatest single intellectual and cultural influence on the literature of his period." Despite being blind almost from birth and coming from an unprivileged peasant background, he was able to attain the very highest positions in the intellectual and educational fields. He studied at the Sorbonne and became dean of arts at Fouad al-Awwal University (later Cairo University) and then minister of education. As an alternative to the traditional education offered by al-Azhar University (which he himself had attended), he strived to set up for Egypt an educational system built along modern Western lines.

The work for which Taha Hussein is best known is *The Days*, the first part of his autobiography, which became an instant classic upon its publication in 1929. When it was published in English in 1932 (under the title *An Egyptian Childhood*), it may well have been the earliest example of modern Arabic literature to appear in English. In addition to his autobiography, Hussein wrote fiction as well as a number of scholarly works on classical Arabic literature and Islam that still give rise to discussion today. He was also an inspiration to the leading creative minds of his time. With his French wife he held a weekly salon for Egypt's leading writers and critics as well as scholars from abroad interested in Egypt's literary renaissance, and he edited the monthly literary journal *al-Katib al-misri* (*The Egyptian Writer*), whose articles about such writers as Eliot, Sartre, Camus, and Faulkner kept Arab intellectuals in touch with literary culture in the West. Hussein's partly autobiographical novel *A Man of Letters*, excerpted below, was published in Arabic in 1935.

FROM *A Man of Letters*

He became calmer, his voice less loud, and his tone more gentle. He spoke to me, almost in a whisper, in a voice that bespoke a profoundly affected soul and a heart brimming with love and tenderness: were I able to see his face then, I would have undoubtedly recognized tokens of emotion and tenderness.

In this gentle voice he asked me, "Suppose I were now in my village and you were in your city. Suppose I wished to visit you and spend part the day with you. Where could I meet you?"

I said, "People are visited in their homes." He said, "I do not wish to visit you in your home. For I do not wish to stand on ceremony or to be embarrassed. I do not wish to be confined to the constraints that fetter people, especially youths and boys, when they visit each other in their homes, where there are also fathers and elder brothers present. I would like to meet you free and unconstrained, having to take account of nothing and of no one. I would like you to throw off this heavy turban which imposes upon you an air of gravity and which I neither approve of nor accept. I would like you to shed these clothes worn only by those who have reached the noontime of their youth. For you are barely at the sunset of your childhood and on the thresholds of the dawn of youth. Your soul is beginning to open up to life with a smile, beginning to shed the innocence of childhood, seeking to evaluate and weigh matters, to judge them with that charming, lovely arrogance which allows young boys to imagine they are men, and to believe that their views are always correct, their judgments unerring. They feel that grown men are mistaken to underestimate them and to perceive of them as mere youngsters, refusing to allow them to participate in elderly affairs.

"Throw off this turban and reject this flowing outer garment and return to the loose gown you donned before coming to Cairo. Your gown stood out among your peers' in the countryside, with its narrow sleeves, slightly gathered at the ends, its neat pleats at the breast and upper back, and its wide belt at the waist which did not encircle the entire body but consisted of two straps sewn to the right and left and held together at the back with mother-of-pearl buttons. Go back to that gown and put that thin white skullcap on your head. It is called a *takiyya* but that is not really what it is. It is worn by the affluent in the provinces in an attempt at imitating the French beret. They call it the 'European' *takiyya*.

"Return to that costume and I will take off this European one and return to the clothes I used to wear in the countryside when I was not yet attending school. I wore an open-breasted wool costume and put a tarbush on my head, as the affluent sons of village mayors did. For you know I am a mayor's son. I shall come to visit you on foot, riding neither horse nor donkey, for I want to be free and unfettered and to spend time with you where I need not worry about horses or donkeys.

"Return to your old attire, and I shall return to mine, and await my visit. Tell me, where shall I meet you? Let it not be in your home. For I know it too well and do not wish to sit in the antechamber for guests. Nor do I wish to sit in the shade of those grapevines which grow beside it or play in the courtyard before it. You perceive it to be spacious but I perceive it to be small. Your father likes to sit there at noon and the master chooses to recite the Qur'an there every day before sunrise.

"I seek an informal meeting, in an informal place where no censor will overhear us or ask us where we are going, when we choose to move on instead of remaining in one particular place."

Moved by his words, voice, and tone, and by the memories they invoked, memories which carried me back to myself before leaving the town to come to Cairo, which put me back in those clothes he described, those which I returned to whenever I revisited the provinces, I said, "Then meet me on the roadside. I will be sitting in front of Sheikh Muhammad Abd al-Wahid's shop on one of those two crates flanking it to the right and left. People sit there to pass the time. They talk or observe the passersby or the customers. They also like to watch the women as they go to the Ibrahimiya canal to fill their jugs and as they return, these jugs now heavily balanced on their heads. They whisper amongst themselves as they return in the morning and sing in chorus when they set out at dawn. These observers also divert themselves by listening to these two women on the right and left of the shop. One of them lives right next to the shop while the other one's home is across the street. Do you know them?" He said, "As well as you do. The first is Zannuba and the other is Umm Mahmud. Each of them sits at her door and speaks to her friend of various things in a loud, jesting, teasing, and tender voice. The young men of the town are very fond of sitting before the shop and listening to these conversations, participating in them from time to time, especially when they consist, as they quite often do, of jesting. For their only joy in life is jesting and earning money." I said, "Well, you will find me sitting on one of those two crates. I usually spend the day with the proprietor and his brother. I converse with the first about such matters as Sheikh Madi—his achievements, his miracles, and his mysticism—and hear from the second such novels and sermons as he reads to me.

Our conversations and readings are interrupted only when a woman or young girl comes in to buy some salt, pepper, thread, or whatever goods are sold in the shop."

He said, "I come to you from the west. As soon as I descend from the bridge I pass by that house you know. I greet Hasan Kuzu, who is sitting in front of his home surrounded by his wife and his incessantly babbling daughters and sons. Then I pass Amm Husayn's home but fortunately I do not meet him. He would have stopped me and asked me, 'Why have you come? How is your father? Why does he not come into town?' Undoubtedly, he would have detained me and would, perhaps, even have insisted that I have lunch at his home. For he is keen on sustaining the ties of friendship between our families. But I have passed the house safely and have met no one. I am exposed to none of the hospitality I dreaded. I see you from afar and note that you are neither chatting with the proprietor nor listening to his brother's reading. You are alone on your crate, bent down, your head between your hands. There are people around you. Some are buying, some looking around. Some are listening to Zannuba and some to Umm Mahmud. That untamed devil, the mayor's son, is meandering in the road, humming, slyly peeking into that alley to the right of the shop where the master and his young wife and old mother-in-law live, and where Aleya Umm Gharib also lives.

"Now I have reached you. I put my hand on your shoulder. You are startled by my proximity. But as soon as you hear my greeting you are reassured. You smile and invite me to sit down. But I refuse and help you up. I take your arm and we move toward the canal, along this road which roughly faces Zannuba's house.

"Look, here are the two of us. We have reached the canal. To our right is the garden of Girgis Effendi, then the path descending to your house. To our left are the Bedouin tents. They have chosen this land to camp in. They guard this extremity of the town. Which of the two directions do you want to follow? Do you want us to go right toward the town, or left, westward, where we will reach the Ibrahimiya and take shelter in the shade of the blackberry trees? Or should we go straight ahead, and take a stroll in these fields which seem to spread forever? Would you prefer that we cross the canal? It is neither a difficult nor a strenuous task, for these days it is dry. Do you not sense children around you playing in the canal, hunting for the small fish still left in its muddy waters? Where do you want to go? If we cross the canal we need only go a little farther in this wide, free expanse till we reach the railway tracks. When we traverse them we will have reached the town via a shortcut. Where do you want to go?

"I need not await your answer. You, no doubt, wish as I do to turn right. This is a pleasant and familiar route. It is the one used by those coming from or going to town. It promises to offer us the variety of diversions and choice of amusements and distractions we seek. Only a few steps away is the *mu'allim*'s garden. Here, we have reached it. We have chosen to enter it and pick its fruits and seek shelter in the shade of its trees for an hour, discussing such matters as we are accustomed to discuss. This is a truly beautiful garden. It was not meant to be scenic. No landscapers designed it. It is free and unbridled! Flowers and trees sprout as they wish, free of all constriction and order. It is truly most beautiful as it gracefully and nimbly extends its harvest of flowers and fruits, green leaves, and supple branches to the canal, as though wishing to proffer all to these waters which run through it, strong and calm, yet quivering with vitality, like a legendary young god.

"I know you are fond of this garden and enjoy coming here alone to ponder the events and misfortunes you invent or to recount to it those narratives and stories you have heard. I have brought you here because I know you enjoy spending hours here, apart, yet close to, the people. I know you relish neither absolute isolation nor absolute mingling with people. But now I perceive that your surroundings disagree with you. It is as though you are uneasy with the garden or as though the garden does not wish to welcome you with its customary affability, cheerfulness, and tenderness.

"I feel your whole body trembling with aversion to stillness and hunger for activity, driven to motion. What do you spurn in this garden? Or what does this garden spurn in you? Why do you not wish to converse with me as you do with yourself, or to narrate to me as you do to yourself what your memory recalls or your imagination contrives?

"Here you are then, most similar to a bolting horse, biting at its bridle, stamping the ground with its hoofs, almost jumping out of its skin with gaiety and a longing to gallop. Where do you wish to go?"

He says all this with such earnestness, confidence, and conviction as to cause me to forget where he and I are, to forget that we are now in Cairo. He persuades me that we are still two young boys, or two adolescents, out on a promenade in that faraway countryside of ours. I listen to him, warm to him, and start to answer him. But he is set free and does not wish to stop, effusive, refusing to abate. He asks and does not await the answer. He answers himself and proceeds with his soliloquy, pausing for nothing. And I listen to and follow him. He accelerates his words as though he were accelerating his movements; still I am breathless from listening, no longer able to follow him. Yet he proceeds with his words, proceeds with his dream, stopping at nothing, abating for nothing. What is strange is that, as he speaks, he arouses in me the very same memories he is arousing in himself. Then he speaks of me and of what I like and it is as though I am speaking of myself.

He says, "So, you do not wish to remain in this garden because your spirit is neither disposed to solitude nor to calm, tranquil conversation. Today you are bent on movement and physical activity. I perceive that you will attain no peace till you have imposed a vigorous walk on yourself. In fact, were you not very shy, and fearful of pitfalls and obstacles, you would have chosen to run or even to sprint. So let us proceed to the public roads. Today you have no need for this garden.

"Let us then move on, let us hurry, run. But you obey me only for a little while. Now I feel your step slackening, your energy waning. Now you prefer to walk at a sedate pace, dallying instead of marching. You realize that you are now close to these four houses which beautifully line the canal bank, their vast gardens spreading before them, their winding trees and branches bending over the gates. You wish to walk slowly along these gates and to caress these vibrant, green leaves with your hand. You find comfort, pleasure, and rapture in touching them, and your heart attains the tranquility it so seldom attains.

"You wish to stop and toy with this hyacinth bean which twines around the superintendent's gate. You want to caress and play with it, straightening its bends and undoing its coils. Yet you know it will not straighten and does not like to stand erect. Then you want to linger at the superintendent's home. I suspect that you are tempted to knock on the door and call Usman or Mahmud. Who knows? Perhaps one of them will answer and invite you in. You would chat with him, or with him and his brother, for part of the day. You are very sly, and have quite a tortuous mind. Why do you lie to yourself and to me? You do not seek Usman, nor do you like to talk with Mahmud. You wish to enter the house, to traverse its vast garden, lingering a little, assuming nonchalance and calm, till you have entered the house and are seated in that modest room where one's foot does not tread on bare ground as it does when you play in your home or when you sit by the store. It touches a floor paved with stone and covered with carpets. There, in that room, you lend your friends only one of your ears or that part of it which you must lend them. As for your other ear, it is sent forth to the end of the house, along with your whole soul. Say the truth! You do not want Usman nor do you seek to chat with Mahmud. In reality, you wish to hear one of those two voices saturated with sweetness, as the vivid color saturates the leafy, supple branches. In fact, you are the happiest of men when you are able to listen to both voices together!

"Which do you prefer and cherish more? The voice of that full, rounded girl called Aziza who would readily play with you and with her brothers were it not for her Turkish mother and Albanian father whose upbringing demands modesty and decorum? She sits with you and listens to you. She may join you in conversation and may laugh at what you say. Her laughter vibrates in the room, radiant, pure, glittering like crystal. Or do you prefer her sister Amina's voice? She is over twenty and has outgrown playing. She was married then divorced by her husband, then returned to her family, melancholic and sad, her voice subdued. Yet her subdued voice arouses consternation in your heart, trouble in your soul, and, in the depths of your being, an anxiety, the source and secret of which you are ignorant, but which you nevertheless both fear and covet. Which of the two voices do you prefer and cherish most? I fear that you have a lecherous soul and a brazen heart. I fear that you are extravagant in the liberties you allow yourself. For you cherish both voices equally, and are equally fond of both sisters. You would like to luxuriate as much as you can in those intense, vague, and mysterious emotions they stir in your soul. You listen to and observe them if they speak or laugh or make any movements and you virtually memorize all this and diligently record it. Then, when you are back in your home, and have retired to your customary corner, you replay the words, laughter, and singing you have heard. You visualize the movements you have sensed. You scrutinize all this closely and extract countless—endless—images, meanings, sentiments, and thoughts which cause you to become oblivious to yourself, your family, and your home. They transport you to a strange world, one a thousand times more dear to you than this one in which you live. Say the truth! Am I not portraying your reactions, describing your sentiments, and speaking of that which you wish to hear? But you have been sitting between Usman and Mahmud, listening to Aziza and Amina for too long. For here is the muezzin's voice calling us to the noon prayers. The superintendent will be home shortly. If we stay, we shall be invited to lunch. I know that although your bashfulness and good manners prevent you from accepting this invitation, your heart begs you to stay. I am also certain that were you to obey your heart's whims, you would stay, endure this dreary lunch hour so that you may later delight in long hours, exulting in these two voices, in their allure, awesomeness, and tenderness. But there is no excuse for staying. What should we do with our discretion? What should we do with our good manners? How would you face your mother? How would you answer her? How would you sustain her harsh reproaches which would assert that well-behaved youths do not extend a visit till it is lunchtime, nor do they accept on-the-spot invitations?

"Let us go, my miserable, wretched friend. Bid Amina and Aziza farewell. You may have occasion to see them tomorrow or this evening. As for now, believe me, we have no place in this house.

"Now that we have passed the entrance of the house, and the door has been closed behind us, now that Usman and Mahmud have found their way back into the garden, we turn toward the canal. We pause at its banks for a moment, hesitating. Should we return now that the day has advanced? Or should we turn right, toward the town, although this will expose us to some reproach?

"We have opted for playfulness and frivolity and turned right toward the railway, walking calmly. Now I praise your sobriety, your self-discipline, your courage, and your insistence that we leave the superintendent house when we did. I thank you for having declined Usman and Mahmud's, and especially Aziza and Amina's, invitation. They all insisted we stay, tempting us. Usman and Mahmud offered to display the wonders they had brought back from Cairo, such toys as are uncommon in the countryside and unusual in the provinces. Aziza offered to play the piano and Amina offered to read some stories. Yet you insisted on leaving in spite of yourself which cruelly beseeched you to stay.

"But I do not understand your fondness of listening to Aziza and Amina nor your infatuation with their conversations. Their tongues twist in a Cairene accent, carrying all of elegance, affectation, and intent to charm. It is as though each of them wishes to distinguish herself and let us know that she is not one of us and that we are nothing compared to her. They belong to that select group which neither pronounces the *gim* as we do nor transforms the *qaf* to an accented *gim*. Instead, it embellishes it with a delicate, light *hamza*, agreeable to the ear. This select group does not fill the mouth with words which it rumbles out as do cattle. It lets them drop from a narrow mouth, gracefully releasing them, allowing them to flow elegantly. It thus vocalizes them most agreeably instead of letting them gush out as though they were crashing cataracts and rocks. I dislike all this because I find it affected and precocious. Who knows, perhaps if we were to see them in Cairo and were to listen to them in their natural habitat, we would find them less affected, more natural. Perhaps, then, they may find their way into my intransigent heart. But, at the present time, my heart is totally shut to them. I prefer, a thousand times over, our peasant girls with their distinctive, sweet modesty and soft bashfulness, their amiable although coarse speech, and their appealing although slightly rough voices. You will be angered. You will rebel and you will object to my taste most vehemently. But, notwithstanding, I do not hesitate to maintain that I prefer Kalima, Aleya's daughter and Gharib's sister, to that affected, false Aziza of yours. I prefer Khadija, daughter of Mahbuba and sister of Ali, to that Amina of yours with her conviction that there is no woman on Earth capable of equaling or surpassing her delicacy and beauty.

"I am a believer in natural beauty, which is neither acquired nor bought, beauty which is provided by nature, lent to faces and souls, this beauty of which al-Mutanabbi spoke. Do you remember his verse? It is famous:

> *"The beauty of urbanity is procured by praise*
> *In the desert, it is beauty unprocured."*

Translated by Mona El-Zayyat

Gamil Atia Ibrahim
(b. 1937)
EGYPT

Gamil Atia Ibrahim was born in Cairo. He took a degree from the Faculty of Commerce at Cairo University, then a diploma in art appreciation from the Academy of Arts. For two years he taught in Morocco; his first novel, *Asila*, draws on this experience. He presently lives in Basel, Switzerland, where he is married to a Swiss schoolteacher and works as a correspondent for several Arabic publications. He has published short stories and several novels, one of which, *Down to the Sea*, is available in English translation.

The Old Man

The old man is in the corner of the room. His period of service in the government has come to an end and the procedures and papers for retirement are being completed. While in the service and at an age of over fifty he had graduated in law, but in terms of promotion he had not benefited greatly from the qualification. Without uttering a word, the man runs his eyes over the men and women working there.

When he had entered the faculty of law he had been preoccupied by the question of justice. Why should his wife have died when she was still young? Why had she not given him any children? Was he entitled to have divorced her? Why did she die during the air-raids on Cairo in 1956?

The doctor had told him that the war had frightened her and had affected her weak heart. He was, however, not entirely sure about that because in the last two weeks her state of health had been extremely bad.

The burial grounds of the Imam Shafie in Cairo are full of the living who have taken up residence in the rooms specially built for those visiting the dead. At the time he told himself that directly the war ended he would move her body to the burial grounds of Port Said, but till now he had not carried out his promise.

He had learnt during his long life in government service that nothing was so harmful to an employee as becoming attached to a young girl at work.

He speaks to himself, addressing the depths of his soul, and sees himself standing on a high rock in a wasteland and talking to a group of people, declaiming at them and shouting for justice. He would have liked to have donned a judge's robes and have dispensed justice amongst people. He keeps control of himself, paying particular attention to his hands lest he wave them about in the air as he shouts silently and draws to himself the gaze of those sitting in the room. One hand he puts in a pocket and the other under his chin as he sits relaxed, gazing ahead of him and leaning back against the chair.

He too had been a young man. His wife had been in her prime when he had married her. Later on everyone would say: An old man whose wife had died and who remained a widower the rest of his life, then he went mad during the few hours before he was to go on pension. Let him go off to the lavatory and talk to himself there to his heart's content.

The woman who was deputy head of the department suddenly said to him in a voice that betrayed a dislike of him:

"Mr. Abdul Azeem, you can leave. You are now on pension."

The man realized what was going on in her mind. He decided to ignore her invitation to go, to be driven away from the office. He took refuge in silence and, as usual, did not turn his face to her. Everyone was sitting and looking at him. They all knew that today he would be going back home and would not again put in an appearance. He had retired on pension—and Leila too knew that.

The man began asking himself why he hadn't yet moved his wife's body to the burial grounds in Port Said. Leila wished him good health and a long and happy life, and he said to her, "That's life." He wasn't, though, altogether sure that he had said anything to her or whether he hadn't contented himself with looking at her, with staring into her ever-radiant face.

Before leaving the room and saying goodbye to the others he told himself that he hadn't failed his wife, for after the 1956 war there'd been the 1967 war in which both the dwellings of Port Said and its burial grounds had been laid waste. Then had come the war of 1973 which had ended with the liberation of part of Sinai, and it hadn't been possible for him throughout these wars to move the body. He also told himself that it was just as well for there were still many wars to come.

Translated by Denys Johnson-Davies

Sonallah Ibrahim

(b. 1937)

EGYPT

Sonallah Ibrahim studied law and drama at Cairo University, and worked as a journalist until his arrest and imprisonment in 1959 for his political activities. He was released in 1964 and left Egypt shortly afterward to take up residence in Berlin and then Moscow. He returned to Egypt in 1976 and has since devoted himself to writing. In 1999 he was invited to teach at the University of California. His first novella, *The Smell of It*, was published in 1966 and has been translated into English; it has been described by the critic Samia Mehrez as "one of the landmarks of modern Arabic literature." Among his novels published since then and available in English are *The Committee*, a Kafkaesque depiction of regimes in power in Egypt and other Arab countries, and *Zaat*, which tells the story of an Egyptian woman living under the reigns of three Egyptian presidents; it casts a black look at the changes that have occurred in Egypt over the past few decades and is a highly readable social comedy. Extracts are given below from both of these novels. In view of his highly critical writings directed against the establishment in Egypt, it is perhaps surprising that Sonallah Ibrahim was put forward for the State Award of Merit in Literature in 2004. At the ceremony itself, he gave his reasons for rejecting the award.

FROM *Zaat*

This momentous night came after long months of gradual convergence between Zaat and Abdel Maguid Hassan Khamees, during which time they frequented the places of amusement available in those days (the mid-sixties): the Casino Fontana on the Nile, the

Fish Garden, the Tea Island, and the Cairo Tower (which Gamal Abdel Nasser had erected, as a substitute for the well-known "finger in the air gesture," using the three million dollars that America had tried to buy him off with). The most important role in their courtship, however, was played by the miracle child itself, which assumed gigantic proportions from the moment of its birth, i.e., the television. It was to play a major role in the life they would share, until it became the only tie that held them together. (Such an outcome had been totally unexpected by Zaat's father when he brought home the set, bearing the brunt of its monthly payments in the hope that he would be able, through its intercession, to avoid any kind of contact with her mother.)

Zaat and future husband would sit in front of the set for hours on end under the watchful eyes of the mother, while their interest was divided between the acting of Abdel Ghany Amar in the soap opera and keeping the cushions in place. It was the era of the seductive miniskirt, which created for cushions a whole new function above and beyond their customary functions (the innocent among them and the not so innocent). For by placing a cushion on her knees it was possible for Zaat to sit back on the sofa as she wished without revealing what it was not yet the right time to reveal. This also enabled the mother to occupy herself exclusively with following the events of the soap, sufficing herself with a sideward glance from time to time to reassure herself that the cushion remained firmly in position. Nevertheless, it so happened that this swift glance was enough to distract her, since her eyes could not help but wander to the thighs of the expectant groom and the corresponding cushion which had settled on his own lap, and at whose purpose she was most perplexed, since Abdel Maguid possessed a natural screen in the form of the trousers of his smart suit. With the passing of time the naive woman, who was distinguished by her meagre experience and tiny imagination, and who had a narrow mind and the feelings of a stone, became filled with pity and sympathy for Zaat, since she concluded that the need of her daughter's fiancé for an extra screen was a result of the enormous size of the thing he was compelled to hide from view.

The thing he was not compelled to conceal was much larger, and here we mean his backside or his buttocks or his posterior (the classical dictionary does not provide us with a word approaching, in its morphological precision and accuracy, the more obscene one which is now on the tip of every reader's tongue), and it was this part of his anatomy which shrunk and diminished with the passing of time in direct inverse proportion to the flowering expansion of Zaat's own.

Apart from that there was nothing wrong with him. He was handsome, smart, and fitted out with all the gold accoutrements: cigarette case and lighter (Ronson), ring, Old Spice aftershave, and winkle-picker shoes. He knew different kinds of food and the protocol for each, and was always ready to complain about the nation's politics and its bias towards the public sector and industrialization. He had a distinguished way of hailing taxis which always made them stop and which filled Zaat with pride, and he alloted great importance to every word that issued from his lips. His incontrovertible views on various subjects were delivered with such confidence that others (or at least Zaat) were compelled to be convinced by them, and they normally ended with a word that perplexed Zaat and her father, with his limited culture, for a long time, before she finally became familiar enough with Abdel Maguid, after the wedding of course, to muster the courage to inquire about its meaning. Raising his eyebrows with such amazement that she was embarrassed, he kindly offered the explanation, pronouncing the English word in his own impeccable way: "*Oov koors?*, naturally." In addition to all this there were his chivalrous Antar escapades, and battles fought in defense of honor and reputation, not to mention the truth, none of which Zaat was allowed to witness, since they took place in the bank where he worked, and the university which he did (not) attend.

Yes indeed. One dark cloud in Abdel Maguid's clear sky: he did not have a university degree, although only one exam, which he had been unable to attend due to illness, stood between him and it. In any case, he now received a sufficient salary, and the doors of the future lay wide open before him.

It was a period of great hopes, bold aspirations, and dreams:

night dreams and day dreams in all their varieties (the dry and the wet). By the duck pond in the Merryland Gardens, she said to him: "Washing clothes is no longer a chore thanks to Omo. Just a little in a bowl of water, and a quick swish to make lots of foam, then you throw in a shirt or a blouse and go off to make the tea or do some cooking, and after that a scrub or two, no need to shred your fingers or wear out the washer" (she means here the woman who washes, not the machine, for its time had not yet arrived).

Abdel Maguid received this announcement of her intentions with little enthusiasm. This was because the image of the washerwoman sitting at the tub, revealing her thighs, and sometimes her breasts, as she bent over to firmly grab a shirt collar or the gusset of a pair of knickers, and give either one a deliberate scrub, first with a hard block of co-op soap then with her fists, had nestled in a corner of his mind, not only as a memory of his first glimpse upon *that* world, but as a very realistic possibility for the long-term future.

As well as the Omo there were anti-perspirant sticks and contraceptive pills, of course, and the holy trinity, which the modern home could no longer do without, and which Abdel Nasser had placed within everyone's reach: a water heater, a stove from the war department factories, and an Ideal fridge. This brings us to the crux of the matter: the nest.

Translated by Anthony Calderbank

FROM The Committee

I took off aimlessly through the streets, my gaze wandering among passersby, storefronts, and entrances to houses. Even so, I was able to notice how most of the passersby had caught the urge to seek wealth and happiness. Crates of Coca-Cola were everywhere. Everyone stood behind them, grocers, doorkeepers, carpenters, and even pharmacists.

I felt thirsty and stopped in front of one of the vendors, whose shop was stocked exclusively with crates of these bottles. He had put a large, lidless cooler on the sidewalk. The thirsty crowded around it.

The cooler was full of bottles floating in water. Snatching one up, the vendor seemed in seventh heaven as he held it toward the outstretched hands. Before any hand grabbed it, he would remove the cap with the opener held ready in his other hand, then hurriedly pick up another one.

I noticed his hand holding a bottle out toward me. I quickly intervened before he popped the cap, asking, "Is it cold?"

Looking at me disapprovingly, he said, "As ice."

I touched the bottle and found it warm, so I said, "No, I'd like a cold one."

While making his displeasure with me clear, he held out the bottle toward the crowd. I reached out and rummaged among the bottles. I discovered that not only were most of them warm, but there was no sign of ice in the water. The vendor kept his eyes on the thirsty, who were wiping sweat from their brows and panting in the heat. He ministered to them with the warm bottles.

I watched them drink the magic liquid. They touched the bottles as though to assure themselves of their ability to distinguish hot and cold. Then, resigned, they swallowed the contents to the last drop and paid the price the vendor demanded. He had doubled the listed price on the pretext of the imaginary ice. He scowled and everyone paid it submissively.

I transferred my attention to the vendor, who was moving energetically and somewhat aggressively. I guessed he would attain his ambition quickly; the store would soon be filled with foreign cigarettes and candy, then with other imported commodities, including cassettes, tape recorders, and canned goods.

I was caught up in my thoughts and didn't notice what was happening until there was a warm opened bottle in my hand. I automatically raised it to my lips.

I paid the price the others had paid and continued walking in a leisurely fashion to the bus stop. I stood with the others until the "Carter" bus came.

The rationale behind using the name of the American president for this type of bus can't be attributed to its particular shape, which resembles a long, sad-faced worm, or to its unusual length, or to the great roar it makes as it runs, or to its higher fares (five times the usual fare), or to its being made in the USA. Rather, it has to do with the insignia on its side, right next to the door, which consists of an American flag emblazoned with two hands clasped in friendship.

In all likelihood, this insignia is the source of the people's delight in the buses' appearance during the last two years or so. They consider the buses the herald of the promised prosperity, which has been so long in coming. They seem prepared to overlook the noise on the grounds that noise is something commonplace in an underdeveloped country like ours. Higher fares are overlooked on the grounds that world prices are rising, and the thick polluting exhaust on the grounds that environmental pollution is only a problem in developed countries. The absence of bars and straps, which leaves the standing passengers swaying and dancing, is excused on the premise that our dull life needs some recreation.

However, it wasn't a week before the buses developed strange symptoms. Their interior support had begun to collapse and the rivets holding the walls to pop out. The automatic doors stuck open and the wall panels fell off. The rubber gaskets in the windows were torn and the screws holding the dashboard came off, revealing the inner workings.

Translated by Mary St. Germain and Charlene Constable

Ulfat Idilbi
(b. 1912)
SYRIA

Ulfat Idilbi, one of Syria's best-known writers, was born in Damascus. She has published five collections of short stories and two novels, both of which are available in English. Her first novel, *Sabriya: Damascus Bitter Sweet*, was published in 1980. In 1991, when the author was seventy-nine years old, her second novel, *Grandfather's Tale*, was published. The first novel deals with Damascus in the 1920s and the struggle against the occupying French. The central character, Sabriya, tells her story of love and frustration, and in the short extract below has a secret meeting with the man with whom she plans to elope.

FROM *Sabriya: Damascus Bitter Sweet*

But when did lovers ever despair? They alone know how to devise ways of getting together, regardless of the obstacles and of the vigilance of others. Adil found a way.

One Thursday we were leaving college at midday for the weekend. I found him waiting for me on the sidewalk in front of the college. He gave me a sign to follow him. I slipped away from my fellow students. He went into a narrow street near the college and I followed. We went down a long street, a few feet only separating us. We had no wish to arouse any suspicion.

At the end of the street there was a garden enclosed by an earth wall. In the middle of the wall was a wooden gate. Adil brought out a piece of wood and opened the gate. I went in after him and closed the gate. I raised my veil and looked at him. He took me in his arms.

"At last we've been able to get together," he said. "I can gaze at those lovely eyes that have so tormented me."

He stole a kiss on my eyes.

I said nothing, but there must have been signs of anxiety on my face for he said, "Why are you so anxious? Don't be afraid. Nobody knows where we are."

"I'm afraid my family will find out what's going on between us and we will be kept apart forever."

"How will they know? This garden is walled and nobody but the owners ever comes here. I know the owner's son. He's an old friend and has given me the key so we can come here whenever we like."

I felt a bit better and looked at the key in amazement. I had never seen one like it before. It was made of planed wood and was at least one foot long. At its head were three nails in the form of a triangle. This piece of wood and its nails performed the function of a key. Adil saw the look of amazement on my face.

"I don't suppose you've ever seen a garden key before."

"I've hardly ever seen the gardens themselves, so how can I be acquainted with the keys?"

He laughed, his black eyes sparkling. The dimple in his right cheek deepened and his white teeth flashed in the middle of his swarthy face. How often had I longed to see this wonderful laugh of his. He pulled me to him.

"From now on," he said, "you're going to see it a lot, my love. Every Thursday when you leave college at midday, come here. I'll be here already. I'll have opened the gate and will be waiting for you behind it."

"But I cannot be more than half an hour late getting home. Otherwise they'll find out. My family are always on the watch."

He smiled.

"Let us at least be grateful for small mercies," he said. "It's better than not seeing each other at all, isn't it?"

"Don't ever mention the idea. I can't bear the thought of not seeing you after having tasted what I have tasted."

We sat on two stones that faced each other beneath the gnarled branches of an old willow tree. We talked and talked. We recalled the tragedy of Sami's untimely death. We reminisced about the cups of coffee we had drunk in the Eyrie and books we had read together, and the mutual longing we had for each other. We wept, and he wiped the tears away with his lips. It was balm. I had never known such a short half hour. The time sped by. I left the garden before he did, went off quickly, and caught a tram to get home on time, for I usually walked home. Nobody noticed that I was a bit late.

Translated by Peter Clark

Yusuf Idris
(1927–91)
EGYPT

Yusuf Idris is regarded as the foremost short story writer in Egypt. Like many of Egypt's writers he spent time in prison during King Farouk's regime. He studied medicine and drew on his experiences as a doctor for many of his stories. In 1960 he became editor of the Cairo daily newspaper *al-Gumhuriya*. As a playwright he brought to the form a particularly robust appreciation of the rich colloquial language of Egypt.

Several collections of Idris's stories are available in English translation. His two novels, both available in English, are *The Sinners* and *City of Love and Ashes*. The first is the better known in Arabic and tells the story of a young peasant woman from a group of migrant workers who accidentally smothers her illegitimate child when giving birth to him, and later dies of childbed fever. The novel, melodramatic though it is, contains some excellent character portrayals. The events of *City of Love and Ashes* take place in 1952, when Egypt was struggling to throw off the yoke of British occupation. In the second passage below, taken from *City of Love and Ashes*, Hamza, a young anti-British activist and organizer, is hiding out in the apartment of his well-off and avowedly apolitical friend Bedeir.

House of Flesh

The ring is beside the lamp. Silence reigns and ears are blinded. In the silence the finger slides along and slips on the ring. In silence, too, the lamp is put out. Darkness is all around. In the darkness eyes too are blinded.

The widow and her three daughters. The house is a room. The beginning is silence.

The widow is tall, fair-skinned, slender, thirty-five years of age. Her daughters too are tall and full of life. They never take off their flowing clothes which, whether they be in or out of mourning, are black. The youngest is sixteen, the eldest twenty. They are ugly, having inherited their father's dark-skinned body, full of bulges and curves wrongly disposed; from their mother they have taken hardly anything but her height.

Despite its small size, the room is large enough for them during the daytime: despite the poverty of it, it is neat and tidy, homey with the touches given to it by four females. At night their bodies are scattered about like large heaps of warm, living flesh, some on the bed, some around it, their breathing rising up warm and restless, sometimes deeply drawn.

Silence has reigned ever since the man died. Two years ago the man died after a long illness. Mourning ended but the habits of the mourners stayed on, and of these silence was the most marked, a silence long and interminable, for it was in truth the silence of waiting. The girls grew up and for long they waited expectantly, but the bridegrooms did not come. What madman will knock at the door of the poor and the ugly, particularly if they happen to be orphans? But hope, of course, is present, for—as the proverb says—even a rotten bean finds some blind person to weigh it out, and every girl can find her better half. Be there poverty, there is always someone who is poorer, be there ugliness, there is always someone uglier. Hopes come true, sometimes come true, with patience.

A silence broken only by the sound of reciting from the Koran; the sound rises up, with dull, unimpassioned monotony. It is being given by a Koranic reciter and the reciter is blind. It is for the soul of the deceased and the appointed time for it never changes: Friday afternoons he comes, raps at the door with his stick, gives himself over to the hand stretched out to him, and squats down on the mat. When he finishes he feels around for his sandals, gives a greeting which no one troubles to answer, and takes himself off. By habit he recites, by habit he takes himself off, and so no one is aware of him.

The silence is permanent. Even the breaking of it by the Friday afternoon recital has waiting, like hope, a hope that is meager yet permanent, which is at least hope. However little a thing may be, there is always something less, and they are not on the lookout for anything more: never do they do so.

Silence goes on till something happens. Friday afternoon comes and the reciter does not come, for to every agreement however long it may last there is an end—and the agreement has come to an end.

Only now the widow and her daughters realize what has occurred: it was not merely that his was the only voice that broke the silence but that he was the only man, be it only once a week, who knocked at the door. Other things too they realized: while it was true that he was poor like them, his clothes were always clean, his sandals always polished, his turban always wound with a precision of which people with sound eyesight were incapable, while his voice was strong, deep, and resonant.

The suggestion is broached: Why not renew the agreement, right away? Why not send for him this very moment? If he's busy, so what—waiting's nothing new? Towards sunset he comes and recites, and it is as if he recites for the first time. The suggestion evolves: Why doesn't one of us marry a man who fills the house for us with his voice? He is a bachelor, has never married, has sprouted a sparse mustache and is still young. One word leads to another— after all he too is no doubt looking for some nice girl to marry.

The girls make suggestions and the mother looks into their faces so as to determine to whose lot he shall fall, but the faces turn away, suggesting, merely suggesting, saying things without being explicit. Shall we fast and break that fast with a blind man? They are still dreaming of bridegrooms—and normally bridegrooms are men endowed with sight. Poor things, they do not yet know the world of men; it is impossible for them to understand that eyes do not make a man.

"You marry him, Mother. You marry him."

"I? Shame on you! And what will people say?"

"Let them say what they like. Whatever they say is better than a house in which there is not the sound of men's voices."

"Marry before you do? Impossible."

"Is it not better that you marry before us so that men's feet may know the way to our house and that we may marry after you? Marry him. Marry him, Mother."

She married him. Their number increased by one and their income increased slightly—and a bigger problem came into being.

It is true that the first night passed with the two of them in their bed, but they did not dare, even accidentally, to draw close to one another. The three girls were asleep but from each one of them was focused a pair of searchlights, aimed unerringly across the space between them: searchlights made up of eyes, of ears, of senses. The girls are grown up; they know; they are aware of things, and by their wakeful presence it is as if the room has been changed into broad daylight. During the day, however, there is no reason for them to stay there, and one after the other they sneak out and do not return till around sunset. They return shy and hesitant, moving a step forward, a step back, until, coming closer, they are amazed, thrown into confusion, are made to hasten their steps by the laughter and guffaws of a man interspersed by the giggling of a woman. It must be their mother who is laughing, also laughing is the man whom previously they had always heard behaving so correctly, so properly. Still laughing, she met them with open arms, her head bared, her hair wet and combed out, and still laughing. Her face which they had instinctively perceived as nothing but a dead lantern where spiders, like wrinkles, had made their nest, had suddenly filled with light; there it was in front of them as bright as an electric bulb. Her eyes were sparkling; they had come forth and shown themselves, bright with tears of laughter; eyes that had previously sought shelter deep down in their sockets.

The silence vanished, completely disappeared. During dinner, before dinner, and after dinner, there are plenty of jokes and stories, also singing, for he has a beautiful voice when he sings and imitates

Umm Kulthoum and Abdul Wahhab; his voice is loud and booming, raucous with happiness.

You have done well, Mother. Tomorrow the laughter will attract men, for men are bait for men.

Yes, daughters. Tomorrow men will come, bridegrooms will make their appearance. Yet the fact is that what most occupied her was not men or bridegrooms but that young man—albeit he was blind, for how often are we blind to people just because they are blind—that strong young man full of robust health and life who had made up for her the years of sickness and failure and premature old age.

The silence vanished as though never to return and the clamour of life pervaded the place. The husband was hers, her legitimate right in accordance with the law of God and His Prophet. What, then, was there to be ashamed about when everything he does is lawful? No longer does she even worry about hiding her secrets or being discreet, and even as night comes and they are all together and bodies and souls are set loose, even as the girls are scattered far apart about the room, knowing and understanding, as though nailed to where they are sleeping, all sounds and breathing aquiver, controlling movements and coughs, suddenly deep sighs issue forth and are themselves stifled by more sighs.

She spent her day doing the washing at the houses of the rich, he his day reciting the Koran at the houses of the poor. At first he did not make it a practice to return to the house at midday, but when the nights grew longer and his hours of sleep less, he began to return at midday to rest his body for a while from the toil of the night that had passed and to prepare himself for the night to come. Once, after they had had their fill of the night, he suddenly asked her what had been the matter with her at midday: why was she talking unrestrainedly now and had maintained such complete silence then, why was she now wearing the ring that was so dear to him, it being the only thing by way of bridal money and gifts the marriage had cost him, while she had not been wearing it then?

She could have risen up in horror and screamed, could have

gone mad. He could be killed for this, for what he is saying has only one meaning—and what a strange and repulsive meaning.

A choking lump in the throat stifled all this, stifled her very breathing. She kept silent. With ears that had turned into nostrils, tactile sense and eyes, she began listening, her sole concern being to discover the culprit. For some reason she is sure it is the middle one: in her eyes there is a boldness that even bullets cannot kill. She listens. The breathing of the three girls rises up, deep and warm as if fevered; it groans with yearning, hesitates, is broken, as sinful dreams interrupt it. The disturbed breathing changes to a hissing sound, a hissing like the scorching heat that is spat out by thirsty earth. The lump in the throat sinks down deeper, becomes stuck. What she hears is the breathing of the famished. However much she sharpens her senses she is unable to distinguish between one warm, muffled heap of living flesh and another, all are famished; all scream and groan, and the moaning breathes not with breathing but perhaps with shouts for help, perhaps with entreaties, perhaps with something that is even more.

She immersed herself in her second legitimate pursuit and forgot her first, her daughters. Patience became bitter-tasting, even the mirage of bridegrooms no longer made its appearance. Like someone awakened in terror to some mysterious call, she is suddenly stung into attention: the girls are famished. It is true that food is sinful, but hunger is even more so. There is nothing more sinful than hunger. She knows it. Hunger had known her, had dried up her soul, had sucked at her bones; she knows it, and however sated she is, it is impossible for her to forget its taste.

They are famished, and it was she who used to take the piece of food out of her own mouth in order to feed them; she, the mother, whose sole concern it was to feed them even if she herself went hungry. Has she forgotten?

Despite his pressing her to speak, the feeling of choking turned into silence. The mother kept silent and from that moment silence was ever with her.

At breakfast, exactly as she had expected, the middle one was silent—and continued in her silence.

Dinner-time came with the young man happy and blind and enjoying himself, still joking and singing and laughing, and with no one sharing his laughter but the youngest and the eldest.

Patience is protracted, its bitter taste turns to sickness—and still no one shows up.

One day, the eldest one looks at her mother's ring on her finger, expresses her delight in it. The mother's heart beats fast—and beats yet faster as she asks her if she might wear it for a day, just for one single day. In silence she draws it off her finger; in silence the eldest puts it on her own same finger.

At the next dinner-time the eldest one is silent, refuses to utter.

The blind youth is noisy, he sings and he laughs, and only the youngest one joins in with him.

But the youngest one, through patience, through worry, through lack of luck, grows older and begins asking about when her turn will come in the ring game. In silence she achieves her turn.

The ring lies beside the lamp. Silence descends and ears are blinded. In silence the finger whose turn it is stealthily slips on the ring. The lamp is put out: darkness is all-embracing and in the darkness eyes are blinded.

No one remains who is noisy, who tells jokes, who sings, except for the blind young man.

Behind his noisy boisterousness there lurks a desire that almost makes him rebel against the silence and break it to pieces. He too wants to know, wants to know for certain. At first he used to tell himself that it was the nature of women to refuse to stay the same, sometimes radiantly fresh as drops of dew, at other times spent and stale as water in a puddle; sometimes as soft as the touch of rose petals, at other times rough as cactus plants. True, the ring was always there, but it was as if the finger wearing it were a different finger. He all but knows, while they all know for certain, so why does the silence not speak, why does it not utter?

One dinner-time the question sneaks in upon him unawares: What if the silence should utter? What if it should talk?

The mere posing of the question halted the morsel of food in his throat.

From that moment onwards he sought refuge in silence and refused to relinquish it.

In fact it was he who became frightened that sometime by ill chance the silence might be scratched; maybe a word might slip out and the whole edifice of silence come tumbling down—and woe to him should the edifice of silence tumble down!

The strange, different silence in which they all sought refuge.

International silence this time, of which neither poverty nor ugliness nor patient waiting nor despair is the cause.

It is, though, the deepest form of silence, for it is silence agreed upon by the strongest form of agreement—that which is concluded without any agreement.

The widow and her three daughters.

And the house is a room.

And the new silence.

And the Koran reciter who brought that silence with him, and who with silence set about assuring for himself that she who shared his bed was always his wife, all proper and legitimate, the wearer of his ring. Sometimes she grows younger or older, she is soft-skinned or rough, slender or fat—it is solely her concern, the concern of those with sight, it is their responsibility alone in that they possess the boon of knowing things for certain; it is they who are capable of distinguishing while the most he can do is to doubt, a doubt which cannot become certainty without the boon of sight and so long as he is deprived of it just so long will he remain deprived of certainty, for he is blind and no moral responsibility attaches to a blind man?

Or does it?

Translated by Denys Johnson-Davies

FROM **City of Love and Ashes**

He rang the bell, and Bedeir opened the door wearing his bathrobe over a brushed-cotton gallabiya. A white woolen skullcap was fastened to his head, a scarf turbaned around it.

"Brother," said Bedeir, as he returned to his seat, "my knees are like jelly! I was sure you must have been arrested. Where have you been?"

"I was looking for work."

"Find anything?"

"Yes."

"What?"

"I'm going to give private lessons."

"Where?"

"Here."

Bedeir roared with laughter. The armchair shook accordingly, as did the newspaper he was reading, and his robe was in turmoil.

"Here where, may I ask?"

"Here in the apartment."

"Oh, that's a good one! You do have a sense of humor! So why do they talk all this nonsense about you? . . . Anyway, have you had your supper?"

"I've no appetite."

"I don't believe it! You've never in your life had no appetite. It must be a miracle. What are you talking about, no appetite? You have to have supper! Have some supper—I want to talk to you."

Hamza could offer no more resistance; he had no choice but to sit down and swallow the food.

Bedeir's expression became serious as he spoke. "Listen, Hamza. You know I have your interests at heart, and you're just like a brother to me. And we've been colleagues and friends for what, fifteen years? I want to tell you something."

"What?"

"Hamza, brother, settle down. Put an end to all this. It's enough that you've wasted years of your life, and there's less left of it than you've used up already. You'll spend your whole life on the run, cast out, nowhere to go. No offense, you understand. Perhaps what I'm saying is a little harsh, but it's the truth."

"Exactly what my mother says," said Hamza with a smile. "Settle down how?"

"Settle down—work, do the right thing, get married, make yourself a home and a family, snap out of it! It's not right for an educated man like you to live like this."

"But I'm very happy with my life as it is."

"Happy? How?"

"I'm happy because the important thing is not how or where you live, but why. The important thing is, what are you doing for other people?"

"I don't understand. Humor me, brother. What are you talking about?"

"Well, of course you wouldn't understand. You're a man with your own life, your own home, your own work. I don't have a life of my own. I've put myself and my life at the service of the people. If necessity dictates I run, I run . . . go to jail, I go to jail . . . die, I die."

"This is unbelievable. So that's it, you've become a prophet, a saint? You don't want anything in this world? You don't have any ambitions of your own?"

"My private aspirations are exactly the general aspirations of the people."

"What fine words! Am I supposed to understand then that you're never going to marry, never going to have your own home?"

"Certainly I'll marry, and have children. But my marriage must serve our cause, not be at its expense. And certainly I'll have a home, but a home that will allow me more opportunity to serve the people."

"So you're going to remain rootless like this forever."

"Not at all. What made me rootless is what made millions of Egyptians rootless, and millions can't remain rootless forever."

Bedeir was silent for a long time, then said, "Hmm. Fine. Looks like it's no use. Hmm. Good night." He pulled up the cover, and it was not long before his snores rose up and he was asleep.

Hamza could not sleep. The conversation had reminded him of the alienation he had felt since coming to this luxurious apartment. Even the word "people" sounded strange on his lips. It hardly had a place among the chandeliers, carpets, and ornate furniture. The visions that had begun to well up in his mind's eye multiplied. His mother. His father. His father the rail worker, with his ample, thick mustache that turned up suddenly at each end. The rail camps that were the pasture of his childhood and boyhood, the camps that the rail authority set up between stations for the workers repairing the tracks. The closed, sealed community of workers. People faced life together. Secrets were the property of all; poverty was fairly distributed among all. The wives bathed together on Friday mornings, boasting about the events of the night before, and the husbands dived together in the irrigation channel to purify themselves. The camp was in the hands of the women in the mornings, and the endless arguments would begin over lost geese or ducks. Eggs were the currency among the women, hand-rolled cigarettes among the men, but real money had to change hands between the men and the women, or else. In every camp there was a wolf who showed his beard then hid behind his wife; the men did not know, but the children and the women watched out for him. In every camp there was an outcast miser who piled millieme upon millieme in the hope of buying a small patch of land in his home village. In every camp there was a religious visionary whom the men mocked and from whom the women took blessings. In every camp there was a beautiful wife, there was jealousy, and there were feuds; children were born by the dozen; there were mosquitoes and millions of insects; dogs and their howlings guarded the poverty, the water jugs, the subsistence.

Every day a problem, quarrels, yelling, scrapping, attempts by the foreman to assert his authority, attempts by the workers to wrest it from him. Talk of pay scales, talk of wages docked. Women in search of conception, men in search of a loan. Patched yellow trousers. Tall woolen caps and heavy Egyptian army-surplus boots. The whistle of trains coming and going: a virgin opens her window, contemplates the trains, sighs, and dreams of the local town, its educated men, and three gold-plated bracelets.

Every day a problem, quarrels, yelling, scrapping. As soon as the day is finished and the sun disappears and the smoke from the stoves dies down and the smoke from the trains stops, the men return to their houses, in winter, or in summer to the spaces in front of them. The low, round table is put down, mouths all around it. Supper is over almost before it starts and is followed by languor and occasional brief exchanges between husband and wife, in which there is more sleep than wakefulness, more optimism than pessimism. The wife is restless, the husband steady. The woman is afraid, the man reassuring. The wife yawns, the husband mumbles tiredly, "It'll all be all right in the morning."

As for Hamza and the other children, the day was theirs. Theirs for running, jumping, and swimming in the irrigation channel; for counting sleepers; for trying to walk unaided along a single rail; for using pebbles as flints to make sparks, in imitation of their fathers; for hunting sparrows with catapults and small stones; for the best game of all, of putting a nail on the track and waiting for a passing train to squash it flat, thin, and sharp as a knife; for the plentiful prickly pears that covered both sides of the track; for the prickly pear season and the endless chases with the trader who bought the fruit from the rail authority and guarded it.

Like him, all the children became ill with bilharzia, hookworm, measles, malaria, and conjunctivitis. Some of them came down with jaundice, never to regain their natural color, or with splenitis.

Sheikh Zidan's Quranic school was followed by compulsory state schooling and its beatings. Primary school brought his first uniform and the somber, vile tarboosh. He passed the primary certificate with 85 percent, entitling him to free secondary education. His father was delighted; his mother wanted him to learn a trade, nothing more. His father wanted him to be an engineer and work in the rail company like his boss's boss's boss's boss. His mother used incantations to protect him against envy. His father showed him his sieve-like trousers and said, "Top of your class, or it's these for you." And he was top.

After the secondary certificate came the calamity, the pain, the terrible struggle to find a pound or fifty piasters for Hamza in his exile far away in Alexandria. A year passed: only three years to go—O Lord, make things easy! But he acquired bad habits: poker, rummy, sour rum, curly-haired women with brilliant red lipstick like the abattoir stamps on slaughtered meat. He lied to his father and swindled his friends. He failed a year and hid his failure. His father believed the star student had passed. He deceived and dissembled.

His father was desperate: Hamza's needs were strangling him. His mother learned to make decorated headscarves. The whole settlement helped out—even the foreman paid fifty piasters each month. His father took Hamza's younger brother out of school so that Hamza could go on, because he was older and closer to earning a salary. The sixth of March: demonstrations, committees, conferences. Meanwhile, his brother was working in the shunting yards, where one morning a train took off his foot; he spent six months in the municipal hospital, then returned to work, one-footed, as a crossing attendant.

Hamza graduated and worked in a factory. With his first salary he printed the union broadsheet. His life was politics, meetings, discussions, the cause, appointments. He was trailed by the political police. His first conviction was on trumped-up charges: he became internee number forty-eight and spent twenty months in al-Tur, Hikestep, and the Alexandria Foreign Prison. Then he was released, but every time a British government official or high-ranking officer came to Egypt, he was arrested, and on every occasion of national or international importance he was detained in the police station for days that stretched into weeks, until at the beginning of the year he was able to make a list of the days on which he would visit the station, as another might mark the public holidays on a calendar.

He owned one suit, which he had had made on his graduation; his eyeglasses he had bought from the university medical center for one pound; he was the second owner of his shoes. He sometimes

sent money to his father, but he was unable to send the pair of black
slippers his mother asked for. His mother still embroidered scarves;
his father's mustache had become white as he had grown older, and
he had still not made foreman. His brother still limped and closed
the gates for the trains and opened them when they passed, his sister, Nabawiya, was still unmarried, and they had moved to yet another rail camp. His mother prayed for his guidance; his father
spoke to the men of his exploits and cursed the government and the
rail authority. The whole settlement wove tales of heroism around
him, and when a train passed the small children would say, "That
train's going to Hamza."

"Aren't you going to sleep, Hamza?"

"Yes, Bedeir, I'm going to sleep."

Translated by R. Neil Hewison

Walid Ikhlassi
(b. 1935)
SYRIA

Walid Ikhlassi was born in Alexandretta, Syria. A book of
his short stories, *Whatever Happened to Antara?* has been
translated into English. The stories take place in Aleppo,
Syria's second city, and deal with the struggles of ordinary
men and women in a shifting political landscape.

The Dead Afternoon

The wall-clock struck five, filling the house with its ringing.

I was watching the swallows from my window as they crossed the
city sky; thousands of swallows, black moving specks.

The evening, meanwhile, prepared to occupy its place in a
new day.

"May they find favour with God," I said to my grandmother,
who had finished her prayers.

"I was late performing the afternoon prayer," she answered sadly.

"Never mind, there will be other afternoons."

My grandmother did not hear me.

I looked at an enormous fly squatting on the outside of the window-pane: it seemed to be defying me, sitting there so close to my nose.

"This fly has annoyed me all day," I said, "and I haven't been able to kill it."

My grandmother did not reply: she had started on a new prayer.

I was not conscious of the passage of time: the fly had taken up so much of it. I had threatened it by tapping on the glass, but it had not stirred. Looking at my fingernails and seeing that they were long, I produced a pair of scissors and began to pare them.

The sky was being engulfed in soft darkness, and the only sound to cut across my grandmother's voice as she recited her prayers, seated in her gazelle-skin chair, was the clock striking six.

My young sister came in from the other room.

"Today we'll be eating *kunafa* with walnuts," she announced.

"I don't like it."

My sister laughed. "This morning you said you wanted *kunafa*."

"I just don't like it."

Turning again to the window, I was surprised to find that the fly was still asleep.

My grandmother, caressing my young sister, said to her:

"Turn on the radio so we can listen to Feiruz."

"We listened to her at midday," I said firmly. The darkness outside prevented me from seeing the swallows. Even so, though, I liked Feiruz's voice.

"We'll listen to her again," said my grandmother.

I did not reply: I was contemplating the sleeping fly.

A frightening thought occurred to me: what if one of them should watch me as I lay sound asleep?

I heard my sister asking my grandmother to tell us the story of the Singing Nightingale this evening and my grandmother saying, "Didn't we finish it yesterday?"

The little girl cried out petulantly.

"Yesterday! Yesterday's over."

"You won't hear the story of the singing nightingale any more," I whispered to myself and I was filled with sadness.

"I'll tell you a new one today," said my grandmother.

"We don't want a new story," exclaimed my sister.

"But the old one's finished."

"It's not finished," shouted my sister.

I tried to excuse my sister, as she jumped off my grandmother's lap and hurried out of the room, but I too felt annoyed; I too wanted the old story.

After a while I complied with my grandmother's request to switch on the radio, and searched round for a station. I found one as the clock struck seven.

"This is Aleppo."

I drew a veil of silence over the voice.

"Let's hear the news," protested my grandmother.

Flicking through the pages of the morning paper, I said:

"It's stale news."

"New things may happen, my son," exclaimed the old lady, suddenly conscious of her age.

I began reading the headlines: having already done so at midday, they did not affect me.

All at once I wanted to get out of that room, but I had nowhere particular to go, so I changed my mind and stayed where I was.

The little girl returned with her large doll.

"Will you tell Suzanne a story?" she asked, looking at her grandmother with a challenge in her eyes.

The old lady laughed.

I went back to the window: the darkness had settled down completely in the vastness of the sky.

I felt a great desire to tease the sleeping fly coming over me. I no longer felt any resentment against it and had forgotten its impudence.

"Won't you tell Suzanne a new story?" asked my sister.

The fact was that I did not know any story. Then I remembered one I had heard on the radio at noon.

"I'll tell you the story of the Bear and the Honey," I replied.

"But it's an old one," cried my sister.

Confused, I returned to observing the fly.

"What is it?" asked the little girl, coming towards me as I sat by the window.

"A sleeping fly."

"A sleeping fly?" my sister asked, knitting her brows. "Is that a new story?"

"It's asleep, it's tired."

"Will you tell it to Suzanne?" she said.

"All right, I'll tell it."

My sister drew close to me.

"What are you looking at?" she demanded.

"I'm looking at the fly."

She climbed onto a chair and stared at it. Then she proclaimed triumphantly in her shrill voice:

"But it's dead!"

I felt uneasy as I looked at the girl who was suddenly as tall as I was.

"It's asleep."

"It's dead!" said my sister, amazed at my ignorance.

I opened the window cautiously and blew softly on the fly: it fell off like a wisp of paper.

I remembered it flying around me, remembered that I had hated it and then loved it.

"Won't you tell Suzanne the story of the Sleeping Fly?"

I didn't answer her: I was listening to the striking of the clock which reverberated through the house.

Translated by Denys Johnson-Davies

Jabra Ibrahim Jabra
(1919–94)

PALESTINE

Jabra Ibrahim Jabra was born in Bethlehem and died in Baghdad, his adopted home. A man of singular talents, he was awarded a scholarship to study at Cambridge, where he took a degree in English. Following World War II he taught at the University of Baghdad, married an Iraqi, and later worked as the public relations representative for the Iraq Petroleum Company. His house in Baghdad became a meeting-place for Iraqi intellectuals. Full of books and paintings, his own and those of his artist friends, it was a place where the music of Bach and Mozart could be heard, and where, he was advised, it would be wise to give a finely framed picture of Saddam Hussein the place of honor. Jabra worked as a poet and novelist (in both Arabic and English), a literary critic, an art critic, and a painter. His translations into Arabic include some six plays by Shakespeare, Faulkner's *The Sound and the Fury*, and an experimental translation into colloquial Iraqi Arabic of Beckett's *Waiting for Godot*. He wrote a novel in English, *Hunters in a Narrow Street*, which was published by Heinemann in 1960, and two Arabic novels, *The Ship*, published in 1969, and *In Search of Walid Masoud*, published in 1978. With *In Search of Walid Masoud*, Jabra, essentially a Palestinian writer, joined the ranks of the finest writers in modern Arabic literature.

FROM *In Search of Walid Masoud*

I could find happiness only with you, you, you, Shahd, my Shahd. Everything I said was directed at you. I kept looking for the other half of me till I found you, and then I came to realize the utter horror of your separation from me: I was, in truth, cut into two segments wanting to come together again. I was waiting for my reunification with you, the woman with whom, so the fates decreed, I could be united in only a few moments of a rapture as profound as the oceans themselves and as swift as the sweep of a hurricane.

Walid, how could you bring yourself even to mention Jinan, even though you were trying to use her to prove you loved me? That day you managed once more to tear me apart; but whereas before it had been love, this time it was jealousy. You forced me to come running back to you, out of jealousy, nothing else. I wanted you to enter a monastery, to suffer, to be deprived of all women after me. Off you went with your half of our relationship and tried to get my half back through Jinan! I made a firm resolution on the spot, that very day, that I'd never get married, just to keep you for myself even if I didn't come back to you. I did come back. Did I ever ask you about Jinan! Did I argue with you about her? Any other woman but me would have left you as soon as she found out another woman was involved, whatever excuses were made. With me it was just the opposite. I came back to you, but this time with feelings of doubt I hadn't known before. Were you still seeing Jinan every time I had to go away? I kept all this to myself, pretending your letter hadn't revealed anything new.

Did you run away from everything at the last moment, just to rid yourself of your wavering over Jinan and myself? Is that possible, even conceivable? Am I supposed to believe you were able to put me in a balance with another woman, Jinan or whoever? I went back to my delirium. Why should I make myself a focus for your tragedy, knowing full well it did indeed have a focus that I dearly wanted not to have to believe in. Flawed angels botched the job of forming the universe, so the universe was full of flaws, too. That's what one of your Greek authors said. Now here I am confirming the truth of what he said. You arrived as a stranger, at war; and that's the way you stayed, a stranger fighting on various fronts in a world molded with flaws. Oh God! "Wasted is the time that we do not spend in love . . ." But the losses were great indeed, my beloved, and time wasn't the only thing wasted. When you lost Marwan, I, too, realized I'd lost everything. Yet, the world stayed the way it was with all its flaws; nothing changed. You came as a stranger and left the same way. You turned me into a stranger in the midst of my own family and friends. Only I have changed. The bougainvillea at our house is in full bloom, and I don't understand why. It's almost as though it wants to spur me on to lift the receiver and call you again to arrange to read my poetry, with my body firing all your senses. Miracles! A purse filled with pearls, dropped from the heavens into my lap. Yes indeed! Now here's another purse dropped from heaven, but this one's full of scorpions.

It was no easy task finding Marwan in Beirut, even though Walid's friend Khalid Abu Matar had given me directions. In the end Khalid went with me himself to the Sabra refugee camp, and after a lot of questions we found Marwan there. "What do you want?" he asked, looking curiously at me. I didn't know what to say. His eyes, gorgeous eyes, were exactly like his father's, but they had a brighter gleam to them and a cruelty totally missing from Walid's. I wanted to imagine it was Walid I was seeing in khaki camouflage uniform and fedayeen headdress, carrying a Kalashnikov. But all I saw was Marwan, tall, unsmiling, rejecting everything except his new comrades in this tented city, which I could feel taking me back to the forgotten essence of life.

"I'm Wisal Raouf," I said, "and I've come from Baghdad. I've got a letter for you from your father."

He took the letter and read it. We were standing in the middle of a roadway crowded with people. I kept looking at his youthful face and the slight moustache barely visible over his lip. He took Khalid and me to a small office, where we sat down on wooden chairs. He's asked me about his father, and introduced us to two of his colleagues who were wearing the same uniform; they brought us some tea. The whole encounter was awkward, but the conversation kept going and gradually became more heated. We toured the camp, and Marwan introduced me to a number of people. "Welcome to the lady from Baghdad!" I could imagine any one of them as a mother for Walid. We met some young people, too, who knew Baghdad;

some of them had studied there. I wanted them to let me stay with them.

"Teach me how to fire a gun," I said to Marwan.

He looked at me in my tight-fitting pants. "Whenever you want to try it!" he replied.

Next day at lunchtime he came to the hotel and we went out to a seaside restaurant. The waiter filled the table with hors d'oeuvres. "Marwan," I said, when the waiter had left, "you've no idea how much your father loves you; you're all he has in the world. Why don't you come to Baghdad?"

He glanced at me for a brief moment, then looked out to sea. He was shy, and hardly said or ate anything. "I've no need to go to Baghdad," he said. "My life's here in the camp. We have lots to do."

"Well, take care of yourself, anyway," I said.

"Why on earth did I join the front then?" he asked in astonishment. "To take care of myself?"

I wanted to tell him to finish his university studies first and then come back to the front, but realized that would just annoy him. I took a packet of banknotes out of my handbag and handed them to him. "These are for you," I whispered. "Your father sent them with me."

He stared at them, there in my hand, as though they were some strange creatures he was afraid to touch. "What's that?" he said.

"Two hundred dinars. You may need them."

"No thanks," he replied, shaking his head. "I don't want them."

"Please!"

"I don't want them."

"I beg you! Please, take them before the customers notice."

"No! I've got quite enough. Really!"

"How strange you are!"

"No, I'm not! I don't need any money. What am I supposed to do with it anyway?"

"Come on, Marwan! Just take it and stop arguing!"

"Forget it! I'll throw it all in the sea if you like!"

"For heaven's sake! If you don't take it now, I'll throw it in the sea for you."

"Go ahead. I hope the fish enjoy it!"

"You're just like your father. Stubborn as hell! You Palestinians, you're all stubborn!"

I put the money back in my handbag. "Do you know anything about my relationship with your father?" I asked him abruptly.

"Are you in love with him?" he asked coldly.

I felt a pain piercing to my very core. "I adore him," I replied. "I'd die for him."

He looked at me silently, then raised his hand from the table and put it on top of mine; I could feel it trembling. "I love him, too," he said, "and my mother used to worship him. But . . ."

Tears welled in my eyes, and my voice broke. "But what . . . what?" I asked.

He withdrew his hand. "He's been fighting the whole of his life," he said with a sigh, "and he's tired. He refuses to give up. Do you think you can help him . . . ease up, at least a little bit?"

I wasn't certain what he meant exactly.

"Oh Marwan!" I answered, my voice breaking again. "If only I could! Life's so complicated and always asks so much of us. If only you knew what a man he is!"

He took out a handkerchief and handed it to me. "Well, then, help him, will you?!"

I dried my eyes with the handkerchief, then paused. "Help him? Me?"

"He insists on going on with the fight himself. He keeps demanding they include him in operations. Don't you realize that?"

"I'm not the slightest bit surprised. But he doesn't talk to me about things like that. He's so secretive."

"When he was here last winter, he brought the matter up with his group, and then with me, too; it really annoyed me. Operations involve a lot of hard training beforehand; they need young men who can run hard, jump, go hungry, and put up with hardship. My father thinks he's still the young man he was twenty-five years ago. I told him if he wanted to commit suicide, to find some other way of doing it. He got very angry and we had a big fight; he swore at me and then went back to Baghdad. He hasn't written a word to me all these past months, and the letter you brought with you is the first one I've had from him since that day. I hear he's renewed his request to be involved with the fighting . . ."

I kept looking at Marwan and imagining to myself that it was Walid talking. The son had the same forceful tone in his voice as the father.

"But how can you deny your father the very things you've chosen for yourself?" I asked.

His face flushed in anger. "Because my role's completely different from his," he replied. "We're in a different phase of operations now. A fifty-year-old carrying an RPG is of no use to us. He's needed for organizing, financing, and making the necessary connections as a background to the fighting. Isn't all that enough for him? He's spent a lot of time fighting in any case . . ."

I didn't answer. As we sat there, silent, I saw the sea pounding the shore beside us, gleaming and restless. That sea belonged to Marwan, and to Walid. I felt at that particular moment it belonged to me, too, because I longed to plunge into the depths of both of them. What kind of fighting had my own father had to do to be appointed minister in the 1950s? What ideas had he put forward, what struggle had he articulated, except, that is, for his struggle against disease ever since he married my mother? What yearning, what passion, what agony had there been?

I put these thoughts out of my mind, so as to concentrate on the roaring mass of blue that seemed to encircle Marwan's face.

"What about now?" I asked. "Are you happy with your father?"

He looked astonished, as though the question had come straight at him from nowhere. "Am I happy with him? The main thing is: is he happy with me? That's what I'd like you to help me with. Can't you see?"

With a laugh I handed him back his handkerchief. "But you're not being any help to me."

"How can I be?"

"Don't you realize that by refusing to take this money you'll annoy him all over again? Marwan, please take it."

I opened my handbag again and was on the point of taking the package out when he pushed my hand back and closed the bag. "No, no," he said. "I told you, I don't want money."

I looked at him in silent despair. He was smiling; yes, for the first time I actually saw him smile! "Marwan!" I exclaimed, giving full vent to my shout. "You actually smiled!"

"What of it?" he asked with a chuckle. "Is that such a miracle?"

"It certainly is! My life's full of miracles these days. Do you know what I mean?"

"You should say thank God for that, then."

"Oh, I do, a thousand times a day! Now what are you going to get me to eat in this glorious spot?"

"Anything your heart desires."

"How about some fish? What's it called here: Sultan Ibrahim?" The waiter came over and took our order.

"Wisal," he said, calling me by my name for the first time.

"Yes!"

"You have beautiful hair. Do you always keep it short like that?"

"But Marwan, you amaze me! You've actually started noticing me."

"So? Another miracle!"

"True enough! I cut it two days ago. Do you like it?"

"Very much. It reminds me of . . ."

"Of what? Who? One of your girlfriends?"

"Of another Iraqi woman who came to visit me with my father when I was a schoolboy at Brummana; that was about four years ago."

"What was her name?" I asked without the least attempt at subterfuge.

"I can't remember," he replied, "but she had really long, beautiful hair. I was twenty-four then."

"Was she Iraqi?"

"Yes. She had green eyes, too. Do you know who she is?"

My heart sank. "Maryam, was that her name? Maryam al-Saffar?"

"Maryam! Yes, that's it!"

"She came to visit you with your father?"

"Yes. I think they'd met accidentally in Beirut."

"Could be," I commented. In fact, I was thinking the very reverse; it certainly hadn't been an accident. Marwan, I thought to myself, are you really trying to remind me I'm just another woman in Walid's life? But why should I be bothered about what woman he loved, or what woman was in love with him, four long years ago?

"Oh, she's one of our many acquaintances," I told Marwan. "She's a professor at Baghdad University now. Do you have any special message for her?"

"Oh no! I don't think she'd even remember me."

I laughed. "I don't think she'd forget anything to do with your father," I said as though to poke fun at myself.

The waiter took the hors d'oeuvres away and brought the fish. "Do you have any girlfriends here?" I asked.

At first he frowned, then his expression relaxed. "The . . . er . . . there are plenty of women around here, even in the camp, but I'm too busy with other things that are more important." For a moment he was silent, then he went on: "My platoon and I go through really tough drills. I can't wait to cross the border. The situation in Amman's extremely tense." There was an abrupt flare of anger in his eyes, then he looked out to sea again with his jaw set in a strange way.

"Marwan," I said, trying to put him in a happier mood again, "this fish is superb."

He turned and looked at me again, determination still written all across his face. "I'll make you a promise," he said.

"A promise?"

"One day I'll make fish for you from Lake Tiberias, with myself, you, and my father sitting by the shore. It may take five or ten years. Do you accept?"

"With all my heart. I'll be waiting . . ."

At this point he took up his knife and fork, and so did I. My heart was pounding with all kinds of emotion, and I didn't know whether to admire or be afraid of this young man who'd made me feel the sea was roaring and pounding all around my head.

The waves kept crashing down on the rocks nearby, turning the headlong rush of blue into a laughing cascade of white that dwindled away into foam, only to confront yet another onslaught of waves.

I sent Walid many cards and letters. Then, when I got back to Baghdad at the beginning of September, I found he'd already left. His "disappearance," without any notice given to his friends, was nothing unusual in itself. He could have been pursuing his interests in Abu Dhabi, London, or even Beirut itself; that, at least, was what people were assuming. But this time he was actually in Jordan, and about two months later he came back, exhausted and broken. Eventually, he revealed some of his secrets to me. I spent another October morning with him, but this time it was agonizing. He started to tell me about the insane, disgusting massacre he'd been involved in, carrying a Kalashnikov he'd never even dreamed of knowing how to fire.

"Don't you ever think of me?" I asked furiously. "Don't you realize how selfish I am about you? Here you are close to fifty . . ."

He let out such a scream as I'd never heard from a human being before. "Shut up," he yelled, "shut up!" and put both his hands over his face, then he turned to the closest wall and leaned on it, sobbing and moaning horribly. I was riveted to the spot in terror, as I watched him banging his head against the wall. His body was shaking and trembling. The room felt small for the two of us, as though the walls were collapsing in on us. I felt my head spinning; I wanted to stop but couldn't. I fell to the ground, grabbing at it to keep myself steady, then crawled over toward him, till my face sank down at his feet and I found myself retching and sobbing, with no idea of what was happening. Much later—I have no idea whether I fainted or what—I found him collapsed over me, piled in a heap on top of me. I took his wan face in my hands. "Walid," I whispered, "oh Walid." I found it difficult even to utter his name, my throat felt so exhausted.

He fell into my arms and put his lips to my ear. "If I have the right to make love to you and fight the whole world for your sake, and all this when I'm pushing fifty, don't I have the right to love my

country, too, and fight the rest of the world for its sake, too, even if
I were ninety?"

"Of course you do," I said, laying him down beside me on the
floor and resting his head on my chest. Was it one hour, two hours?
The whole day went by, with us like a pair of corpses, wrapped one
around the other. The world doesn't understand and never will; and
accordingly, I reject a world that doesn't understand me. I must
keep my wounds to myself, not tell anyone else about them; I must
continue my rejection and join the other rejectionists.

Translated by Roger Allen and Adnan Haydar

Said al-Kafrawi
(b. 1939)

EGYPT

Said al-Kafrawi was born in the Nile Delta. In his writing he
has confined himself to the short story, of which he has published twelve volumes. Most of his stories deal with peasant
life. A representative volume of his stories in English translation appeared in 1998 under the title *The Hill of Gypsies*.
Collections of his stories have also been published in French
and Italian.

The Hill of Gypsies

"How old is the date palm, Grandpa?"
   "Very old, as old as your forefathers."
   "And you, how old are you, Grandpa?"
   "Very old."
   "From the days of Orabi, for instance?"
   "And who's told you about Orabi?"
   "We have him in our history book."
   He smiled and patted me on the back. "Good for you."
   There were some stones lying about below the wall, and the

light of dusk was emptying itself into the sky before the sunset
prayer of Ramadan. I looked into his face and remembered that
whenever my father scolded me harshly for neglecting my studies, I
would run to my grandfather and take refuge in his embrace. I
would hear him telling my father off: "You'll go on at him till you
do for him."

He used to seat himself, then take my head and put it on his lap,
and I would hear him reviling unknown persons. I'd see him point
toward the shade traced on the wall, while with his leg he would
rock me to sleep and would not wake me until I had woken up of
my own accord.

Plunging his hand into his cloak, he brought it out and waved it
in front of me.

I was astonished when I saw the colored sun glowing behind
him. Clapping my hands together, I called out, "Hey! A Ramadan
lantern! A Ramadan lantern!"

I jumped to my feet. Whenever I stretched out my hand to take
it, my grandfather raised it higher.

"God keep you, Grandpa—let me have the lantern, don't
tease me."

He burst out laughing and said to me, "It cost twenty piasters,
you rascal. You don't deserve it. Guard it like your eyes and enjoy
yourself, my dear fellow."

He removed with his hand the stones that were on the ground,
then took off his broadcloth cloak and spread it out along the
stretch of shade and placed his turban on the stump of the branch
of the mulberry tree. He lay down on the cloak, placing his right
arm over his eyes, and his beard looked to me as though it were
teased cotton.

"Run off," he said to me, "to where your father and uncles are
and see if they've finished irrigating the Mirza field or whether
they'll be spending the night in the fields."

"Right away, Grandpa. Right away."

"Tell your grandma to moisten the dates and the licorice. I'm
really thirsty today."

"Right away, Grandpa."

Sleep made its stealthy way to him from the mulberry tree. He became distracted, then closed his eyes, yet he still went on talking.

"Mind you, wake me before the sunset prayer, for I shall be paying a visit to the departed."

When he talked of things I didn't understand he would be on the threshold of sleep.

"Light the lantern, but beware of going to the hill of the gypsies."

His breathing became regular and his chest began moving up and down; he snored softly.

I said to myself: The hill of the gypsies—what had brought it to his mind? And why should I go there? And who would show me the way up to where the houses ended, to where one cannot walk and the wind howls in the graveyard trees?

"Beware of the hill of the gypsies. They snatch children and make tattoo marks on their chests and call them by names other than their own."

He began to dream, to talk nonsense.

I left him and went off, waving the colored lantern.

At the door I was met by my mother with her head covered. When she saw the lantern she said, "Congratulations, Abdul Mawla." I told her joyfully that my grandfather had brought it for me from the town, and she smiled at me. I said to her, "Why, when he goes to sleep, does my grandfather talk about the gypsies?" My mother said to me, "The gypsies are also God's servants—they are not to be feared." She mentioned Galeela to me and said, "And have you forgotten Galeela the gypsy, Abdul Mawla?"

"Galeela . . . Galeela." I repeated the name to myself and looked at the yellowed sun. My chest was filled with the smell of scalding milk.

Galeela the gypsy. Ah!

Three tattoo lines on her chin and the green spot to one side of her straight nose; a beauty spot like a raisin that death itself would not erase. The crescent earrings, glistening, shook when she moved her head. Eyes of divine kohl in which wandered a mysterious inscrutability. The appeal they had in the hearts of my mother and her aunts was one of life's secrets.

"We make divination in sand, we tell fortunes in seashells. We reveal all."

"Come here, Galeela."

And on the ground of the alleyway, and under the male mulberry tree, she would spread the handkerchief and place on it the grains of soft sand. The kohl-black eye looks into the eyes of the village women, who are captivated by her hidden magic. The fingers mark out life's pathways, bringing into being the destinies of people: roads opened to good fortune, ending in weddings for virgins; peace of mind at the return of the absent. A year of bounty, udders abundant with milk, the grain stores full of the good things and the blessings of the fields. But perils, like predators, are lying in wait in the womb of the unknown, envious and hating. And the Lord is the Savior of His servants, and His Messenger a guardian, and the righteous are not harmed. And you are good and righteous, O Ameena, daughter of al-Mursi, and your son Abdul Mawla is protected from the evil eye and from the iniquities of the devils.

I listen to her voice and emerge from sleep. Passing through the door, I look for an instant into her eye, which was not the color of ashes but of light. I am pinned to the ground at the threshold, between the darkness of the house and the blaze of the sun.

Her dress is of light linen, fashioned with circles that reveal a slip the color of garden roses.

She takes me in her arms and the smell of her sweat fills me to overflowing. She says to me, "O son of the precious." I feel my head in her bosom and my heart racing madly. She kisses me on the mouth and my aunts laugh. "Leave the boy alone, you saucy wench. Sister, she's brazen and has no shame; she doesn't give a damn."

The gypsy girl laughs and my good-natured mother says to her, "Don't stay away—we miss you, Galeela." The gypsy replies, "Earning one's daily bread is full of hardship, mother of Abdul Mawla."

When she draws away from me I shudder and hear my heart beating. I see her lifting her dress and revealing the calf of her leg as she looks toward me. "Let's be seeing you, Abdul Mawla"—and she disappears in the bend of the road. Her voice carries across the valley: "We make divination, we tell fortunes in seashells. All is revealed."

She disappears and there remains in my heart her voice and the promise that I shall see her. After the meal for breaking the fast, and drinking tea, and performing the prayer, I light the lantern. When its light is dispersed, my grandfather is delighted and he gazes at the splendor of colors spread out on the ground. I push the gate of the fence and go out into the lane.

I hear my uncle's voice warning me, "Take care of the lantern."

The lane was crowded with children and a gathering of young girls. In the houses they were busy with making pastries for the Feast, and the café radio blared out religious formulas and the glorification of God.

Seeing my lantern, the children gathered around me. They walked along behind me, their shadows falling on the ground. We went up to where the tomb of Abu Hussein stands on the canal.

"There's Sidi Abu Hussein," I shouted.

The wind roared in the high branches.

"My mother says his secret powers are fantastic and that he has performed miracles."

"And he has done favors and miracles for the whole village."

"And he sets the clouds in motion so that the rain falls."

"It's God who does that, you ignorant thing. And it's God who will raise you up on the Day of Final Judgment so that you and your father go to Hell and my grandfather and I go to Heaven."

The children laughed and looked at the lantern, whose light had grown dim. Shafika said, "The candle spluttered and the light's gone out."

"Tomorrow you'll buy a candle, Abdul Mawla, and you'll give light to the lantern."

"Tomorrow's the night of the twenty-seventh, the Night of Power."

The Night of Power, which is to say that tomorrow celestial light will be opened, prayers will be answered, and we'll go to the hill of the gypsies. I mentioned this to the children and they answered in one voice, "The hill of the gypsies? Not likely!"

They were silent, then quickly rejoined, "And why not? We'll go."

In the morning I said to my father, "Give me five piasters." And when he asked me "Why?" I said to him, "To buy a candle." He shouted at me, "And what about yesterday's candle?" I said to him, "It's finished."

Again he barked, "So, you son of your mother, you'll be wanting five piasters every day." I said, "Father, tonight's the Night of Power, and I must give light to the lantern."

My father raised the head of the ax and I screamed. I backed away and my foot sank into the mud of the cattle-pen, and I noticed the baby calf sucking at the teat of its restless mother, which was turning around on itself. I heard my grandfather's voice near the door saying to my father, "What's wrong with you?" and I heard my father reply, "By God, Father, you've brought us a real headache—he wants a candle."

He unfolded his old brown purse and undid the buttons. I could hear the click of the buttons as they were opened, and I was full of happiness. No sooner did I see the five-piaster piece than I grasped hold of His Majesty the King and heard my father shout, "That's how you'll spoil him." Then I went around all the village shops asking for a candle, from the river lane to the other side, and from the lowland right up to Marees's land. And I shouted inwardly, "What a lousy day!"

I arrived at the house shaking, and screamed at my mother, "I want a candle," and I kicked up the dust and threw a stone at the window of the upper floor. My mother stopped kneading the dough and bawled at me, "And what's got into you, Abdul Mawla? Calm down. Where do you think we'll get you a candle from?"

My uncle Ahmed shouted at me, "The devil take you, you never finish asking for things. Go up to the room on the roof and you'll find a small tin lamp, just the size of the lantern. Clean it and fix a wick in it, then fill it with oil and give us a bit of peace from your crazy idea."

I stopped crying and went up to my uncle and said to him, "And this lamp, where is it, Uncle?" He answered me, "Up above—in the window to the right of the door as you enter."

I rushed up the stairs and opened the door of the room on the roof. I searched on the windowsill and came across the lamp. I found it to be old, knocked about until it was the size of a large frog. It was covered with rust and dust from being left there so long, lurking amid wooden spoons, a ball of string, old seals bearing names that had long disappeared, and contracts for land dated ages ago. I actually found a dagger with a gleaming blade inside a leather scabbard. I whispered to myself, "A dagger and a lantern."

I gathered up bolls of cotton and a complete wick, and I washed the lamp with mud and dust, and scoured it with petrol, then filled it and fitted the wick.

At night I lit the lantern and gathered the children behind me, and we hurried off to where the hill of the gypsies was. We left the village behind us and plunged into the darkness by the light of the lantern. I saw a small quantity of smoke rising up from the burning wick and blackening the sides.

We passed by the shack of Umm Bilal, that good-for-nothing woman who had no relatives. I saw her standing by her shack close to the water pump. I greeted her and she returned my greeting and asked, "Where are you off to, children?" and we replied in one voice, "To the hill of the gypsies." The woman laughed in a voice that scared us. Waving her hand at us, she called out, "The hill of the gypsies? You, you undersized, worthless lot. Go back, you naughty boys. You're not up to gypsies. If you go there they'll kidnap you and castrate you like goats. They'll open up your stomachs and take out your intestines, then fill them with salt, embalm you, and hang you up at the doors of their tents."

We were frightened, and our feet were rooted to the ground. The night around us seemed to stretch away. Said Badr made off, with Madi behind him, and they went back home.

We hastened on, penetrating deep into the night. As we walked, the light dwindled; the flame was imprisoned within the layer of soot that covered the colored glass.

A wind blew up and the trees shook. From afar, from among the graves, rose the howling of a wolf. Stars twinkled in the sky. Our voices were held captive as we clasped hands in fear.

"The worst is over, boys," I said. "The hill's close by."

I heard my voice but no reply.

The lantern's wick quivered and went out. Darkness as black as kohl descended. Shafika wept and called out, "I'm frightened."

I raised the lantern and said to them, "God will cast celestial light upon the ground."

"I want to go back."

"I shall ask of God to lengthen my grandfather's life. What will you ask of Him, Shafika?"

"I'm going home," cried out Othman, the youngest of us, and pleaded with Mongi: "Come back with me, Mongi—my mother will kill me."

The children left me and hurried back toward the village. I went on alone to my destination. In my right hand I held my lantern, whose colors had disappeared. I whispered to myself, "I'll go on by myself even if the earth be filled with devils"—and when I mentioned the devils my whole body shuddered.

The fields closed in on me and I saw the trees stretching out their branches toward me, and I heard a rustling within the alfalfa grass. I took courage and said to myself, "The devils are imprisoned in Ramadan. Calm yourself." The voice of a curlew came to me, as though saying, "Sovereignty is Yours. Sovereignty is Yours." Relaxing, I said to myself, "It is I who am wrong, I was misled by the light of the lantern going out, and that which was ordained for me"— and I walked on, following in the footsteps of the light from the stars.

I wanted to return but it was no longer possible. From afar I heard the beating of drums carried by the wind. I noticed a crescent moon, like a slice of watermelon, withdrawing into the sky. I whispered, "The hill's far away and the moon is no guide."

The hill came into view, tattooed with a few trees scattered on the sides. Three tents were illuminated by lamps attached to posts, palpitating and revealing hair tents huddled up close together.

I went up the hill. When I felt tired I sat down on a stone.

I saw them forming a circle and beating on drums and singing to the music of a flute and a reed pipe. The tune wafted to me, intimate and friendly.

I drew closer and saw the Mawawi, the chief of the gypsies, standing under the large lamp. When I looked closely I found that he had braided locks and in his left ear a silver earring, from which dangled small bells. When he raised his hands I saw that he wore on his fingers rings with bezels in the form of scarabs. Above his eyes the brows met, delineating the eyes of a hawk, while his teeth were capped with golden crowns and sparkled in the light of the gypsy fire whenever he laughed.

A gypsy of short stature moved to poke the fire with an iron prong and it blazed up. Another man had a snake, with raised head, curled about his arm; it bared its fangs and stared about it with unblinking eyes. A small monkey stood silently on his shoulder, its face expressing the wisdom found in old men.

I grew tired of looking and of my apprehensions. It was as though I had nodded off. Had I been overcome by sleep? Or had the fire, the thumping of the drums, and the smiling Mawawi cast a spell over me as I saw the celestial light opening out and winged angels descending and roaming around in the place, with the perfumes of paradise being diffused? I said to myself, "I'll pray for my grandfather. On the Night of Power no prayer is left unanswered"—and I saw a gypsy greeting the angels with drums, while the Mawawi pushed his way into the circle of gypsies, taking the hand of a gypsy girl of comely face and sleek figure, clothed in a silk dress, her waist drawn in with a green belt, an end of which hung down to her thigh. She had taken up a position in the middle of the circle and had begun to dance to the rhythm of the drum. Behind her there were opened up before me gateways to flowering gardens in which the angels still circled.

"Galeela. Galeela," I called out and the Mawawi became aware of my presence. He approached me. "You came?" he said, smiling. "Ah," I said.

He drew me by the hand and I threw myself down on my back on a table. He placed his right hand on my chest and the woman with the tattoo and the crescent earrings brought the big cast-iron bowl, with the steam rising from the warm water. I whispered, "Galeela." The Mawawi asked for rosewater, ginger, saffron, camphor, and white sandalwood, and he dissolved them in the water. I heard his voice mumbling, "The letter is the origin of speech, and the Throne stands on the letter"—and I did not understand.

When I inhaled the odor of the scent, I closed my eyes and said, "Perfume." I saw him opening his knife and putting a mark on my chest, and my alarm increased. He said, "Don't be frightened," and he cleaved my chest and I groaned. Then I heard them intoning, "A speedy recovery."

I saw my heart that had been plucked out throbbing in the palm of his hand. Blood flowed from it. I heard him calling to me, "Here you are seeing your own heart." I tried to stand up, but he stopped me. He said, "Guard your secret." I said, "I'm thirsty," and he said to them, "Give him something to drink."

He placed my heart in a container and its blood floated on the water. He washed it and cleaned it and wrote letters and words on it with a reed pen, and when I asked him what he was writing he replied that he knew what he was doing.

The beating of the drums and the sounds of the flute and the reed pipe continued. Moths made their appearance above the gypsy fire, and the hill was illuminated by a heavenly resplendence.

He placed my heart in my chest and the stars that I would track until the end of my life were scattered about. I said to my grandfather, who was wearing a colored loincloth and a vast turban on his head, and clasping a scepter in his hand, "Look, Grandpa, they are my stars." But he did not look. "Debility," he said, "and long traveling is the heart's punishment." Then he placed some dates in my hand and said, before his face disappeared, "Satisfy your hunger."

The Mawawi shook me and asked me my name. Caught unawares, I forgot my name. The gypsy girl answered, "Abdul Mawla," and the Mawawi said, "You'd gone a long way away, Abdul Mawla," and he put a candle in the lantern after washing it, and once again the colored lights of the lantern came back. He said to me, "Be careful of the stones and the runnels across the pathways. Go to your right at the next bend and you'll reach the village at daybreak."

I went down the slope of the hill and walked between the cypresses and the eucalyptus trees, inhaling the night smell of perfume and hearing the sound of singing, while to my right there gushed forth a flow of running water.

Translated by Denys Johnson-Davies

Ghassan Kanafani
(1936–72)
PALESTINE

Ghassan Kanafani was born in Acre, Palestine, and was killed in Beirut when his car was booby-trapped. Before moving to Beirut, where he worked as spokesman for the Popular Front for the Liberation of Palestine, he taught and worked as a journalist in Damascus and Kuwait. Though deeply involved in politics, he was also devoted to literature, publishing five novels and five collections of stories, as well as studies of Palestinian literature. He is best known for *Men in the Sun*, a short novel about refugees from Palestine who seek to make a new life in Kuwait. The second selection below is an excerpt from the novel, a scene in which the refugees are hiding, in the blistering heat, inside an empty water tank, hoping to be smuggled across the border.

The Slave Fort

Had he not been so sadly shabby one would have said of him that he was a poet. The site he had chosen for his humble hut of wood and beaten-out jerry cans was truly magnificent; right by the threshold the might of the sea flowed under the feet of the sharp rocks with a deep-throated, unvarying sound. His face was gaunt, his beard white though streaked with a few black hairs, his eyes hollow under bushy brows; his cheekbones protruded like two rocks that had come to rest either side of the large projection that was his nose.

Why had we gone to that place? I don't remember now. In our small car we had followed a rough, miry, and featureless road. We had been going for more than three hours when Thabit pointed through the window and gave a piercing shout:

"There's the Slave Fort."

This Slave Fort was a large rock the base of which had been eaten away by the waves so that it resembled the wing of a giant bird, its head curled in the sand, its wing outstretched above the clamour of the sea.

"Why did they call it 'The Slave Fort'?"

"I don't know. Perhaps there was some historical incident which gave it the name. Do you see that hut?"

And once again Thabit pointed, this time towards the small hut lying in the shadow of the gigantic rock. He turned off the engine and we got out of the car.

"They say that a half-mad old man lives in it."

"What does he do with himself in this waste on his own?"

"What any half-mad old man would do."

From afar we saw the old man squatting on his heels at the entrance to his hut, his head clasped in his hands, staring out to sea.

"Don't you think there must be some special story about this old man? Why do you insist he's half-mad?"

"I don't know, that's what I heard."

Thabit, having arrived at the spot of his choice, leveled the sand, threw down the bottles of water, took out the food from the bag, and seated himself.

"They say he was the father of four boys who struck it lucky and are now among the richest people in the district."

"And then?"

"The sons quarreled about who should provide a home for the father. Each wife wanted her own way in the matter and the whole thing ended with the old man making his escape and settling down here."

"It's a common enough story and shouldn't have turned the old man half-mad."

Thabit looked at me uncomprehendingly, then lit the small heap of wood he had arranged, and poured water into the metal water-jug and set it on the fire.

"The important thing in the story is to agree about whether his flight was a product of his mad half or his sane half."

"There he is, only a few yards away—why not go over and ask him?"

Thabit blew at the fire, then began rubbing his eyes as he sat up straight, resting his body on his knees.

"I can't bear the idea which the sight of him awakens in me."

"What idea?"

"That the man should spend seventy years of his life so austerely, that he should work, exert himself, existing day after day and hour after hour, that for seventy long years he should gain his daily bread from the sweat of his brow, that he should live through his day in the hope of a better tomorrow, that for seventy whole years he should go to sleep each night—and for what? So that he should, at the last, spend the rest of his life cast out like a dog, alone, sitting like this. Look at him—he's like some polar animal that has lost its fur. Can you believe that a man can live seventy years to attain to this? I can't stomach it."

Once again he stared at us; then, spreading out the palms of his hands, he continued his tirade:

"Just imagine! Seventy useless, meaningless years. Imagine walking for seventy years along the same road; the same directions, the same boundaries, the same horizons, the same everything. It's unbearable!"

"No doubt the old man would differ with you in your point of view. Maybe he believes that he has reached an end which is distinct from his life. Maybe he wanted just such an end. Why not ask him?"

We got up to go to him. When we came to where he was he raised his eyes, coldly returned our greeting and invited us to sit down.

Through the half-open door we could see the inside of the hut; the threadbare mattress in one corner, while in the opposite one was a square rock on which lay a heap of unopened oyster shells. For a while silence reigned; it was then broken by the old man's feeble voice asking:

"Do you want oyster shells? I sell oyster shells."

As we had no reply to make to him, Thabit enquired:

"Do you find them yourself?"

"I wait for low tide so as to look for them far out. I gather them up and sell them to those who hope to find pearls in them."

We stared at each other. Presently Thabit put the question that had been exercising all our minds:

"Why don't you yourself try to find pearls inside these shells?"

"I?"

He uttered the word as though becoming aware for the first time that he actually existed, or as though the idea had never previously occurred to him. He then shook his head and kept his silence.

"How much do you sell a heap for?"

"Cheaply—for a loaf or two."

"They're small shells and certainly won't contain pearls."

The old man looked at us with lusterless eyes under bushy brows.

"What do you know about shells?" he demanded sharply. "Who's to tell whether or not you'll find a pearl?" and as though afraid that if he were to be carried away still further he might lose the deal, he relapsed into silence.

"And can you tell?"

"No, no one can tell," and he began toying with a shell which lay in front of him, pretending to be unaware of our presence.

"All right, we'll buy a heap."

The old man turned round and pointed to the heap arrayed on the square rock.

"Bring two loaves," he said, a concealed ring of joy in his voice, "and you can take that heap."

On returning to our place bearing the heap of shells, our argument broke out afresh.

"I consider those eyes can only be those of a madman. If not, why doesn't he open the shells himself in the hope of finding some pearls?"

"Perhaps he's fed up with trying and prefers to turn spectator and make money."

It took us half the day before we had opened all the shells. We piled the gelatinous insides of the empty shells around us, then burst into laughter at our madness.

In the afternoon Thabit suggested to me that I should take a cup of strong tea to the old man in the hope that it might bring a little joy to his heart.

As I was on my way over to him a slight feeling of fear stirred within me. However, he invited me to sit down and began sipping at his tea with relish.

"Did you find anything in the shells?"

"No, we found nothing—you fooled us."

He shook his head sadly and took another sip.

"To the extent of two loaves!" he said, as though talking to himself, and once again shook his head. Then, suddenly, he glanced at me and explained sharply:

"Were these shells your life—I mean, were each shell to represent a year of your life and you opened them one by one and found them empty, would you have been as sad as you are about losing a couple of loaves?"

He began to shake all over and at that moment I was convinced that I was in the presence of someone who certainly was mad. His eyes, under their bushy brows, gave out a sharp and unnatural brightness, while the dust from his ragged clothes played in the afternoon sun. I could find not a word to say. When I attempted to rise to my feet he took hold of my wrist and his frail hand was strong and convulsive. Then I heard him say:

"Don't be afraid—I am not mad, as you believe. Sit down, I want to tell you something: the happiest moments of my day are when I can watch disappointment of this kind."

I reseated myself, feeling somewhat calmer.

In the meantime, he began to gaze out at the horizon, seemingly unaware of my presence, as though he had not, a moment ago, invited me to sit down. Then he turned to me.

"I knew you wouldn't find anything. These oysters are still young and therefore can't contain the seed of a pearl. I wanted to know, though."

Again he was silent and stared out to sea. Then, as though speaking to himself, he said:

"The ebb tide will start early tonight and I must be off to gather shells. Tomorrow other men will be coming."

Overcome by bewilderment, I rose to my feet. The Slave Fort stood out darkly against the light of the setting sun. My friends were drinking tea around the heaps of empty shells as the old man began running after the receding water, bending down from time to time to pick up the shells left behind.

Translated by Denys Johnson-Davies

FROM Men in the Sun

The lorry, a small world, black as night, made its way across the desert like a heavy drop of oil on a burning sheet of tin. The sun hung high above their heads, round, blazing, and blindingly bright. None of them bothered to dry their sweat any longer. Assad spread his shirt over his head, bent his legs, and let the sun roast him without resistance. Marwan leaned his head on Abu Qais's shoulder and closed his eyes. Abu Qais stared at the road, tightly closing his lips under his thick gray moustache.

None of the four wanted to talk anymore, not only because they were exhausted by their efforts, but because each one was swallowed up in his own thoughts. The huge lorry was carrying them along the road, together with their dreams, their families, their hopes and ambitions, their misery and despair, their strength and weakness, their past and future, as if it were pushing against the immense door to a new, unknown destiny, and all eyes were fixed on the door's surface as though bound to it by invisible threads.

We'll be able to send Qais to school and buy one or two olive shoots. Perhaps we'll build a cottage to live in, which will be ours. I'm an old man; I may arrive or I may not. And do you think that the life you lead here is better than death? Why don't you try, as we do? Why don't you get up off that cushion and set out through God's world in search of a living? Will you spend the whole of your life eating the flour ration for one kilo of which you sacrifice all your honor at the doors of officials?

The lorry traveled on over the burning earth, its engine roaring remorselessly.

Shafiqa is an innocent woman. She was an adolescent when a mortar bomb smashed her leg and the doctors amputated it from the top of the thigh. And his mother didn't like anyone to talk about his father. Zakaria has gone. There, in Kuwait, you'll find everything out. You'll learn everything. You're still a boy, and you know no more of life than a babe in arms knows of its house. School teaches nothing. It only teaches laziness. So leave it and plunge into the frying pan with the rest of humanity.

The lorry traveled on over the burning earth, its engine roaring with an intolerable noise.

Perhaps it was buried in the ground, the bomb he trod on as he was running; or maybe it was thrown in front of him by a man hidden in a nearby ditch. None of that is important now. His legs were suspended in the air and his shoulders were still on the comfortable white bed, and the terrible pain was still plunging between his thighs. There was a woman there, helping the doctors. Whenever he remembered it, his face was suffused with shame. And what good did patriotism do you? You spend your life in an adventure, and now you are incapable of sleeping with a woman! And what good did you do? Let the dead bury their dead. I only want more money now, more money.

The lorry traveled on over the burning earth, its engine roaring loudly.

The policeman pushed him in front of the officer, who said to him: "You think you're a hero when the donkeys carry you on their shoulders, demonstrating in the street." He spat in his face, but

Assad didn't move as the saliva ran slowly down his forehead and gathered on the tip of his nose in a nasty viscous mess. They led him out, and when he was in the corridor he heard the policeman who was grasping his shoulder say in a low voice: "Damn this uniform!" Then he let him go, and Assad ran off. His uncle, wishing to marry him off to his daughter, wanted him to make a start in life. Otherwise he would never have collected fifty dinars in the whole of his life.

The lorry traveled on over the burning earth, its roaring engine a gigantic mouth devouring the road.

The sun in the middle of the sky traced a broad dome of white flame over the desert, and the trail of dust reflected an almost blinding glare. They used to be told that someone wasn't coming back from Kuwait because he'd died; he'd been killed by sunstroke. He'd been driving his shovel into the earth when he fell onto one knee and then on both. And then what? He was killed by sunstroke. Do you want him buried here or there? That was all, sunstroke. It was quite right. Who called it "sunstroke"? Wasn't he a genius? This desert was like a giant in hiding, flogging their heads with whips of fire and boiling pitch. But could the sun kill them and all the stench imprisoned in their breasts? The thoughts seemed to run from one head to another, laden with the same suspicions, for their eyes suddenly met. Abul Khaizuran looked at Marwan and then at Abu Qais, whom he found staring at him. He tried to smile, and failed, so he wiped the sweat from his forehead with his sleeve, murmuring:

"This is the Hell that I have heard of."

"God's Hell?"

"Yes."

Abul Khaizuran reached out his hand and turned off the engine; then he slowly got down, followed by Marwan and Abu Qais, while Assad remained perched above them.

Abul Khaizuran sat in the shade of the lorry and lit a cigarette. He said in a low voice:

"Let's rest a little before we begin the performance again."

Abu Qais asked:

"Why didn't you set out with us yesterday evening so that we would be saved by the cool of the night from all this trouble?"

Without raising his eyes from the ground, Abul Khaizuran replied:

"The road between Safwan and Mutlaa is full of patrols at night. During the day no patrol can run the risk of making a reconnaissance in heat like this."

Marwan remarked:

"If your lorry is sacrosanct and never searched, why can't we stay outside that terrible prison?"

Abul Khaizuran replied sharply:

"Don't be silly. Are you so afraid of spending five or six minutes inside? We've done more than half the journey, and only the easiest part is left." He stood up, went over to the water skin hanging outside the door, and opened it. "I'll put on a splendid lunch for you when we arrive. I'll have two chickens killed . . ." He raised the water skin and poured the water into his mouth until it began to trickle out at the corners onto his chin and his wet shirt. When he had quenched his thirst he poured the rest of the contents over his head, letting the water run down over his forehead, neck, and chest, which gave him an extraordinary appearance. He hung the water bottle outside the door again, spread his big hands and cried:

"Come on, you've learned the art well. What time is it now? Half past eleven. Think, in seven minutes at the outside I'll open the cover for you. Remember that, half past eleven."

Marwan looked at his watch and nodded. He tried to say something but it was beyond him, so he took a few steps over to the iron ladder and began to climb it.

Assad rolled up his shirt and plunged into the opening. Marwan hesitated a little and then followed him, leaning with his stomach on the edge and then skillfully sliding down with a sharp movement. Abu Qais shook his head, saying: "Seven minutes?"

"At the outside!"

Abul Khaizuran patted Abu Qais on the shoulder and looked straight into his eyes. They stood there together streaming with sweat, neither of them able to speak.

Abu Qais climbed the ladder with firm steps, and let his legs down through the opening. The two younger men helped him down.

Abul Khaizuran closed the cover and turned the curved metal handle twice before jumping quickly down and rushing to his seat.

Only a minute and a half later he had driven his lorry through the big open gate in the barbed-wire fence round the post of Mutlaa. He brought it to a stop in front of the wide steps leading to the tiled one-story building flanked on both sides by small rooms with low, closed windows. Opposite it were a few stalls selling food, and the noise of air conditioners filled the air.

There were only one or two cars parked waiting at the edge of the big square. The silence hung heavy and unbroken, except for the hum of the air conditioners attached to all the windows looking out onto the square. Only one soldier was standing in a small wooden hut beside the side flight of steps.

Abul Khaizuran hurried up the steps and made for the third room on the right. Immediately he opened the door and went in; he felt, from the glances directed at him by the officials, that something was going to happen. But he didn't pause, pushing his papers in front of the fat official sitting in the center of the room.

"Aha! Abu Khaizurana!" shouted the official, as he slid the papers to one side with deliberate carelessness, and crossed his arms on the metal desk. "Where have you been all this time?"

Abul Khaizuran panted:

"In Basra."

"Haj Rida asked after you more than six times."

"The lorry had broken down."

The three officials in the room broke into loud laughter and Abu Khaizuran turned round, at a loss. Then he fixed his eyes on the fat man's face.

"What is it that amuses you this morning?"

The three officials exchanged glances and then burst out laughing again. Abul Khaizuran said tensely, shuffling from one foot to the other:

"Now, Abu Baqir, I've no time for jokes. Please . . ."

Stretching out his hand he moved the papers closer in front of the official, but again Abu Baqir pushed them away to the edge of the desk, folded his arms and smiled wickedly.

"Haj Rida asked about you six times."

"I told you, the lorry was not working. And Haj Rida and I can come to an understanding when we meet. Please sign the papers. I'm in a hurry."

He slid the papers closer again, but once more Abu Baqir pushed them away.

"Your lorry wasn't working?"

"Yes. Please! I'm in a hurry."

The three officials looked at one another and quietly gave a knowing laugh. The desk of one of them was completely bare except for a small glass of tea; the other had stopped working to follow what was happening.

The fat man called Abu Baqir said, belching:

"Now, be sensible, Abu Khaizurana. Why do you hurry your journey in terrible weather like this? The room here's cool, and I'll order you a glass of tea. So enjoy the comfort."

Abul Khaizuran picked up the papers, took the pen lying in front of Abu Baqir and went round the table to stand beside him. He pushed the pen towards him, nudging his shoulder with his arm.

"I'll spend an hour sitting with you when I come back, but now let me leave, for Baqir's sake and Baqir's mother's sake. Here!"

Abu Baqir, however, did not move his hand but continued to stare stupidly at the driver, on the point of bursting out laughing again.

"Ah, you devil, Abu Khaizurana! Why don't you remember that you are in a hurry when you are in Basra? Eh?"

"I told you, the lorry was in the garage."

Again he pushed the pen towards Abu Baqir, but he didn't move.

"Don't lie, Abu Khaizurana, don't lie! Haj Rida has told us the story from A to Z."

"What story?"

They all exchanged glances, as Abul Khaizuran's face turned white with terror, and the pen began to tremble in his hand.

"The story of that dancer. What's her name, Ali?"

From the other side of the empty desk, Ali answered:

"Kawkab."

Abu Baqir hit his desk with his hand and gave a broad smile.

"Kawkab. Kawkab. Abu Khaizurana, you devil. Why don't you tell us what you get up to in Basra? You make out to us that you are a decent, well-behaved fellow, and then you go to Basra and commit mortal sins with that dancer, Kawkab. Yes, Kawkab, that's the name."

"What's all this rubbish about Kawkab? Let me go before Haj Rida gives me the sack."

Abu Baqir replied:

"Impossible. Tell us about this dancer. The Haj knows the whole story and he's told it to us. Come on."

"If Haj Rida's told it to you, why do you want me to tell it again?"

Abu Baqir stood up and gave a bull-like roar.

"Ah! So it's true. It's a true story." He walked round the desk and came to the middle of the room. The story of depravity had excited him. He had thought about it day and night, endowing it with all the obscenity created by his long, tormenting deprivation. The idea that a friend of his had slept with a prostitute was exciting, and worth all those dreams.

"You go to Basra and make out that the lorry isn't working, and then you spend the happiest nights of your life with Kawkab. Good heavens, Abu Khaizurana! Good heavens, you devil! But tell us how she has shown her love for you. Haj Rida says that she loves you so much that she spends her money on you and gives you checks. Ah, Abu Khaizurana, you devil!"

He came up to Abul Khaizuran, his face red. Obviously, he'd enjoyed himself thinking about the story as Haj Rida had told it to him over the telephone. He leaned over and whispered hoarsely in his ear:

"Is it your virility? Or aren't there many men about?"

Abul Khaizuran laughed hysterically and shoved the papers at Abu Baqir's chest. He picked up the pen and began signing them automatically, shaking with suppressed laughter. But when Abul Khaizuran stretched out his hand to take them, Abu Baqir hid them behind his back, warding off Abul Khaizuran with his other arm.

"Next time I'll go with you to Basra. Agreed? You'll introduce me to this Kawkab. Haj Rida says she's really beautiful."

Abul Khaizuran said in a trembling voice as he stretched out his arm, trying to reach the papers:

"I agree."

"On your honor?"

"On my honor."

Abu Baqir collapsed into renewed laughter, shaking his round head as he went back to his desk, while Abul Khaizuran rushed outside with his papers, pursued by Abu Baqir's voice:

"You devil, Abu Khaizurana! He's deceived us for two years, but now he's been shown up. Ah, you devil, Abu Khaizurana!"

Abul Khaizuran burst into the other room, looking at his watch. A quarter to twelve. The signing of the other papers didn't take more than a minute. When he shut the door after him the heat lashed him again, but he took no notice, jumping down the wide steps two at a time until he stood in front of his lorry. He looked at the tank for a moment and he had the impression that the metal was about to melt under that fearful sun. The engine responded to the first touch, and he instantly closed the door, not waving to the guard. The road now was completely level and he had a minute or a minute and a half before he could round the first bend, hiding him from the post. He was forced to slow down a little when he met a large lorry, but then he put his foot down till the vehicle was going at top speed. When he reached the bend the wheels set up a screech like a howl and almost touched the sand verge as they made their enormous turn. There was nothing in his mind but terror, and he thought he would collapse over his steering wheel in a faint. The wheel was hot and he felt it scorch his hard hands, but he didn't slacken his hold on it. The leather seat burned under him and the glass windscreen was dusty and blazed with the sun's glare.

A loud hiss came from the wheels as though they were flaying the asphalt. Did you have to talk so much rubbish, Abu Baqir? Did you have to spew up all your filth onto my face and theirs? The curse of almighty God be upon you. The curse of almighty God, who doesn't exist anywhere, be visited upon you, Abu Baqir! And on you, Haj Rida, you liar! A dancer? Kawkab? God damn you all!

He stopped the lorry sharply, and climbed over the wheel to the roof of the tank. When his hands touched the metal roof he felt them burn, and couldn't keep them there. He moved them away and leaned his elbows, in their sleeves, on the metal roof, crawling to the angular lock. He took hold of it with a corner of his blue shirt and turned it, so that it burst open and the rusty metal disk stood vertical over its hinge.

As he let go of the disk he caught sight of the heads of the watch on his wrist. They pointed to nine minutes to twelve. The round glass had cracked into little pieces. The uncovered opening yawned empty for a moment. Abul Khaizuran's face, drawn to it, twitched compulsively, his lower lip trembling as he panted for breath, overcome with terror. A drop of sweat from his forehead fell onto the metal roof of the tank and immediately dried. He put his hands on his knees, bent his soaked back until his face was over the black hole, and shouted in a dry, grating voice:

"Assad!"

The sound reverberated in the tank and almost pierced his eardrums as it came back to him. Before the echo of the rumble that his first cry had set up had died away, he shouted again:

"Hey there!"

He put two firm hands on the edge of the opening and, supporting himself on his strong arms, slid down inside the tank. It was very dark there, and at first he couldn't make out anything, but when he moved his body away from the opening a circle of yellow light fell into the depths and showed a chest covered with thick gray hair that began to shine brightly as though coated with tin. Abul Khaizuran bent to put his ear to the damp gray hair. The body was cold and still. Stretching out his hand, he felt his way to the back of the tank. The other body was still holding on to the metal support. He tried to find the head but could only feel the wet shoulders; then he made out the head, bowed on the chest. When his hand touched the face, it fell into a mouth open as wide as it could go.

Abul Khaizuran had a choking sensation. His body had begun to run with sweat at such an amazing rate that he felt he was coated in thick oil, and he couldn't tell whether he was trembling because of this oil covering his chest and back or whether it was caused by fear. Bending down, he felt his way to the opening, and when he put his head through it, Marwan's face came into his mind for some reason, and wouldn't go away. He felt the face take possession of him from within, like a fresco shimmering on a wall, so he started to shake his head violently as he slipped down from the opening and the merciless sun burned it. He stood for a moment breathing in fresh air. He couldn't think of anything. Marwan's face had surged up to take complete possession of his mind, like a spring that bursts from the earth and sends its water high into the air. When he reached his seat he remembered Abu Qais, whose shirt was still lying on the seat beside him. He took it in his long fingers and threw it far away. He switched on the lorry's motor and it began to roar again, as the lorry made its slow, majestic way down the slope.

He turned round to look through the small, wire-netted window, and saw the round disk open, standing straight over its hinge, with its inside corroded with rust. Suddenly the metal disk disappeared behind drops of salt water, which filled his eyes. He had a headache and vertigo such as he had never felt before. Were those salty drops tears, or sweat running from his burning forehead?

Translated by Hilary Kilpatrick

Sahar Khalifeh
(b. 1941)

PALESTINE

Sahar Khalifeh was born in the West Bank city of Nablus. A
former Fulbright scholar, she holds a B.A. from Bir Zeit
University and a Ph.D. in women's studies and American
literature from the University of Iowa. She is the director of
the Women's Training and Research Center in Nablus. Two
of her novels, *The Inheritance* and *Wild Thorns*, have been
translated into English. *Wild Thorns*, excerpted here, describes life in the Israeli-occupied West Bank. In the following passage, Usama, a young Palestinian, is returning home
from the Gulf, where he has worked as a translator, to help
with the movement against Israel.

FROM *Wild Thorns*

Usama hid in a dark corner of the street. He unwound the *kufiyya*
from his head and threw it to the ground; looking carefully left and
right, he moved off into the crowd. He felt eyes devouring his face
and imaginary fingers pointing at his hand, which felt as though he
were still gripping a dagger. He ran on to the end of the street. The
patrol cars were coming. He climbed the steps to his uncle's house.
Basil was waiting. Without saying a word, they ran across the open
courtyard and down a passage behind the marble pillars. Basil
moved a stone in the wall, and a secret door opened that led into an
ancient vault.

Basil lit a small flashlight and went down the crumbling steps.
Usama followed him.

"Did anyone recognize you?" Basil asked.

Usama drew a deep breath. A pungent odour of decay was all
about him. Crates of explosives lay along one side of the vault. He

felt their cold wood. "I'm not sure," he answered. "Saafan may have been there."

Basil turned abruptly and shone the flashlight in his cousin's face. "Saafan? That's a disaster! Are you sure?"

"No, I'm not. Come on, let's get moving. We have to hide quickly. We can't take risks. It was probably Saafan. And he must have recognized me. I saw him in the shop once. What's more important is that some of our men are waiting over there. You know what you're supposed to do?"

"Trust God and me," said Basil. "Hani and I will distribute what's necessary. And I know the password."

Usama took him by the shoulders.

"Be careful, Basil," he warned. "This is a serious business. You know the consequences. I won't repeat the advice I gave you earlier. But don't make any decisions without consulting Lina. That's crucial. She's a very solid girl. And she's had lots of experience. Now, let me kiss you goodbye. I may not see you again. Be a man, Basil. Don't trust anyone. Especially the people in this house."

They moved off down the long, cold vault. At the end Basil opened a piece of the wall from the inside and Usama found himself in the ablutions area of the Great Mosque. He emerged along with the worshippers and hired a taxi to take him to a village. Soon he could no longer see the city behind him.

He walked for an hour without stopping, clambering along rough mountain paths, then finally sat down on the edge of a rock. He took off his shoes and sweater, and opened the neck of his shirt.

The sun was setting. The May breezes moved through the cypress and olive groves. He stretched out on the grass, resting his head on a smooth rock. He felt lost, wanted to break down and weep. His eyes swam up into the blue space above him. Shadows of oak trees. The olive trees and umbrella pines that grew deep in the mountains. Grapevines on the slopes.

He raised his hand and stared at it. The same hand that had written poetry about love and peace. And about the sacrificial lamb!

He watched the play of light on the veins of his hand. Amazement.

Confusion. He was sensitive and confused, like many other men. He touched the earth he loved. Yes, but. The time for poetry and dreams of passion was past. And this hand. This very hand! Those two other hands that had covered the shocked face of a little blonde girl. The mother had screamed "Get him!" An unseen hand seemed to grip his heart. Loneliness, isolation, silence. Far away a peasant played his flute while another sang:

> Mountain, greet the plain and the valley.
> Greet the trees that line the flanks of my country.
> Though the enemy harvests our fields,
> I will seed the ground again with my sons.

A mist of poetry seemed to hover above his head. Why are we so moved by songs of loss? Are we a nation of romantics? Well, not any more. Love lying broken at your feet makes your soul a commodity in the market of blood. But I'm here. On this earth, in spite of everything. I'm here. And I'll stay here. Let the leader push me onto the dirtiest plane in any Arab airport and let fire-spitting engines bear me to Lisbon or America or the oil states. Let any force on this earth transport me wherever its mood decides, to any spot as yet unknown in time and space. I'm here. I've returned. To this rock. To this hollow. And this hand, stained with blood, is still a bridge of freedom over a river of pain. Now I raise it, now I let it drop, it's an eagle's wing, swift enough to cut the sound barrier with its edge. My voice thunders; the Katyushas and the napalm roar. May the earth shake when I walk. May unheeding eyes watch me if I sleep. I'm moving towards the light along the dark paths of anger.

He laced up his shoes and walked away, whistling cheerfully.

Translated by Trevor Le Gassick and Elizabeth Fernea

Edwar al-Kharrat
(b. 1926)

EGYPT

Edwar al-Kharrat was born in Alexandria. For some years he worked as the deputy secretary-general of the Afro-Asian Writers' Association. His first book, a collection of stories, was published at his own expense in 1959. Since then he has written prolifically and has been awarded a number of prizes for his contribution to Arabic literature. He has also worked on translations from English and French. The events of his two recent novels, *The City of Saffron* and *Girls of Alexandria*, take place in the city of his birth, which has inspired much great literature. Al-Kharrat's novel *Rama and the Dragon* was awarded the Naguib Mahfouz Medal for Literature in 1999, which led to its translation into English. The increasing difficulty of much of his writing has meant that he has not been as widely translated as he deserves.

FROM *Rama and the Dragon*

Water drops fall from the long, rusty wound in the stone of the centuries-old statue. The murmuring water flows cheerfully, without quivering, under the light poured from a strong, high-pitched, firmly radiant lamp. The iron surrounding the fountain is low, circular, presenting an island in a street gushing with two streams of shiny cars—one in each direction—hurrying with their noisy, exploding, fluctuating emissions.

The new friends, Mikhail and Rama, having come out of the cinema, are overlooking the statue from behind a broad windowpane inside a large modern restaurant practically without customers. Their comfortable seats were mounted with ribbed, black plastic resembling leather, Formica armrests dappled with splendid cunning to imitate wood. The hollow, round aluminum, resembling commonplace silver, emits hushed echoes whenever a leg accidentally grazes it.

They have been to the cinema. Her warm and subdued whispering—unfolding vague images that possess distinctly erotic features—draws the side of her face, radiant with captivating appeal, near to his eyes. He glances at her as if she were part of the film itself, his arm in his short-sleeve shirt touching her soft, bare arm whose fullness increases as she presses it on the rough woolly armrest cover. Between them stands a kind of physical affection, a warm, undeclared sensual understanding.

After the disappearance of the last traffic wave over the crosswalks used by the nocturnal crowds and the dispersal of the last show viewers gathered in their intimate circles, the lit city became theirs, as if its empty, clean, wide streets were welcoming avenues into the mind for a gentle night wind that promised unlimited good things. Having left the restaurant they passed an endless series of dazzling ponds of light, gravely empty and quiet, choosing to amble toward islands of still shades with tree leaves fluttering harmoniously.

He said to her: I have known streets of many cities in almost all hours of day and night. There is nothing more beautiful than empty streets at night with the city lamps lighting them in a practically useless way. Public lights fall on buildings and on the black asphalt—vast, shiny, free—which can be crossed and walked on without penalty. Despite the heaving danger and the unknown, the city seems as if healed forever of hidden evil and violence, from the wrangles of a herd of mechanical and electrical armors gushing without stopping. How beautiful is this city!

Just before their walk, they had ordered hamburgers and beer; she said she liked beer. They ate with an appetite for everything. She spoke spontaneously and heatedly about her fear of death, though not her own. She said that death was horrible and unimaginable. He said: no one ever believes inside himself that he will die. Death is simply an abstraction, something that happens to others, and does not happen to me at all. It is the only thing that no one knows, for I think that even at the very unimaginable moment of loss of consciousness, no one knows, no one believes that he will die, nor would he know the meaning of death even if he knew and believed that it would happen. For a person remains convinced, in-tuitively certain, that he will live, until he crosses the boundaries. And he is right, for even in crossing he lives. After that no con-sciousness, nothing. Yes, death is the only thing that can never be known, neither before nor after. What is known about it are things related to it, associated with it, that precede it or surround it, but not the reality itself. Death—simply—does not exist.

She said in a bout of strange passion that this was exactly what she had been thinking about all the time without saying it, for no one would believe it or be convinced by it. She said: The frighten-ing thing is the death of a loved person. And she asked: How can someone live if his truly beloved person dies? She said: This is the death that a person feels and knows intimately through a loss that cannot be made up for at all. This is the diffused suffering, gratu-itous, filling the corners of earth and heaven. And she asked: Why? Why? The flowers of such suffering are so thorny.

Her eyes watered. She was swept by terrible fear, provoked, maintained by the fact that her loved ones were still living, that they had not died. She said that she was ready to die for the sake of those she truly loved. She said that she prayed, never knowing whether she was a believer or not, but nevertheless pleading vaguely and daily to a divine power to protect and keep alive those whom she loved.

He said to her: As if you were talking with my voice, expressing what I sense without having given it a form or definition!

Their happiness in this rare, enabling articulation was complete and untarnished. They celebrated in the refreshing, faint glow of the beer mugs, in the light meal, and in the warmth of the sensuous closeness in the cool night air blowing from the open window, open onto the wet statue and fountain—gushing in geometrically intri-cate trajectories: its drizzle radiating on the husky, muscular male body in a challenging position, entrenching his exploding legs in the earth, two tree trunks of undecaying stone.

He saw on her bare arm, as if embroidered on her skin, the trace of the cinema armrest with its rough woolly cover.

She said to him: I always need human warmth, human relations, I cannot stand for any substitute. I can't live in a furnished apartment, day in, day out by myself, cooking on Fridays for the week, washing my pantyhose on Saturdays, going to the hairdresser on Sundays. I am not this kind. I want to meet people, talk and live with them, get out in the world and encounter new types of men. This is why you find me looking for inspection trips in my job, so that I can embark to any place without hesitation.

He said without complaint, without disapproval: As for me, I am a loner. I can—and at times I love to—stay in my room for a week without seeing streetlights.

She said thoughtfully: Yes, that is possible for you. You can be cut off from people.

He said: No, no. I need people badly, especially those I love, even if at a distance. The most important thing is that they are there. Being cut off, like monks are, troubles me and gives me insomnia.

One day, he said to himself: Was her interest in me in the beginning simply to pick up a new type of man? A new naive type that seemed uncontaminated, simply for the hobby of her collection? How does she best get to know new types of men? Is this an accusation of cheapness I'm launching?

He said to himself: Why does the traditional reaction of an Eastern man, of a southern Egyptian, persist in you? Isn't it an outdated and medieval sensibility, no matter what philosophical and contemporary views and positions—existentialism, Marxism—are involved?

It never occurred to him to answer the question, which, in the final analysis, constituted a process: admission of the fact, then the doubting of it, then the admission of it again: an endless cycle.

He said to her: The need for human warmth triggers your many friendships?

She leaned toward him, in the fervor of an opening up between two new friends. The pressure of her breasts on the bra beneath the light blouse was evident. She pushed her face close to his unintentionally, relaxing her bosom on the Formica table next to the empty beer mug on whose lip a slight white foam was attached, and, on the other side the shiny metal box from which white paper napkins come out, also the small ceramic hamburger plate with its brown color and traces of dark red, dry ketchup.

I don't know how to maintain relations with women, she said. There's nothing in common between us. I can't, I really can't, enter into a conversation about fashion, recipes, types of make-up, problems with servants, or gossiping about others. I don't know how to put on half a ton of powders and creams every day, tarnishing or beautifying my face with them. As you can see, I don't use lipstick. There is something masculine in me. They say I am a policeman, an old guard.

He laughed and said: You are sheer femininity.

She said: May God bless you for the compliment.

He said: No, I mean what I said.

After dinner, when having coffee, she said to him: I have an appointment with a Sudanese friend, an exile visiting this country. He phoned me this afternoon and invited me to an unofficial diplomatic soirée. These invitations usually bore me, but I couldn't refuse. I haven't seen him for a while, and he is a dear friend, an elderly gentleman. I ask you for a favor. Kindly take me in a taxi to the Clock Square. You are not so busy, are you? This request humbles me, but I have to say I don't dare take a taxi alone at night.

He said: Is that all? Your wish is my command, my lady, from the bottom of my eyes. I shall apologize and delay my appointment for half an hour.

She said: O my God! You have an appointment? Then no need.

He said: No, no! It is very simple. I'll take you.

No sooner had the taxi moved away with them—in the intimate, private darkness typical of narrow spaces, while he was gazing at the city, with its people and lights disappearing soundlessly behind the windowpane as the engine roared softly with its hushed, internal, mechanical power—than he had stretched his hand to hers at the same time her hand was moving toward his. The fingers touched, clasped firmly. He felt blood rising to his face for the first time in their friendship. Her voice quivered as she called on him pleading and anxious: Mikhail! He said: Rama, what is happening to us? She said: Mikhail, Mikhail, I don't know. This was their first and last mutual confession, then a charged silence fell upon them, pregnant with all possibilities.

She tried to pay for the taxi, but he refused, laughing. The driver hesitated for a moment in front of the two different hands, each extending a large sum. Then as a matter of male solidarity the driver quickly took his money. She said to him: Go back in the same taxi, so you can make it to your appointment. He said: No, I will walk you to your destination and enjoy the air. She said: But your appointment? He said: I have time.

He stepped down, they walked together. She clung to his arm with new familiarity and spontaneity. She said: I'll phone you when I get back. I'll talk to you; at least wish you good night. He pressed her hand as he parted from her and stood watching as she entered a residential building full of quiet windows. He walked aimlessly, a bit distraught as various scenarios filled his head. Under his feet the streets felt like waves. He was plowing their waters, sailing with spread sails pushed by abundant and prosperous wind.

He said to himself: No, she will probably forget or else it will be too late. She will not call tonight. Tomorrow, she will talk and I will hear her story.

It was one in the morning when he went to bed. Exhausted, his senses were yet alert. A lightness and joy fluttered within him. He had not known such feelings for a long time, and as yet they were vague, without content.

Suddenly, in the profound and enclosed silence the telephone rang loudly. He stretched his hand—alarmed, anxious, not fully awake—as if knowing it was she. The light, he discovered, had been left on and shone brightly. With an unimaginable effort he responded with an awkward but alert voice: Hello!

Her voice came to him, unsteady, low, and womanish: Hello, Mikhail! Have I awakened you? He said: Not at all. I was waiting for your telephone call. How was your evening? She said: Horrible. Let's not talk about it. I miss you. He said: I miss you too. He

looked at his watch. It was after 2:30. She said: Mikhail, I need you.
I can't sleep and I want to talk to you. He said: Now? She said: Yes,
now of course. I am in an unbearable state of anxiety and I propose
we talk.

Having had the matter slip out of his hand, he said: Do you
know what the time is? It's 2:30. She said: What does it matter what
time it is? I am resorting to you. He said: I don't know. There are
certain things we have to take into consideration: we are Egyptians,
after all. We'll talk as you wish, surely, but tomorrow morning. He
did not comprehend what was going on. He was frightened. She
said: All I want is to talk together, talk, t-a-l-k, like two mature, ra-
tional persons, one to the other. One person who needs the other. I
need you. That's all. Her voice was shaking—drinking more than
she should have? Sweat oozed from all the pores of his body. His
face blazed. He fell silent, didn't say a thing.

She said: All right, I understand. You are right. No doubt. I am
mistaken.

Her voice began to crack. No resistance could stop its breakdown. She said: Please forgive me—as the tears gathered, amplified,
exploded over the phone—I apologize, I didn't mean—the words
got lost, buried in her unbearable crying bout, in the pain and sense
of rejection and loss, in the night and in the loneliness without
hope of comfort. Sweat continued dripping from him without
stint, without resistance. He said: Don't cry. Please, please, Rama,
don't cry. She said intermittently: I am not crying, I am not crying.
He said: I will be with you in minutes. Please, I am coming. She
could not get her tears to cease flowing, as she said with a tired, surrendered, thankful, and grateful voice: No, no reason to bother
yourself. I understand. I am better now. He said: No, that's enough,
Rama. I'll come right away. I want to come. I wanted to come all
along. She said, while the last hushed sighs were making her voice
present in his own room as her femininity enveloped and embraced
him in its soft, captivating tone: I'll wait for you.

He changed his night flannels, as they had become moist with
sweat. In few moments, which he took to be hours, he dressed.
When he went out, he was confounded again. First, he went down

to the dark lobby: in his agitation he thought the appointment was there. He was surprised by sleeping chairs, extinguished lights, a detained nocturnal emptiness. He went back perplexed and self-questioning.

He entered her room. But after she opened the door in a hurry, she did not close it herself. Instead, she said to him: Close the door behind you, Mikhail. A single wall window was their only sky, their only light. Agitated, his eyes were slightly blinded in the darkness. She said to him: No, don't turn on the light. I don't want light now. I cannot stand it.

The bathroom was lit behind the glass of the closed door. The light was stealing in like trickling water.

She said to him: Come! Sit next to me on the bed.

She was under the white sheet while preparing a place for him on the edge of the bed with her hands. He sensed the bronze color of her bare arms in the faint darkness. The church dome in the window frame seemed to him heavy and flattened.

In her face, the anxiety of the tearful storm lingered. Her cheeks and eyelids seemed round, slightly puffed, adding to her appeal.

She said: We will talk now. Nothing but talk.

This was followed by a belated tearful sigh. He leaned over and kissed her under the eyes. He patted her cheeks and eyelids with his hands in a silent, comforting gesture. She raised her arms and slid his glasses away from his eyes in a deliberate, slow gesture, putting them down next to keys and a cigarette pack under the shade of the turned-off table lamp.

She said: Come, let's talk. If we analyze the problem objectively and logically we will . . .

He put his hand on her lips and said: No, no, Rama. No need for logical, objective analysis or for a non-logical, non-objective analysis.

She said: From the dialectical angle, we can look at the issue from the point of view of . . .

Smiling lightly and affectionately, he said: I don't want to discuss the issue from any point of view.

Her lips held on to his: the appeal of the lightly fragrant wine breath of her mouth was immediate and sudden. Their first kiss was sudden, unexpected. His lips came to know the freshness of the open, slow-moving, and clinging mouth. In her mouth was a light sugary taste—the sweetness of a mature fruit plucked from a mother tree.

He leaned to take her between his arms, and he felt on his chest the weight of her naked breasts under the light nylon, white gown. The music of the spheres was grandly mellow, and heavens resounded with glorious, lofty melodies. The juxtaposition of chests was a fulfillment, a realization of a deep primordial demand that could not be questioned. His arm behind her shoulder held the magnificence of that which he did not know the world could contain.

She said to him: Come next to me.

His move was quick, without thought.

She said to him: Put your hand on my breast.

He felt the virginity of her blooming bosom, its strange innocence while she looked at him with gentle ecstatic eyes. No present, no future, and no past. The moment that does not end is everything. There was no discovery, nor the rush into new recognition. Their knowledge of each other was as old as time: entrenched, having its own principle as if eternal. This determined voracity, this burning desire, this distilled eroticism devoid of the weakness of humane affection. The boat of craving rose with them above deep waves with quiet surface amid the reed stalks. His hands knew their way to the wet and rich jungles as he sailed in no time between the two full and soft legs that he could not see: his face was buried between her breasts.

She said: Tomorrow you will return, and we will talk formally as required by good manners. As for now, we have a few moments together.

She said: We will wait for our pleasure together, one after the other: each in its turn. We will not hurry.

There was nothing between them except a joy with steady music—its uproar controlled by a strict, spontaneous, uncalculated rhythm.

She said: Wait, till we come simultaneously together.

The waves were lapping between their embracing bodies. Her full thigh on his leg was a spread-out sail of heavy fabric filled by the blowing of joyful wind. Just the same, he was listening from afar to the fluttering of vast wings filling the blocked sky, in a frame of radiant but faint fire, above the joyful bells twinkling: the annunciation of the coming of a new resurrection. Death, where is your darkness? Then the dams broke after their soft rocks trembled under the unbearable anxiety of pleasure. The roaring of the last waves broke out: her abrupt cry from the pain of pleasure was sharp and hushed. The boat that carried them together was shaking in its final shudder in the jungles. It staggered and drowned in the warm pond whose waters streamed off, and on which the breeze collapsed amid the soft reed stalks, burnt and dried up by the sun.

They were traveling once by train when she said to him unexpectedly: I seduced you. Had I not cried when I phoned, you would not have come.

His friend Ibrahim once said to him: Ah, Rama. This woman is incredible. Everything with her goes through there, from below, everything. What a loss! Such intelligence, education, brilliance, self-sacrifice! All of it passes through there: all her mind, her work, her play, her archaeological expertise, her radicalism—all are in the service of the lower part. He added: She used to be, indeed, very beautiful in the past. When she went to Port Said, she became a legend, but now . . . Who would look at her now?

Mikhail said to himself: For the cynics, everything spirals into a repetitive cynical mold. Is this the story of a woman-nymph, like any other? The flesh of truth is something alive, gentle, soft. It cannot be reduced to a cynical formula; it cannot be a mold among other judgmental molds—ready-made, cheapened by hands, made commonplace by gossip.

He said to himself: I, I look at her and I fully see her, I know a beauty in her that no one else can see: a gentleness that hurts the heart, a childish weakness, also a rocklike force, a hunger not of this earth. I know through her a woman's body pouring into my arms as well as a stony, harsh wall that cannot be possessed. She has both indescribable affection and absolute indifference—an indifference not even aware of itself. What does it matter if the feet of conquering armies have stepped on the fresh flesh of your truth, endless times? The rock stays, the fertility of the flesh is renewed in the jungles of Manzala swamps and down to the drowned cataracts. The hippopotami, with ugly mouths, gobble tons of dry grass of shooting stars. The Nile waters disappear behind the great dam, and the earth cracks, opening up a network of wound marks without blood. Ghosts, ghouls, and monsters surround me, surround you, you, nymph, you, dark river houri. Phantoms in the gardens of Circe disappear in the burning noon sun on the mountain of Aswan. The crooked tree trunks are laid bare, black, leafless. These are not her sins; they are not her sins. She has no sins. It is my sin that I did not know how to teach her my reality. I remained for her without substance, a chiaroscuro. What, then, is my reality? Do I have any? If so, why do I wish to see it reflected in her green mirror alone?

She said to him: I love you this way, when you are gentle and sweet; I don't love your fierceness.

He said to her: I want you to open up for me all your inner life, even those things that shock, torture, and frighten. I'll live them again with you. I will share with you the mad frenzy, if that is what it is called. Perhaps I shall be wounded deeply. Yes, but the wounds are open now, anyhow, and they might never heal as it is. What I mean is that I am ready to live with you. I am capable of it. A shared healing might be in this. I don't know. What I know is that you're staying alone inside your loneliness, a relentless loneliness within loneliness, each with its own flavor of cruelty. Your solitude is made by your own hands inside a self-enclosed planet. When will it end? Is this what you want? Or is it that you possess nothing but this? It is not, and it cannot be, your will. Nothing is forced upon us from outside. You know this. There is no need for me to say it.

He said: You share with me all the moments of my life . . . I want complete sharing.

She said without accepting, not even for a moment: Total sharing is very demanding.

He said: Yes.

She said: Haven't we agreed that perfection is not of this world? It is enough that we get what we can, if we can.

In his fancy, it was possible to arrive at this absolute love within the prison of conventions that people erect for their lives. In the heart of such impossibility, he wanted to reach her totally, and to give himself totally.

He said: Knowledge for me is love.

She said: What do you want to know? Nothing. Void and emptiness.

He said: You? In the midst of your crowded activity?

She said: The worst kind of void is that in the midst of crowds; in the midst of people, urgent issues, successive problems, and everything emptied on the inside.

He said: It is not emptiness then, but escape.

She said: I want to escape from you.

He said: Isn't there a kind of escape forward through confrontation?

She said: Last night I did not sleep because of the heat.

He said: You told me you slept well.

She said: I slept well, yes, but not enough, only a little.

She yawned and put her hand on her mouth, looking at him with a half-apologetic glance.

He asked himself, he doesn't know how many times he had asked himself: Was that an act of self-destruction or an act of self-liberation from the rubble of a previous, repetitive, and unending destruction?

She said: I leave matters to unfold on their own. I take things as they come. Most things do not ever get completed. How many things around us, inside us, are half-made things, partially completed, thus partially incomplete!

Of course he did not tell her: Do you know anything about the long, long hours passing by in which I think of you, for you, in you—talking to you confidentially and at length, with utter bitterness? I shy from such naïveté, from the fact that all this is half-cooked, half-raw, half-crude and wasted, of no interest at all to anyone.

He said to himself: Music tortures me these days. It invades me without resistance, a sort of sensual conquest on the level of blood and guts. It possesses me instantly, opening up all locks and flowing heavily into my veins, as if it were a poison of a very deadly kind, absorbed by every cell in my guts, welcomed and demanded. Music's indefinite language is a resounding cry. Where are the music of the mind and the spell of its pure geometric lines?

He said to her: You are fortunate, at least for not being romantic at all. I don't know if you resort to certain escapes from romanticism?

He meant escapes into sensuality, the continuous, diligent search for relaxation of organic tension that can never be quieted, escapes into a non-romantic absorption and drowning. At times, he was surprised and shocked by her calmness, her acceptance, her surrender, and immobility. The morning would stretch into a slow, alienating rhythm, as if it would never leave off. Even the taste of her kisses changed, lacked sharpness and responsiveness, lacked the slightly sugary taste.

With the absence of certainty, numbness creeps into him. His mind falls into a heavy stillness. Even his heart gives up on expressiveness.

She said to him: When someone loves, usually one's energy gushes at every moment. Creation, creativity, and discovery spring out, even as you drink your cup of coffee, as if you are remaking the world.

He did not mention to her his confusion in the perplexing waves of unanswerable questions: small waves, turbid and blocking the horizon, without hope of reaching the vast surface of the sea toward the unlimited and extended borders, melding with the open skies.

Sorrow lies in your eyes while cool air and pure blue radiance fill the November sky. This Sea City is my city, diffused in the high noon of its paved road. Your stabbing eyes carry a weight, which cuts the surface of my self to the very bottom, while I am a step apart from you in the high noon of the road. And you, my love so distant—more illusory than my love fancies. What do I observe in your glances? Is this look, with its alienated depth, yours or my own

fancy? And this love that troubles me, possesses me, murders me—
is this love my own delusion? What is in your mind, Rama? A depressing, fragile sorrow or a void? The void of a November noon? I
don't know, I don't know anything about you, my enigmatic love. I
don't know the meaning of your glance. I don't know who I am for
you. I don't know who you are. The winter void of my taciturn
noon. My city escapes me: Fancies, people and their cars, traffic
lights and horns, the rattle of trams and the eyes of the people
buried in the secrets of their troubles, all silent on the road. All disappearing in November clarity, in distant white clouds hanging on
the city ceiling in al-Raml Station. Nothing is left but your gaze—
a secret I will never decipher.

Translated by Ferial Ghazoul and John Verlenden

Betool Khedairi
(b. 1965)
IRAQ

Betool Khedairi was born in Baghdad to an Iraqi father and
Scottish mother, and now lives in Amman, Jordan. She took
a degree in French literature and then divided her time
among Iraq, Jordan, and the United Kingdom. Her novel *A
Sky So Close*, excerpted below, was published in Lebanon in
1999. Its narrator, growing up between two cultures, feels
that she belongs neither to Baghdad nor to England.

FROM *A Sky So Close*

I say goodbye to my mother at sundown from the back door, when
she hears the tooting of David and Millie's car horn. She walks out
on tiptoe, trying to stop her high heels from sinking into the mud
pillows where you had planted some mint seedlings that morning.
You enjoy the leaves with your cup of tea, or on a slice of the local
white cheese. I watch their greeting ritual from where I'm standing

by the garden tap. The car stops, David gets out, giving my mother a hug and a wide smile. Millie gets out of the front seat quickly, vacating it for my mother, then takes up her place in the back seat quite happily. Another brief hug before the car moves off. A quick glance backward from my mother. She looks toward me, but doesn't see me.

I spend Friday finishing my school homework. I then clean my glass fish tank and change its water. I watch the dancing many-colored, scaly creatures inside it. I speak to them but get no reply. Eyes without lashes stare back at me through the glass; they're continuously sending out kisses and bubbles. We had river fish and rice for lunch. In the afternoon depression sets in, until we dispel it with the flavorings game.

Together we prepare a bag of popcorn and take it up to your room. You say to me:

—Today we'll be working only with colors, which is why I allowed you to eat the popcorn, as its salty taste would spoil your ability to pick out the various flavors. This week I received a contract from a new company that produces paints and emulsions. They want to compete in the local market and have asked me to come up with unusual and exotic names for them, and to give them suggestions for how to promote their products. I want you to help me. Today we need to let our imagination go free, to the end of the rainbow.

—What about tasting the products? I've been looking forward to that all week!

—There are many projects, my little one, and there will be a lot of that in the weeks to come. Now, let us start work.

You take out the largest collection of colored squares I've seen in my life. Meters of samples, shades that can't be imagined. Fluorescent ribbons, shiny ones, and others with rough surfaces wait for us to give them names. Rectangles, triangles, and circles of color compete in the degree of their purity. We spread them out on the floor in your room and start with the most appealing ones. You point to the first color and ask me:

—So what do you think, my assistant, what is this?

I reply without any hesitation:

—Blue.

—What name do you want it to have?

I thought for a while:

—Light blue.

You laugh and your eyes sparkle.

—No, no, no . . . that's no good. I'll give you an example. It's like: the Spray from the Ocean, the Blue of Dolphins, a Silver Mist, Dry Ice. The name has to be poetic and unusual. That is the secret! Don't you think?

I read your glinting eyes and reply:

—Exactly, but how are we going to come up with names like that for all these other colors?

—Don't worry, they'll come. Now look at this color—what is it called?

—Orange.

—That's not enough. It could be called Inspiration of Rust, Desert Bronze, Golden Honey, Fragments of Autumn.

I was astonished. I didn't know what to say. You start to make some notes in your little book. I put some popcorn in my mouth and gaze at you.

—This is a pretty color, it's a pleasant brown. Let's call it Bleached Brown, Dust from the Little Mountains, Eastern Spice, or Crusty Bread. What do you think?

—Excellent.

—It's your turn now with this color.

—Very good, and I see it as Angel's Wings, Oyster's Pearl, Waterfall's Froth, or an Ice Cave.

I laughed,

—In this heat, Father?

—Hmm, you have a point. You see, you've started to associate the color with the name.

You then pick up a yellowish brown color and say:

—I defy you to name this color.

I reply:

—Caramel.

You add:

—Or maybe Dusky Skin, or Wild Mushroom Peel.

I couldn't keep up with your wealth of ideas. I preferred to just listen.

—Don't give up. You'll learn how to do this very quickly. I'm sure of that. This yellow color, what do you think?

—A lemon.

—Yes, but it's an impure yellow. It could be called Pineapple Scales, or Banana Mousse.

—But Father, these colors are paints!

—That's what makes it more exciting.

Each name takes at least ten minutes of thinking. Sometimes it takes you more than half an hour to choose a certain name. It's only now that I'm getting to know you. This secret world of yours had never dawned on me. I'd been engrossed in my school routine, my uniform, and my training. I never thought that I could imagine the color pink as Cherry Gel, or that I could call the color green a Lazy Forest, a Fermented Apple Skin, or a River Pebble. How do you come up with such magic, Father? Is this what my mother meant when she said that you seduced her with your descriptions of the East?

The weeks pass; we compete to find new names for our colors. Fridays have become less depressing. We giggle at the breakfast table when you cut through a boiled egg and say:

—Ah, a Grainy Yolk.

I reply:

—No, it's Woven Amber.

You cry out:

—You cheeky girl; the professor's student has become a professor and a half!

My mother casts a bemused look in our direction from behind her newspaper. She lifts up her knife. It has some dark berry jam on it. She spreads it on her slice of toast. I turn toward you.

—Baba, what do you think?

You say with a smile:

—A Turkish Plum.

I say:

—No, Wild Berries.

You add:

—Well done, but it's more like a Unique Grape.

I say:

—No, that's a very ordinary name. What about Ground Ruby?

You reply:

—Excellent.

It was thus that we colored our day. We spent a whole evening on the shades of the color gray. I'd never seen such beauty before. I say to you:

—How do they make these colors in the laboratories?

—Science and technology are constantly making great advances. If we learn how to put science to good use, the future for humankind holds great promise.

You suggested to me:

—Volcanic Ash, Gray Cloud.

—Did you not say that we should avoid using the name of the color itself?

—Yes, but gray is not a color; it's a puzzling nuance.

—Alright, then, Smoky Haze.

—Well done, or Froth on the Beach, Powdered Stone.

I jump up and shout:

—Yes, Powdered Stone fits perfectly, as if it's the color of concrete.

—I think you'll excel in this field, my little one.

—Does that mean I'll have to study chemistry like you, Baba?

—You may not need to do that if you want to remain my assistant. Anyway, this is just some preliminary experience for you. There are specialized courses in the field of advertising that you may want to do when you grow up.

I ask you:

—What about Seal's Fur?

You reply:

—That will be its trade name. You've now registered a color in your name for the first time.

You take me into the world of colors and flavors—some of them lived in my dreams; some dwelled, with all their crystals, under my tongue.

You look up at the clock on the wall. It's past one o'clock. You say:

—My God, I forgot that you have to go to school tomorrow. Hurry up and get ready for bed.

I kiss you, leaving you in your room. My mother's room is totally silent.

That night, for the first time, I awoke from my sleep, startled. I could hear my mother shouting downstairs, at three-thirty in the morning, and you're shouting at the top of your voice:

—It seems I've given you too many liberties, which you don't deserve!

—I don't care what you say. I'm fed up with this sham relationship. I enjoy spending my evenings with my foreign friends, staying up late with them; I will not let you spoil it for me when I get back. I'm not Cinderella—I don't have to be back by midnight. Can't you understand that my life is now separate from yours? We don't live together, nor do we even get along together, we merely reside in the same house!

—As long as you live in this house, you'll respect its traditions. I don't think I've left you lacking for anything. Don't make our lives more confused.

—So we're back to it's all my fault. Can't you understand? I want a final separation. I don't want your favors, nor do I want you to remind me that you're the master of this house. I'm content with my job, my friends, and my daughter.

—Where will you live? In Basra?

—Why not? Isn't it better than this hell I'm living in now?

—You don't even bother to deny your relationship with him!

At this point I felt you were going to explode with anger. I could hear crying. You threw something at her. It was the ashtray. It struck my glass fish tank with a crack. I could hear the water start to trickle out from it slowly.

You were coughing violently, you were saying:

—If this is what you want, woman, then I'll divorce you. You can have what you want. Go to him, or go back to England! The child is mine, she'll stay with me, I promise you that. The law is on my side. I'll keep it on my side whether you like it or not!

Translated by Muhayman Jamil

Elias Khoury
(b. 1948)
LEBANON

Elias Khoury is one of the major novelists of the Arab world. Not content to write in the conventional narrative style and structure, he requires a certain amount of collaboration from his reader. As in *The Arabian Nights*, Khoury's novel *The Journey of Little Gandhi*, a story of the Lebanese civil war and the invasion of Beirut by the Israelis, employs a series of embedded stories in the development of the central one. Three other novels by Elias Khoury are available in English: *The Gates of the City*, the earlier *Little Mountain*, and his most ambitious work to date, *Gate of the Sun*, which has been made into a successful film.

FROM *The Journey of Little Gandhi*

One of those mornings, Gandhi was sitting alone in front of his box. He had placed the metal shoe trees on the ground, waiting for some shoes. He saw Dr. John Davis coming in the distance. The American professor was walking, his dog next to him, a big dusty-colored German shepherd that growled and barked. Gandhi asked God for refuge from seeing him so early in the morning. Dr. Davis stopped in front of the shoe-shine box, holding the rope tied to the dog's neck, and the dog moved left and right, sniffing and putting his mouth on the shoe trees. The American pulled his dog back. And the dog would go close to the shoe trees and head in Gandhi's direction, sniff at the sitting man's feet, and Gandhi would try to get away from the dog, move his feet away, pretend to be busy with the shoe trees and shoes, and wipe his face with his long black sleeve. Dr. Davis asked how things were going, while the dog roamed about, with his master holding the rope. Then the dog got away from Davis's hand. The dog ran off, and Davis called him— "Fox! Fox!"—and the dog ran as if he'd found something. Dr. Davis left Gandhi and chased after his dog. A woman came and placed three pairs of men's black shoes in front of the box. Gandhi put them up on the shoe tree and started working. Gandhi didn't like to dye shoes until he'd stretched the leather out on the shoe tree. The original way of doing it, he believed, was to dye the shoes without taking them off the person's foot. The foot gave the shoe its form and stretched it out, and so the color would spread equally over the entire shoe. But when the shoe is without a foot, the leather gets wrinkled, and it becomes difficult to dye it, because the transformation to mirror becomes impossible.

Gandhi had finished mounting the shoes on the shoe trees when he saw Dr. Davis coming back with his dog. That day, John Davis made the suggestion that would make Gandhi leave his profession for the first time. He would leave it for the second and last time, based on a suggestion made by Hasan Zaylaa, when he would become responsible for keeping the quarter clean.

Mr. Davis stopped and asked him if he would help him feed his dog.

"I don't have anything, just shoes," Gandhi said.

Gandhi agreed to Mr. Davis's idea without ever imagining it would lead him to leave his trade.

Gandhi went into the American University cafeteria with a big burlap bag in his hand. Davis told him he'd made an arrangement with the kitchen manager and the American director of the kitchen to allow Gandhi to take the leftovers every day, take them to his house near Bakhaazi Hospital as food for Fox, who seemed he could never get enough to eat. He agreed with Gandhi to pay him one lira a day, and at that time a shoe shine was a quarter-lira. In other words, filling the bag was as good as shining four pairs of shoes.

When Gandhi entered the kitchen, he was shocked by the amount of food. The cook, who was wearing a white shirt and a long white cap on his head, led him through the inner rooms of the kitchen and pointed to the plates. Gandhi would empty everything from his bag. He'd fill the bag, and there would still be a lot of food left that was to be thrown away.

He took the bag to Mr. Davis's house, and that day he decided.

On the second day, he came with two bags—one for the dog and one for himself.

In the first bag he put the leftovers, and in the second one, which was stuffed with empty sardine tins he'd picked up the night before and had his wife wash out, he tried to sort out the food and place it in the little tin cans. Then he put them carefully into the bag.

On the third day, he brought, in addition to the two bags and the empty sardine tins, an empty bottle and tried to fill it with oil left in the plates of labneh.

On the fourth day, Fawziyya came with him, and she did the sorting and organizing of the food before it was placed into the tin cans.

On the fifth day, the routine was regulated, and he agreed with the kitchen manager to pay him six liras a day, after he'd refused Gandhi's offer to share the food.

On the sixth day, he opened a restaurant.

And on the seventh day, the day the American University cafeteria is closed, Gandhi rested in his house, and didn't go to work. That was the first time in his life he didn't go to work on a Sunday.

Gandhi placed some small chairs and handmade straw trays in front of his house in Nabaa and turned the stone bench into a restaurant.

"Those were the days," Gandhi would say. "In those days there was a lot of prosperity. We all ate, we and the dog. The dog had enough, and we had enough, and everyone ate . . . The Houranis started coming, Houranis, Kurds, all kinds of people, cement workers, port laborers, you name it, they'd come every day and buy. A plate of labneh, ten piasters, a plate of hummus, twenty-five, a plate of kefta, fifty, things just worked out. Muhammad al-Hariri, God rest his soul, started coming regularly. He'd come and bring a bottle of arak with him, and he'd pour some for himself and the other customers. I refused, I said no way, nothing sacrilegious in my restaurant, but how can you fight sacrilege when it's everywhere? So I drank, I had tons of money. Those were the days, I even forgot all about shoe shining—no, I didn't forget, I stopped sitting there all day, breaking my back behind the shoe-shine box. I worked a little on the side, for special customers. I'd take the box and sit beneath Madame Lillian Sabbagha's staircase, and enjoy seeing the beautiful Russian woman in the morning. I'd shine her shoes, the Reverend Amin's, Davis's, the Assyrian's, al-Munla's, and very few others. The real work, however, was in the restaurant."

Then came the catastrophe.

The dog died.

Gandhi was prepared for anyone's death, but not the dog's. Gandhi, like everyone, thought about death, and death, according to him, resembled his father, lying in the open coffin, teardrops stuck to his lower eyelids. He thought about his wife's death, and other people's deaths. Gandhi lived with death, the babies died before being born, death came before all things. Death was life. But the death of the dog never crossed his mind, and when the dog died, and Gandhi saw Mr. Davis transform into a ghost, he was beset with fear and worry. He tried to console the American, he tried to say to him what the Reverend Amin used to say when he'd visit him after all those stillbirths that happened to Fawziyya, his wife. "The Lord giveth, and the Lord taketh away." He tried to console him but Mr. Davis went nuts. Davis would talk about how the murderer got out and spat, and he'd say he wanted to leave the country. His blond wife, who had some white strands in her hair like pieces of cloth planted on her scalp, sat with her head down in the corner of the house, curled up like a snail, hardly moving. Gandhi would go in and out, serve coffee to the few people who'd come to offer their condolences, and Davis would refuse to be consoled.

Translated by Paula Haydar

Mohamed Khudayir
(b. 1942)

IRAQ

Mohamed Khudayir was born in Basra and works as a school-master. One of Iraq's outstanding literary talents, he has pub-lished three collections of stories and a novel, *Basriyatha*, about the town where he now lives. Several of his stories have been translated into English, but there has yet to be a complete volume of his work available in translation. In 2003 he was awarded the prestigious Owais Prize.

Clocks Like Horses

This meeting may take place. I shall get my watch repaired and go out to the quays of the harbour, then at the end of the night I shall return to the hotel and find him sleeping in my bed, his face turned to the wall, having hung his red turban on the clothes hook.

Till today I still own a collection of old watches; I had come by them from an uncle of mine who used to be a sailor on the ships of the Andrew Weir company; old pocket watches with chains and silver-plated cases, all contained in a small wooden box in purses of shiny blue cloth. While my interest in them has of late waned, I had, as a schoolboy, been fascinated by them. I would take them out from their blue purses and scrutinize their workings in an at-tempt to discover something about them that would transcend "time stuffed like old cotton in a small cushion," as I had recorded one day in my diary.

One day during the spring school holidays it occurred to me to remove one of these watches from its box and to put it into the pocket of my black suit, attaching its chain to the buttonholes of my waistcoat. For a long time I wandered round the chicken mar-ket before seating myself at a café. The waiter came and asked me the time. I calmly took the watch out of its blue purse. My watch was incapable of telling the time, like the other watches in the box; nothing in it working except for the spring of the case which was no sooner pressed than it flicked open revealing a pure white dial and two hands that stood pointing to two of the Roman numerals on the face. Before I could inform him that the watch was not working, the waiter had bent down and pulled the short chain towards him; having looked attentively at the watch he closed its case on which had been engraved a sailing ship within a frame of foreign writing. Then, giving it back to me, he stood up straight.

"How did you get hold of it?"

"I inherited it from a relative of mine."

I returned the watch to its place.

"Was your relative a sailor?"

"Yes."

"Only three or four of the famous sailors are still alive."

"My relative was called Mughamis."

"Mughamis? I don't know him."

"He wouldn't settle in one place. He died in Bahrain."

"That's sailors for you! Do you remember another sailor called Marzouk? Since putting ashore for the last time he has been living in Fao. He opened a shop there for repairing watches, having learned the craft from the Portuguese. He alone would be able to repair an old watch like yours."

I drank down the glass of tea and said to the waiter as I paid him: "Did you say he was living in Fao?"

"Yes, near the hotel."

The road to Fao is a muddy one and I went on putting off the journey until one sunny morning I took my place among the passengers in a bus which set off loaded with luggage. The passengers, who sat opposite one another in the middle of the bus, exchanged no words except for general remarks about journeying in winter, about how warm this winter was, and other comments about the holes in the road. At the moment they stopped talking I took out my watch. Their eyes became fixed on it, but no one asked me about it or asked the time. Then we began to avoid looking at each other and transferred our attentions to the vast open countryside and to the distant screen of date palms in the direction of the east that kept our vehicle company and hid the villages along the Shatt al-Arab.

We arrived at noon and someone showed me to the hotel which lies at the intersection of straight roads and looks on to a square in the middle of which is a round fenced garden. The hotel consisted of two low storeys, while the balcony that overlooked the square was at such a low height that someone in the street could have climbed up on to it. I, who cannot bear the smell of hotels, or the heavy, humid shade in their hallways in daytime, hastened to call out to its owners. When I repeated my call, a boy looked down from a door at the side and said: "Do you want to sleep here?"

"Have you a place?" I said.

The boy went into the room and from it there emerged a man whom I asked for a room with a balcony. The boy who was showing me the way informed me that the hotel would be empty by day and packed at night. Just as the stairway was the shortest of stairways and the balcony the lowest of balconies, my room was the smallest and contained a solitary bed, but the sun entered it from the balcony. I threw my bag onto the bed and the boy sat down beside me. "The doors are all without locks," said the boy. "Why should we lock them—the travelers only stay for one night."

Then he leaned towards me and whispered: "Are you Indian?"

This idea came as a surprise to me. The boy himself was more likely to be Indian with his dark complexion, thick brilliantined hair and sparkling eyes. I whispered to him: "Did they tell you that Basra used to be called the crotch of India, and that the Indian invaders in the British army, who came down to the land of Fao first of all, desired no other women except those of Basra?"

The boy ignored my cryptic reference to the mixing of passions and blending of races and asked, if I wasn't Indian, where did I live?

"I've come from Ashar," I told him, "on a visit to the watchmaker. Would you direct me to him?"

"Perhaps you mean the old man who has many clocks in his house," said the boy.

"Yes, that must be he," I said.

"He's not far from the hotel," he said. "He lives alone with his daughter and never leaves the house."

The boy brought us lunch from a restaurant, and we sat on the bed to eat, and he told me about the man I had seen downstairs: "He's not the owner of the hotel, just a permanent guest."

Then, with his mouth full of food, he whispered: "He's got a pistol."

"You know a lot of things, O Indian," I said, also speaking in a whisper.

He protested that he wasn't Indian but was from Hasa. He had a father who worked on the ships that transported dates from Basra to the coastal towns of the Gulf and India.

The boy took me to the watchmaker, leaving me in front of the door of his house. A gap made by a slab of stone that had been removed from its place in the upper frieze of the door made this entrance unforgettable. One day, in tropical years, there had stopped near where I was a sailor shaky with sickness, or some Sikh soldier shackled with lust, and he had looked at the slab of stone on which was engraved some date or phrase, before continuing on his unknown journey. And after those two there perhaps came some foreign archaeologist whose boat had been obstructed by the silt and who had put up in the town till the water rose, and his curiosity for things Eastern had been drawn to the curves of the writing on the slab of stone and he had torn it out and carried it off with him to his boat. Now I, likewise, was in front of this gateway to the sea.

On the boy's advice I did not hesitate to push open the door and enter into what looked like a porch which the sun penetrated through apertures near the ceiling and in which I was confronted by hidden and persistent ticking sounds and a garrulous ringing that issued from the pendulums and hammers of large clocks of the type that strike the hours, ranged along the two sides of the porch. As I proceeded one or more clocks struck at the same time. All the clocks were similar in size, in the great age of the wood of their frames, and in the shape of their round dials, their Roman numerals, and their delicate arrow-like hands—except that these hands were pointing to different times.

I had to follow the slight curve of the porch to come unexpectedly upon the last of the great sailors in his den, sitting behind a large table on which was heaped the wreckage of clocks. He was occupied with taking to pieces the movement of a clock by the light of a shaded lamp that hung down from the ceiling at a height close to his frail, white-haired head. He looked towards me with a glance from one eye that was naked and another on which a magnifying-glass had been fixed, then went back to disassembling the movement piece by piece. The short glance was sufficient to link this iron face with the nuts, cogwheels and hands of the movements of the many clocks hanging on the walls and thrown into corners under dust and rust. Clocks that didn't work and others that did, the biggest of them being a clock on the wall above the watchmaker's head, which was, to be precise, the movement of a large grandfather clock made of brass, the dial of which had been removed and which had been divested of its cabinet so that time manifested itself in it naked and shining, sweeping along on its serrated cogwheels in a regular mechanical sequence: from the rotation of the spring to the pendulum that swung harmoniously to and fro and ended in the slow, tremulous, imperceptible movement of the hands. When the cogwheels had taken the hands along a set distance of time's journey, the striking cogwheel would move and raise the hammer. I had not previously seen a naked, throbbing clock and thus I became mesmerized by the regular throbbing that synchronized with the swinging motion of the pendulum and with the movement of the cogwheels of various diameters. I started at the sound of the hammer falling against the bell; the gallery rang with three strokes whose reverberations took a long time to die away, while the other clocks went on, behind the glass of their cabinets, with their incessant ticking.

The watchmaker raised his head and asked me if the large clock above his head had struck three times.

Then, immersing himself in taking the mechanism to pieces, he said: "Like horses; like horses running on the ocean bed."

A clock in the porch struck six times and he said: "Did one of them strike six times? It's six in America. They're getting up now, while the sun is setting in Burma."

Then the room was filled again with noisy reverberations. "Did it strike seven? It's night-time in Indonesia. Did you make out the last twelve strokes? They are fast asleep in the furthest west of the world. After some hours the sun will rise in the furthest east. What time is it? Three? That's our time, here near the Gulf."

One clock began striking on its own. After a while the chimes blended with the tolling of other clocks as hammers coincided in falling upon bells, and others landed halfway between the times of striking and yet others fell between these halfway so that the chimes hurried in pursuit of one another in a confused scale. Then, one after another, the hammers became still, the chimes growing further apart, till a solitary clock remained, the last clock that had not discharged all its time, letting it trickle out now in a separate, high-pitched reverberation.

He was holding my watch in his grasp. "Several clocks might strike together," he said, "strike as the fancy takes them. I haven't liked to set my clocks to the same time. I have assigned to my daughter the task of merely winding them up. They compete with one another like horses. I have clocks that I bought from people who looted them from the houses of Turkish employees who left them as they hurried away after the fall of Basra. I also got hold of clocks that were left behind later on by the Jews who emigrated. Friends of mine, the skippers of ships, who would come to visit me here, would sell me clocks of European manufacture. Do you see the clock over there in the passageway? It was in the house of the Turkish commander of the garrison of Fao's fortress."

I saw the gleam of the quick-swinging pendulum behind glass in the darkness of the cabinets of the clocks in the porch. Then I asked him about my watch. "Your watch? It's a rare one. They're no longer made. I haven't handled such a watch for a long time. I'm not sure about it but I'll take it to pieces. Take a stroll round and come back here at night."

That was what I'd actually intended to do. I would return before night. The clocks bade me farewell with successive chimes. Four chimes in Fao: seven p.m. in the swarming streets of Calcutta. Four chimes: eight a.m. in the jungles of Buenos Aires . . . Outside the den the clamour had ceased, also the smell of engine oil and of old wood.

I returned at sunset. I had spent the time visiting the old barracks which had been the home of the British army of occupation, then I had sat in a café near the fish market.

I didn't find the watchmaker in his former place, but presently I noticed a huge empty cabinet that had been moved into a gap between the clocks. The watchmaker was in an open courtyard before an instrument made up of clay vessels, which I guessed to be a type of water-clock. When he saw me he called out: "Come here. Come, I'll show you something."

I approached the vessels hanging on a crossbeam: from them water dripped into a vessel hanging on another, lower crossbeam; the water then flowed on to a metal plate on the ground, in which there was a gauge for measuring the height of the water.

"A water-clock?"

"Have you seen one like it?"

"I've read about them. They were the invention of people of old."

"The Persians call them *bingan*."

"I don't believe it tells the right time."

"No, it doesn't, it reckons only twenty hours to the day. According to its reckoning I'm 108 years old instead of ninety, and it is seventy-eight years since the British entered Basra instead of sixty. I learned how to make it from a Muscati sailor who had one like it in his house on the coast."

I followed him to the den, turning to two closed doors in the small courtyard on which darkness had descended. He returned the empty clock-cabinet to its place and seated himself in his chair. His many clothes lessened his appearance of senility; he was lost under his garments, one over another and yet another over them, his head inside a vast tarbush.

"I've heard you spent a lifetime at sea."

"Yes. It's not surprising that our lives are always linked to water. I was on one of the British India ships as a syce with an English trader dealing in horses."

He toyed with the remnants of the watches in front of him, then said: "He used to call himself by an Arabic name. We would call him Surour Saheb. He used to buy Nejdi horses from the rural areas of the south and they would then be shipped to Bombay where they would be collected up and sent to the racecourses in England. Fifteen days on end at sea, except that we would make stops at the Gulf ports. We would stop for some days in Muscat. When there were strong winds against us we would spend a month at sea. The captains, the cooks and the pilots were Indians, while the others, seamen and syces, were from Muscat, Hasa and Bahrain; the rest were from the islands of the Indian Ocean. We could have with us divers from Kuwait. I remember their small dark bodies and plaited hair as they washed down the horses on the shore or led them to the ship. I was the youngest syce. I began my first sea journey at the age of twelve. I joined the ship with my father who was an assistant to the captain and responsible for looking after the stores and equipment. There were three of us, counting my father, who would sleep in the storeroom among the sacks and barrels of tar, the fish oil, ropes and dried fish, on beds made up of coconut fibre."

"Did you make a lot?"

"We? We didn't make much. The trader did. Each horse would fetch 800 rupees in Bombay, and when we had reached Bengal it would fetch 1,500 rupees. On our return to Basra we would receive our wages for having looked after the horses. Some of us would buy goods from India and sell them on our return journey wherever we put in: cloth, spices, rice, sugar, perfumes, and wood, and sometimes peacocks and monkeys."

"Did you employ horses in the war?"

"I myself didn't take part in the war. Of course they used them. When the Turks prevented us from trading with them because they needed them for the army, we moved to the other side of the river. We had a corral and a caravanserai for sleeping in at Khorramshahr. From there we began to smuggle out the horses far from the clutches of the Turkish customs men. On the night when we'd be traveling we'd feed and water the horses well and at dawn we'd proceed to the corral and each syce would lead out his horse. As for me I was required to look after the transportation of the provisions and fodder; other boys who were slightly older than me were put in charge of the transportation of the water, the ropes, the chains and other equipment. The corral was close to the shore, except that the horses would make a lot of noise and stir up dust when they were being pulled along by the reins to the ship that would lie at the end of an anchorage stretching out to it from the shore. The ship would rock and tiny bits of straw would become stuck on top of our heads while the syces would call the horses by their names, telling them to keep quiet, until they finished tying them up in their places. It was no easy matter, for during the journey the waves, or the calm of the invisible sea, would excite one of the horses or would make it ill, so that its syce would have to spend the night with it, watching over it and keeping it company. As we lay in our sleeping quarters we would hear the syce reassuring his horse with some such phrase as: 'Calm down. Calm down, my Precious Love. The grass over there is better.' However this horse, whose name was Precious Love, died somewhere near Aden. At dawn the sailors took it up and consigned it to the waves. It was a misty morning and I was carrying a lantern, and I heard the great carcase hitting the water, though without seeing it I did, though, see its syce's face close to me—he would be returning from his voyage without any earnings."

Two or three clocks happened to chime together. I said to him:

"Used you to put in to Muscat?"

"Yes. Did I tell you about our host in Muscat? His wooden house was on the shore of a small bay, opposite an old stone fortress on the other side. We would set out for his house by boat. By birth he was a highlander, coming from the tribes in the mountains facing the bay. He was also a sorcerer. He was a close friend of Surour Saheb, supplying him with a type of ointment the Muscati used to prepare out of mountain herbs, which the Englishman would no sooner smear on his face than it turned a dark green and would gleam in the lamplight like a wave among rocks. In exchange for this the Muscati would get tobacco from him. I didn't join them in smoking, but I was fond of chewing a type of olibanum that was to be found extensively in the markets of the coast. I would climb up into a high place in the room that had been made as a permanent bed and would watch them puffing out the smoke from the *narghiles* into the air as they lay relaxing round the fire, having removed their dagger-belts and placed them in front of them alongside their coloured turbans. Their beards would be plunged in the smoke and the rings would glitter in their ears under the combed locks of hair whenever they turned towards the merchant, lost in thought. The merchant, relaxing on feather cushions, would be wearing brightly-coloured trousers of Indian cloth and would be wrapped round in an *aba* of Kashmir wool; as for his silk turban, he would, like the sailors, have placed it in front of him beside his pistol."

"Did you say that the Muscati was a sorcerer?"

"He had a basket of snakes in which he would lay one of the sailors, then bring him out alive. His sparse body would be swallowed in his lustrous flowing robes, as was his small head in his saffron-coloured turban with the tassels. We were appalled at his repulsive greed for food, for he would eat a whole basketful of dates during a night and would drink enough water to provide for ten horses. He was amazing, quite remarkable; he would perform bizarre acts; swallowing a puff from his *narghile*, he would after a while begin to release the smoke from his mouth and nose for five consecutive minutes. You should have seen his stony face, with the clouds of smoke floating against it like serpents that flew and danced. He was married to seven women for whom he had dug out, in the foot of the mountain, rooms that overlooked the bay. No modesty prevented him from disclosing their fabulous names: Mountain Flower, Daylight Sun, Sea Pearl, Morning Star. He was a storehouse of spicy stories and tales of strange travels and we would draw inspiration from him for names for our horses. At the end of the night he would leave us sleeping and would climb up the mountain. At the end of one of our trips we stayed as his guest for seven nights, during which time men from the Muscati's tribe visited us to have a smoke; they would talk very little and would look with distaste at the merchant and would then leave quietly with their antiquated rifles.

"Our supper would consist of spiced rice and grilled meat or fish. We would be given a sweet sherbet to drink in brass cups. As for the almond-filled *halva* of Muscat that melts in the mouth, even the bitter coffee could not disperse its scented taste. In the morning he would return and give us some sherbet to drink that would settle our stomachs, which would be suffering from the night's food and drink, and would disperse the tobacco fumes from the sailors' heads."

An outburst of striking clocks prevented him momentarily from enlarging further. He did not wait for the sound to stop before continuing:

"On the final night of our journey he overdid his tricks in quite a frightening manner. While the syces would seek help from his magic in treating their sick horses, they were afraid nonetheless that the evil effects of his magic would spread and reap the lives of these horses. And thus it was that a violent wind drove our ship onto a rock at the entrance to the bay and smashed it. Some of us escaped drowning, but the sorcerer of Muscat was not among them. He was traveling with the ship on his way to get married to a woman from Bombay; but the high waves choked his shrieks and eliminated his magic."

"And the horses?"

"They combated the waves desperately. They were swimming in the direction of the rocky shore, horses battling against the white horses of the waves. All of them were drowned. That was my last journey in the horse ships. After that, in the few years that preceded the war, I worked on the mail ships."

He made a great effort to remember and express himself:

"In Bahrain I married a woman who bore me three daughters whom I gave in marriage to sons of the sea. I stayed on there with the boatbuilders until after the war. Then, in the thirties, I returned to Basra and bought the clocks and settled in Fao, marrying a woman from here."

"You are one of the few sailors who are still alive today."

He asked me where I lived and I told him that I had put up at the hotel. He said:

"A friend of mine used to live in it. I don't know if he's still alive—for twenty years I haven't left my house."

Then, searching among the fragments of watches, he asked me in surprise:

"Did you come to Fao just because of the watch?"

I answered him that there were some towns one had to go to. He handed me my watch. It was working. Before placing it in my hand he scrutinized its flap on which had been engraved a ship with a triangular sail, which he said was of the type known as *sunbuk.*

I opened the flap. The hands were making their slow way round. The palms of my hands closed over the watch, and we listened to the sea echoing in the clocks of the den. The slender legs of horses run in the streets of the clock faces, are abducted in the glass of the large grandfather clocks. The clocks tick and strike: resounding hooves, chimes driven forward like waves. A chime: the friction of chains and ropes against wet wood. Two chimes: the dropping of the anchor into the blue abyss. Three: the call of the rocks. Four: the storm blowing up. Five: the neighing of the horses. Six . . . seven . . . eight . . . nine . . . ten . . . eleven . . . twelve . . .

This winding lane is not large enough to allow a lorry to pass, but it lets in a heavy damp night and sailors leading their horses, and a man dizzy from sea-sickness, still holding in his grasp a pocket watch and making an effort to avoid the water and the gentle sloping of the lane and the way the walls curve round. The bends increase with the thickening darkness and the silence. Light seeps through from the coming bend, causing me to quicken my step. In its seeping through and the might of its radiation it seems to be marching against the wall, carving into the damp brickwork folds of skins and crumpled faces that are the masks of seamen and

traders from different races who have passed by here before me and
are to be distinguished only by their headgear: the Bedouin of Nejd
and the rural areas of the south by the *kuffiyeh* and *'iqal*, the Iraqi
effendis of the towns by the *sidara*; the Persians by the black tarbooshes made of goat-skin; the Ottoman officers, soldiers and government employees by their tasseled tarbooshes; the Indians by
their red turbans; the Jews by flat red tarbooshes; the monks and
missionaries by their black head coverings; the European sea captains by their naval caps; the explorers in disguise . . . They rushed
out towards the rustling noise coming from behind the last bend,
the eerie rumbling, the bated restlessness of the waves below the
high balustrades . . . Then, here are Fao's quays, the lamps leading
its wooden bridges along the water for a distance; in the spaces between them boats are anchored one alongside another, their lights
swaying; there is also a freighter with its lights on, anchored between the two middle berths. It was possible for me to make out in
the middle of the river scattered floating lights. I didn't go very close
to the quay installations but contented myself with standing in
front of the dark, bare extension of the river. To my surprise a man
who was perhaps working as a watchman or worker on the quays
approached me and asked me for the time. Eleven.

On my return to the hotel I took a different road, passing by the
closed shops. I was extremely alert. The light will be shining
brightly in the hotel vestibule. The oil stove will be in the middle of
it, and to one side of the vestibule will be baggage, suitcases, a water
cooling box and a cupboard. Seated on the bench will be a man
who is dozing, his cigarette forgotten between his fingers. It will
happen that I shall approach the door of my room, shall open the
door, and shall find him sleeping in my bed; he will be turned to the
wall, having hung his red turban on the clothes hook.

Translated by Denys Johnson-Davies

Ibrahim al-Koni
(b. 1948)
LIBYA

Ibrahim al-Koni was born in Ghadames, Libya, to Tuareg parents. He graduated from the Gorki Institute in Moscow and has held several important governmental positions in Libya, as well as in Warsaw and Moscow. He presently lives in Switzerland and devotes himself full-time to writing. He has published more than thirty books, including collections of stories, novels, and books of essays and criticism. Much of his writing is available in German translation. Two novels, *The Bleeding of the Stone*, from which the following extract is taken, and *Anubis*, are available in English translation.

FROM *The Bleeding of the Stone*

John Parker, a captain at the Hweilis Base, had been chosen to run a subsidiary camp, set in a strategic spot on the Naffousa mountain. In his student days he'd studied Zoroastrian, Buddhist, and Islamic Sufi thought at the University of California, and he'd kept his fondness for Eastern philosophies. Upon joining the Marines and moving to North Africa in 1957, he'd seized the chance to plunge himself into a study of Sufi ways. When they'd landed in Tunisia on the way to Tripoli, he'd left his comrades (who'd gone to spend the evening in a bar), choosing instead to visit a *dhikr* circle. Although it was strictly against Marine rules to visit "doubtful" places of religion, the embassy official had seen no harm in meeting his wish, and together they'd gone to witness the rituals of dervishes chanting and ecstatically invoking God's name. It had, though, been a wretched experience. When they'd been standing by for just a few minutes, some young boys began throwing stones at them, driving them out of the circle. He'd returned to his ship with a fair number of bruises to show. His drunken comrades had made fun of him, telling him it was an old Eastern tradition for curious strangers to be stoned.

What fascinated him above all was an idea advanced by a French writer: that it was the Maghreb that had brought Sufism down from its throne of heavenly philosophy, to the common soil of everyday life. Here in these countries, in contrast to the Arab east, there seemed no difference between the wise sage, the simple dervish, and the pious saint—they all looked like wandering beggars! And so Sufism here, as an esoteric philosophy, was actually closer to Buddhism. There was no difference between God in heaven and the poor vagabond on earth, so long as God Himself was prepared to take up His abode in such holy fools.

In the same book he'd found the thrilling text that led to his passion for gazelle meat. The author had quoted a passage from an obscure Sufi traveler, who'd written as follows: "The truth lies in grazing beasts. In gazelles God has placed the secret and sown the meaning. For him who tastes the flesh of this creature, all impotence in the soul will be swept away, the veil of separation will be rent, and he will see God as He truly is."

This mystical passage would never have evoked such an echo in him had he not been interested, too, in the Buddhists' bold ideas on dumb animals. When at university, he'd repeated to Caroline an inscrutable passage from Zen teaching, to which he was deeply attached in those days. Man's search for union with God could, it said, only be realized when he'd passed through the animal state. He must live apart until he became an animal himself, silencing his tongue until he lost the ability of speech, eating grass until he forgot the taste of food. The Creator was more inclined to enter a creature living deep in the wilderness, secluded even from those animals that seek the company of humans.

He'd said many things of this sort to Caroline (who'd been infatuated with him), but he'd very stupidly failed to acknowledge he'd taken them from Buddhist teachings. As a result she'd supposed he was crazy and left him!

The obscure Sufi text brought him back to these outlandish no-tions, which had shattered his first relationship with a woman. Now he decided to use his isolation, here in the western mountain, to try to unravel the secret: to taste the flesh of this legendary animal, in the hope that God would open the door to him, that he'd know the bliss of seeing Him as He truly was. He was surprised by the Sufis' agreement that grazing creatures were specially worthy to receive God's holiness and presence, but he saw a strong parallel with Zen teachings, which set a greater value on animals than on man. They too had preferred some animals to others, placing savage beasts beyond the pale of mercy and ascribing holiness to those that were peaceful. The obscure Sufi took his vision still further, listing numerous strange illnesses whose only known cure was the eating of gazelle flesh. He needed gazelles, he told people—and right away they told him about Cain the son of Adam.

"If disaster ever struck," they said, "and all the gazelles in the desert perished except one, then Cain would find it and eat it up." They told tales, too, of Cain's legendary passion and greed for the meat. A dervish expressed it in cryptic fashion. "There's a worm in this creature's mouth," he said, "that makes him eat his very self if he finds no meat to eat." This dervish was a solitary old man who sat each day with his back against the wall of the mosque, facing the rays of the twilight sun. He didn't mix with others, and people avoided him because of his odd ideas on religion and the world. Although the general at the Tripoli headquarters had warned against mixing with local people, Parker couldn't resist the temptation, and he spoke with the old man everyone accused of being an outlandish dervish and heretic—he was shunned, apparently, because he'd fallen out with the other Sufi shaykhs. Once, when the two had gone together to a *dhikr* session, where dervishes tore at their faces and breasts, and brandished knives in the fire of their passion, the old man had led Parker right away.

"Look at those Tijani heretics!" he'd said. "Look at the heresies they're contriving, the way they're wrecking Sufism and Islam!"

On the way back, John had asked, suddenly: "According to your order, does God dwell in gazelles?"

The old man had been silent for some time. Then he'd said, as if talking to himself: "God dwells in all souls. To limit it to gazelles is heresy."

He'd turned to John and added: "That's one of the Tijani heresies."

Parker had read of the controversies between North African Sufis. This dervish, he'd learned already, belonged to the Qadiri order—which was why the Tijani shaykhs incited people against him, and he'd become an outcast. The man produced further surprising ideas that evening, as he went on talking about God's incarnation in earthly beings.

"That's our difference with you people," he said. "With you Christians. You say Christ is God, limiting God's glory to one creature, while we see Him present in all creatures. Our religion's more just than yours."

The wise dervish urged him, too, to change his view of the Sufi ways of life. The deeper he went in his quest, the man added, the more vitally important the things he was likely to discover. This Qadiri Sufi taught him many secret things. And as he came to know Cain better, and Cain went on supplying him with gazelle meat, he discovered that the dervish, like the Buddhists of Tibet and the Himalayas, ate no meat at all, but lived on barley bread. One day, even so, the old man made a passing reference to the *waddan*. He told him, in that mysterious tone he used when about to impart some secret knowledge known to no one else: "Take oil from Gharyan, dates from Fezzan. And meat? The *waddan*." He laughed. "Oh," he went on, "if the Tijani heretics only knew I was revealing the secrets of the desert to Christians! They'd stone me!" He gazed at him for some time, then went on in the same tone: "The *waddan*'s truly remarkable. I tasted it in the old days, when I used to eat meat. The divine secret's in the *waddan*."

He remembered this exchange when Cain, coming and telling him how the gazelles had died out in the desert, asked for the use of a helicopter to scour the Hasawna mountains.

"There've been some stray gazelles sighted there," he said. "The Hasawna mountains are the gazelles' last stronghold."

"It's not allowed to fly search helicopters over the desert," Parker said. "You know that as well as I do. The rules are clear enough."

"If a man wants roses," Cain said, "he'll put up with their thorns. Do you know that saying?"

Parker laughed.

"If a man wants roses," he repeated, "he'll put up with their thorns. Well, that's true enough. I don't know which of us loves roses more. Me—or the creature whose teeth are eaten by worms and can't live a single day without meat!"

Cain laughed in his turn, but the joke struck home even so.

"We've done with gazelles," he said, red-faced, but managing to hide his anger. "It's the *waddan*'s turn now."

"The *waddan*!"

Cain sipped his tea in silence. Then he said: "The *waddan*'s difficult to hunt. It hides away deep in the mountains, down in the southern desert. A journey there takes preparation, fleets of vehicles, specialists. And you won't give me one helicopter to search the Hasawna mountains. If a man wants roses, he'll put up with their thorns. The thorns of the *waddan* are stronger than gazelles'!"

"I wonder if either of us could put up with them!" John retorted. "You can't stand the desert thorns, I know. You'd like to reap the fruits without the sun and the dust. You'd like to hunt gazelles in silk gloves." He laughed sarcastically. "You don't love the desert," he went on. "Shaykh Jallouli, the one the other shaykhs in your town call a heretic dervish, says water cleanses the body and the desert cleanses the soul. I've never come across anyone here who's more faithful to the desert—and yet he doesn't savor its bounty the way you do. He doesn't eat its gazelles. You, Cain, eat the fruit and curse what produces it. The desert hasn't cleansed you, because you've never truly loved it. And now you demand whole fleets of vehicles to take you off in search of the *waddan* down in the southern deserts. You want to blackmail me the way you did with the gazelles all those years. You're not just selfish and greedy. You're lazy too."

Again Cain held himself in. He simply smiled. "If I wiped out the gazelles," he said evenly, "you helped me do it. You gave me the trucks and the guns, and you ate your fair share of the bag—more than your fair share. You're the one who wiped out the desert gazelles, after hammering my ear with all those fairy tales about the poor beast's meat having divine secrets lurking in it. You're the biggest criminal of the lot. You say how marvelous gazelles are, how innocent they are, then you sink your teeth in their flesh, in search of some secret that doesn't even exist outside your own weird head. You pretend to be kind to animals, and yet you're greedier than me, greedier than all the meat eaters in the desert. The worm tickling your teeth's fiercer than the one in mine."

But there was no other way of reaching the Hasawna mountains and combing it for the gazelles the wandering herdsmen said they'd seen. They flew off in the helicopter, on a secret mission Shaykh Jallouli anointed with curses. Ever since hearing of the slaughter of the gazelles, he'd refused to have anything to do with Parker. First he stopped shaking hands with him and returning his greetings, then he started sending people to him with warnings and curses. One Friday the two came suddenly face-to-face by the old souk. Jallouli lowered his head and tried to move on, but Parker wouldn't let him.

"How can you claim," the shaykh murmured then, pain in his eyes, "to belong to the religion of Christ? You're no part of him. You've nothing to do with him, or he with you."

With that he wrapped his cloak around his head and disappeared into the crowd. Parker never saw him again, but he couldn't forget the look of pain in the man's eyes as he'd uttered those harsh words. Only then did he sense the hateful crime he'd committed against one of the loveliest of creatures. But what could he do? Gazelle meat was like opium. Once a man tasted it, he got used to it; and once he'd got used to it, he'd go mad without it!

Translated by May Jayyusi and Christopher Tingley

The Ill-Omened Golden Bird

Abdullah worshiped for four hundred years, then occupied himself with the singing of a bird on a tree in the garden of his house. He was repaid for this by God ceasing to love him.

—Farid al-Din al-'Attar al-Nisaburi,
The Conference of the Birds

No sooner had it alighted on a scraggy wild bush than, standing bolt upright in front of the tent, she saw the poor child staring at its fabulously bright feathers. Like someone stung, she leapt up and hurled herself at the boy, encircling him with her arms. The tears coursed down from her eyes as she lamented, "No, no, don't look at it like that! It's a delusion. It's a trick. It steals children from their mothers."

But the child was able to detach himself from his mother's embrace with the litheness of a snake and to follow the extraordinary colored bird with the golden wings, the like of which he had never previously seen. He walked toward it fascinated.

The golden bird did not move, did not heed his approach. It waited for him until he was standing in front of it. The child stretched out his hand until it was almost touching the bird's feathers, which glowed under the rays of dusk, then it adroitly flew down and moved a couple of paces beyond the reach of his hand. The mesmerized child advanced farther, almost grasping hold of it. Again it evaded his hand and ran a few more steps. The child was breathless with curiosity and longing, and the extraordinary bird prepared itself for a long chase.

The mother wailed. "Woe is me! Now the chase has begun. Did I not tell you that it is a bird of ill-omen? It lures away children and draws them into the desert. Come back, child! Come back!"

The boy did not come back. He rushed off behind the golden messenger of enticement, which moved coquettishly, flirtatiously, as it made its escape. The child rushed after it, breathing hard, baffled by his desire to grasp it, to take possession of it. On that day his mother rescued him. Running behind them, she caught hold of him and forcibly took him back.

Night fell and darkness reigned. The father returned and she informed him in alarm of what had occurred. He declared with peremptory roughness, "If the bird comes back, shut the boy in. Tie him to a rope and fasten it to that peg."

The bird did not return on the following day, nor for several days after. It then seized the opportunity of the father being away and the mother having gone to visit a friend in the neighboring hamlet, and it advanced upon its confused victim. In the late afternoon it led him on, crossed with him the southern plains, traversing hills and valleys in an astounding chase. The wonderful golden bird would wait proudly until the child reached it and was about to grasp hold of it, when it would slip away, gracefully move off a pace or two, or three at the most, and then stand waiting as it turned to right and left. Sometimes it would direct toward the child an enigmatic look from its small, slyly lustrous eyes and spread its brilliant wings in womanly enticement until the child drew close and was bending over it, certain that this time he would grab hold of it, when it would again slip away with astonishing agility and forge ahead.

The chase continued.

Darkness advanced and finally covered the everlasting desert, and the bird disappeared.

The child found himself soiled with sweat, urine, and fatigue. He collapsed under a bush and fell asleep. At night he was woken by the howling of wolves and heard the conversation of the djinn in the open air. He recited the Chapter of Unity, which he had learned from his mother, as he watched the stars scattered in the darkness of the skies. The stars entertained him with their secret language, speaking to him of things he did not understand. Finally, he became sleepy again.

In the morning, he wandered for a long time in the desolate waste before they found him in a small wadi, lying under a sparse genista shrub with bloodied feet and cracked lips, exhausted and shattered by fatigue.

After the father had forced her to cease her long weeping and she was able to hold back her tears, the mother said that night, "Have you seen what the bird of ill-omen has done to you? It's Satan. Do you not understand?" She shook him violently as, driven by what had happened, she repeated, "It steals children from their mother. It's Satan—the accursed Satan."

The father stopped her with a brusque movement, and she went back to her sobbing. They were gathered around the stove before repairing to sleep. The boy fell asleep. The boy fell asleep as he sat there.

They had been blessed with him after they had despaired.

They had made the rounds of all the quacks, sorcerers, and holy men known in the oases of the desert until they had despaired of compassion. Talismans had been of no use, nor had amulets. She had procured the rarest of herbs and people had brought her, from the central parts of the continent, preparations made from snake poisons and the brains of wild beasts.

When they were close to the climacteric, they had been taken to the frightening Magian fortune-teller, who had become famous through dealing with the heathen company of the djinn in the oasis of Adrar.

Had they not sought him out in the plains of faraway Red Hammada he would not have deigned to meet them. The Magian fortune-teller had ceased to receive people and had gone into isolation a long time ago after a continuous series of battles and encounters organized by the Mustansir dervishes against the companies of believing djinn, who had taken possession of the last of the strongholds of wisdom in the desert, claiming that it was armed with talismans and amulets inspired by texts from the Quran. The group announced that the age of idols had come to an end and that the Magian's profession was an abomination, an act of Satan, so he had suffered persecution and was forced to cease practicing his readings that possessed understanding of the darkness and the unknown. He was likewise shunned by people through fear of the violence of the newly converted groups, so the leading pagan fortune-teller found himself isolated and besieged. He sought refuge in a cave in the mountain of Adrar and lived with his followers, in hiding from the arrogant, unbelieving djinn, who vie in breaking open talismans and sometimes in exchanging insulting names among themselves. Often people heard the eminent fortune-teller guffawing in his cave at the jokes of his loyal followers who had applied themselves tirelessly to keeping him amused so as to ease his loneliness.

He received the two of them at the entrance to the desolate cave that had been hacked out of the mountain top. He addressed them in Hausa. On realizing that they did not understand it, he condescended to talk to them in the Tuareg tongue of Tamahaq. As for the language of the Quran, he uttered not a word of it, and they knew that he was doing this in outrage at the Isawi dervishes, who had swept away his glory in the oasis. His complexion was tanned despite his isolation within the darkness of the cave. He was dressed from tip to toe in black, so that in the darkness he looked like a djinn from the company of unbelievers.

The people of the oasis had come to tremble at his followers, saying that the djinn had become hostile in their behavior ever since the dervishes had entered the Sufi orders and the assemblage of djinn had split into two companies: one that followed the true religion and believed in the dervishes, and one that had remained as they were—unbelieving, idolatrous, and following the fearsome Magian fortune-teller.

Perhaps it was such reports that affected the woman and caused her to tremble at merely seeing this idol sent from the homeland of caves and darkness.

He slaughtered a white chicken at her bare feet and stained her body with blood. He handled her rounded buttocks and toyed with her swelling breasts as he muttered the talismans of ancient idols and tilled her body with his rough fingers daubed with the blood of the snow-white chicken.

The husband followed these rites in a daze. The fortune-teller warned him against uttering any Quranic verses or traditions of the prophets before beginning his pagan recitations in the language of the Hausa and the djinn. He had said, "My helpers do not like that—Quranic verses and biographies of the messengers and prophets are forbidden in my house!"

Then he scattered a powderlike incense in the stove. Clouds of evil-smelling vapor rose up. The woman experienced vertigo, while her husband had a sensation of nausea. Then the bronzed Magian again fingered her body, staining it with the remnants of the blood. Finally he said, "We have finished the first stage. Tomorrow you will go with me and I shall show you the tomb in whose presence you must both sleep for three consecutive nights."

After mumbling some cryptic incantations, he concluded by saying, "It is the oldest grave in the desert. It is the oldest grave in the world—the tomb of tombs and the goal of the universe, a goal before people knew of the goal of the dervishes and the beaters on tambourines."

The tomb was a heap of black stones clinging to the foot of the mountain, below the gloomy cave. The first night passed calmly, and the second, and on the third night she saw her shameful dream, which bashfulness prevented her from recounting to her husband. She saw herself being given in marriage to the King of the Djinn. He penetrated her, unusually, in the morning and made her taste such an experience that she still reels at the memory of its frenzy. The frightening king had used her as no human man had ever used a woman. The two of them crossed the vast wadi, making their way on the stones, and she could not free herself of his blazingly feverish body.

She hid the great secret from her husband without knowing that he too had hidden his secret from her, for on that final night she was groaning and twisting and giving vent to her pain from her excessive, agonized pleasure. Neither of them was able to look the other in the eye for the space of several whole months. The fortune-teller had bestowed on them a pagan spell for the awaited heir apparent and he refused to take payment for his rites.

A few weeks later he saw that she had cravings for certain food and was devouring white mud.

No sooner was the boy born than she quickly hung the spell

around his neck, after securing it in a wrapping of leather and dec-
orating it with magical mosaic colors. When the charm was lost, a
year ago on one of their journeys across the desert, the woman was
distraught, but the stupid husband calmed her down by saying that
he would arrange for her to have a spell from a holy man at the
neighboring hamlet, not knowing that the spells of holy men do not
replace the charms of the pagan fortune-teller. As soon as the bird
of ill-omen came, the poor mother remembered her lost charm.

She felt distress and portents of evil.

The golden bird is the messenger of Satan to entice children and
steal them away from their mothers. The old women in the desert
say that it appears only rarely but when it does, many victims will
fall to it, for its appearance is linked to drought and lean years. The
old wise women in the deserts of Timbuktu confirm that the secret
of its evil omen lies in its golden feathers. Thus, wheresoever the
sparkle of the devilish gold flashes, ill-luck makes its appearance,
blood flows, and the accursed Satan is at work.

Today the bird has again made its appearance and has lured the
wretched boy to his destruction, the mother unaware, for she has
gone to the nearby hamlet to borrow a full waterskin.

In the days following its first appearance, precautions were
taken. She carried out her husband's order by tying the boy to a peg
with rough fiber threads, and she never went out to the pasture or
to visit women neighbors in the nearby plains without making sure
that the fetters around the bleeding leg of the child were firmly secured. He cried when she was away and would try to escape from
the cruel shackle, for the rough rope had carved a bloody collar
around his young leg. Secretly at night in her bed, she felt pity for
him, but would go back in the morning to secure the rope in her
fear for him.

But time is the bane of the memory, the temptation of extinction
and forgetfulness. Weeks passed and she grew complacent and relaxed her vigilance. Going away to borrow water, she left the boy
loose in the house. The ill-omened bird came after she had gone
and abducted the child.

He pursued it in the plains and the wadis; he ascended the heights and went down the hills. The pursuit continued into the late afternoon, and when the time for siesta came the child collapsed, his face set in the dust, panting for breath. The cruel sun was seated on its throne; its rays were released from their hiding-place and burnt the boy with their fire. His tender feet were dyed with blood, his lips were dry, his throat parched of the last drop of saliva.

The bird did not vanish until that moment. It witnessed the shudderings and tremblings of the child, at which it alighted on a wild bush with faded branches and started to spread its fabulous wings and preen them with its amazing beak.

The child regained consciousness before dusk and continued the chase, crawling on hands and knees over the savage stones. He did not turn his gaze to his bleeding limbs and had no sensation of his flesh being lacerated as the stones mangled it, strewing blood on the rocks.

They found the rotting body on the following day under a solitary and desolate lotus tree.

Through the days and nights she wept for him. She mourned him to the desert, the vastness, the wild trees, and the sacred crane. She did not cease moaning until the man took her on a journey to the cave of the fearsome Magian fortune-teller, craving to obtain another boy. There they told her that the detestable fortune-teller had died, and they expressed pride that Adrar had been cleansed for evermore of the filth of idols, but she went to the foot of the mountain where the oldest grave in the world had been erected, and there she lamented as she repeated her misfortune. "Why did you give him to me if You wanted to take him from me? Why?"

The Isawi dervishes answered her questions as they swayed ecstatically, beating on tambourines and raising their voices in Sufi panegyrics about divine love, there at the foot of the mountain. "He takes only from those He has liked, and He gives only to those He has loved."

Translated by Denys Johnson-Davies

Naguib Mahfouz
(1911–2006)
EGYPT

Naguib Mahfouz was born in Cairo in the distinctive historic district of Gamaliya, which provides the setting for many of his novels. He worked in various government posts until he retired in 1971. His first novel appeared in 1939, and in all he has published more than thirty novels and fourteen collections of short stories. Many of his novels have been made into successful films. In 1988 he was awarded the Nobel Prize in literature. Most of his writings are now available in translation.

Mahfouz's *Cairo Trilogy* is generally agreed to be his outstanding achievement. Like Galsworthy's *Forsyte Saga* or Thomas Mann's *Buddenbrooks*, it tells of the lives of a single family, in this case that of the patriarchal Ahmad Abd al-Jawad. When the English translation of the first book of the *Trilogy* appeared, the English critic Howard Brenton observed with acute insight that "Mahfouz does not seem to have heard of the sin of readability." It is in fact the sheer unpretentious readability of all his writing that makes him such an outstanding writer and allows him to be read with pleasure even in translation. Other novels by Mahfouz that deserve special attention include *Midaq Alley*—a starkly realistic narrative about an alley in Gamaliya and the extraordinary individuals who inhabit it—*The Thief and the Dogs*, *Adrift on the Nile*, *The Harafish*, *Arabian Nights and Days*, and *Miramar*. The English novelist John Fowles wrote an introduction to the first English-language edition of *Miramar*, published in 1978—no less than ten years before Mahfouz was awarded the Nobel Prize—pointing out that a distinguished writer had made his appearance on the literary scene. Mahfouz's *Children of the Alley*, about the inhabitants of a district of modern Cairo acting out the lives of their spiritual forebears, was considered too daring by many and provoked his attempted assassination in 1994 by an Islamist extremist. The extract from the *Cairo Trilogy* included here comes near the beginning of the first volume, *Palace Walk*; it is a description of Amina, the mother of the family, and shows the skill with which Mahfouz brings to life the simplest material.

Mahfouz's gifts as a short story writer are evident in the story below from *The Time and the Place*, a selection of stories drawn from the fourteen volumes he has published in this genre. Also below is an excerpt from his novel *Arabian Nights and Days*, a scene as compact as one of his short stories.

The Conjurer Made Off with the Dish

"The time has come for you to be useful," said my mother to me, and she slipped her hand into her pocket, saying:

"Take this piastre and go off and buy some beans. Don't play on the way, and keep away from the cars."

I took the dish, put on my clogs and went out, humming a tune. Finding a crowd in front of the bean-seller, I waited until I discovered a way through to the marble table.

"A piastre's worth of beans, mister," I called out in my shrill voice.

He asked me impatiently:

"Beans alone? With oil? With cooking butter?"

I didn't answer and he said to me roughly:

"Make way for someone else."

I withdrew, overcome by embarrassment, and returned home defeated.

"Returning with an empty dish?" my mother shouted at me. "What did you do—spill the beans or lose the piastre, you naughty boy?"

"Beans alone? With oil? With cooking butter?—you didn't tell me," I protested.

"You stupid, what do you eat every morning?"

"I don't know."

"You good-for-nothing, ask him for beans with oil."

I went off to the man and said:

"A piastre's worth of beans with oil, mister."

With a frown of impatience he asked:

"Linseed oil? Nut oil? Olive oil?"

I was taken aback and again made no answer:

"Make way for someone else," he shouted at me.

I returned in a rage to my mother, who called out in astonishment:

"You've come back empty-handed—no beans and no oil."

"Linseed oil? Nut oil? Olive oil?—you didn't tell me," I said angrily.

"Beans with oil means beans with linseed oil."

"How should I know?"

"You're a good-for-nothing and he's a tiresome man—tell him beans with linseed oil."

"How should I know?"

I went off quickly and called out to the man while still some yards from his shop:

"Beans with linseed oil, mister."

"Put the piastre on the counter," he said, plunging the ladle into the pot.

I put my hand into my pocket but didn't find the piastre. I searched round for it anxiously. I turned my pocket inside out but found no trace of it. The man withdrew the ladle empty, saying with disgust:

"You've lost the piastre—you're not a boy to be depended on."

"I haven't lost it," I said, looking under my feet and round about me. "It's been in my pocket all the time."

"Make way for someone else and don't make trouble."

I returned to my mother with an empty dish.

"Good grief, you idiot boy!"

"The piastre . . ."

"What of it?"

"It wasn't in my pocket."

"Did you buy sweets with it?"

"I swear I didn't."

"How did you lose it?"

"I don't know."

"Do you swear by the Koran you didn't buy anything with it?"

"I swear."

"There's a hole in your pocket."

"No there isn't."

"Maybe you gave it to the man the first time or the second."

"Maybe."

"Are you sure of nothing?"

"I'm hungry."

She clapped her hands together in a gesture of resignation.

"Never mind," she said. "I'll give you another piastre but I'll take it out of your money-box, and if you come back with an empty dish I'll break your head."

I went off at a run, dreaming of a delicious breakfast. At the turning leading to the alleyway where the bean-seller was I saw a crowd of children and heard merry, festive sounds. My feet dragged as my heart was pulled towards them. At least let me have a fleeting glance. I slipped in amongst them and found the conjurer looking straight at me. A stupefying joy overwhelmed me; I was completely taken out of myself. With the whole of my being I became involved in the tricks of the rabbits and the eggs, and the snakes and the ropes. When the man came up to collect money, I drew back mumbling, "I haven't got any money."

He rushed at me savagely and I escaped only with difficulty. I ran off, my back almost broken by his blow, and yet I was utterly happy as I made my way to the seller of beans.

"Beans with linseed oil for a piastre, mister," I said.

He went on looking at me without moving, so I repeated my request.

"Give me the dish," he demanded angrily.

The dish! Where was the dish? Had I dropped it while running? Had the conjurer made off with it?

"Boy, you're out of your mind."

I turned back, searching along the way for the lost dish. The place where the conjurer had been I found empty, but the voices of children led me to him in a nearby lane. I moved round the circle; when the conjurer spotted me he shouted out threateningly:

"Pay up or you'd better scram."

"The dish!" I called out despairingly.

"What dish, you little devil?"

"Give me back the dish."

"Scram or I'll make you into food for snakes."

He had stolen the dish, yet fearfully I moved away out of sight and wept. Whenever a passer-by asked me why I was crying I would reply:

"The conjurer made off with the dish."

Through my misery I became aware of a voice saying:

"Come along and watch."

I looked behind me and saw a peep-show had been set up. I saw dozens of children hurrying towards it and taking it in turns to stand in front of the peepholes, while the man began making his commentary on the pictures:

"There you've got the gallant knight and the most beautiful of all ladies, Zainat al-Banat."

Drying my tears, I gazed up in fascination at the box, completely forgetting the conjurer and the dish. Unable to overcome the temptation, I paid over the piastre and stood in front of the peephole next to a girl who was standing in front of the other one, and there flowed across our vision enchanting picture stories. When I came back to my own world I realized I had lost both the piastre and the dish, and there was no sign of the conjurer. However, I gave no thought to the loss, so taken up was I with the pictures of chivalry, love and deeds of daring. I forgot my hunger; I forgot the fear of what threatened me back home. I took a few paces back so as to lean against an ancient wall of what had once been a Treasury and the seat of office of the Cadi, and gave myself up wholly to my reveries. For a long while I dreamt of chivalry, of Zainat al-Banat and the ghoul. In my dream I spoke aloud, giving meaning to my words with gestures. Thrusting home the imaginary lance, I said:

"Take that, O ghoul, right in the heart!"

"And he raised Zainat al-Banat up behind him on his horse," came back a gentle voice.

I looked to my right and saw the young girl who had been beside me at the performance. She was wearing a dirty dress and coloured clogs and was playing with her long plait of hair; in her other hand were the red and white sweets called "Lady's fleas," which she was leisurely sucking. We exchanged glances and I lost my heart to her.

"Let's sit down and rest," I said to her.

She appeared to be agreeable to my suggestion, so I took her by the arm and we went through the gateway of the ancient wall and sat down on the step of a stairway that went nowhere, a stairway that rose up until it ended in a platform behind which there could be seen a blue sky and minarets. We sat in silence, side by side. I pressed her hand and we sat on in silence, not knowing what to say. I experienced feelings that were new, strange and obscure. Putting my face close to hers, I breathed in the natural smell of her hair, mingled with an odour of earth, and the fragrance of breath mixed with the aroma of sweets. I kissed her lips. I swallowed my saliva which had taken on a sweetness from the dissolved "Lady's fleas." I put my arm round her, without her uttering a word, kissing her cheek and lips. Her lips grew still as they received the kiss, then went back to sucking at the sweets. At last she decided we should get up. I seized her arm anxiously.

"Sit down," I said.

"I'm going," she said simply.

"Where to?" I asked irritably.

"To the midwife Umm Ali," and she pointed to a house at the bottom of which was a small ironing shop.

"Why?"

"To tell her to come quickly."

"Why?"

"My mother's crying in pain at home. She told me to go to the midwife Umm Ali and to take her along quickly."

"And you'll come back after that?"

She nodded her head in assent. Her mentioning her mother

reminded me of my own and my heart missed a beat. Getting up from the ancient stairway, I made my way back home. I wept out loud, a tried method by which I would defend myself. I expected she would come to me but she did not. I wandered from the kitchen to the bedroom but found no trace of her. Where had my mother gone? When would she return? I was bored with being in the empty house. An idea occurred to me: I took a dish from the kitchen and a piastre from my savings and went off immediately to the seller of beans. I found him asleep on a bench outside the shop, his face covered over by his arm. The pots of beans had vanished and the long-necked bottles of oil had been put back on the shelf and the marble top washed down.

"Mister," I whispered, approaching.

Hearing nothing but his snoring, I touched his shoulder. He raised his arm in alarm and looked at me through reddened eyes.

"Mister."

"What do you want?" he asked roughly, becoming aware of my presence and recognizing me.

"A piastre's worth of beans with linseed oil."

"Eh?"

"I've got the piastre and I've got the dish."

"You're crazy, boy," he shouted at me. "Get out or I'll bash your brains in."

When I didn't move he pushed me so violently I went sprawling onto my back. I got up painfully, struggling to hold back the crying that was twisting my lips. My hands were clenched, one on the dish and the other on the piastre. I threw him an angry look. I thought about returning with my hopes dashed, but dreams of heroism and valour altered my plan of action. Resolutely, I made a quick decision and with all my strength threw the dish at him. It flew through the air and struck him on the head, while I took to my heels, heedless of everything. I was convinced I'd killed him, just as the knight had killed the ghoul. I didn't stop running till I was near the ancient wall. Panting, I looked behind me but saw no signs of any pursuit. I stopped to get my breath back, then asked myself what I should do now that the second dish was lost. Something warned me not to return home directly, and soon I had given myself over to a wave of indifference that bore me off where it willed. It meant a beating, neither more nor less, on my return, so let me put it off for a time. Here was the piastre in my hand and I could have some sort of enjoyment with it before being punished. I decided to pretend I had forgotten my having done wrong—but where was the conjurer, where was the peep-show? I looked everywhere for them but to no avail.

Worn out by this fruitless searching, I went off to the ancient stairway to keep my appointment. I sat down to wait, imagining to myself the meeting. I yearned for another kiss redolent with the fragrance of sweets. I admitted to myself that the little girl had given me sensations I had never experienced before. As I waited and dreamed, a whispering sound came to me from far away behind me. I climbed the stairs cautiously and at the final landing I lay down flat on my face in order to see what was behind it, without anyone being able to spot me. I saw some ruins surrounded by a high wall, the last of what remained of the Treasury and the Chief Cadi's house. Directly under the stairs sat a man and a woman, and it was from them that the whispering came. The man looked like a tramp; the woman like one of those gypsies that tend sheep. An inner voice told me that their meeting was similar to the one I had had. Their lips and eyes revealed this, but they showed astonishing expertise in the extraordinary things they did. My gaze became rooted upon them with curiosity, surprise, pleasure, and a certain amount of disquiet. At last they sat down side by side, neither of them taking any notice of the other. After quite a while the man said:

"The money!"

"You're never satisfied," she said irritably.

Spitting on the ground, he said: "You're crazy."

"You're a thief."

He slapped her hard with the back of his hand, and she gathered up a handful of earth and threw it in his face. Then he sprang at her, fastening his fingers on her windpipe. In vain she gathered all her strength to escape from his grip. Her voice failed her, her eyes bulged out of their sockets, while her feet struck out at the air. In

dumb terror I stared at the scene till I saw a thread of blood trickling down from her nose. A scream escaped from my mouth. Before
the man raised his head, I had crawled backwards; descending the
stairs at a jump, I raced off like mad to wherever my legs might
carry me. I didn't stop running till I was out of breath. Gasping for
breath, I was quite unaware of my whereabouts, but when I came to
myself I found I was under a raised vault at the middle of a cross-
roads. I had never set foot there before and had no idea of where I
was in relation to our quarter. On both sides sat sightless beggars,
and crossing it from all directions were people who paid attention
to no one. In terror I realized I had lost my way and that countless
difficulties lay in wait for me before I would find my way home.
Should I resort to asking one of the passers-by to direct me? What,
though, would happen if chance should lead me to a man like the
vendor of beans or the tramp of the waste plot? Would a miracle
come about whereby I'd see my mother approaching so that I could
eagerly hurry towards her? Should I try to make my own way, wandering about till I came across some familiar landmark that would
indicate the direction I should take? I told myself that I should be
resolute and take a quick decision: the day was passing and soon
mysterious darkness would descend.

Translated by Denys Johnson-Davies

FROM *Arabian Nights and Days*

He was truthful in what he said: his sorrow for Sanaan's family did
not dissipate, and the origin of that did not lie solely in passionate
love. He had liked the man before he had liked his daughter. He
was not always devoid of good sentiments and religious remem-
brances, but he found no objection to practicing corruption in a
corrupt world. The truth was that in the quarter there was no heart
like his for mingling black with white. So it was that he invited
Fadil Sanaan to his house on a visit shrouded with secrecy.

The young man came in his new attire, consisting of a gallabiya and sandals, the garb of a peddler. Gamasa seated himself beside him in the reception room and said, "I am pleased, Fadil, that you are facing up with such courage to the way things have turned out for you."

"I thank God who has preserved my faith after the loss of position and wealth."

Truly impressed, Gamasa said, "I summoned you in deference to our long acquaintance."

"May God bless you, sir."

He looked at him for a while, then said, "If it weren't for that I would have allowed myself to arrest you."

In amazement Fadil inquired, "Arrest me? Why, sir?"

"Don't pretend not to know. Has not the evil that engulfed you been enough for you? Seek your livelihood far from associating with destructive elements who are the enemies of the sultan."

"I am nothing but a peddler," said Fadil with a pallid face.

"Stop dissimulating, Fadil. Nothing is hidden from Gamasa al-Bulti, and my first task, as you know, is to pursue the Shiites and the Kharijites."

"I am not one of them," said Fadil in a low voice. "Early in my life I was a student of Sheikh Abdullah al-Balkhi."

"I too was a student of his. Many graduate from the school of al-Balkhi—people of the Way and people of the Prophet's Sunna, Sufis and Sunnis. Some devils who deviate from the Path also graduate."

"Be sure, sir, that I am as far as can be from those devils."

"You have very many companions from among them."

"I have nothing to do with their doctrines."

"It starts as innocent friendship, then comes degeneration—they are madmen, they accuse the rulers of unbelief and they delude the poor and the slaves. Nothing pleases them, not even fasting in the month of Ragab. It is as though God had chosen them to the exclusion of His other worshipers. Be on your guard against falling into the same fate as your father, for the Devil has all kinds of ways and means. As for me, I know nothing but my duty. I have pledged my loyalty to the sultan, as I have to the governor of the quarter, in exterminating the apostates."

"Be assured, sir," said Fadil in a listless tone, "that I am very far distant from the apostates."

"I have given you fatherly advice, so keep it in mind," said Gamasa.

"Thank you for your kindness, sir."

Gamasa began scrutinizing his face in search of points of similarity between him and his sister Husniya. For some moments he was lost in the ecstasy of love. Then he said, "There's one more matter: I would ask you to inform your mother that to present a petition for the return of the family property would be regarded as a challenge to the sultan. There is no power or strength other than through God."

"That is also my opinion, sir," said Fadil meekly.

The meeting ended secretly, as it had begun. Gamasa wondered whether one day he would be given the chance of summoning him that he might ask for Husniya's hand.

Translated by Denys Johnson-Davies

FROM *Palace Walk*

When they had finished breakfast, the mother said, "Aisha, you do the laundry today and Khadija will clean the house. Afterward meet me in the oven room."

Amina divided the work between them right after breakfast. They were content to be ruled by her, and Aisha would not question her assignment. Khadija would take the trouble to make a few comments, either to show her worth or to start a quarrel. Thus she said, "I'll let you clean the house if you think washing the clothes is too much. But if you make a fuss over the washing so you can stay in the bathroom till all the work in the kitchen is finished, that's an excuse that can be rejected in advance."

Aisha ignored her remark and went off to the bath humming. Khadija commented sarcastically, "Lucky for you that sound reverberates in the bathroom like a phonograph speaker. So sing and let the neighbors hear it."

Their mother left the room and went through the hall to the stairs. She climbed to the roof to make her morning rounds there before descending to the oven room. The bickering between her daughters was nothing new to her. Over the course of time it had turned into a customary way of life when the father was not at home and no one could think of anything pleasant to say. She had tried to stop it by using entreaty, humor, and tenderness. That was the only type of discipline she employed with her children. It fit her nature, which could not stand anything stronger. She lacked the firmness that rearing children occasionally requires. Perhaps she would have liked to be firm but was not able to. Perhaps she had attempted to be firm but had been overcome by her emotions and weakness. It seemed she could not bear for the ties between her and her children to be anything but love and affection. She let the father or his shadow, which dominated the children from afar, straighten them out and lay down the law. Thus their silly quarrel did not weaken her admiration for her two girls or her satisfaction with them. Even Aisha, who was insanely fond of singing and standing in front of the mirror, her laziness notwithstanding, was no less skillful and organized than Khadija.

Amina would have been justified in allowing herself long periods of relaxation, but she was prevented by a natural tendency that was almost a disease. She insisted on supervising everything in the house, no matter how small. When the girls finished their work, she would go around energetically inspecting the rooms, living areas, and halls, with a broom in one hand and a feather duster in the other. She searched the corners, walls, curtains, and all the furnishings to eliminate an overlooked speck of dust, finding as much pleasure and satisfaction in that as in removing a speck from her eye. She was by nature such a perfectionist that she examined the clothes about to be laundered. If she discovered a piece of clothing that was unusually dirty, she would not spare the owner a gentle reminder of his duty, whether it was Kamal, who was going on ten, or

Yasin, who had two clear and contradictory approaches to caring for himself. He was excessively fastidious about his external appearance—his suit, fez, shirt, necktie, and shoes—but shockingly neglectful of his underwear.

Naturally this comprehensive concern of hers did not exclude the roof and the pigeons and chickens that inhabited it. In fact, the time she spent on the roof was filled with love and delight from the opportunities it presented for work, not to mention the joys of play and merriment she found there. No wonder, for the roof was a new world she had discovered. The big house had known nothing of it until she joined the family. She had created it afresh through the force of her spirit, back when the house retained the appearance it had always had since being built ages before. It was her idea to have these cages with the cooing pigeons put on some of the high walls. She had arranged these wooden chicken coops where the hens clucked as they foraged for food. How much joy she got from scattering grain for them or putting the water container on the ground as the hens raced for it, preceded by their rooster. Their beaks fell on the grain quickly and regularly, like sewing-machine needles, leaving little indentations in the dust like the pockmarks from a drizzle. How good she felt when she saw them gazing at her with clear little eyes, inquisitive and questioning, while they cackled and clucked with a shared affection that filled her heart with tenderness.

She loved the chickens and pigeons as she loved all of God's creatures. She made little noises to them, thinking they understood and responded. Her imagination had bestowed conscious, intelligent life on all animals and occasionally even on inanimate objects. She was quite certain that these beings praised her Lord and were in contact, by various means, with the spirit world. Her world with its earth and sky, animals and plants, was a living, intelligent one. Its merits were not confined to the blessing of life. It found its completion in worship. It was not strange, then, that, relying on one excuse or another, she prolonged the lives of the roosters and hens. One hen was full of life, another a good layer. This rooster woke her in the morning with his crowing. Perhaps if it had been left entirely to her, she would never have consented to put her knife to their throats. If circumstances did force her to slaughter one, she selected a chicken or pigeon with a feeling close to anguish. She would give it a drink, seek God's mercy for it, invoke God's name, ask forgiveness, and then slaughter it. Her consolation was that she was exercising a right that God the Benefactor had granted to all those who serve Him.

The most amazing aspect of the roof was the southern half overlooking al-Nahhasin Street. There in years past she had planted a special garden. There was not another one like it in the whole neighborhood on any of the other roofs, which were usually covered with chicken droppings. She had first begun with a small number of pots of carnations and roses. They had increased year by year and were arranged in rows parallel to the sides of the walls. They grew splendidly, and she had the idea of putting a trellis over the top. She got a carpenter to install it. Then she planted both jasmine and hyacinth bean vines. She attached them to the trellis and around the posts. They grew tall and spread out until the area was transformed into an arbor garden with a green sky from which jasmine flowed down. An enchanting, sweet fragrance was diffused throughout.

This roof, with its inhabitants of chickens and pigeons and its arbor garden, was her beautiful, beloved world and her favorite place for relaxation out of the whole universe, about which she knew nothing. As usual at this hour, she set about caring for it. She swept it, watered the plants, fed the chickens and pigeons. Then for a long time, with smiling lips and dreamy eyes, she enjoyed the scene surrounding her. She went to the end of the garden and stood behind the interwoven, coiling vines, to gaze out through the openings at the limitless space around her.

She was awed by the minarets which shot up, making a profound impression on her. Some were near enough for her to see their lamps and crescent distinctly, like those of Qala'un and Barquq. Others appeared to her as complete wholes, lacking details, like the minarets of the mosques of al-Husayn, al-Ghuri, and al-Azhar. Still other minarets were at the far horizon and seemed phantoms, like those of the Citadel and Rifa'i mosques. She turned her face toward them with devotion, fascination, thanksgiving, and hope. Her spirit soared over their tops, as close as possible to the heavens. Then her eyes would fix on the minaret of the mosque of al-Husayn, the dearest one to her because of her love for its namesake. She looked at it affectionately, and her yearnings mingled with the sorrow that pervaded her every time she remembered she was not allowed to visit the son of the Prophet of God's daughter, even though she lived only minutes away from his shrine.

She sighed audibly and that broke the spell. She began to amuse herself by looking at the roofs and streets. The yearnings would not leave her. She turned her back on the wall. Looking at the unknown had overwhelmed her: both what is unknown to most people, the invisible spirit world, and the unknown with respect to her in particular, Cairo, even the adjacent neighborhood, from which voices reached her. What could this world of which she saw nothing but the minarets and roofs be like? A quarter of a century had passed while she was confined to this house, leaving it only on infrequent occasions to visit her mother in al-Khurunfush. Her husband escorted her on each visit in a carriage, because he could not bear for anyone to see his wife, either alone or accompanied by him.

She was neither resentful not discontented, quite the opposite. All the same, when she peeked through the openings between the jasmine and the hyacinth bean vines, off into space, at the minarets and rooftops, her delicate lips would rise in a tender, dreamy smile. Where might the law school be where Fahmy was sitting at this moment? Where was the Khalil Agha School, which Kamal assured her was only a minute's trip from the mosque of al-Husayn? Before leaving the roof, she spread her hands out in prayer and called on her Lord: "God, I ask you to watch over my husband and children, my mother and Yasin, and all the people: Muslims and Christians, even the English, my Lord, but drive them from our land as a favor to Fahmy, who does not like them."

Translated by William Maynard Hutchins
and Olive E. Kenny

Mohamed Makhzangi
(b. 1950)

EGYPT

Mohamed Makhzangi was born in the town of Mansura in the Delta of Egypt. He studied to become a doctor and later specialized in psychology and alternative medicine in Kiev, Ukraine. After practicing as a doctor, he turned to journalism and writing. He spent time in Kuwait working on the magazine *al-'Arabi*, and he currently works in Cairo on the children's edition of *al-'Arabi*. He has published several volumes of short stories; translations of his stories have appeared in English, French, German, Russian, and Chinese. He divides his time between Egypt and Syria.

The Pilot

Aboard a slim boat among the forests of reeds at the lake's edge I stood watching what was happening. I was using binoculars to observe this method of hunting duck, though without really believing my eyes. It seemed to me a simple, unnatural contrivance, aptly named "submersion." The noses of the hunters practicing it reminded me of the Hyksos. I knew that long ago they had infiltrated to this spot, settling on the lake shore. The memory of Tanis, submerged somewhere in the water in front of me, gave me the idea that something unpleasant would perhaps repeat itself. I jeered at the sight of the hunter I was following getting his equipment ready: tying his pocket knife by the handle to a string dangling from his wrist, he put on his cap made of leather and duck feathers and began to push his way into the water. He submerged himself up to his nose. In the middle of the lake it looked as if a wild duck were swimming about. But it was a very poor sort of a duck, a travesty of a duck for anyone giving it a moment's scrutiny.

The flight of duck wove into sight on the lake's horizon, led by the drake, the pilot. The flight advanced like a large dark arrowhead against the clear, luminous surface of the sky. It seemed to me something sublimely cosmic in its sweep. But I felt ill at ease when I saw it suddenly changing course from winging its way in the heavens to dipping down toward the water, toward the fake swimming bird. It was with a trembling heart that I waited for the eyes of the pilot bird to grasp the sheer crudity of the deception. There was no doubt that this might occur, be it at the very last moment. But the pilot bird did not turn back and the arrow carried on in its descent. All at once I heard the splash as the feet and bellies of the birds came into contact with the water. The arrow put down on the waters of the lake, becoming a triangle of closely packed birds, with the ambush lying in the very heart of the triangle.

The birds close to the fake duck gave out a small collective pulsation. In a flash one of them vanished, leaving in its place a gap that was quickly filled by the closely packed birds. The Hyksos hunter in this flash of time gently stretched out his hand under the water, catching hold of the feet of the duck nearest him. Pulling it under the water before it could cry out or struggle, he busied himself with cutting its throat. Then he tied it by the feet to the belt around his waist so that it hung down, trailing blood.

The birds were quickly dwindling in number. I was astonished that they were not alarmed by their startling reduction in number or by the water around them becoming stained with blood.

It was clear that the Hyksos hunter made a point of leaving the leader, the pilot bird, to the end. The other birds, as they diminished in number, would move automatically to crowd together again, retaining the shape of a triangle, with the pilot bird at its apex. It became apparent to me that in their long flight and when they were swimming, the birds never looked around them. It was enough for each to keep its mind on where the pilot was and to follow it. Flying in arrowhead formation and crowding together into a triangle were merely instinctive measures to allow each bird to have a commanding view of the pilot. Seeing the pilot, each bird is reassured. Whether its neighbor vanishes or remains in place, nothing worries the bird so long as the pilot is there: the pilot flies and the bird flies behind, the pilot alights and the bird too alights. The Hyksos hunter no doubt understood this, so would leave the pilot alone. Did the pilot not notice?

But how should the pilot notice? As I watched it through my binoculars for a long time, it looked neither around nor behind itself. It seemed to look out only for itself, just so long as it felt that there was a bird of like species following it. But the bird that remained was not following it—there was only the cap of the Hyksos hunter, hidden under the water, that travesty of a duck that jumped to his feet with a cry of total victory. This time the hunter did not drag his prey under the water to cut its throat. He grasped hold of it, keeping it alive. But what sort of a life for the pilot bird in the grasp of the hunter, who had emerged exultantly from the bloodied water, around his middle the bodies of the rest of the birds, swinging by their tied feet, the slaughtered covey that was?

Translated by Denys Johnson-Davies

Alia Mamdouh
(b. 1944)
IRAQ

Alia Mamdouh was born in Baghdad. After taking a degree in psychology, she became the editor of a weekly magazine. She left Iraq in 1982 and has since lived in Beirut, Tunis, Morocco, and Paris. Her novel *Naphtalene* has appeared in translation in English, French, Italian, German, Spanish, Dutch, and Catalan, and her latest novel, *The Loved Ones*, won the Naguib Mahfouz Medal for Literature in 2004.

Presence of the Absent Man

And another day . . .
(This evening will have a different taste.)

Since early morning the woman had been constantly walking about, on the move. She washed the passageway leading to the small garden in which were rows of sparse bushes, short, flaccid, and drooping. She removed the cat from its shelter and took hold of one of the kittens. It tried to get away from her. It squatted on the ground, then gently let go its claws.

"Meiow . . . Meiow."

After she had cleaned the dirt from inside the small wooden shelter, she took hold of the mother cat and began talking to it. The cat's face bore that look that would turn to invective if the woman increased the amount of tenderness she was showing.

"Puss . . . Puss."

The woman is afflicted by a strange feeling of numbness. She fingers her wrinkled face and unties from her head the blue headscarf patterned with white and red circles. She takes it in her hand and folds it lengthways, then begins swinging it to right and left, playing with the kittens, while the mother cat looks on warily. The headscarf shakes between the woman's fingers, sometimes becoming the object of a tug-of-war in the teeth of one or other cat.

(Ah, I want to have someone to confide in.)

She leaves the door of the shelter open, and her face becomes grave with a certain sense of frustration and the dialogues she opens up with herself and for which she vainly waits for answers.

From morning she has been setting aside some of the furniture. This couch had not brought much luck: her husband had sat down on it and died. And this chair: whenever she sits on it, her thoughts become disrupted and she cannot say what she wants to say to those around her, a problem she does not know how to solve. What furniture, then, is left?

All she possesses are three bamboo chairs, a long sofa with rickety back legs, and another small one (which, however, is like a cavern in that whenever anyone sits in it they go off into a semitrance). There is also an old carpet that covers quite a bit of the house, and curtains the color of dust that are in fact clean. Drawing back the curtains, she opens the large window that looks onto the garden. The cat is licking its kittens piled up on top of her like the gum that piles up over the fissures in a tree.

This evening she will be conversing with a real voice, and she trembles with delight. She leaves the window, enters her room, and extracts from a large, carefully wrapped bundle some white towels, a wooden comb with broad teeth, and a large cube-shaped cake of soap redolent with the scent of chicory. She looks at herself in the mirror: A woman in her forties, tall and with a dark complexion, sturdily built, her black hair slightly coarse, her muscles strong, giving the impression of severity, her eyes black and sharp, bespeaking a certain wildness. Carrying all her things, she puts them down on a small chair with short legs outside the bathroom door.

(Oh, if only I had some girl, I'd call her to gather up all these things for me, and I'd leave her standing outside until I came out of the bathroom.)

She quickly takes off her clothes. Despite herself, and with an unhurried movement, she looks with distaste at all the parts of her body. The bathroom was the sole place where she would gasp and cry out, not troubling to hide her embarrassment at seeing herself. Nor would she shrink from admitting that she had begun to age.

She opens the tap and hot tongues descend. The steam from the hot water dazes her and she begins first of all to scrub her face.

On her wedding night she had scrubbed her face so hard with some sort of stone that she had made it bleed. They told her it would fill the vessels of her face with pure, healthy blood. They also told her that a red face would be a green light for the man to satisfy all her desires. But while her face had continued to be radiant, luck had held aloof.

She scrubs her back with a piece of wood in the shape of a hand, moaning and laughing. She will remain a respectable woman, for no one expects her to be otherwise.

It was on her last visit to the big market: every Thursday the big market rises up in her head like the Prophet's Midnight Journey, and the new things she imagines she will be wearing cling to her mind, and the unknown man who will while away her time from

home to market in the expectancy of something, and all the possibilities she used to see as impossible she would imagine as happening with every visit to the big market.

It was there that she saw her. A star in her haughtiness, obscenely
and insolently beautiful. Her *abaya* gave out a revealing light,
through which she quivered like someone who has lost her way. She
was gazing in all directions; then, at last, her eyes came to rest on
hers. When, suddenly, she bumped into her, the *abaya* fell down
from a head that trembled with shyness and a face that veered between recalcitrance and chastity. "I didn't mean to embarrass you."

The other woman did not reply. She remained silent, innocent,
alarmed about something that was going to occur. Leaning forward, she became, amid that throng of people, a ball being hurled
about by buyers and sellers. And when the other opened her arms
and quickly clasped her, fearful she would fall, the two of them
looked at each other. The two pairs of eyes were pierced by the light
from a match that had just been struck, and the two bodies released
a blaze of high tension, while between their fingers crept cold damp
sweat.

"Every Thursday I come here—and you?"

The other woman did not reply.

"I've not seen you before. Are you from here?"

Like a sting, gripped by what was around her, the other woman
answers, "I'm on a visit."

"Anyone with you?"

"My husband and the children are waiting for me at the entrance
to the market."

How was it that she had not seen this face before, this reticent,
alert, suspicious face, a face made for passion? When she proceeded
to free herself from her, she clung to her, saying—the words all
mixed up with the voices of vendors, the screaming of children, the
clamor of women doing their shopping, and the mewing of cats
standing far off waiting for somewhere to take shelter—"Every
Thursday I come here."

And her voice was lost amid the din of passers-by.

But the other woman takes herself off like hallowed sin, and all these scenes evaporate and she is moving about alone, with despair gathering inside her head like a hemorrhage.

Her eyes are half-closed, and the soap flows over her pores, the bubbles losing themselves on the naked brown flesh. She stretches out her legs, the brown froth bespattered on her knees.

(First of all I'll look into her eyes, and then I'll get to know her. I want to be sure she's in front of me, for the time between looking at someone and getting to know them is a new departure.)

She wants to begin from her toes. She will tickle them first, so as to see her smile. Maybe she will cry out with joy: joy is like death, and for her nothing but death remains.

She leans against the bathroom wall and sings an old folk song. She places her dirty clothes in an ancient washbowl, scouring them with her hand while continuing to sing.

And she will seat her in front of her and at first will look into her eyes and will not wait for any sign of the screen being raised. Like her, she will be on her own.

She will bring the food for the cat and its kittens so that their mewing will not disturb them, and she will put all the clocks out of action and will sit waiting for her like a child waiting for its New Year present.

She squeezes out her clothes.

(First of all I'll squeeze her knees, because the only time I saw her knees they looked like two solitary fruits on a lofty tree.)

She leans against the wall for a while.

She will not put on the strong light, so she will not be suddenly startled.

She stands upright in the middle of the bathroom and her shadow looks solid and solitary.

The breasts are heavy, the shoulders broad, the hips full, the thighs taut. The hair falls sedately down to the neck; the neck itself is smooth, the face giving itself up completely to becoming, after a while, the half-circle that will become complete with the semicircle that will shortly be coming.

On the second Thursday she did not come, neither on the third, the fourth, the fifth, or the sixth. She would hurry to the market, with the noon heat approaching fifty degrees. Her eyes would be bloodshot, her stomach saturated with the smell of sweat and that physical desire she did not want to be dispersed after having come so close to it.

She would hurl herself at the vendors, shouting unreasonably about the rise in prices, then buying unnecessary things. A cat crouched against the wall, its tongue dry, its body ablaze with the heat. At home the cat stays for days without food: in retribution for all these times of dejection, she deprives the cat and its kittens of food. She looks at herself in the mirror.

(I've aged six weeks all at once.)

She had not got to know her name, and all names were jostling in her head in a nightmare. She did not know her address and all addresses took turns in destroying her because of her separation from her.

They had come to know one another in a feverish manner. Every morning she would pile up the sheets on the floor, throw the pillows against the wall, strike her head with a fierce blow of her fist, and tell herself that she was emotionally bankrupt.

After the first meeting she stayed a week without washing, lest the other woman's signature be erased from her body, and every Thursday would bring her defeat and the ordeal of futile hopes.

When, once again, she seats herself on the wooden sofa, she curls her legs into a triangle, lets down her hair, and begins combing it. The smell of henna and infused chicory, the steam from the hot water, the female presence, all impose themselves strongly on her: she wants to remain alive, youthful, desirable.

(We shall be alone and no one will have any suspicions about us. The neighbors will say she's my woman friend, and the vendors at the souk will catch their breath when she arrives there.)

Anyone hearing her humming to herself would think that Paradise was being taken by storm, and anyone seeing her coming out of the bathroom daubed with silky perfume would know that she will shortly be betrothed: a woman concealed behind a black childhood, a naïve adolescence, and an uncourageous youth.

She is a woman who has wallowed in grief and become liable to collapse but who had not wanted to mutilate her life, had wanted neither to disappear like so much vapor nor to shine like some star; she is beginning to become capable of achieving continuity with some creature, be it a cat, a spider, a woman, even a jungle animal or a snake.

And this place of banishment, what magically gaudy toys it has, and what despair to make captive the heart and body, and what a way by which to attain tranquility.

On the seventh Thursday she quivered like the short-branched pomegranate tree as she looked into the face of the other woman, a face that was wax-white.

"Do you want to go to the back street?"

They walked together, two specters that had grown weary through remembering and love-sickness, two visible, waking beings dazzled by the infernal fire that they would shortly be entering. They came to a stop and the passers-by around them were like the vibrations of a radio tuner that is caught between two stations.

"The very evening I left you my husband left me."

This penetrating blackness was slowly flowing out of the night, and objects ceased to come between them; fear, this taboo that was spread between them, did not touch them. They were two beings without equal.

"And the children?"

"I left them at my mother's."

"And you?"

"I want you."

She took her hand. When they were apart she used to say to herself: So everything's been revealed, but now everything's begun.

On the seventh Thursday hands will touch with greater sweetness. She took her by the hand and they walked in the back street and boarded the large bus and sat together.

"I want to touch you now."

"No, not now."

She pointed to her house and got off. The total moment will come, and she will recollect with what bashfulness people had previously encircled her. For several years she had been pierced through with trembling, and she had chased it away as white corpuscles chase away germs. The blood, though, had not been poisoned and would, once again, gush forth, carrying with it all these accumulations of emotions. All this life that has passed is a falsehood, all that aged history a falsehood, and absurd those small alliances that begin in one place and end in another.

Slowly she turns her head in the room and sits drying her body. An unspoken question seizes hold of her. What if she refuses, what if she bids her farewell by withdrawing into herself?

What a stratagem it is that comes about from a clash of fires! Hurriedly she rises and puts on a long red woolen nightdress. After squeezing her hair dry, she allows it to fall down to her shoulders. She sinks onto the couch. The smell of the bath, filled with soap, henna, and chicory, permeates the room like a sort of incense.

The gown is easy to pull off, the nightdress long, with buttons at the breast and nothing more.

Suddenly she hears the door open and then close quietly without banging. "Who is it?"

The other woman peers around the doorway.

"You?"

"Me."

Her face is grief-stricken, defeated, as though she had emerged from a snare. She remains standing. She takes in all the objects with an all-embracing glance. She throws her *abaya* to the ground and seats herself on it. She leans against the wall and takes a deep breath: it seems to her that the room has become so restricted it is turning into a tomb, while the woman is still on the sofa, as silent as an angel in panic.

Thus they remain, speechless for more than several minutes, their breathing constricted, not knowing where things will start or how the evening will turn out. Both of them are frightened, as the woman sits on the floor, her knees cracking, her face paralyzed by fever, and she herself turns her head slowly and casts apprehensive yet conclusive glances at the earthly creature sitting close by her.

The anticipation of this moment is the contract binding this sublime partnership. Is not everything in the end mere desires, with which we adorn these unions that we can put into effect only in dreams?

The mewing of the cat increases the nervousness of the two women.

"What a noise—it's hungry."

How can they say that the body gets pensioned off? This mucus locked within the gullet and the veins, from where does it come? And the cat's saliva, does it not have a sanguine nerve? What incompatibility is there between the prick of a pin and the whiplashes of thoughts? What is the significance of a great victory over a small force? She believes that the discovery of magic is more powerful than magic itself, and all of a sudden she rises to her feet and at that moment it seems to her that embarking upon magic is the bringing together of the small particles that are entangled inside her. She seats herself on the floor close to the other woman, and the mewing outside begins to break up this small pleasure. What honor is this that she herself will know of and what hellish temptation leads the two of them to revolt?—and the cat, with its proficiency at continuing to diminish the elation, is peering through the window with hurt eyes and a madly brandishing tail.

Thirst and the quenching of it, hunger and satiety, night and morning, birth and death, flight and presence. What a dark coming together despite the harmony of it!

"Did you pass by the children?"

"I visited them before coming here."

"And him?"

"The So-and-so got himself married right away."

"He didn't tell you why?"

"Yes—don't you see what I look like now? He dislikes pregnant women."

"And are you miserable?"

"Very."

"But why? Did you love him all that much?"

She grew pale. Love stays only for a little while, and banal endings become frozen, as do the big disappointments; and so that people may come to know one another without any law, everything is expressed through pallor.

The woman continues what she had to say. "But I . . ."

Her pulse beats harder, the cat's mewing rains down, and this continuous pricking has afflicted the three faces: two women whose bodies reveal a certain plumpness and a cat that invents kinds of clamor designed to bring it security.

"I still think of him. You don't know how he used to watch me when I was among people, and when we were on our own, and how he used to rule over me, and how he would control me. O sister mine—man is a beautiful curse that we cannot pretend to do without. Look at this dress, he bought it for me before the break-up and said to me jokingly, 'Make it so that it can be taken off quickly'— and so many other things."

"That's enough, enough, enough."

The maddening mewing, the throbbing heartbeats, the sudden irritation, the memories that have followed without interruption for the last hour, the long moment of frustration, the cat's thirst, the woman's pain, and the force of this aggression among the three of them.

She turns toward the window, looks at the cat triumphantly. The cat is scrutinizing the two of them. The other woman takes hold of her *abaya*, drawing it out from under her, and sits comfortably. The rustling of her dress sighs with this naked joy. She radiates beams of light.

She murmurs between her teeth, "How close you are to me: your arm is like his, your muscles strong like his, your glances overflowing with this frenzied inferno." Shifting backward, she raises her head to the light. The cat renews its mewings. A white line gleams between mouth and mouth, and the lips mumble words. The cat bursts through the glass of the window and enters, covered in blood and bringing with it cravings of hunger and thirst.

Translated by Denys Johnson-Davies

Hanna Mina
(b. 1924)
SYRIA

Hanna Mina is one of the best-known Syrian novelists. Two of his novels, *Fragments of Memory* and *Sun on a Cloudy Day*, have been translated into English.

FROM *Fragments of Memory*

Father tried to work as a cobbler. He constructed legs for a wooden crate to convert it into a shoemaker's box and sat under a tree awaiting what would turn up. At that time, I believed that Father was a cobbler and that he would earn something; that the village would bring their shoes to him to mend as he did ours. Every time a man or a woman came, I expected to see something in their hands. But all my expectations were disappointed, not because the villagers failed to bring their shoes to be fixed, but because they did not have shoes. They were barefoot. It was summer, they were barefoot, and in the winter this state of affairs did not change very much. It only changed for the men and some of the women. As for the children of my age, they were without shoes in all seasons. Being without shoes made life pleasurable for me, and I had to do without shoes for three years.

While Mother was confined to her bed under that damned fig tree, she would send my sister and me to see how Father was getting along, if he was doing anything. We would go to find him sitting idle, and brooding. We would stay beside him a short while. Presently, he would order us to go back to our sick mother who might need us.

He finally mended a shoe. Was it out of pity? Possibly! Or it may have been that some of them had to go to the city. They brought some old shoes that had to be fixed. We were happy that day; Mother muttered her thanks to God saying that she had not been afraid of starving as much as she had of Father leaving if that *fellah* had not brought his shoe to be mended.

Where had he learned this trade? Had he learned it? Had he ever learned a trade and mastered it? With the exception of clearing out and drinking, the answer is negative, and even when he left, it was as a vagabond and his drinking was an addiction not for pleasure or sport. I doubt that he knew how to drink wine or talk about it knowledgeably. He never mentioned it. He sipped it on the spot, when he was walking along, and, when he sat, he drank it quickly. No ritual! No distinction between good or bad wine. The appetizers were anything that was on hand: a pinch of salt if there was nothing else. He drank. He repented. He drank. Denial when sober or no talk about drinking. He would take an oath. Who would believe him? He would swear an oath with the bottle in his pocket and the smell on his breath. He would go out in the cold in the open air to drink his bottle. He understood that Mother knew. He would take an oath, curse and beat her, then be wretched. Mother hated him, pitied him. He deserved the kind of pity afforded to one who never mastered anything, neither virtue nor vice.

He mended the *fellah*'s shoe, repaired a *fellaha*'s shoe and was summoned to the *mukhtar*'s house. He returned with a pair of old shoes that he mended. We had something to eat. Above all else he was working. The *fellah* gave him something from his house. But, as for money, it was a rarity. He only got it from the *mukhtar*. The *fellahin* didn't hold him responsible for skilled workmanship any more than he held them responsible to pay him. Both sides look circumstances into account and were tolerant towards each other. As far as Father was concerned, he wanted to do something no matter what the return or even without any, because work in itself kept his mind and ours from dwelling on the terrible reality of our condition that we had no means of escaping or at least improving.

However, the dividends of mending shoes, even in this intermittent, miserable manner, came to an end in the middle of the summer. Cursing his luck, Father said, "If it were only winter!" Mother looked at him from her bed, smudged with particles of brick-red dust that rose in clouds on the path and wind that blew in our direction, but did not say anything. Not having the strength to speak, she closed her eyes, groaning in pain, then grew quiet, succumbing to her illness.

Translated by Olive E. Kenny and Lorne Kenny

Ahlam Mosteghanemi
(b. 1953)
ALGERIA

Ahlam Mosteghanemi received a B.A. in Arabic literature from the University of Algiers in 1973 and a doctorate in sociology from the Sorbonne in 1982. Two of her novels have been translated into English: *Memory in the Flesh*, which won the Naguib Mahfouz Medal for Literature in 1998, and *Chaos of the Senses*. Mosteghanemi has also published two collections of poetry.

FROM *Memory in the Flesh*

All these ideas passed through my mind as I tramped through the streets and came upon—after thirty-seven years—the prison walls that I had once known from the inside.

Does a prison become something else when we look at it from the outside? Is it possible for the eye to wipe out memory? Can one memory deface another?

Al-Kudya prison was part of my first memories that time cannot delete. It was a memory that made me stop suddenly in front of those prison walls.

I entered them again as I had one day in 1945 with fifty thousand other prisoners who were arrested after the demonstration of the Eighth of May: it is with sadness that I remember.

I was luckier than those who did not enter it that day. Forty-five thousand martyrs fell in a rebellion that shook the whole of eastern Algeria, between Constantine and Setif, Qalima and Kharrata.

They were the first formal group of Algerian martyrs. Their martyrdom came years before the War of Liberation. Can I forget them? Should I forget those who entered the prison and never emerged? Their bodies remaining in the torture chambers? Can I forget those who died the worst kind of death—our comrades who chose to die alone?

There was Isma'il Sha'lan. He was a simple construction laborer. He had the task of looking after the documents and secret archives of the Peoples' Party. He was the first to have a call from the secret police who knocked at the door of his little room, shouting, "Police. Open up."

Instead of opening the door, Isma'il Sha'lan opened the window, the only window, and threw himself out into Wadi al-Rammal. He died with his secrets in Constantine's deep valleys.

Is it possible today, even after half a century, to remember Isma'il without weeping? He died to avoid giving away any names under torture.

Then there was 'Abd al-Karim bin Wattaf, whose screams under torture reached our distant cells. Each electric shock they gave him was like a dagger stabbing at our flesh. He swore at his torturers in French, and called them dogs, Nazis, murderers. His shouts came to us, punctuated by the electric shocks. We would respond to him with cries and an enthusiastic rendering of our anthems. His voice then fell silent.

And there was Bilal Husain, Si Tahir's closest friend, one of the forgotten victims of history. Bilal was a carpenter. He was no scholar, but a whole generation learned their nationalism from him. His workshop was under Sidi Rashid's bridge, a base for secret activity.

I remember him stopping me as I was passing his workshop on my way to the Constantine Secondary School. He made me read the newspaper, *al-Umma*, or some other clandestine publication.

I remembered how, during two whole years, I was being politically prepared for becoming a member of the Peoples' Party. They put me through more than one field test. Every member was supposed to pass these before taking the party oath. Many started their party activities in one of the cells created by Bilal.

In that workshop, of which no trace remains today, he used to meet the political leaders. Msali al-Hajj gave his last instructions there. It was there that slogans were written onto banners for demonstrations to surprise the French.

Bilal planned a demonstration to take place for tactical reasons on Sidi Rashid Bridge. It was easy to gather people there and then disperse them on all the roads that led to the bridge. The French authorities had not expected the sense of organization and were taken aback at the precision of the planning. Bilal was the first to be arrested and tortured as an example to others.

Bilal Husain did not die as others died. He spent two years in prison under torture. He lost his skin to the machines of torture.

I remember that for several days he was unable to put on a shirt. It would have stuck to his open wounds. The hospital doctor refused to take on the responsibility of treating him.

He left prison and was sent into exile under close surveillance. Bilal Husain lived on as a fighter in unknown battles and on the run after independence. He died quite recently at the age of eighty-one on May 27, 1988. He died in hospital, blind, destitute, and childless.

Translated by Baria Ahmar Sreih

Sabri Moussa
(b. 1932)
EGYPT

Sabri Moussa received his degree in fine arts and has written novels, plays, and film scripts, in addition to short stories. His novel *Seeds of Corruption* has received several awards and was published in English translation in the United States.

Benevolence

The woman noticed that her daughter had slowed down and her movements were sluggish as if she had to drag her body along. Her body was not big enough to be heavy. Her neck was slender and her breasts were like two peaches.

The woman paused at her daughter's breasts and was surprised that the two peaches were extraordinarily ripe for her fourteen years of age. As the woman stood studying her daughter her anxiety grew. The girl walked with her legs apart even though her thighs were not fat enough to make her walk that way. On her face, usually pale from undernourishment, were two small apples sparkling with near-bursting skin which set free the blood underneath. The girl's eyes were bright and wide, as if she were feverish, while her body appeared full and well fed.

The mother's eyes travelled to her daughter's stomach and she became alarmed. The stomach did not appear out of the ordinary and it told her nothing, but the girl seemed to pay great attention to it as she moved about, as if something within irritated her.

The mother was sure her daughter was pregnant without being married. She stretched out her hand, took the girl's small hand and drew her into an inner room where she inspected her body. Only then were her doubts confirmed and a stone fell on her heart. The girl was three months pregnant.

Weeping, the girl explained that she had not willingly taken part in what had happened. She had been under the old tree on the hill while the sheep were grazing a stone's throw away. Just before sunset a man suddenly appeared and raped her. The act took a while but she did not care very much.

The woman was not listening. Her face darkened and became gloomy for she was absorbed in thinking about her husband who had died without leaving a son behind. For this reason she cried bitterly and blamed him. Had he left a son, she would not now be poor, weak and lonely.

The girl slept because she was tired, even though she knew her mother was having a breakdown as she sat in front of the stove and stared with haggard eyes at its fiery opening. Her imagination drove her to fantasize what her coming days would be like when her daughter passed through the village, stomach protruding.

Before dawn, the woman rose, having made a decision. She gathered together her things and woke the girl. She went out in her big, black robe with her daughter following. Before daylight came, they had left the village behind.

By the time the sun had risen high they were climbing down a hill to level ground. The woman was old, worn out, and overburdened with cares and wants but she gathered her strength and went on her way.

Now and then she turned her stony face to the girl who hastened behind, lowering modest eyes at such moments, as if shame were chasing them.

The day passed without them stopping. Sunset found them at the outskirts of a village near the end of the valley. The woman dropped onto the river bank, unable to walk further. She rubbed her swollen feet, wailed and complained of her misfortune. The girl walked down the bank of the river and brought back some water for her mother to drink. She washed her mother's face and wrapped her feet. But the woman did not stop wailing.

A man passed by them and saw the woman crying. He stopped and asked what the matter was. He was big, his bones were well defined, and his neck thick. She told him her story.

The man looked towards the girl who lowered her face. He contemplated the situation while the woman continued complaining that her husband had died without leaving her a boy.

The man said to himself, "Be kind for once. Here is a weak woman with no man to help her."

He was a professional killer, robber and thief, but times change.

He said to himself, "Old age has begun to creep up on me and

I have nothing left. Any action I take, I pay the price even more now."

He patted the woman's shoulder and comforted her. He carried her belongings and led the procession to his home. At home he served them food, which they ate, and then prepared a bed for them, telling the woman to sleep peacefully and let him take charge of her worries.

As night descended on the village, the man approached the girl and broke her neck. He put the body into a sack, carried it to the river and dumped it in. He then lightheartedly returned home.

In the morning he prepared breakfast for the woman and placed her and her belongings on a donkey. As he walked beside the donkey back to the village the woman raised her face to heaven and muttered prayers thanking God for the man.

Translated by Elizabeth Bloeger and Vivien Abadeer

'Abd al-Rahman Munif
(1933–2004)
SAUDI ARABIA

'Abd al-Rahman Munif was born in Amman, Jordan, to a Saudi father and an Iraqi mother. He earned a degree in Jordan and then studied law at Baghdad University, from which he was expelled in 1955 because of his political activities. He left Iraq for Egypt, earning a law degree from Cairo University, and then went to Yugoslavia for a doctorate in oil economics at the University of Belgrade. After taking his degree in 1961, he worked for the Syrian Oil Corporation. In 1963, after becoming active in the Pan-Arabist movement, he was stripped of his Saudi nationality. Disenchanted with politics, he moved to Lebanon, where he published his first novel in 1973 and worked on a Lebanese newspaper. He then moved to Baghdad and worked for the Iraqi Ministry of Oil, editing its magazine. During this period Munif concentrated on writing fiction. He published a

novel exposing the physical and psychological horrors of
torture carried out in Arab prisons, and with the Palestinian
writer Jabra Ibrahim Jabra he wrote the novel *'Alam bila
khara'it* (*A World without Maps*), which appeared in 1982.
From 1981 to 1986 he lived as a political refugee in Paris,
where he wrote his magnum opus, *Cities of Salt*. Some 2,500
pages in length, it tells the story of a desert community
where the discovery of oil brings about the destruction of
traditional bonds of social life. When Munif was finally allowed to return to Syria, his wife's native country, he stayed
there for the remaining years of his life. The selection below
is from his novel *Endings* (1977), about village life on the
edge of the desert. This scene describes the sandstorm in
which the hunter 'Assaf and his dog meet their death.

FROM *Endings*

The sun is beating down from the heavens like molten lead. The
sand feels hotter than coals. Even the dog yelps as it lifts up its paws;
it sounds almost like a call for help or a protest, as though it is being
made to walk on sharp thorns or broken glass.

When the two vehicles took off, they trailed a huge cloud of dust
behind them which completely enveloped 'Assaf and turned him
into a part of the desert itself as it stretched away to infinity. The
dog let out a howl of protest. For a while it ran after one of the cars,
but then slowly made its way back to its master.

There exist places where nature can be seen in all its unbridled
power: in seas and oceans, at the summits of mountains, in the
depths of valleys, in the frozen ice floes, in the darkness of jungles.
In all these locales nature gives all sorts of warnings of changes to
come. There is an internal charge present which cannot remain the
same for long and will inevitably change at any moment. The
desert, on the other hand, the mysterious, cruel, savage desert with
all its surprises, transcends the normal laws of nature simply in
order to corroborate them.

Within an hour the entire scene had been turned upside down.
A violent wind blew up, and a huge sandstorm transformed everything. Storms like this would push the sand into dunes in much the
same way as winds do with the waves of the sea. The sands rolled
over and over just like a bale of fresh cotton or the ashes of burnt
paper. No sooner did anyone turn to face this sudden onslaught
than both throat and eyes were filled with those tiny, soft grains of
sand which managed to feel like cinders falling out of an ever-
burning coal fire.

The things that happened on that summer day deep in the desert
and yet such a comparatively short distance away from al-Tiba are
such that no one can recall them without bursting into tears. The
fear which gripped everybody during those tense hours of waiting
was so strong and utterly debilitating that no one can remember
what happened. The words which people try to use to describe
events sound curiously weak and befuddled, with no real meaning
to them. The people from al-Tiba knew by instinct how cruel the
desert can be; they could tell from the smell in the air, from the
harsh glare of the sky, from the storms which came out of the valley
and across the plain to al-Tiba. They were all well aware of this, and
yet even they could not believe the sheer force of the storm facing
them now. They had never seen anything like it in their lives before.
Their guests were totally panic-stricken and lost all ability to function; they simply turned into a group of human puppets, weeping
and pleading. There was just one thing they wanted: not to die!

When fear reaches its peak, men can no longer act. They should
have just stopped where they were and waited. But the cruel sandstorms were in control of everything now, leading them ever onwards. On those few occasions when the men stopped, savage
winds came roaring down, bringing burning hot sands. Everyone
started yelling in panic; they could all sense death's hand tightening
its grip on their necks. But they did not stop. Instead, driven on by
natural instincts, they tried to escape from the storm. The jeep
managed to keep both its traction and power intact, but the other
car was like a blind tortoise which had lost its way and had no idea
either of where it was going or when it would die. One of the men

from al-Tiba suggested that things were so risky that the two cars should stay close together. At that everyone felt a certain sense of relief. In fact, the driver of the Volkswagen was not satisfied merely staying close to the jeep, but insisted on driving in front of it, and just a few metres at that.

In the desert waiting like this for death to arrive is one thousand times worse than death itself. Here death does not come suddenly or in disguise. There is no question of it appearing quickly and finishing everything off. At first it just bares its teeth and sits there on the car windows. From time to time it may kick up a fuss and scream, buffet you in the face and blow a grain or two of sand into your mouth and eyes. When this bit of fun is over, it will retire for a while and start prowling round like a wolf, waiting for the next round to start. And it is not a long wait. Like smoke it soon rises up quickly and forcefully. The mouth goes dry, and eyes assume an expression of panic. Yet another cruel, nerve-wracking wait begins. The same searing agony is there and the same overwhelming power. There is no going back. Once again it starts pounding on the car windows, loudly and continuously. With all this waiting and waiting, a man dies slowly; a thousand times over he dies. He loses all self-confidence; his will dissipates. He falls, picks himself up again, and then totters. His mouth is full of panic-stricken prayers, although he has no idea of where they have come from. He shouts, but there is no sound. He looks at the faces of his companions, only to see his own. He remembers, he resists, he collapses, he falls. Yet again he dies, and rises again from death. He looks out at the few metres of ground which are visible through the windows. He can feel the sand covering everything. He takes a mouthful of water and holds it in his mouth for as long as possible in the hope of getting more energy to put up some resistance and remain in control. He can no longer talk or swallow the water which in any case has turned into salt and saliva. He longs to shout out, to die once and for all. He wishes the earth would suddenly open up and swallow him. He longs for water and shade. And he waits . . . !

In the desert even time assumes its own special meaning. It turns into tiny atoms; the second, the minute, these represent the whole of time. Then it starts breaking up into infinitesimal parts, just like the desert itself. Like some coarse, soaking wet cord it starts relentlessly tightening its grip on the neck and making incisions, but without ever severing it or simply leaving it as it is. The whole thing turns into a prolonged death, assured, expected yet deferred and forever mocking. Men come to feel as though they are being strangled. The heart-beat gets faster, temperatures start to rise, and people's faces turn a blue colour. No one dares look at anyone else for fear of either cracking up completely or bursting into tears.

The heat comes up from the ground and down from the searing orb of the sun high in the sky. There is not even a single moment to take stock or think. When darkness comes, it makes people feel extremely weak and increases their sense of panic a hundredfold.

It is a long, long wait. But then the wind starts up again and the atmosphere clears. The sun sinks towards the west, although no one notices it sliding its way down as one would at sea. The air is full of sand, but gradually a faint light can be made out. The temperature begins to fall. All day the sun has stayed there high up in the sky like the noose of a gallows hanging over everyone, but now people begin to realize that it is going down.

At times like these any thought of conversation is utterly impossible. The struggles going on inside everyone were so intense and contradictory that anything might happen or indeed its exact opposite; and men might behave in exactly the same way. The heat from the sun, the worst enemy of all, began to seem almost gentle and radiant as the huge orb began its descent towards the horizon. The brilliant glare which had enveloped everything during the daytime now became a dream to be forgotten along with the gradual onset of darkness. The winds which in daytime would define direction and lead men to a specific location were transformed in the early darkness of evening into a few random blasts of air accompanied by a wailing sound.

So this is death, each one of them told himself, death and nothing else. In moments of absolute despair such as these, man accepts anything, even death itself; he wills it to come in a flash, complete and terminal. But this situation was not like that. What was happening in this case was a harsh exposure, a stripping away of everything, a process of destruction which gradually split cells apart with a cruelty akin to the hunger of a wild animal. Only the desert at night-time could come up with such a death as this, while the winds continued their never-ending rampage.

Here then is man, that weak and transient creature, faced with a crushing force which neither destroys him nor leaves him to his own devices!

"God help you, 'Assaf!" said one of the men from al-Tiba, his voice choking.

"That's right," said the man sitting in 'Assaf's place next to the driver, "where's 'Assaf?"

Once again words simply dissipated in people's mouths. Silence reigned, but it was nevertheless that particular kind of echoing silence that is no silence at all; at every moment and in every place it bursts at the seams. The sound of its moaning can be sensed through every pore of the body.

Then came the moment—no one could say with any certainty when it happened or how much time had passed—the wind started dying down. Gradually the sandstorm abated, although the sky was still wrapped in its heavy and overbearing black mantle. The driver started switching the car lights on and off, and that was regarded as a shrewd and meaningful gesture.

"Someone's bound to see us," said the man sitting beside him. "They'll come and rescue us."

"Why don't you start the car?" suggested the man from al-Tiba who was sitting in the back seat behind the driver. "Circle round a few times in case 'Assaf spots us or we him. Then we can head towards him or vice versa!"

No questions were asked, nor was there any argument. The car was started and began circling like a tethered animal. Once in a while the driver would turn the lights on in case something happened or a rescue team showed up.

"If we find 'Assaf," the man from al-Tiba said, "he'll be able to rescue us. He'll have no trouble taking us all back to al-Tiba. But, if we don't find him . . ."

He fell silent. People looked at him, but said nothing. The darkness had already triggered a new type of fear, and any notion that they were about to be rescued sounded like the beating of a sickly heart. As a result, these words echoed around the inside of the car like a warning of impending doom!

Translated by Roger Allen

Muhammad al Murr
(b. 1955)
UNITED ARAB EMIRATES

Muhammad al Murr was born in Dubai and received his university education in the United States. The best-known writer from the United Arab Emirates, he has published thirteen collections of short stories. He is also a journalist and is chairman of the prestigious Dubai Cultural Council. Two volumes of his selected stories have been published in English translation.

Your Uncle Was a Poet

"Your uncle was a poet."

Khalifa's mother did not know that the words she uttered would have such an impact on her son. She was having dinner with him and they were watching television. A programme had started about Nabati poetry. She was talking to her son about the divorce of a neighbour's daughter and then suddenly said, prompted by something on the television, "Your uncle was a poet."

That sentence stuck in Khalifa's mind. There was earlier poetic talent in the family.

Khalifa was a young junior official and read lots of magazines and newspapers. He knew that plenty of things were due to heredity. His voice, for example, was high like that of his mother's brother. His father was bald and here he was, his hair beginning to recede. His eyes were grey like those of his mother. Talent was also hereditary. His uncle was a poet. There was no doubt that in the family there would be people who were ready to recite poetry. When he went that night to a neighbour's house he lost terribly at rummy, even though he was a master of the game. His mother's sentence went dancing through his brain, making it impossible for him to concentrate.

"Your uncle was a poet."

He was only able to lay his hands on two poems said to have been written by his uncle. He started to read all the Nabati poetry pages in the Emirates and Gulf newspapers.

"Your uncle was a poet."

Yes, he could become a poet like his uncle. The talent ran in the family. His friend, Jasim, dropped by. He had just bought a new Japanese car and wanted to celebrate with him. Jasim had half a carton of beer. They went to the beach. Khalifa drank three cans. He was not listening to Jasim's chatter about the specifications of his new car. He was gazing at the sunset, absorbed in its fascination.

"Your uncle was a poet."

At nine that evening Jasim brought him home. He told his mother that he had already eaten. He shut himself up in his room and took from the wardrobe some notepaper. The pages were pink and each page had a border of coloured hearts. He began to write. Four hours went by. At exactly one o'clock in the morning he finished, tired and happy at the same time. He had written his first poem with thirty verses. A love poem. Poems with a moral and poems with riddles would have their turns in the future. He had to start with a poem of love.

Next morning Khalifa went to see his friend, Muhammad, the secretary to the man in charge of the department he worked in. He asked him to type out the verses. His own handwriting was very untidy and the people at the newspaper to whom he was going to send his poem would not be able to read it. The secretary did not understand poetry, or anything else, but agreed. The only hobby in which his feelings and interest were engaged was fishing. Khalifa looked at the typed poem and was at first quite pleased. Then he remembered that one of his colleagues in the Department of Financial Affairs, the Egyptian, Sami, was an excellent calligrapher. He took the poem to him to write out in his beautiful hand. Sami read it and burst out laughing, "What's this rubbish?"

Khalifa said, indignantly, "My dear chap, all I want is a simple service from you. There's no need for such remarks. Anyway you don't know anything about Nabati poetry."

Sami wrote it out for him in the ruq'a script. It looked really beautiful. Khalifa put it in a pretty envelope and typed the newspaper's address on it. He did not trust the department's messenger. He took it along himself to the central post office which was near the department's building.

After he sent his poem to the newspaper to publish on the Nabati poetry page, his heart was full of expectation. The editor of the page was sure to like it and find it amazing. He would certainly know that his uncle was a poet and that the poetic talent ran in the family. Where would they publish it? At the top of the page, of course. Or in the middle with a picture of a beautiful Bedu girl or of gazelles. Gazelles would be better. Without any doubt one of the well-known entertainers would like it and sing it. "And after that other poets will write poems of criticism. Of course they'll want to criticize me and I'll reply to them and blacken their reputations. People will say, 'Have you heard and read the reply of Khalifa, the famous poet, to the poem of So-and-so or Such-and-such?' And the girls, how could I forget about them? After my poems are published, lovely girls will pester me by phone. I'll have to write to the telephone exchange. 'The girl who is asking for me and refuses to give you her name. Don't transfer her call to me. Say I'm not in. I cannot waste time talking on the phone. Any girl who wants me must come and see me.' And radio and TV. 'I don't like appearing on the television screen. It's true my mum says I'm the best-looking boy in the quarter, but I know she's exaggerating somewhat.'

"The radio's OK, so long as the programmes are only about poetry and are broadcast at midnight. Lots of girls listen to the radio last thing at night. After a little while I'll have to publish a collection of my poems on glossy paper, of course, with coloured pictures. Cassettes of my poems could be distributed with the books, sung by one of the best-known artistes." He thought of his mother with affection. He owed it all to her wonderful sentence.

"Your uncle was a poet."

In the first week the poem did not appear. There was of course a delay in the post. A letter from London to Dubai took four days. A letter from Dubai to Dubai could take over ten days. A strange business. The next week also there was nothing. Khalifa got very angry with the post. In the third week the following appeared on the page of Nabati poetry in a corner of short messages from the editor: "To Khalifa Muhammad. Your poem is feeble in content and flawed in its metre. It is a long way from Nabati poetry but we would like to praise you for your beautiful handwriting."

Translated by Peter Clark

Buthaina Al Nasiri
(b. 1947)
IRAQ

Buthaina Al Nasiri was born in Baghdad and took a degree in English literature from Baghdad University. Her first volume of short stories was published in 1974. Her stories have been translated into German, French, Spanish, and Danish, and a representative volume of her work was published in English translation under the title *Final Night*.

I've Been Here Before

I know this lane. After the first bend there's a date palm growing at such an angle you'd think it would fall down. A white house with windows painted in red makes its appearance.

This is the house. I'll step across the threshold and knock at the door. When no one answers I'll go around the fence, and in the back garden I'll see the swing, which is also red.

Have I seen all that a long time ago in some dream? But where's the man who suddenly bursts out of the back door to tell me roughly, "Get away from the swing, child—the paint isn't dry yet."

The door unexpectedly flies open and a heavily built man appears. In a sullen voice he says, "Get away from the swing, child—the paint isn't dry yet."

I put out a tentative finger and touch the swing support, drawing back as though stung: my finger is dyed red as though with blood.

I stand in confusion trying to collect myself: everything has happened as before, with one tremendous difference—a half century has elapsed. Hasn't the paint dried yet?

I have in mind to ask the man. I stare into his eyes: they are the blue of the sea at dawn. I look into them. The dark blueness invites me in, so I enter.

I enter and am met by the dawn breeze brushing against me. Shivering, I wrap the overcoat around me. How much time has elapsed with me standing here on the sea shore?

I feel the smooth coolness of the sand inviting me. It tickles the soles of my bare feet, the ground below spreading out and my feet little by little sinking in. I lift them up and look at their imprints filling up with sea water.

How much time has passed as I walk along the shore line? There comes over me a sensation that I walked like this years ago and that when I reach that rock I'll find a young boy behind it casting his hook into the sea and waiting patiently, while in the small basket by his side will be two fish: one large and one small.

I shall stand by him and inquire, "Have you been on your own all this time?"

He'll look suspiciously at me and shrug his shoulders. When I ask him about the sort of fish in the basket, he'll again shrug his shoulders and I'll mutter, "You don't want to talk to me," and I'll let my shoes fall to the ground so I can put them on, thinking that I'd like to return home before my mother misses me.

Before moving away from the sea I take a look behind me and stare at the young boy's back.

He is still holding the hook but he is no longer that young boy.

I find the features of a man I know. I hesitate about going back and looking into his face. But the moment I think of doing so I feel a fear that his eyes would meet mine. I remember, as though in something like a dream, that long years ago he was on the deck of a ship that went down with everyone on board.

I hasten to climb the sandy slope up to the street. Doing so, I almost fall on my face, but when I recover and reach the pavement, I look behind me apprehensively; the young man is carrying his basket and moving away.

My gaze is struck by the blueness of the sky, which has begun to contract. Whenever I gaze at it, it contracts further still, until it becomes two lakes that grow smaller. Then I find myself staring into eyes the color of the sea at dawn. I awake to the man's voice: "You're very late—there's no one here."

He says it with the brusqueness of a door being slammed in my face and I feel dejected at the sensation of loneliness I am left with.

As I step backward, the house quickly vanishes from sight and becomes a dot that hurries to some place on the horizon.

I find myself once again walking in the lane. At the end of it a white sail comes into view, swelling in the late afternoon breeze. Coming closer, I make out that the sail is a white gown worn by a tall, solemn-looking man standing at the edge of a hole, carrying a vast hoe with which he is digging the ground. The hole grows larger and takes on a rectangular shape. Seeing me, he points at the hole with a commanding gesture.

Without uttering a word, I step down into the hole. The man gestures again and I lean backward and stretch out in the rectangle submissively, crossing my arms across my chest as though commencing to pray.

Something is poured down onto my legs. I open my eyes to see the man heaping earth onto me. This is one of those nightmares that sometimes beset me, but each time I open my eyes wide I wake up.

More earth is heaped over my body. When was the last time I had such a dream? My pupils widen till my eyelids become taut. Earth covers my chest and the hole grows narrower. I breathe with difficulty. I am dreaming. I shall open my eyes like this, forcibly. Like this. But I find, after the hole is completely closed, that I am not dreaming.

Translated by Denys Johnson-Davies

Emily Nasrallah
(b. 1931)
LEBANON

Emily Nasrallah grew up in a small village in southern Lebanon and attended the American University of Beirut. A journalist and writer, she has published six novels and five collections of stories. Her novel *Flight Against Time* is available in English translation, as is a book of her stories, *A House Not Her Own*. Among the topics she has written about are the civil war in Beirut and the struggle of women for independence in a male-dominated country. She divides her time among Beirut, Cairo, and Canada.

A House Not Her Own

The key is in her hand yet the door remains locked. The key does not find its way into the lock nor does the door respond. And for the tenth time she remembers: This is not the key to this door. It is the key that glues itself to her fingers every time she puts her hand in her purse. It is attracted to her by a magnetic power. She banishes it again to a separate pouch in her bag and looks for the other key.

The door opens and she hesitates for a moment before entering the apartment. She listens intently, for fear there may be someone inside. "Someone" who does not know her, who will pounce at her and ask her who she is. Her words would trip over each other.

She stands bewildered and confused. What would she tell her interrogator? Would she say why she is here? The questioning voice would come back to her from the inside and she would remain on the doorstep, silent. She would decide not to say anything, for there are no words to explain why she is here.

"So, why . . . ?" She hears the voice of the beautiful woman, emanating from the picture in the gilded frame in the centre of the salon. It screams at her and she trembles, and shivers run from her head down to her toes.

"I thought you knew," she mutters.

The beautiful woman retreats and her voice loses its harshness. *"They told me. They wrote to me from Beirut and they told me."*

"So they wrote . . ."

"Yes, but I forgot . . . I thought you were another."

"You are right. How are you to know me, we have never met." She hangs her head low.

This is not the first time she enters this strange apartment. She has been here for more than a week. That is, since a rocket, of a calibre she does not remember, hit her house; her beautiful house in the middle of its glorious garden in the suburb of Beirut. The rocket took it upon itself to erase all traces of her house and eradicate her garden. She can but thank the Lord that she and her family managed to escape unscathed.

A thousand thanks to God.

They had been hiding in the basement of a neighbouring building. Small houses such as hers were not built for war. Nor were the bigger houses, she muses, thinking of the sights she had witnessed on her way from the ruins of her home to the city centre. Those sights convinced her that neither palaces nor skyscrapers nor fortresses were made to withstand the might of the modern artillery

being experimented with in her country. Nothing could stand up
to the concentrated shelling, the random shelling, the sporadic
shelling. She witnessed the incredible and said to her sorrowed soul,
"Your anguish is equal to that of others."

She repeats the adage to herself often. Not because she feels she
is above other people or her despair is more important but because,
at certain points in their lives, people forget that they are but ashes
and dust. There are times when they believe they are omnipotent
giants, their shadows extending as far as their eyes can see. And one
day they receive a blow, they know not from where, and they
awaken and they look around them and they are finally aware of
their time and their place.

She has lost her home. She is now in this strange dwelling that
was offered to her and her family by an old friend from college. "It
is fully furnished," the friend told her. "The owners asked me to
take care of it while they're away." Her friend gave her the key.

She is lucky. She has not ended up on the streets, nor out in the
open, sleeping on the beaches like the thousands of destitute. She
was lucky to have had a friend in her time of need.

She takes another step towards the living room. Instinctively she
places her package on the hall table. The package tilts, it is too big
for the table. It topples the statue of a Greek god. She rushes back
to the table, rights the *objet d'art*, gathers her purchases and retreats
to the bedroom with them, muttering apologies.

Her guilt has been constant since she set foot in the strangers'
apartment, since she first attempted to open the door with the
wrong key. She walks through the apartment, apologizing to the
tiles as she treads heavily on them. She places her possessions on a
table. She hears the ghosts around her grumble. Children poke
their heads out of the picture frames and shout at her, "*This is our
place . . . You belong elsewhere.*" Their innocent smiles become fero-
cious, like shrapnel they cut into her flesh.

And the pretty woman in the big framed picture, holding up the
cascading folds of the wedding dress she wore half a century ago,
runs towards her, "*What hole did you creep out of?*"

Her groom shakes his head, tugs at his bow tie and speaks softly, "*She might have lost her way. Be gentle with her. Don't frighten her.*"

Then they all shout from the walls, from behind the masks of time and dust. The voices of parents and grandparents, aunts and uncles, the living and the dead intermingle, "*Throw her out. She's a stranger. This house is not her own.*"

"You are right. All of you are right. I am only here for a short while. My house was demolished by a rocket . . ." But she does not continue for they have turned away and become deaf to her explanations.

She moves her things to the dressing table and is confronted by the army of bottles and jars lined up there and the souvenirs hanging on both wings of the mirror. She moves some of them to make room for her hairbrush and her few toiletries. "Excuse us," she murmurs. "We are only here for a short time." And she catches herself in her little dramatic moment and wants to laugh and cry at once. She collapses onto the nearest chair.

In her dreams, during her childhood and youth, she imagined many scenarios, drew many images for her life, but never did she imagine her present situation. She never thought, not in her wildest dreams, that she would one day take refuge in a house not her own.

She always thought the house that would hold her, and the one she loved, would be hers forever. In childhood she had pictured it as a mud hut, on the banks of a stream among the orchards in her village. And as she grew so did her dream house. It grew taller as she grew taller. But even when it was only a tree house in her father's garden, or a tent atop their summer house, it remained special. Hers. The place where she could rest and dream, to which she could invite her friends. It remained open and welcoming.

Her words tumble and fall into the bottomless void. All that is left of her past now are words. Words and memories to be planted in the silence of this place and the emptiness of this time. She tells herself, "We are but passers-by on this earth. No sooner do we arrive than we are carried away by wings that lift us to a place where neither our plans nor our schemes matter. A place even our imagination is powerless to describe."

And a voice answers her, "*But people are like trees whose branches cannot grow the leaves of life unless their roots are firmly planted in the soil.*"

Ever since she had been pulled out by her roots and implanted in this new soil she has felt dizzy and numb. She holds her head in her hands, lest it, too, should fall off. Her head reels with the voice and its echo. She has to learn how to cope with the new reality.

A quarter of a century written with blood and tears, in which she built her home like a female bird builds her nest. She and he, both, against the fates. A blessed life it had been. The seeds of blessing having been planted beneath the foundations of her home, for stone and steel and wood do not make a home. Nor does luxurious furniture dictated by the fancy and whim of decorators and creative strangers. What good is it for a house to withstand the elements if the gentle breeze of love and life does not blow within? What is the meaning of a home if it is a cocoon closed to the world, and the world's dreams and magic? What is the meaning of her existence in this strange place where the walls are but stone and the doors planks of wood? And what if it were an expensive ebony? It is still only wood, and the marble is icy beneath her feet and the ceiling threatens to cave in on her.

She rises from her seat and moves aimlessly through the rooms and onto the balcony. There is the sea, a blue expanse, cold and remote. It reminds her of the Arctic ocean that she had once visited. And the buildings, shoulder to shoulder, hugging, each trying to hide the other's faults, the roads winding around them, grey and paved in dust. She can hear the children's cries coming at her from every direction. They hang in the air, strangely devoid of childish joy. In front of her are the balconies of neighbouring buildings, decorated with clotheslines—the trademarks of the dispossessed. She remembers that she is but a drop in this vast ocean of misery, a grain of sand on its shores. Yet she gives herself and her feelings so much importance. She wraps herself in her cloak of misery and turns this apartment into a cocoon that threatens to suffocate her. What is wrong with her? She, who even in her first home, the little village on the slopes of Mount Haramoun, had an unquenchable thirst to better herself, to learn, to rise in the world, to delve into the mysteries of the universe.

Her feet lead her around the apartment. Questions rise from deep within her, turn in an empty circle, and remain in search of answers. From which direction will her answers come?

From the West? Where the warships are anchored, spewing fire and destruction onto the land? From the North where the north winds blow icy cold, cutting into the flesh like the blade of a knife? Or from the East where the battles rage and the fronts are aflame; where explosives roar like thunder and ululating bullets write, in red and yellow fire upon the night sky, the names of those that have fallen? Or is it from the South that she will get her answers? The South!

She wraps her arms around herself as though hiding from the danger around her. Her body has become weak as a child's, left unprotected, at the mercy of the elements. She holds her body with her arms, trying to build fences around it. Then she realizes that her arms are powerless to protect her battered body, for they are part of it. And the protection she so dearly desires at this moment will not come from any earthly source.

She is awakened from her deep thoughts by a fierce banging on the door. She turns around and automatically walks towards the door, not asking who it is. She reaches out to open it, then retreats. She remembers where she is. She remains in her place, fixed, listening to the banging growing louder and fiercer, beating at her like a hammer. Slowly, she withdraws to the farthest corner of the house, for she is not expecting anyone . . . and the house is not her own.

Translated by Thuraya Khalil-Khouri

Ibrahim Nasrallah
(b. 1954)
PALESTINE

Ibrahim Nasrallah grew up in a Palestinian refugee camp.
Today he lives in Amman, Jordan. He is known primarily
for his several volumes of poetry, for which he has been
awarded the Owais Prize. After graduating from college, he
worked for two years as a teacher in the Qunfudha region of
Saudi Arabia; the experience inspired his first novel, *Prairies
of Fever*, an experimental, postmodern work about identity.

FROM *Prairies of Fever*

You stood there at the beginning of things. You looked around.
Sabt Shimran looked almost empty, and the graveyard lay silent and
deserted on the southern side of the village.

This was a large cemetery for a small village like Sabt Shimran.
It was like a city, a metropolis that had swallowed scores of villages
in the centuries that had passed over this one village.

You felt your heart contract at the thought that graveyards out-
grow the local inhabitants.

Damp mounds of earth, still unscorched by the sun, were indi-
cations of freshly dug graves. You approached, but they were all
graves without names. Wide villages without gravestones.

You thought of going to Fatima, but changed your mind. You
prepared yourself for the inevitable crossing between the cemetery
and the police precinct. How could truth be ascertained in this no-
man's-land?

You climbed the stone steps heavily—three miles dragged their
distance under the exposure of the flaming May sun. At last, the
precinct stretched in front of you.

You shouted your greetings.

No one answered.

An officer, who's the head of the precinct, and two policemen. Four naked walls; an aura of boredom and viscosity. Here time revolves between ash flicked into the air and the dormant sitting on long wooden seats like those in cafés.

The officer looked at you as though you didn't exist. One of the policemen scratched his leg robustly, and the third turned his head to the wall.

You sat down.

You knew in advance it would take time. After a few minutes you lost hope anyone would ask you anything, so you said: "I woke up today, and there was no trace of my roommate. All I found was his briefcase on the bed."

The officer turned his head to the wall, and said, "And then?"

You said, "Yesterday he was sick. He was feverish in the afternoon. His condition wasn't cause for undue alarm until they came after midnight and asked him to pay one thousand riyals toward his funeral expenses; but he refused. I discovered this today when I counted his money. Imagine, they wanted him to pay for his own burial. This morning he was gone."

"Who were these men?"

"I don't know. I only heard their voices."

"What's your roommate's name?"

You couldn't discern who was questioning you, whether it was the officer or one of the two policemen. Two faces outlined against the wall, and a voice steeped in lethargy.

"His name is Muhammad Hammad."

The head of the precinct fidgeted slightly in his wooden chair, and waved his two naked feet with their wiry hairs. Then he placed his right foot on the floor.

"And what's your name?"

Already you'd realized the impossibility of being comprehended. You were shaking all over like a leaf about to separate from its branch and fall.

You said, "Muhammad Hammad."

The duplication went unnoticed, and the officer continued his questions:

"You're a stranger to Sabt Shimran, aren't you?"

Before you had time to answer, one of the policemen, the one who'd scratched his leg, approached his chief and whispered something. "Oh, I see!" the chief answered, and turning to you, he said: "But tell me, how do you two have the same name?"

"I don't know. It must be a coincidence, Sir."

You cursed yourself inside for saying that. It was shameful for a man like you to address the chief of a small precinct in Sabt Shimran as "Sir."

The officer adjusted his manner of sitting in the chair. "Why don't you come back later in the afternoon? There's nothing in your story that calls for immediate action. Go back home; you may find your roommate waiting for you there."

And for a brief moment his words instilled in you the hope that you would find him. But secretly you were annoyed at their disrespectful manner of dismissing you.

You stood up, and, without saying a single word, you rushed out. The heat bounced back off the sidewalks, slammed the houses, fumed on the roads and chased the passersby.

Translated by May Jayyusi and Jeremy Reed

Haggag Hassan Oddoul
(b. 1944)
EGYPT

Haggag Hassan Oddoul was born in Alexandria to parents who had left their native village in the Nubian region of southern Egypt. He was a construction worker on the Aswan High Dam and then served in the Egyptian armed forces during the War of Attrition and the October 1973 War. He began writing at the age of forty, and has written short stories, novels, and plays. His story collection *Nights of Musk* was awarded the State Prize for Short Stories in 1990.

Nights of Musk

Long, long ago, south of the rapids, the nights exuded incense and oozed musk. They were watered by the celestial majesty of the Nile and nourished by the green strip of life that lined its banks. Their sky was pure and their air invigorating. There was born generation after generation, dark, dark. We would say: "We are dark, dark, for our sun shines upon our faces."

Aaaaaah Aaaaaah Aaaaaah

My wife was screaming in pain inside the house. Outside, in the wide courtyard, I sat under the arbor with my family around me. Anxiety gnawed like a frozen blade in my heart. The experienced men offered the usual words of encouragement. "Don't worry, they are the pains of a first birth. You'll soon be a father, Ibn Zibeyda." My uncle Bilal said, "Take this cigarette. Smoke it and learn patience." He leaned over and whispered in my ear, "It's packed with the best bango. It'll calm your nerves."

Salha's screams and groans came from the distant room and seared me. She walked up and down the room wailing, supported by the shoulders of her mother and my sister, waiting for the fetus to fall and the swollen belly to relax. Water was boiling on the fire. Salha would not lie down until the time came. I was waiting to hear a sound sweeter than the roll of a drum:

Waaaaah waaaaah waaaaah

Duum-taka dum-tak duum-taka dum-tak

In the groom's house that night, the young men were warming up the drums, trying them out, *duum-taka dum-tak*. Even before we reached puberty I was trying to woo Salha, sometimes politely and

other times rudely. I pursued her constantly. I strutted proudly before her at every wedding and danced for her. I sang her the ballad
"Your breasts are firm like oranges." She had a magnificent chest.
Her bouncing breasts drove me wild. They kept me awake at night
and haunted me during the day.

The sunset twilight drew a line of watery red along the horizon.
A young girl ran across the low sands up toward the village. I
jumped out from behind a wall. She fell onto me and I was delighted. She was horrified and screamed: "Bismillah!" Sweat ran
down her face and neck like branches of the Nile. She pushed me
away and cursed me. "Devil, you're always on fire, Ibn Zibeyda."

I answered as I did every time. "Don't blame me. Blame the sun
that won't let us cool down. Blame your bouncing breasts."

She hid a smile and ran off, and the hot thud of the tambourine
resounded with the beat of my heart:

Duum-taka dum-tak duum-taka dum-tak

Aaaaaah Aaaaaah Aaaaaah

She screamed in the room, leaning on shoulders, moving exhausted
up and down. Outside in the yard, I was waiting for the expected
one to appear. My sister's son Habboub was learning to walk. He
fell over and his vest came up and revealed his ebony body. He
smiled at me. His tiny soft penis was covered with specks of sand. I
went over to him. "You, my lad, are three years older than my
daughter who's going to be born any minute now. I wonder . . . will
she be for you? Will you chase her across the sand dunes and behind
the palm trunks? I wonder if you'll woo her politely or provoca-
tively? Habboub, she will have heavy breasts like her mother's. Will
you sing for her 'Your breasts are firm like oranges'?" I lifted him
up, and he was still smiling at me, trying to take the cigarette out of
my mouth. "Little bastard. Make sure you don't go pestering my
daughter rudely." I slapped him playfully on the thigh. A fresh wave
of screaming brought me to my senses.

Weeeek weeeek weeeek

Hooooi hooooi hooooi

Fawziya hooi, Binyamin hooi, Salha hooi, Ibn Zibeyda hooi. That's how we called to one another as children, boys and girls, running over the soft glowing sand. We drew pure air into our chests and counted the colors of the magic Nile. From the top of the mountain, it wound its way into the distant blueness of the sky. Parts of it were sheets of silver reflecting the sun's rays. As we ran down toward it, its color darkened to intermingling shades of gray. We ran to it through the green bank, and it turned muddy brown. Naked we dove in and found it clear and pure. Wonderful Nile, mighty as the sea. When we got tired, we would stretch out on the bank, and the sun would take us in a warm embrace. The burning fiery rays caused a reaction inside us, and we grew up fast. The girls ripened in a few years, still young, and the older boys snatched them up at fabulous weddings. No one can imagine how delicious the taste of those weddings was without actually experiencing them. Wonderful, sweet, and wild are the weddings of the south.

And on the palm-stalk bed, leg wraps around leg and embrace follows embrace. Bellies swell and the dark-skinned generations come forth, carrying the sun in their faces, screaming:

Waaaaah waaaaah waaaaaah

Eeeeshshshsh eeeeshshshsh eeeeshshshsh

The rustle of the ears of corn, the branches of the trees, the leaves of the blessed palm, and the ripple of the Nile's gentle waves are questions that do not wait for answers.

The floods passed quickly. The women ululated joyfully at the luscious bunches of dates. Real seasons. We grew up in an instant,

Salha. So many presented themselves to your father, and of all the lads obsessed with that magnificent chest, you smiled bashfully only when my name was mentioned. Ibn Zibeyda. You were mine and I was yours. And the happy wedding day finally arrived.

We don't know where the days come from.

And we don't know where they go.

Eeeeshshshsh eeeeshshshsh eeeeshshshsh

Ya salaaaaam ya salaaaaam ya salaaaaam

On moonlit nights, my friends and I, young lads happy at the first hairs sprouting on our lips, would sit under the two doum trees, singing the ballad of "The Dark Beauty," which lavishly celebrated the face of the dark-skinned beloved without naming her. Nearby, under the towering sycamore, you were sitting with the girls, virgins full of desire, enraptured by the effusive beats of the tambourine. Each one of you thought the ballad was for her. There was passion in the hoarse voice of our singer, who began like all balladeers south of the rapids begin: *Ya salaaaaam*. Everyone becomes enraptured, and why not? For al-Salaam is one of the names of God. We joined in enthusiastically, singing *Ya salaaaaam* after every line, like real professionals. The opening *ya* took our bodies forward, leaning toward you. The *s* was from Salsabeel, wellspring of Paradise. The *l* poured full and fat from moistened mouths, the long *aaaaa* ascended with the rising of our hands to our temples, next to our eyes and dropping lashes. The wide sleeves of our gallabiyas hung calmly, relaxing with the sweet long vowel, as it took away the heat from our loins and soothed our passion. And with the final *m* the hands fell quickly down to show how much, how much we enjoyed the song. We captured your hearts, and they poured forth a flood of potent giving. Your bodies swayed from side to side, and you clapped your henna-dyed hands to the rhythm of the tambourine's beat. We communicated, and in spite of the sandy distance between the doum and the sycamore, we were one harmonious group, swimming altogether through the heaving sea of the night. We dissolved, sparkling with burning desire and an ardent longing to be lawfully joined on a day we prayed would come soon.

Our grandmothers sat close by. They saw our shapes clearly and smiled. They whispered of their own days that had passed like a sweet dream whose moon has evaporated behind a single sunny day. They looked at the new generation blooming, and with their gleaned wisdom, anticipated what would come to pass between us one day. "Fawziya is for Binyamin, Nebra Tari is for Husayn the Omda's son, Hawa is for Selimto, Salha is for Ibn Zibeyda . . ."

Ya salaaaaam ya salaaaaam ya salaaaaam

Waaaah waaaaah waaaaah

Good news at last. I threw down the joint and leapt to my feet shouting, "He is the Giver, He is the Granter of all things, praise be to Him." My uncle Bilal, Salha's father, laughed and said: "Didn't I tell you to be patient?" Then, in tears, he embraced me. My sister Miska came out of the room drenched in sweat. She threw her arms around me and kissed me. "Congratulations to us all; you have a daughter, Ibn Zibeyda."

Waaaah waaaaah waaaaah

Dark dark dark

Dark faces, pure eyes, white teeth, and consciences. Our colors are primary and well-defined. We know nothing of twisted words and half measures. The crowning turban is as white and clear as the dawn, the gallabiya a cup of milk to cover us, the shoes bright red, the young women's kohl as black as night, the tattoos deep and dark. The gold is amber, dangling in rings from ears and noses, hanging upon the forehead, treasure upon a young treasure. It shines from the neck and falls playfully onto the unfettered chests, yellow and lucky, plunging, leaping about between the firm round hills. From the top of the head hangs the shaw-shaw, two bands of gold thread covered in beads that follow the movement of the head, dancing and colliding in the air, and making a *shaw shaw* sound.

Shaw shaw shaw

Taraaak trak-trak taraaak

The people are clapping, Salha. They are our people, the people of the south. It is the hands dance. They dance to the beat of their own hands, bringing their palms together with power and zeal. The resounding *taraaak* splits the air in the sandy courtyard under the gentle light of the lamps and the silver moon. *Taraaak trak-trak taraaak*. Everyone is here: men, women, children, old folk, and even the sick. There isn't a Nubian on earth who would miss a wedding. Our grandparents' souls watch contentedly from the cemetery, and when the dance heats up, they come down and mingle with us, longing to be among us again. A wedding party draws the whole village. Even the River People, inhabitants of the cool depths, emerge dripping from the water alone and in groups. We can feel them down on the bank of the river sitting in the branches and among the palm fronds. Their young alight on ears of corn, which dance in ecstasy beneath them and scatter drops of dew, like pearls, *eeeeeeshshsh eeeeeeshshsh*. We call to them. "Welcome amon nutto, welcome People of the River." The dance flares up and draws us into intense rhythmic passion, drowning in the thunderous roar of the tambourines *duum-taka dum-tak* and the explosion of clapping palms *taraaak trak-trak taraaak*. We disturb the spirits, the people of the nether world, Lord preserve us from their evil. They slip from deep under the mountain and burst forth like satanic shells from the cracks and crevices of the high peaks. They circle under the stars and then arrange themselves at the edges of the light, dancing and singing mischievously. Their voices echo through the bounds of space and a massive sound engulfs us. And we, in fear and trepidation, sing a prayer: "O God, O Protector, between them and us let Your protection fall."

Just such a night was our night, Salha. Your old mother and my sister with the women sprinkling salt and Daughter of Sudan perfume in the air. They danced the perch dance amid a crowd of women adorned with gold of all shapes and sizes, gleaming and rustling, *shaw shaw shaw*, and the silver anklets on their feet with a clear ring, *klin-klin klin-klin*.

That night, there wasn't a limp body, nor a languid heart, not a single person who did not take part, nor a single tongue that did not congratulate, not a single weary soul. Everyone joined in the dance.

They had a wonderful procession for us, sweet Salha, the bride and groom, and the women's ululations were like brass bells and bird songs.

Lilililililililililiiiiiy

Dirgid-dirgid dirgid-dirgid

Her sprightly female donkey was carrying her across the rocks. Her mother had sent her to the next village, and now she was coming back. I was lying in wait behind a fold in the mountain, and she rode past me. I followed and she heard the hooves of my male donkey. When she saw me, she gave her donkey a violent slap and off it leapt over the rocky land, four pairs of hooves beating the rhythm, *dirgid-dirgid dirgid-dirgid*. She turned west and my donkey followed in full chase. The sand dunes started and the she-donkey slowed down as she climbed. I dismounted with the hem of my gallabiya between my teeth. Two steps and I put my hands on the donkey's rump, leapt up with my legs open, and landed on the back of the beast, right up against Salha's back. She screamed.

"Ibn Zibeyda, you filthy rascal, leave me alone!"

She cursed me while she tried to undo my hands from around her waist. The donkey was taking us round in circles, and Salha was losing patience.

"Ibn Zibeyda, someone will see us, then there'll be real trouble."

"No one can see us except God."

"Then may God roast you."

"He'll forgive me when I marry you according to His law, and Prophet Taha's law."

"Haa haa haa."

"Your breasts are firm like oranges."

I almost had the oranges in my hands when she sunk in her ivory teeth and elbowed me sharply in the side. My hands let go, and with a push of her back, she sent me rolling down the dune with sand pouring inside my gallabiya.

Salha laughed.

"Haa haa haa. That's so you'll learn some manners, Ibn Zibeyda."

Haa haa haa haa haa haa

Kum-ban-kaash kum-ban-kaash

The children joined in the fun. They drummed on old cans and sang and danced in the courtyard. Dancing and singing are in our blood. We inherit them. Children of the tribe, you have added joy to our joy at the birth of Zibeyda. Two young children came into the yard. One held a bottle between his hands while the other tapped marvelous rhythms with two spoons.

Kin-klin-lin kin-klin-lin kin-klin-lin

Immmmmm immmmmmm immmmmm

The bride was sulking, refusing even to talk to her hot, impassioned groom. She even wanted him to pay her a real Turkish guinea just to start a conversation.

On the bed you were like dark nocturnal velvet to the touch. They had rubbed you all day with dulka oil from Halfa, with extracts of fragrant oils and herbs. Its sweet smell penetrated your pores and radiated from your body, as if the dulka oil was in you, not on you. I touched your shoulder with nervous fingers. They slid to your breast and your perfect stomach. You laughed as if I was tickling you and your braided African locks, shining with oil, danced about your head. *Ah aaaaaaah* what a girl! How gorgeous you were! Your mother had used her own experience to bring you up to be polite and well mannered, and then to teach you how to have fun on the palm-stalk bed. You surprised me, Salha. You were a whirlpool raging in the flood season, a lavish wave of giving, a lusty jet-black mare. When you turned your legs over and I saw you from behind, my heart leapt. Our bodies are so sweet, they need no words. Our weather is so perfect, we need no covers. The house was wide and spacious, warm and still, and the silence utterly complete, exhausted after a wedding that made the universe tremble.

Salha, you were a naughty little devil when you were a child, then you changed into a charming and understanding young woman. Your father Bilal gave his consent, and I took you in lawful marriage. And now here you are with me, naughty again as a bride. You've returned to your naughtiness, and now it is allowed. I prefer you this way.

Aaaaah aaaaah aaaaah

Tudishshsh tudushshsh

In the darkness before dawn, we jumped into the celestial Nile to perform our ablutions in its pure and holy water. It flows from the springs of Salsabeel in Paradise. The rippling water has its effect. It passes over our bodies and we absorb its silt and fertile mud. My pores draw it into my bones, into my marrow, and it kisses the water of life and gives it its dark color. It embraces your sweet body slowly and deliberately and seeps inside until it rests in the womb, enfolding the tiny beginning, giving it color. There it grows and curls up. And outside, the belly looks like a soft, round sand dune. And on the day God wills, our love comes out to us, a blessed child with the sun in his face, crying.

Waaaaah waaaaah waaaaah

Kum-ban-kaash kin-klin-lin kum-ban-kaash

I stood beside the bed. Salha was lying there exhausted, smiling contentedly, holding our child Zibeyda. Her father Bilal stood next to her mother. They were both delighted. Habboub, on his mother's shoulder, was shouting happily and fidgeting. He wanted to get down and play with my daughter. I said, "Bismillah," and picked my daughter up in one arm and Habboub in the other. I whispered into his ear, "Habboub, if the Almighty grant that my daughter be yours, then take her in lawful marriage. Sing to her . . . 'Your breasts are firm like oranges.' She'll like that. And when she screams *weeeek weeek* and brings you the *waaaah waaaah*, a little girl with dark skin, and the sun in her face, call her after your mother, Miska al-Tayib."

Translated by Anthony Calderbank

Yusuf al-Qa'id
(b. 1944)
EGYPT

Yusuf al-Qa'id was born in Egypt to a peasant family. He received his education in Egypt and taught there for three years. One of Egypt's outstanding novelists, he has published eleven novels and four collections of stories. His novel *War in the Land of Egypt*, the basis for a successful film starring Omar Sharif, was originally banned in Egypt.

Three Meaningless Tales

1. A Futile Crossing

The rich man reached the broad river and its raging waters. He heard a voice call out to him, "What is it you're looking for now, sir?"

He replied, "A man who will carry me across the river on his back."

A kindly giant appeared before him at once. The rich man leapt on the strong man's back and shouted to him, "Swim me across."

The strong man swam out into the river. As he neared the far bank he became exhausted and almost perished.

"Don't die before you get me safely to shore," the rich man yelled at him.

The strong man replied, "Your wish is my command."

He did get him to dry land, but then he immediately died. After dying he held out his hand to the rich man. "Give me my wages so I can pay to get buried," he entreated him.

The rich man kicked him so hard that the dead man's hand flew off into the sky, leaving him with only one hand. The rich man screamed at him: "What wages? If I had not been on your back you wouldn't have been able to make the crossing. Times are hard. Your making it all the way was a miracle. You could not have done it without me. Then you talk about getting paid!"

The rich man proceeded angrily upon his way. "What's come over the world?" he asked himself. "Why do poor people think about getting rich? Isn't there a law against that?"

2. Who Sank the Ship

The ship was crossing vast oceans. None of the passengers knew its point of departure or where it was scheduled to land. It just kept on sailing. There were only two types of passengers on the ship: the very rich and the very poor. The rich occupied the upper state-rooms and the poor were in the lower cabins. On the first day one of the rich people died. After performing the autopsy, the doctor declared, "He died from overeating."

The poor people were amazed at his statement. They considered the event one of the wonders of the age. The following day one of the poor people died. After examining him, the doctor proclaimed, "He died of hunger."

The rich people on the boat were amazed and considered this death one of the wonders of the age. After some days there was a change in the weather and life became unbearable on the upper decks of the ship. The captain, who was one of the rich people, issued immediate orders for an exchange of places. The rich went below and the poor came to the upper decks. Both groups were amazed at the strange events on the ship.

Then suddenly the ship's supply of drinking water was exhausted. The question was how to obtain potable water.

The poor people said, "Let's all be patient until relief comes."

The rich, however, raised a ruckus. The captain issued two orders. The first was to exchange places again. So the rich climbed up and the poor went down below. People commented that here was a fourth marvel. After the rich had ascended, the captain put into effect his second order which was to drill a hole in the bottom of the hull so that the poor people could get some water.

The ship began to sink, and some of the poor people drowned. The rich, however, refused to believe it. The ship kept on sinking. The rich people sipped the water as it bubbled up from below. And . . .

3. Hunger Fantasia

The same year that conditions changed in the country and people hoped that life would improve, the family's circumstances deteriorated. They could not find enough to eat. The mother bared her breasts. She asked the head of the household to go to sleep until the situation improved. They would proceed as though there were no man in the family.

She set forth and wandered about aimlessly. The man fell asleep for four years. He was awakened by sirens and patriotic anthems. He asked his children, "Have you found anything to eat?"

They told him they had been fasting since he went to sleep. They had not yet been able to break that fast. The mother was still on her historic journey. The country was at war with its enemies. They hoped they would be able to find something to eat after the war.

The father went back to sleep. After five years he was awakened by the noise of a great commotion in the streets. He noticed that one of his children was missing. The others had still not been able to find anything to eat. The mother was continuing her trip. The country was engaged in a thrilling debate over the best way to break an egg before eating it. Some people said it should be cracked on the right side. Others insisted on cracking it from the left. A group of moderates said it should be broken at the center. The father tried to understand their arguments, but his mind grew tired and he went back to sleep. He had asked them to wake him when they found something to eat, but no one disturbed him.

He awoke after another six years to hear the wail of sirens and battle hymns. When he opened his eyes he discovered that another child had disappeared. He learned the boy had been martyred in a war the country had launched in some distant land. Things were just the way they had been. The mother was absent on her voyage of discovery, and the children were hungry. Enemies had appeared at the borders of the country and had to be combated. A despondent silence reigned over the children. The father grasped the situation without recourse to words. He fell asleep. His nervous system was apparently set for the same number of years this time. Then he awoke to find another child missing and the country plunged into the last of its wars. They had been told that the mother was returning. It was true that they were still hungry, but food, hope, and a new life were on the way. They would have to be patient for only one more year.

The father went back to sleep for three years. He was awakened by voices around him. He opened his eyes to find his surviving children eating each other. When they noticed that he was awake, their mouths sprang open. He leapt up in terror and fled to the main street of the city. It was the avenue used for processions and parades. There was his wife, stark naked. A number of strangers were trifling with parts of her body. She was laughing giddily in a way he had never seen before. More than one man came up to him to eat him. He asked his wife to protect him.

She shouted at him, "Everyone is eating everyone, and I've the greatest right to eat you."

He was the only person still to have all his flesh and bones. Along the avenue people were eating people and some were eating themselves.

The head of the household was revolted by what he saw. He looked around for a place where he could sleep. Hands surrounded him from every direction and began to finger him with gluttonous desire. He had no choice but to surrender to these hands. He fell asleep on top of them. They bore him aloft and carried him down the main thoroughfare as though in a giant funeral procession.

Translated by William Hutchins

Abd al-Hakim Qasim
(1935–90)
EGYPT

Abd al-Hakim Qasim was born in a small village in the Egyptian Delta and attended Alexandria University. In 1967 he was sentenced by a military court to five years' imprisonment for his involvement with underground leftist movements. Upon being released from prison he published his novel *The Seven Days of Men*, which has been translated into

English. A volume consisting of two outstanding novellas was published in English translation under the title *Rites of Assent*. Abd al-Hakim Qasim lived for many years in Berlin before returning to Cairo, where he died.

The Whistle

A long, long line of children slips between the maize stalks putting under them small handfuls of chemical fertilizer; behind them is an overseer with a long cane and a whistle.

The boy Hasan and the girl Hanim are at the end of the line, each of them holding a pot full of fertilizer in one hand; their hands, brown and thin, move like the pendulum of a clock between the pot and the roots of the maize.

The weather is heavy, overcast; spiders' webs hang between the stalks and stick to forehead and temple; the maize leaves, like pliant knives, scratch at neck and cheek, while the sweat breaks out falteringly on back and under arms.

The boy Hasan is tense: he strikes at the earth, kicks at the stems of weeds that become entangled with the hem of his *galabia* and implant themselves in the sole of his foot.

He is glancing at the girl Hanim all the time. She is slightly withdrawn, looking warily at him. He leans towards her and she moves away sideways, and ever so gradually they put a great distance between themselves and the other children.

The boy Hasan began to breathe more quickly, glancing more often furtively towards her, while her coquettishness deepened in significance and the small handfuls of fertilizer began to fall not exactly on the roots.

The weather became heavier, more overcast. Hasan knocked against a maize stalk; its ear shook, raising a small cloud of pollen whose motes sparkled in the sunlight above the tufts of stalks. Then it sent down a fine rain that stuck to his already wet face and neck, the runnels of sweat bearing the minute beads to his chest and back, while the solution of chemical salt ran from the palm of his hand down his arm and, both hands being soiled, he was unable to scratch his skin that was ablaze with fire.

He moaned. Lowering his head, he rubbed, with the top of his shoulder, at a drop of sweat slowly making its way along the inflamed skin behind his ear. He gazed long at Hanim, breathing heavily, audibly, through his nose, the girl small under his gaze, her face lowered, and the fertilizer falling very far from the roots.

"Hey, Hanim!"

The girl squatted down on her haunches directly she heard the harsh sound of his breathing, planting the palms of her hands in the ground behind her, the pot of fertilizer thrown down at a slant beside her. Her lower jaw hung down and her lips were parted; a lock of dusty hair clung to her moist forehead; her dress was drawn up, revealing her long red underclothes.

Supporting his weight on his knees and hands, the boy Hasan began moving towards the girl Hanim. Her small breasts rose and fell.

Suddenly they heard the overseer's whistle. Quickly they took up the pots and went on placing the small handfuls of fertilizer under the roots.

The weather grew heavier and more overcast. Violently he pulled away a maize leaf that had almost passed through his eyelid and pierced his eye.

He was slightly ahead of Hanim. He looked around him. They were so far from the rest of the children they heard no sound from them.

He turned and found that he had overlooked several plants. He returned to them and gave them fertilizer. Had the overseer seen it he'd have given him a beating.

There were very many plants to be done before they reached the canal and he could cleanse his hands of the chemical salt solution which bit into them like fire, and scoop up water and splash it onto his face and be able to scratch his festering skin.

A grasshopper landed on the back of his neck; its saw-like leg clung to his skin. He placed the pot on the ground and, hunching up his shoulders, moved his neck frenziedly from right to left, his teeth clenched, unable to bring his soiled hand up to his neck lest he set it ablaze. The grasshopper flew off, landing on a stalk, then to another and yet another, heedless of the overseer's whistle.

The only sound to be heard was that of the monotonous repeated movements of their hands between the pot and the maize stalks. Suddenly the boy Hasan froze where he was; the girl Hanim froze too, as though part of him. He leaned forward, inclining his head to one side, listening. There was nothing except for the movement of cicadas; they were completely alone.

Hasan looked round furtively, having forgotten about the pot of fertilizer he was holding up in the air. He stretched out his free hand little by little till he had clasped the girl's hand violently, his eyes exploring between the stalks of maize. Very slowly the girl Hanim flexed her knees, and Hasan too. A long, staccato whispering noise escaped from his lips, and then the two of them were squatting on the ground, their knees joined, their foreheads almost touching. He wanted to stretch out his hand to her, but it was soiled with that chemical salt, and he began to rub it, with quick, violent movements on the ground, to wipe it clean.

Suddenly they heard the overseer's whistle and Hasan rose to his feet. A broken piece of glass must have cut his finger because it was pouring with blood.

The repeated movement of their hands between pot and roots was taken up again. The salt solution trickled down into the wound. Hasan's hand tightened on the pot as he clenched and unclenched his wounded hand.

Hanim was gazing at him apprehensively, her eyes fixed on his back, while her hand moved between the pot and the maize roots.

Blood poured from his finger, his eyes watered, yet he continued to scoop up the fertilizer and place it under the stalks.

After a while there was a gleam of light between the maize stalks, then he found a splodge of sun on the ground and rose to his feet and ran towards the canal to plunge his face into the water.

Translated by Denys Johnson-Davies

Somaya Ramadan
(b. 1951)
EGYPT

Somaya Ramadan was born in Cairo. She received her
Ph.D. in English from Trinity College, Dublin, and is a lecturer in English and translation at the National Academy of
Arts in Cairo. The following passage is from *Leaves of Narcissus*, a novel about exile, physical and psychological, that
takes place mainly in Ireland. It was awarded the Naguib
Mahfouz Medal for Literature in 2001.

FROM *Leaves of Narcissus*

I left Mary behind—or perhaps I threw her out, and she complied
without question. I flung my coat around my shoulders, wound my
white scarf around my neck, slammed the door behind me, and
went to find him in his office. There he was, his hair long and deep
black, assailed here and there by gleaming silver threads. The dark
curls practically brushed the sky-blue shirt collar rising from the
neckline of a navy blue pullover. There he was: the eyeglasses, small,
round lenses rimmed in thin gold wire; a mouth that reminded me
of those O-shaped mouths on cherubs ranged around the murals of
the Italian Renaissance. His brown eyes shone mischievously. We
had met at a performance of modern Irish dance at the Abbey The-
atre. As the others went on ahead, he said, "I know you very well.
You are the woman I see in my dreams."

We laughed. I said I didn't like Jung's mystifications, and instantly he replied that he personally was Freudian to the bone, and
we laughed even more. I hadn't laughed at all for quite a long time.
When he asked, "When shall we meet?" that diaphanous veil of deception that separates two strangers fell between us. But then I re-

called a young Arab girl called Maryam, opening the *Sunday Times* on a rainy weekend day in London. The newspaper had been wider than the span of her arms, and she had hidden her face in its folds and cried in silence. So I said, "Sunday. Let's meet on Sunday." And when the time came, I did not go.

When he saw me at midweek, he suppressed a little gleam of delight and swathed his voice in an agreeable, light tone:

"And whom shall I thank for this visit, three days late?"

"Salvador Dalí," I said.

"No joking?"

"No joking."

"Do you want to tell me—when, how, and the rest?"

"I was hanging a poster, a print of the *Metamorphosis of Narcissus*, and suddenly I recalled something you said that made me see."

I went to him in his chair in front of the window, which looked out over the courtyard, and I smelled the fragrance of soap drifting from the collar of his shirt. Through the window I saw the Henry Moore sculpture recently purchased by the university, a different perspective than I had seen it from before. On the soft grass, the figure submissively endured the group of schoolchildren who were popping brightly through and around the gaps between its gentle curves. I kissed him on the cheek and suddenly understood the distance that separates words from communion. You need very many words and even more pauses, and thousands of tiny motions, so slight that they are barely noticeable even to the trained eye; you need an even larger palette of tones, merely to signal misunderstanding; you have to pass through all of this before you reach a state where you know that your meaning and your words are one, no more and no less, and that they are instantaneously grasped by the person for whom they are meant. Before you achieve this, you need recourse to many lies.

In her room, on the small bed, she studies the long pale languid body. She had never liked white flesh: it had always seemed to hint of flabbiness, before this. And it had never happened that she'd known a man untouched by the purifying blade of circumcision. Yet, he left her synonymous with gentle radiance and rich fulfillment, his pleasure a slow, spontaneous, prayerful tenderness, a bodily reverence clothed in a soft tremble, a lesson in worship.

When the doorbell rang, he asked her, "Aren't you going to open the door?"

"No."

"Do you know who is at the door?"

"Yes."

"Did you leave me knocking at the door, when you knew it was me?"

"Yes," she said. She lied and knew then that she loved him dearly, unreservedly.

Quietly she pulled the door shut behind her. The sky was raining mud. She went into O'Neill's Pub and knocked back glass after glass of murky beer, and returned to her room, her clothes clinging to her body. She fell ill and raved deliriously with fever. The doctor arrived.

"Nothing to worry about. It'll all pass, you'll think it was a dream."

As soon as she recovered her strength, she returned to her hours in the library. But no matter what she tried to read, the words were unintelligible. When he arrived on his bicycle, shaking the rain off, he said, "Perhaps it would be better for you to go home. You have all the symptoms."

He was joking, or at least partly so. He knew that she had definite plans to go back. He knew she didn't mean it when she said that the only way she could possibly stay on was for them to get married. But she did not laugh when he mentioned "the symptoms," for it was his way of inviting her to his home, though what he always said was "your home." She surprised him with an anger that compressed her words and expelled them in a barely audible hiss:

"Where is my home? What is this that you call my home? Why do you say that—my home?"

I had a home. I had a home to which I would return, and a homeland.

It was not the newspaper for which her hand reached but Thomas Flanagan, noted authority on Irish literature, quoting *Henry V.* She read to him, a wan, tight smile on her lips: "My nation! What ish my nation? Ish a villain, and a bastard, and a knave, and a rascal? What ish my nation? Who talks of my nation?"

He took her in his arms, trying to dispel her wild alarm. "I don't mean your *homeland*, princess of mine. I mean your *home*—where I am."

And when she stared at him as if he were a stranger whom she had just met for the very first time, he tried harder, differently, and got himself into a deeper fix:

"Where your family is."

"What's the difference?" she shot back, he took her in his arms and stayed until she had fallen asleep.

In the news, Egypt's pulse was quickening; Egypt stifled our breath. The Islamists: there were interminable lists of names, students and professors and officers and soldiers. They were hanged.

The BBC report wondered: Is Cairo calm or is it simply indifferent?

Cairo is a fish with mayonnaise, at an authentic Egyptian afternoon meal for a delegation of foreigners.

On Sunday he arrived on his bicycle. "All right, now I will accompany you to your nation, I mean, your home," he said, laughing.

She laughed, too. She was wearing black. She had been on the point of leaving for the Egyptian embassy to pay her respects, as exile dictated, following the recent death of the "Believer President," Muhammad Anwar al-Sadat, assassinated in the military reviewing stand by Islamists who had disguised themselves as soldiers, when the news came of her father's death. As she was leaving the room, her gaze met the eyes of the sailor in the picture on the wall-map, heading seaward in the little wooden boat.

Translated by Marilyn Booth

Alifa Rifaat
(1930–95)
EGYPT

Alifa Rifaat spent most of her adult life in various parts of the Egyptian countryside as the wife of a police officer, and it is largely from these years that she drew the material for her short stories. A volume of selected stories in translation, *Distant View of a Minaret*, was well received in Britain and the United States for its bold depiction of a woman's place in Muslim society.

An Incident in the Ghobashi Household

Zeinat woke to the strident call of the red cockerel from the rooftop above where she was sleeping. The Ghobashi house stood on the outskirts of the village and in front of it the fields stretched out to the river and the railway track.

The call of the red cockerel released answering calls from neighbouring rooftops. Then they were silenced by the voice of the *muezzin* from the lofty minaret among the mulberry trees calling: "Prayer is better than sleep."

She stretched out her arm to the pile of children sleeping alongside her and tucked the end of the old rag-woven *kilim* round their bodies, then shook her eldest daughter's shoulder.

"It's morning, another of the Lord's mornings. Get up, Ni'ma— today's market day."

Ni'ma rolled onto her back and lazily stretched herself. Like someone alerted by the sudden slap of a gust of wind, Zeinat stared down at the body spread out before her. Ni'ma sat up and pulled her *galabia* over her thighs, rubbing at her sleep-heavy eyes in the rounded face with the prominent cheekbones.

"Are you going to be able to carry the grain to the market, daughter, or will it be too heavy for you?"

"Of course, mother. After all, who else is there to go?"

Zeinat rose to her feet and went out with sluggish steps to the courtyard, where she made her ablutions. Having finished the ritual prayer, she remained in the seated position as she counted off on her fingers her glorifications of Allah. Sensing that Ni'ma was standing behind her, she turned round to her:

"What are you standing there for? Why don't you go off and get the tea ready?"

Zeinat walked towards the corner where Ghobashi had stored the maize crop in sacks; he had left them as a provision for them after he had taken his air ticket from the office that had found him work in Libya and which would be bringing him back in a year's time.

"May the Lord keep you safe while you're away, Ghobashi," she muttered.

Squatting in front of a sack, the grain measure between her thighs, she scooped up the grain with both hands till the measure was full, then poured it into a basket. Coughing, she waved away the dust that rose up to her face, then returned to her work.

The girl went to the large clay jar, removed the wooden covering and dipped the mug into it and sprinkled water on her face; she wetted the tips of her fingers and parted her plaits, then tied her handkerchief over her head. She turned to her mother:

"Isn't that enough, mother? What do we want the money for?"

Zeinat struck her knees with the palms of her hands and tossed her head back.

"Don't we have to pay off Hamdan's wage?—or was he cultivating the beans for us for nothing, just for the fun of hard work?"

Ni'ma turned away and brought the stove from the window shelf, arranging the dried corn-cobs in a pyramid and lighting them. She put it alongside her mother, then filled the teapot with water from the jar and thrust it into the embers. She squatted down and the two sat in silence. Suddenly Zeinat said:

"Since when has the buffalo been with young?"

"From after my father went away."

"That's to say, right after the Great Feast, daughter?"

Ni'ma nodded her head in assent, then lowered it and began drawing lines in the dust.

"Why don't you go off and see how many eggs have been laid while the tea's getting ready."

Zeinat gazed into the glow of the embers. She had a sense of peace as she stared into the dancing flames. Ghobashi had gone and left the whole load on her shoulders: the children, the two *kirats* of land and the buffalo. "Take care of Ni'ma," he had said the night before he left. "The girl's body has ripened." He had then spread out his palms and said: "O Lord, for the sake of the Prophet's honour, let me bring back with me a marriage dress for her of pure silk." She had said to him: "May your words go straight from your lips to Heaven's gate, Ghobashi." He wouldn't be returning before the following Great Feast. What would happen when he returned and found out the state of affairs? She put her head between the palms of her hands and leaned over the fire, blowing away the ashes. "How strange," she thought, "are the girls of today! The cunning little thing was hanging out her towels at the time of her period every month just as though nothing had happened, and here she is in her fourth month and there's nothing showing."

Ni'ma returned and untied the cloth from round the eggs, put two of them in the fire and the rest in a dish. She then brought two glasses and the tin of sugar and sat down next to her mother, who was still immersed in her thoughts.

"Didn't you try to find some way out?"

Ni'ma hunched her shoulders in a gesture of helplessness.

"Your father's been gone four months. Isn't there still time?"

"What's the use? If only the Lord were to spare you the trouble of me. Wouldn't it be for the best, mother, if my foot were to slip as I was filling the water jar from the canal and we'd be done with it?"

Zeinat struck herself on the breast and drew her daughter to her.

"Don't say such a wicked thing. Don't listen to such promptings of the Devil. Calm down and let's find some solution before your father returns."

Zeinat poured out the tea. In silence she took quick sips at it, then put the glass in front of her and shelled the egg and bit into it. Ni'ma sat watching her, her fingers held round the hot glass. From outside came the raised voices of women discussing the prospects at the day's market, while men exchanged greetings as they made their way to the fields. Amidst the voices could be heard Hamdan's laughter as he led the buffalo to the two *kirats* of land surrounding the house.

"His account is with Allah," muttered Zeinat. "He's fine and doesn't have a worry in the world."

Ni'ma got up and began winding round the end of her head cloth so as to form a pad on her head. Zeinat turned round and saw her preparing herself to go off to the market. She pulled her by her *galabia* and the young girl sat down again. At this moment they heard knocking at the door and the voice of their neighbour, Umm al-Khair, calling:

"Good health to you, folk. Isn't Ni'ma coming with me to market as usual, Auntie Zeinat? Or isn't she up yet?"

"Sister, she's just going off to stay with our relatives."

"May Allah bring her back safely."

Ni'ma looked at her mother enquiringly, while Zeinat placed her finger to her mouth. When the sound of Umm al-Khair's footsteps died away, Ni'ma whispered:

"What are you intending to do, mother? What relatives are you talking about?"

Zeinat got up and rummaged in her clothes box and took out a handkerchief tied round some money, and also old clothes. She placed the handkerchief in Ni'ma's palm and closed her fingers over it.

"Take it—they're my life savings."

Ni'ma remained silent as her mother went on:

"Get together your clothes and go straight away to the station and take a ticket to Cairo. Cairo's a big place, daughter, where you'll find protection and a way to make a living till Allah brings you safely to your time. Then bring it back with you at dead of night without anyone seeing you or hearing you."

Zeinat raised the end of her *galabia* and put it between her teeth. Taking hold of the old clothes, she began winding them round her waist. Then she let fall the *galabia*. Ni'ma regarded her in astonishment:

"And what will we say to my father?"

"It's no time for talking. Before you go off to the station, help me up with the basket so that I can go to the market for people to see me like this. Isn't it better, when he returns, for your father to find himself with a legitimate son than an illegitimate grandson?"

Translated by Denys Johnson-Davies

Nawal El Saadawi
(b. 1931)
EGYPT

Nawal El Saadawi was born in a small Egyptian village and trained as a doctor. She became well-known in the 1970s for her books exposing the sexual and cultural oppression of Arab women. She has published many novels and collections of stories; fourteen of her books are available in English translation (her translator is her husband, the writer Sherif Hetata). She is the second most widely read Arab writer in the English-speaking world (after Naguib Mahfouz).

El Saadawi was imprisoned by Egyptian president Anwar Sadat in 1981. In the 1990s she left Egypt for the United States when she was threatened by Muslim fundamentalists. She has taught at a number of American universities. A controversial figure, she is seen very differently in the Arab world from how she is seen in the West. The second selection below is from her best-known novel, *Woman at Point Zero*, and describes the heroine's final revolt against man's domination.

She Has No Place in Paradise

With the palm of her hand, she touched the ground beneath her but did not feel soil. She looked upwards, stretching her neck towards the light. Her face appeared long and lean, the skin so dark it was almost black.

She could not see her own face in the dark and held no mirror in her hand. But the white light fell onto the back of her hand so that it became white in turn. Her narrow eyes widened in surprise and filled with light. Thus widened and full of light, her eyes looked like those of a houri.

In astonishment, she turned her head to the right and to the left. A vast expanse between the leafy trees above her head as she sat in the shade and the stream of water like a strip of silver, its clusters of droplets like pearls, then that deep plate full of broth to the rim.

Her eyelids tightened to open her eyes to the utmost. The scene remained the same, did not alter. She touched her robe and found it to be as soft as silk. From the neck of her gown wafted the scent of musk or good perfume.

Her head and eyes were motionless for she feared that any blink of her eyelids would change the scene or that it would disappear as it had done before.

But from the corner of her eye, she could see the shade stretching endlessly before her, and green trees between the trunks of which she saw a house of red brick like a palace, with a marble staircase leading up to the bedroom.

She remained fixed to the spot, able neither to believe nor disbelieve. Nothing upset her more than the recurrence of the dream that she had died and woken to find herself in paradise. The dream seemed to her impossible, for dying seemed impossible, waking after death even more impossible and going to paradise the fourth impossibility.

She steadied her neck still more and from the corner of her eye stared into the light. The scene was still the same, unaltered. The red brick house, like that of the Omda, the towering staircase leading to the bedroom, the room itself bathed in white light, the window looking out onto distant horizons, the wide bed, its posts swathed in a curtain of silk, all were still there.

It was all so real it could not be denied. She stayed where she was, fearing to move and fearing to believe. Was it possible to die and waken so quickly and then go to paradise?

What she found hardest to believe was the speed of it all. Death, after all, was easy. Everybody died and her own death was easier than anyone's, for she had lived between life and death, closer to death than to life. When her mother gave birth to her, she lay on top of her with all her weight until she died; her father beat her on the head with a hoe until she died; she had gone into fever after each birth, even until the eighth child; when her husband kicked her in the stomach; when the blows of the sun penetrated under the bones of her head.

Life was hard and death for her was easier. Easier still was waking after death, for no one dies and no one wakens; everyone dies and awakens, except an animal which dies and remains dead.

Her going to paradise was also impossible. But if not her, who would go to paradise? Throughout her life she had never done anything to anger God or His Prophet. She used to tie her frizzy black hair with a skein of wool into a plait; the plait she wrapped up in a white headscarf and her head she wrapped in a black shawl. Nothing showed from under her robe except the heel of her foot. From the moment of her birth until her death, she knew only the word "okay."

Before dawn, when her mother slapped her as she lay, to go and carry dung-pats on her head, she knew only "okay." If her father tied her to the water mill in place of the sick cow, she said only "okay." She never raised her eyes to her husband's and when he lay on top of her when she was sick with fever, she uttered only the word "okay."

She had never stolen or lied in her life. She would go hungry or die of hunger rather than take the food of others, even if it were her father's or brother's or husband's. Her mother would wrap up food for her father in a flat loaf of bread and make her carry it to the field on her head. Her husband's food was also wrapped up in a loaf by his mother. She was tempted, as she walked along with it, to stop under the shade of a tree and open the load; but she never once stopped. Each time she was tempted, she called on God to protect her from the Devil, until the hunger became unbearable and she would pick a bunch of wild grass from the side of the road which she would chew like gum, then swallow with a sip of water, filling the cup of her hand from the bank of the canal and drinking until she had quenched her thirst. Then wiping her mouth on the sleeve of her robe, she would mutter to herself, *Thank God*, and repeat it three times. She prayed five times a day, her face to the ground, thanking God. If she were attacked by fever and her head filled with blood like fire, she would still praise God. On fast days, she would fast; on baking days, she would bake; on harvest days, she would harvest; on holy days, she would put on her mourning weeds and go to the cemetery.

She never lost her temper with her father or brother or husband. If her husband beat her to death and she returned to her father's house, her father would send her back to her husband. If she returned again, her father would beat her and then send her back. If her husband took her back and did not throw her out, and then beat her, she returned to her mother who would tell her: *Go back, Zeinab. Paradise will be yours in the hereafter.*

From the time she was born, she had heard the word "paradise" from her mother. The first time she'd heard it, she was walking in the sun, a pile of dung on her head, the soles of her feet scorched by the earth. She pictured paradise as a vast expanse of shade without dung on her head, on her feet shoes like those of Hassanain, the neighbor's son, pounding the earth as he did, his hand holding hers, the two of them sitting in the shade.

When she thought of Hassanain, her imagination went no further than holding hands and sitting in the shade of paradise. But her mother scolded her and told her that neither their neighbor's son Hassanain, nor any other neighbor's son, would be in paradise, that her eyes would not fall on any man other than her father or brother, that if she died after getting married and went to paradise, only her husband would be there, that if her soul was tempted, awake or asleep, and her eye fell on a man other than her husband and even before he held her hand in his, she would not so much as catch a glimpse of paradise or smell it from a thousand meters.

From that time, whenever she lay down to sleep, she saw only her husband. In paradise, her husband did not beat her. The pile of dung was no longer on her head; neither did the earth burn the soles of her feet. Their black mud house became one of red brick, inside it a towering staircase, then a wide bed on which her husband sat, holding her hand in his.

Her imagination went no further than holding his hand in paradise. Never once in her life had her hand held her husband's. Eight sons and daughters she had conceived with him without once holding his hand. On summer nights, he lay in the fields; in the winter, he lay in the barn or above the oven. All night long, he slept on his back without turning. If he did turn, he would call to her in a voice like a jackal's: *Woman!* Before she could answer "yes" or "okay," he would have kicked her over onto her back and rolled on top of her. If she made a sound or sighed, he would kick her again. If she did not sigh or make a sound, she would get a third kick, then a fourth until she did. His hand never chanced to hold hers nor his arm happen to stretch out to embrace her.

She had never seen a couple, human or otherwise, embrace except in the dovecot, when she went up there, on the top of the wall appeared a pair of doves, their beaks close together; or when she went down to the cattle pen or from behind the wall there appeared a pair of bull and cow or buffalo or dogs—and her mother brandishing a bamboo stick and whipping them, cursing the animals.

Never in her life had she taken the black shawl off her head nor the white scarf tied under the shawl, except when someone died, when she untied the scarf and pulled the black shawl around her head. When her husband died, she knotted the black shawl twice around her forehead and wore mourning weeds for three years. A man came to ask for her in marriage without her children. Her mother spat in disgust and pulled the shawl down over her forehead, whispering: *It's shameful! Does a mother abandon her children for the sake of a man?* The years passed by and a man came to ask for her hand in marriage, with her children. Her mother yelled at the top of her voice: *What does a woman want in this world after she has become a mother and her husband dies?*

One day, she wanted to take off the black shawl and put on a white scarf, but she feared that people would think she'd forgotten her husband. So she kept the black shawl and the mourning weeds and remained sad for her husband until she died of sadness.

She found herself wrapped in a silken shroud inside a coffin. From behind the funeral procession, she heard her mother's wailing like a howl in the night or like the whistle of a train: *You'll meet up with your husband in paradise, Zeinab.*

Then the noise stopped. She heard nothing but silence and smelled nothing but the soil. The ground beneath her became as soft as silk. She said: *It must be the shroud.* Above her head, she heard rough voices, like two men fighting. She did not know why they were fighting until she heard one of them mention her name and say that she deserved to go directly to paradise without suffering the torture of the grave. But the other man did not agree and insisted that she should undergo some torture, if only a little: She cannot go directly up to paradise. Everyone must go through the torture of the grave. But the first man insisted that she had done nothing to merit torture, that she had been one hundred percent faithful to her husband. The second man argued that her hair had shown from under her white headscarf, that she had dyed her hair red with henna, that the hennaed heels of her feet had shown from under her robe.

The first man retorted that her hair had never shown, that what his colleague had seen was only the skein of wool, that her robe had been long and thick, under it even thicker and longer underskirts, that no one had seen her heels red.

But his colleague argued, insisting that her red heels had enticed many of the village men.

The dispute between the two of them lasted all night. She lay facedown on the ground, her nose and mouth pressed into the earth. She held her breath pretending to be dead. Her torture might be prolonged if it became clear that she had not died; death might save her. She heard nothing of what passed between them; nobody, human or spirit, can hear what happens in the grave after death. If one did happen to hear, one had to pretend not to have heard or not to have understood. The most serious thing to understand is that those two men are not angels of the grave or angels of any type, for it is not possible for angels to ignore the truth which everyone in the village with eyes to see could know: that her heels had never been red like those of the Omda's daughter, but like her face and palms, were always cracked and as black as the soil.

The argument ended before dawn without torture. She thanked God when the voices stopped. Her body grew lighter and rose up as if in flight. She hovered as if in the sky, then her body fell and landed on soft, moist earth and she gasped: Paradise.

Cautiously, she raised her head and saw a vast expanse of green, and thick leafy trees, shade beneath them.

She sat up on the ground and saw the trees stretching endlessly before her. Fresh air entered her chest, expelling the dirt and dust and the smell of dung.

With a slight movement, she rose to her feet. Between the tree trunks she could see the house of red brick, the entrance before her very eyes.

She entered quickly, panting. She climbed the towering staircase panting. In front of the bedroom, she stopped for a moment to catch her breath. Her heart was beating wildly and her chest heaved.

The door was closed. She put out her hand carefully and pushed it. She saw the four posts of the bed, around them a silken curtain. In the middle, she saw a wide bed, on top of it her husband, sitting like a bride-groom. On his right was a woman. On his left, another woman. Both of them wore transparent robes revealing skin as white as honey, their eyes filled with light, like the eyes of houris.

Her husband's face was not turned towards her, so he did not see her. Her hand was still on the door. She pulled it behind her and it closed. She returned to the earth, saying to herself: *There is no place in paradise for a black woman.*

Translated by Shirley Eber

FROM *Woman at Point Zero*

So he began to share in everything that I earned, in fact to confiscate the larger part for himself. But each time he tried to come near me, I pushed him away, repeating:

"It's impossible. It's no use trying."

Then he'd beat me up. And each time I would hear the same phrase repeated as he struck me: "The word does not exist for me."

I discovered he was a dangerous pimp who controlled a number of prostitutes, and I was one of them. He had friends everywhere, in every profession, and on whom he spent his money generously. He had a doctor friend to whom he had recourse if one of his prostitutes became pregnant and needed an abortion, a friend in the police who protected him from raids, a friend in the courts who used his legal knowledge and position to keep him out of trouble and release any of the prostitutes who found herself in gaol, so that she was not held up from earning money for too long.

I realized I was not nearly as free as I had hitherto imagined myself to be. I was nothing but a body machine working day and night so that a number of men belonging to different professions could become immensely rich at my expense. I was no longer even mistress of the house for which I had paid with my efforts and sweat. One day I said to myself,

"I can't go on like this."

I packed my papers in a small bag and got ready to leave, but suddenly he appeared, standing in front of me.

"Where are you going?" he asked.

"I'm going to look for work. I still have my secondary school certificate."

"And who said that you are not working?"

"I want to choose the work I'm going to do."

"Who says anyone in this whole wide world chooses the work he wants to do?"

"I don't want to be anybody's slave."

"And who says there is anyone who is not someone else's slave? There are only two categories of people, Firdaus, masters and slaves."

"In that case I want to be one of the masters and not one of the slaves."

"How can you be one of the masters? A woman on her own cannot be a master, let alone a woman who's a prostitute. Can't you see you're asking for the impossible?"

"The word 'impossible' does not exist for me," I said.

I tried to slip through the door, but he pushed me back and shut it. I looked him in the eye and said,

"I intend to leave."

He stared back at me. I heard him mutter, "You will never leave."

I continued to look straight at him without blinking. I knew I hated him as only a woman can hate a man, as only a slave can hate his master. I saw from the expression in his eyes that he feared me as only a master can fear his slave, as only a man can fear a woman. But it lasted for only a second. Then the arrogant expression of the master, the aggressive look of the male who fears nothing returned. I caught hold of the latch of the door to open it, but he lifted his arm up in the air and slapped me. I raised my hand even higher than he had done, and brought it down violently on his face. The whites of his eyes went red. His hand started to reach for the knife he carried in his pocket, but my hand was quicker than his. I raised the knife and buried it deep in his neck, pulled it out of his neck and then thrust it deep into his chest, pulled it out of his chest and plunged it deep into his belly. I stuck the knife into almost every part of his body. I was astonished to find how easily my hand moved as I thrust the knife into his flesh, and pulled it out almost without effort. My surprise was all the greater since I had never done what I was doing before. A question flashed through my mind. Why was it that I had never stabbed a man before? I realized that I had been afraid, and that the fear had been within me all the time, until the fleeting moment when I read fear in his eyes.

Translated by Sherif Hetata

Tayeb Salih
(b. 1929)
SUDAN

Tayeb Salih was born in the north of Sudan but has spent the greater part of his life outside the land of his birth. He came to writing relatively late in life. After attending university in England, he joined the BBC Arabic service and became the head of drama. He later became director-general of information in the Arabian Gulf state of Qatar and then worked for UNESCO in Paris. His novella *The Wedding of Zein* was made into an Arabic film. He has also written several short stories, some of which appeared in translation in the magazine *Encounter*. His best-known work is *Season of Migration to the North*, which Edward Said named one of the six best novels in Arabic. The story of Mustafa Sa'eed, a student whose brilliance and thirst for knowledge take him from his Sudanese village to London, only for him to return home, broken by the West that obsessed him, recently became the first Arabic novel to be included in the Penguin Modern Classics series.

Although Salih writes mainly about a particular area of Sudan, he brings to his depiction of its people and their way of life a sophisticated mind that has been honed on his readings of such novelists as Joseph Conrad and Ford Madox Ford and an unusually wide range of classical Arabic poetry and prose. The passage below is from *Season of Migration to the North*, followed by a short scene from his most recent novel, *Bandarshah*, and one of his lesser-known short stories.

FROM *Season of Migration to the North*

"Politics have spoilt you," I said to Mahjoub. "You've come to
think only in terms of power. Let's not talk about ministries and the
government—tell me about him as a man. What sort of a person
was he?"

Astonishment showed on his face. "What do you mean by what
sort of a person?" he said. "He was as I've described him." I could
not find the appropriate words for explaining what I meant to
Mahjoub. "In any case," he said, "what's the reason for your interest in Mustafa Sa'eed? You've already asked me several times about
him." Before I could reply Mahjoub continued, "You know, I don't
understand why he made you the guardian of his children. Of
course, you deserve the honour of the trust and have carried out
your responsibilities in admirable fashion. Yet you knew him less
than any of us. We were here with him in the village while you saw
him only from year to year. I was expecting he'd have made me, or
your grandfather, guardian. Your grandfather was a close friend of
his and he used to enjoy listening to his conversation. He used to
say to me, 'You know, Mahjoub, Hajj Ahmed is a unique person.'
'Hajj Ahmed's an old windbag,' I would reply and he would get really annoyed. 'No, don't say that,' he'd say to me. 'Hajj Ahmed is a
part of history.'"

"In any case," I said to Mahjoub. "I'm only a guardian in name.
The real guardian is you. The two boys are here with you, and I'm
way off in Khartoum."

"They're intelligent and well-mannered boys," said Mahjoub.
"They take after their father. They couldn't be doing better in their
studies."

"What will happen to them," I said, "if this laughable business
of marriage Wad Rayyes has in mind goes through?"

"Take it easy!" said Mahjoub. "Wad Rayyes will certainly become obsessed with some other woman. Let's suppose, at the very

worst, she marries him; I don't think he'll live more than a year or two, and she'll have her share of his many lands and crops."

Then, like a sudden blow that lands right on the top of one's head, Mahjoub's words struck home: "Why don't *you* marry her?" My heart beat so violently within me that I almost lost control. It was some time before I found words and, in a trembling voice, said to Mahjoub: "You're joking of course."

"Seriously," he said, "why don't you marry her? I'm certain she'd accept. You're the guardian of the two boys, and you might as well round things off by becoming a father."

I remembered her perfume of the night before and the thoughts about her that had taken root in my head in the darkness.

"Don't tell me," I heard Mahjoub saying with a laugh, "that you're already a husband and a father. Every day men are taking second wives. You wouldn't be the first or the last."

"You're completely mad," I said to Mahjoub, laughing, having recovered my self-control.

I left him and took myself off, having become certain about a fact which was later on to cost me much peace of mind: that in one form or another I was in love with Hosna Bint Mahmoud, the widow of Mustafa Sa'eed, and that I—like him and Wad Rayyes and millions of others—was not immune from the germ of contagion that oozes from the body of the universe.

After we had had the circumcision celebrations for the two boys I returned to Khartoum. Leaving my wife and daughter in the village, I journeyed by the desert road in one of the Project's lorries. I generally used to travel by steamer to the river port of Karima and from there I would take the train, passing by Abu Hamad and Atbara to Khartoum. But this time I was, for no particular reason, in a hurry, so I chose to go the shortest way. The lorry set off first thing in the morning and proceeded eastwards along the Nile for about two hours, then turned southwards at right angles and struck off into the desert. There is no shelter from the sun which rises up into the sky with unhurried steps, its rays spilling out on the ground as though there existed an old blood feud between it and the people of

the earth. There is no shelter apart from the hot shade inside the
lorry—shade that is not really shade. A monotonous road rises and
falls with nothing to entice the eye: scattered bushes in the desert,
all thorns and leafless, miserable trees that are neither alive nor
dead. The lorry travels for hours without our coming across a single
human being or animal. Then it passes by a herd of camels, likewise
lean and emaciated. There is not a single cloud heralding hope in
this hot sky which is like the lid of Hell-fire. The day here is something without value, a mere torment suffered by living creatures as
they await the night. Night is deliverance. In a state close to fever,
haphazard thoughts flooded through my head: words taken from
sentences, the forms of faces, voices which all sounded as desiccated
as light flurries of wind blowing across fallow fields. Why the hurry?
"Why the hurry?" she had asked me. "Why don't you stay another
week?" she had said. "The black donkey, a Bedouin fellow cheated
your uncle and sold him the black donkey."

"Is that something to get angry about?" said my father. Man's
mind is not kept in a refrigerator. It is this sun which is unbearable.
It melts the brain. It paralyses thought. And Mustafa Sa'eed's face
springs clearly to my mind, just as I saw it the first day, and is then
lost in the roar of the lorry's engine and the sound of the tyres
against the desert stones, and I strive to bring it back and am
unable to.

The day the boys' circumcision was celebrated, Hosna bared her
head and danced as a mother does on the day her sons are circum-
cised. What a woman she is! Why don't *you* marry her? In what
manner used Isabella Seymour to whisper caressingly to him? "Rav-
ish me, you African demon. Burn me in the fire of your temple, you
black god. Let me twist and turn in your wild and impassioned
rites." Right here is the source of the fire; here the temple. Nothing.
The sun, the desert, desiccated plants and emaciated animals. The
frame of the lorry shudders as it descends into a small wadi. We pass
by the bones of a camel that has perished from thirst in this wilderness. Mustafa Sa'eed's face returns to my mind's eye in the form of
his elder son's face—the one who most resembles him.

On the day of the circumcision Mahjoub and I drank more than we should. Owing to the monotony of their lives the people in our village make of every happy event however small an excuse for holding a sort of wedding party. At night I pulled him by the hand, while the singers sang and the men were clapping deep inside the house. We stood in front of the door of that room. I said to him, "I alone have the key." An iron door.

Mahjoub said to me in his inebriated voice: "Do you know what's inside?"

"Yes," I said to him.

"What?" he said.

"Nothing," I said, laughing under the influence of the drink. "Absolutely nothing. This room is a big joke—like life. You imagine it contains a secret and there's nothing there. Absolutely nothing."

"You're drunk," said Mahjoub. "This room is filled from floor to ceiling with treasures: gold, jewels, pearls. Do you know who Mustafa Sa'eed is?"

I told him that Mustafa Sa'eed was a lie. "Do you want to know the truth about Mustafa Sa'eed?" I said to him with another drunken laugh.

"You're not only drunk but mad," said Mahjoub. "Mustafa Sa'eed is in fact the Prophet El-Kidr, suddenly making his appearance and as suddenly vanishing. The treasures that lie in this room are like those of King Solomon, brought here by genies, and you have the key to that treasure. Open, Sesame, and let's distribute the gold and jewels to the people." Mahjoub was about to shout out and gather the people together had I not put my hand over his mouth. The next morning each of us woke up in his own house not knowing how he'd got there.

The road is endless, without limit, the sun indefatigable. No wonder Mustafa Sa'eed fled to the bitter cold of the North. Isabella Seymour said to him: "The Christians say their God was crucified that he might bear the burden of their sins. He died, then, in vain, for what they call sin is nothing but the sigh of contentment in embracing you, O pagan god of mine. You are my god and there is no god but you." No doubt that was the reason for her suicide, and not that she was ill with cancer. She was a believer when she met him. She denied her religion and worshipped a god like the calf of the Children of Israel. How strange! How ironic! Just because a man has been created on the Equator some mad people regard him as a slave, others as a god. Where lies the mean? Where the middle way? And my grandfather, with his thin voice and that mischievous laugh of his when in a good humour, where is *his* place in the scheme of things? Is he really as I assert and as he appears to be? Is he above this chaos? I don't know. In any case he has survived despite epidemics, the corruption of those in power and the cruelty of nature. I am certain that when death appears to him he will smile in death's face. Isn't this enough? Is more than this demanded of a son of Adam?

From behind a hill there came into view a Bedouin, who hurried towards us, crossing the car's path. We drew up. His body and clothes were the colour of the earth. The driver asked him what he wanted.

He said, "Give me a cigarette or some tobacco for the sake of Allah—for two days I haven't tasted tobacco." As we had no tobacco I gave him a cigarette. We thought we might as well stop a while and give ourselves a rest from sitting.

Never in my life have I seen a man smoke a cigarette with such gusto. Squatting down on his backside, the Bedouin began gulping in the smoke with indescribable avidity. After a couple of minutes he put out his hand and I gave him another cigarette, which he devoured as he had done the first. Then he began writhing on the ground as though in an epileptic fit, after which he stretched himself out, encircled his head with his hands, and went stiff and lifeless as though dead. All the time we were there, around twenty minutes, he stayed like this, until the engine started up, when he jumped to his feet—a man brought back to life—and began thanking me and asking Allah to grant me long life, so I threw him the packet with the rest of the cigarettes. Dust rose up behind us, and I watched the Bedouin running towards some tattered tents by some bushes southwards of us, where there were diminutive sheep and naked children. Where, O God, is the shade? Such land brings forth nothing but prophets. This drought can be cured only by the sky.

Translated by Denys Johnson-Davies

FROM Bandarshah

I reckoned that Tureifi must have been thirty-six or thirty-seven, for he was around twelve in the year of the wedding of Zein. At that time Mahjoub was forty-five—I know that for a fact—while Ahmed, who today has become the father of many daughters and whose daughters are of marriageable age, was about twenty in that year. I scrutinized his face as he sat in front of me on the verandah of the diwan, cross-legged, holding a cup of coffee, in the forenoon. There was nothing remarkable about the face apart from the narrow, intelligent eyes and that ironic smile at the left-hand corner of the mouth that speaks of a contradiction between what he says and what he means. There was also something else: that thing that power bestows on those who have it, a mixture of daring and fear, of generosity and greed, of timidity and boldness, of truth and falsehood. It was as though you were confronted by an actor performing a part; you know that what is taking place before you is not real yet you cannot help but give yourself up to the illusion. Tureifi was fully aware of the nature of the role he was performing.

He ended his speech by saying: "The world must go forwards not backwards. There is no doubt that you of all people realize that. Mahjoub had performed his role and that's that. We too will perform ours."

I recollected that Tureifi was not only the son of Mahjoub's sister but was also the husband of his daughter.

He also said: "Mahjoub and his gang imagined they had a divine right to authority. They forgot the village had changed. Many things have happened. Wad Hamid is no longer the Wad Hamid of thirty years ago. New generations have appeared, new demands. In the old days, when the steamer appeared people would gather under the doum tree and look at it as though it were a miracle. Now the situation's changed."

I imagined him as he was when a boy, pouring out water for us in Mahjoub's diwan. He used to perform such traditional tasks carelessly, saying neither "yes" nor "at your service," making you feel that you should be pouring the water yourself. I wondered whether, even at that early age, he knew that the fact that someone was older than someone else means nothing? His teachers at school used to say that he was a sly pupil, at the head of any movement of insubordination or trouble-making and yet escaping punishment: always it was he who committed the offence, while the punishment would be meted out to someone else. It was as though the fates were preparing him for this role. At the time of the wedding of Zein, Mahjoub entrusted him with providing fodder for the guests' donkeys, but he was more inclined towards providing liquor for those who liked to drink. When Mahjoub woke up to the fact that something was amiss, he found the donkeys without fodder and, on searching for Tureifi, discovered him drinking with the revelers. Mahjoub scolded him and slapped him; Tureifi didn't take it silently but shouted back at Mahjoub, saying: "Who do you think you are?" and left the wedding and didn't participate in it. From his early youth he used to do things that weren't done: he would cross his legs in the presence of his elders, would yawn openly when Ali Wad Shayeb told one of his stories, and would elbow himself into the conversations of grown-ups and speak out his mind, always opposing or making fun of the opinions of men old enough to be his father. The consensus of opinion was that he was a good-for-nothing boy, and Mahjoub used to say to his father in company: "May the Lord spare us the mischief of Tureifi your son." Despite this, he always surprised people with his outstanding skill and proficiency in any activity he chose to take up. In the history of Wad Hamid he did several heroic things that had not earned sufficient appreciation from people, because no sooner had he done some laudable action than he would destroy it with an action that was disgraceful in people's eyes, as though doing so on purpose, as though not caring whether people thought he'd acted well or badly.

They were at a loss about him, regarding him with a mixture of admiration and wariness.

"The people," said Tureifi, "want a leader who knows the nature of his role in the village. Mahjoub was making himself into a tribal sheikh—a lot of hullabaloo and nothing to show for it. I know Mahjoub's your close friend, but that's the truth."

I remembered that in the great flood he had rescued Ammouna bint at-Taum from drowning and that he'd stayed up all night swimming between the island and the shore, untying a cow here, setting up a barrier there, or lifting up something that had fallen down, and stretching out a helping hand to someone seeking aid. In the morning, when the people were collectively combating the flood, he was asleep at home. Reckoning up who'd been there and who hadn't, they said: "Tureifi, the son of Bakri, may God frustrate him—on such a day everybody's busy and he's asleep on his back at home."

Ammouna bint at-Taum told them otherwise, but they refused to believe her. When there was a gathering of people, Sa'eed Asha 'l-Baytat would say: "I swear to you, Tureifi, the son of Bakri, is a fine man, but you're blind to it."

Ali Wad Shayeb would laugh with the rest of the scoffers, saying: "Asha 'l-Baytat's making himself into a propaganda broadcasting station for the son of Bakri. It's a case of the blind and the halt."

Despite this, they gathered one forenoon under the big sayyal tree in the centre of the village and elected him as their leader.

He continued his speech with, "The question of kinship and friendship has nothing to do with it. The question's one of principles."

"What's your principle?" I said to him.

He said pompously, as it appeared to me at the time, though I may have been mistaken, "My principle is to extricate this village from the pit of backwardness and underdevelopment. We must keep up with progress. The age is one of science and technology."

Then he looked at me challengingly and asked of me, "And what's your position in what's happening?"

I laughed and my laughter annoyed him, and with, as it seemed to me, great pomposity, he said, "It's a serious matter, not a joke. What's your position?"

It would have been easy in those particular circumstances to have made fun of him, but I resisted and kept quiet. Perhaps he did not realize why I had a soft spot for him, for he was Maryam's son and it was possible that he could have been my son had it not been for the fact that my grandfather had said no. She had supported her brother against him and had left her husband's house and stayed with Mahjoub, though Tureifi was her firstborn son and she loved him very much and was proud of him. After that she never saw him again. Then she died in the month of Amsheer and we had buried her just before sunset. It was a painful occasion. Tureifi was crying as I had never seen a human being cry and we had forcibly taken hold of him—Wad Rawwasi, Abdul Hafeez and I—to stop him entering the grave with her. Poor boy, he too suffered. Man, however ambitious he may be, is still the son of a woman. Perhaps he saw the reflections of those thoughts on my face, for he suddenly sat up straight and put out the cigarette he had in his hand. He stirred restlessly in his chair. He gave a muffled sigh and, lowering his head, examined the ground. Treating him gently, because of all I remembered, I asked him, "Do you remember that dawn in Amsheer?"

"What dawn?" he said, raising his head in alarm.

"That memorable dawn," I said to him, "when the mosque, contrary to custom, was filled with worshippers—in Amsheer after we had buried your mother Maryam at night."

He lowered his head, looking down at the ground, and didn't answer.

"We carried you unconscious from the graveyard after the burial. Do you remember?"

"I don't remember," he said sharply.

"You fainted at the graveside and woke to the weeping of the worshippers in the mosque at dawn. Between sleeping and wakefulness you had a dream. Do you remember?"

"I don't remember," he said violently.

"You heard a voice," I said to him.

"I heard no voice," he said.

"Someone called out to you."

"No one called out to me," he said with irritation.

"Do you remember what happened that dawn?" I said to him. "Do you remember the weeping of the worshippers? Do you remember that you wept till you almost passed out?"

Raising his head, he gathered his wits about him with an obvious effort, for he was shaken, and said in a trembling voice, "I don't remember."

Perhaps I was hard on him, but one of the reasons for my return was to learn the truth of the matter before it was too late, for I too had crossed that bridge and had buried well-loved things, and I had seen things sprout up in the same way as the graves will split open on the Day of Resurrection, and we must come to comprehend the connection between the two halves of the millstone. I said to him— and maybe I was being cruel—albeit unintentionally in those circumstances.

"I shall tell you what happened. A messenger came to you. You rose in a dazed state and walked behind him in the darkness and saw in front of you a fortress, and it was as if the darkness had been cleft open to reveal it. Its lights came and went. You followed the messenger and found yourself where there was noise and the sound of singing and dancing. There was a celebration being held in the midst of that darkness. Doors were opened and you walked through corridor after corridor till you arrived at a spacious hall with lamps and lanterns. In the middle of the place was one in the guise of two. The one welcomed you with smiles, and the two greeted you warmly. And the voice said to you: 'Welcome to Tureifi, the son of Bakri. Welcome to the new leader of Wad Hamid.' He seated you either on the right or the left and they brought you drink. You awoke and heard Asha l'-Baytat giving the call to the dawn prayer in a voice that stirred you and revived your longings and sorrows. You walked between the darkness and the light, not knowing in what time you were, yesterday, today or tomorrow, nor in what place, here or there. You met a great concourse of people who had gathered without reason or prior arrangement, as though they were expecting you. You remembered the people meeting at the grave just before sunset and the people under the large sayyal tree in the centre of the village at forenoon and you remembered a first forenoon, before you were born, or your father, or your grandfather were born by many, many generations. People were rushing about hither and thither, searching for something and for nothing, and you and Bandarshah were holding the threads of chaos, in the middle of it and above it. It was a feast. You wept with the people and the people wept with you. And the stranger by the window was appearing and disappearing. I asked, 'Did you see the person who was there?' Some people said yes and you said no. Do you remember?"

We were silent for a long time and the surface of his face was like a sky whose clouds gather and disperse, then form anew. And I thought I would rescue him from drowning because he was Maryam's son, so I laughed and he too laughed as I had expected in such circumstances.

"And now I'll answer your question," I said to him. "My position is, as you can see, a complicated one."

He had all but regained his composure. He looked at his watch and stood up to leave. I was struck by the similarity between him and Mahjoub: the way of standing and of sitting, the laughter, the expression in the eyes, the gestures. He had nothing of his mother. He had come to persuade me to join his camp. He had not succeeded but perhaps, like me, he had comprehended something.

As he walked towards the door, he said, "I too will answer you. That dawn I saw a vision and I heard a voice, but it was not as you have described it."

Translated by Denys Johnson-Davies

The Cypriot Man

Nicosia in July was as though Khartoum had been transplanted to Damascus. The streets, as laid out by the British, were broad, the desert was that of Khartoum, but there was that struggle between the east and west winds that I remember in Damascus.

It was British from head to toe, despite all that blood that had been spilt. I was surprised for I had expected a town of Greek character. The man, though, did not give me time to pursue my thought to its conclusion but came and sat himself beside me at the edge of the swimming-pool. He made a slight gesture with his head and they brought him a cup of coffee.

"Tourist?" he said.

"Yes."

He made a noise the import of which I did not follow—it was as though he were saying that the likes of me didn't deserve to be a tourist in Nicosia, or that Nicosia didn't deserve to have the likes of me being a tourist in it.

I turned my attention from him so as to examine a woman with a face like that of one of Raphael's angels, and a body like that of Gauguin's women. Was she the wife or the other woman? Again he cut through the thread of my thoughts:

"Where are you from?"

"The Sudan."

"What do you do?"

"I'm in government service."

I laughed for in fact I didn't work for the government; anyway governments have broad shoulders.

"I don't work," he said. "I own a factory."

"Really?"

"For making women's clothes."

"How lovely."

"I've made a lot of money. I worked like a black. I made a fortune. I don't work any longer—spend all my time in bed."

"Sleeping?"

"You must be joking. What does a man do in bed?"

"Don't you get tired?"

"You're joking. Look at me—what age do you think I am?"

Sometimes fifty, sometimes seventy, but I didn't want to encourage him.

"Seventy," I said to him.

This did not upset him as I had presumed. He gave a resounding laugh and said:

"Seventy-five in actual fact, but no one takes me for more than fifty. Go on, be truthful."

"All right, fifty."

"Why do you think it is?"

"Because you take exercise."

"Yes, in bed, I bash away—white and black, red and yellow: all colours, Europeans, negresses, Indians, Arabs, Jewesses; Muslims, Christians, Buddhists: all religions."

"You're a liberal-minded man."

"Yes, in bed."

"And outside."

"I hate Jews."

"Why do you hate Jews?"

"Just so. Also they play with skill."

"What?"

"The game of death. They've been at it for centuries."

"Why does that make you angry?"

"Because I . . . because I . . . it's of no consequence."

"Are they not defeated?"

"They all give up in the end."

"And their women?"

"There's no one better than them in bed. The greater your hatred for them, the greater your enjoyment with their women. They are my chosen people."

"And the negroes of America?"

"My relationship with them has not reached the stage of hatred. I must pay them more attention."

"And the Arabs?"

"They provoke laughter or pity. They give up easily, these days anyway. Playing with them is not enjoyable because it's one-sided."

I thought: if only they had accepted Cyprus, if only Balfour had promised them it.

The Cypriot man gave his resounding laugh and said:

"Women prolong one's life. A man must appear to be at least twenty years younger than he is. That's what being smart is."

"Do you fool death?"

"What is death? Someone you meet by chance, who sits with you as we are sitting now, who talks freely with you, perhaps about the weather or women or shares on the stock market. Then he politely sees you to the door. He opens the door and signs for you to go out. After that you don't know."

A grey cloud stayed overhead for a while, but at that moment I did not know that the divining arrows had been cast and that the Cypriot man was playing a hazardous game with me.

The wave of laughter broadened out and enfolded me. They were a sweet family which I had come to like since sitting down: the father with his good-natured face and the mother with her English voice which was like an Elizabethan air played on the strings of an ancient lyre, and four daughters, the eldest of whom was not more than twelve, who would go in and out of the pool, laughing and teasing their parents. They would smile at me and broaden the compass of their happiness till it included me. There came a moment when I saw on the father's face that he was about to invite me to join them; it was at that moment that the Cypriot man descended upon me. The eldest girl got up and stepped gracefully towards the pool. With the girl having suddenly come to a stop as though some mysterious power had halted her, the Cypriot man said:

"This one I'd pay a hundred pounds sterling for."

"What for?" I said to him in alarm.

The Cypriot man made an obscene gesture with his arm.

At that moment the girl fell facedown on to the stone and blood poured from her forehead. The good-natured family started up, like frightened birds, and surrounded the girl. I immediately got up from beside the man, feeling for him an overwhelming hatred, and seated myself at a table far away from him. I remembered my own daughters and their mother in Beirut and was angry. I saw the members of the delightful family making their departures, sadly, the daughters clinging to their mother, the mother reproaching the father, and I became more angry. Then I quietened down and the things around me quietened down. The clamour died away and there came to me my friend Taher Wad Rawwasi and sat beside me: on the bench in front of Sa'eed's shop. His face was beaming, full of health and energy.

"Really," I said to him, "why is it that you haven't grown old and weak though you're older than all of them?"

"From when I first became aware of the world," he said, "I've been on the move. I don't remember ever not moving. I work like a horse and if there's no work to be done I create something to busy myself with. I go to sleep at any old time, early or late, and wake up directly the *muezzin* says 'God is great, God is great' for the dawn prayer."

"But you don't pray?"

"I say the *shahada*[1] and ask God's forgiveness after the *muezzin* has finished giving the call to prayers, and my heart finds assurance that the world is going along as it always has. I take a nap for half an hour or so. The odd thing is that a nap after the call to prayers is for me equal to the whole night's sleep. After that I wake up as though I've been woken by an alarm clock. I make the tea and wake Fatima up. She performs the dawn prayer. We drink tea. I go down to meet the sun on the Nile's surface and say to God's morning

---

[1] The doctrinal formula of Islam: "There is no god but God and Muhammad is the messenger of God."

Hello and Welcome. However long I'm away I come back to find the breakfast ready. We sit down to it, Fatima and I and any of God's servants that destiny brings to us. For more than fifty years it's been like this."

One day I'll ask Taher Wad Rawwasi about the story of his marriage to Fatima bint Jabr ad-Dar, one of Mahjoub's four sisters. His loyalty was not to himself but to Mahjoub, and he used to make fun both of himself and of the world. Would he become a hero? It was clear that if it really came to it he would sacrifice himself for Mahjoub. Should I ask him now? However, off his own bat, he uttered a short phrase compounded of the fabric of his whole life:

"Fatima bint Jabr ad-Dar—what a girl!"

"And Mahjoub?"

Taher Wad Rawwasi gave a laugh that had the flavour of those bygone days; it indicated the extent of his love for Mahjoub. Even mentioning his name would fill him with happiness, as though the presence of Mahjoub on the face of the earth made it less hostile, better, in Taher Wad Rawwasi's view. He laughed and said, laughing:

"Mahjoub's something else; Mahjoub's made of a different clay."

Then he fell silent and it was clear to me that he didn't, at that time, wish to say any more on that particular subject. After a time I asked him:

"Abdul Hafeez said you'd never in your whole life entered a mosque. Is that so?"

"Just once I entered a mosque."

"Why? What for?"

"Only the once. It was one winter, in Touba or Amsheer, God knows best."

"It was in Amsheer," I said to him, "after you'd buried Maryam at night."

"That's right. How did you know?"

"I was there with you."

"Where? I didn't see you that morning, though the whole village had collected on that day in the mosque."

"I was by the window, appearing and disappearing till you said
'And not those who are astray. Amen.' "[2]

"And then?"

"God be praised. Poor Meheimeed was calling out 'Where's the
man who was here gone to?' "

"And then?"

Suddenly the dream bird flew away. Wad Rawwasi disappeared,
as did Wad Hamid[3] with all its probability. Where he had been sitting I saw the Cypriot man, I heard his voice and my heart contracted. I heard his shouting and the hubbub, the slapping of the
water against the sides of the swimming-pool, with specters shaped
in the form of naked women and naked men and children leaping
about and shrieking. The voice was saying:

"For this one I'd only pay fifty pounds sterling."

I pressed down on my eyes so as to be more awake. I looked at
the goods on offer in the market. It was that woman. She was drinking orange juice at the moment at which the Cypriot man had said
what he did. She spluttered and choked; a man leapt to his feet to
help her, then a woman; servants and waiters came along, people
gathered, and they carried her off unconscious. It was as if a magi-
cian had waved his wand and, so it seemed to me, the people instantly vanished; and the darkness too, as though close at hand,
awaiting a signal from someone, came down all at once. The
Cypriot man and I on our own with the light playing around on
the surface of the water. Between the light and the darkness he said
to me:

"Two American girls arrived this morning from New York.
They're very beautiful, very rich. One's eighteen and she's mine, the
other's twenty-five and she's for you. They're sisters; they own a villa
in Kyrenia. I've got a car. The adventure won't cost you a thing.
Come along. They'll be really taken by your colour."

The darkness and the light were wrestling around the swimming-

---

[2] The final words of the *Fatiha*, the equivalent in Islam of the Lord's Prayer.
[3] The village in which most of the writer's novels and short stories are set.

pool, while it was as if the voice of the Cypriot man were supplying the armies of darkness with weapons. Thus I wanted to say to him all right, but another sound issued from my throat involuntarily, and I said to him, as I followed the war taking place on the water's surface:

"No, thank you. I didn't come to Nicosia in search of that. I came to have a quiet talk with my friend Taher Wad Rawwasi because he refused to visit me in London and I failed to meet him in Beirut."

Then I turned to him—and what a ghastly sight met my eyes. Was I imagining things, or dreaming, or mad? I ran, ran to take refuge with the crowd in the hotel bar. I asked for something to drink; I drank it, without recollecting the taste of it or what it was. I calmed down a little. But the Cypriot man came and sat down with me. He had bounded along on crutches. He asked for whisky, a double. He said that he had lost his right leg in the war. What war? One of the wars, what did it matter which one? His wooden leg had been smashed this morning. He had climbed up a mountain. He was waiting for a new leg from London. Sometimes his voice was English, sometimes it had a German accent; at others it seemed French to me; he used American words.

"Are you . . ."

"No, I'm not. Some people think I'm Italian, some that I'm Russian; others German . . . Spanish. Once an American tourist asked me whether I was from Basutoland. Just imagine. What's it matter where I'm from? And Your Excellency?"

"Why do you say to me Your Excellency?"

"Because you're a very fine person."

"And what's my importance?"

"You exist today and you won't exist tomorrow—and you won't recur."

"That happens to every person—what's important about that?"

"Not every person is aware of it. You, Excellency, are aware of your position in time and place."

"I don't believe so."

He put down his drink in one gulp and stood up, on two sound legs, unless I was imagining things, or was dreaming or mad, and it was as though he were the Cypriot man. He bowed with very affected politeness, and it was as though his face as I had seen it at the edge of the pool made you sense that life had no value.

"I won't say goodbye," he said, "but *au revoir*, Excellency."

It was ten o'clock when I went to bed. I did everything possible to bring sleep about, being tired and having swum all day. I tried talking to Taher Wad Rawwasi. I asked him about the story of his marriage to Fatima bint Jabr ad-Dar. I asked him about his attendance at dawn prayers on that memorable day. I asked him about that singing which was linking the two banks with silken threads, while poor Meheimeed was floundering about in the waves in pursuit of Maryam's phantom, but he did not reply. Music was of no help to me, neither was reading. I could have gone out, gone to a night club or for a walk, or I could have sat in the hotel bar. There was nothing I could do. Then the pain began: a slight numbness at the tips of the toes which gradually began to advance upwards until it was as though terrible claws were tearing at my stomach, chest, back and head: the fires of hell had all at once broken out.

I would lose consciousness then enter into a terrible vortex of pains and fires; the frightful face would show itself to me between unconsciousness and a state of semi-wakefulness, leaping from chair to chair, disappearing and reappearing all over the room. Voices I did not understand came to me from the unknown, faces I did not know, dark and scowling. There was nothing I could do. Though in some manner in a state of consciousness, I was incapable of lifting up the receiver and calling a doctor, or going down to reception in the hotel, or crying out for help. There was a savage and silent war taking place between me and unknown fates. I certainly gained some sort of a victory, for I came to to the sound of four o'clock in the morning striking, with the hotel and the town silent. The pains had gone except for a sensation of exhaustion and overwhelming despair, as though the world, the good and the evil of it, were not worth a gnat's wing. After that I slept. At nine o'clock in the morning the plane taking me to Beirut circled above Nicosia; it looked to me like an ancient cemetery.

On the evening of the following day in Beirut the doorbell rang. It was a woman clad in black carrying a child. She was crying and the first sentence she said was:

"I'm Palestinian—my daughter has died."

I stood for a while looking at her, not knowing what to say; however, she entered, sat down and said:

"Will you let me rest and feed my child?"

While she was telling me her story the doorbell rang. I took a telegram and opened it, with the Palestinian woman telling me her formidable misfortune, while I was engrossed in my own.

I crossed seas and desert, wanting to know before all else when and how he had died. They informed me that he had as usual worked in the garden in his field in the morning and had done those things he usually did during his day. He had not complained of anything. He had entered his relations' homes, sat with his friends here and there; he'd brought some half-ripe dates and drunk coffee with them. My name had cropped up in his conversation several times. He had been awaiting my arrival impatiently, for I had written to him that I was coming. He supped lightly as usual, performed the evening prayer, then about ten o'clock the harbingers of death had come to him; before the dawn prayer he had departed this world, and when the aeroplane was bearing me from Nicosia to Beirut they had just finished burying him.

At forenoon I stood by his grave, with the Cypriot man sitting at the side of the grave, in his formal guise, listening to me as I gave prayers and supplications. He said to me in a voice that seemed to issue from the earth and the sky, encompassing me from all sides:

"You won't see me again in this guise other than at the last moment when I shall open the door to you, bow quietly and say to you 'After you, Your Excellency.' You will see me in other and various guises. You may encounter me in the form of a beautiful girl, who will come to you and tell you she admires your views and opinions and that she'd like to do an interview with you for some paper or magazine; or in the shape of a president or a ruler who offers you some post that makes your heart lose a beat; or in the form of one of life's pranks that gives you a lot of money without your expending any effort; perhaps in the form of a vast multitude that applauds you for some reason you don't know; or perhaps you'll see me in the form of a girl twenty years younger than you, whom you desire and who'll say to you: 'Let's go to an isolated hut way up in the mountains.' Beware. Your father will not be there on the next occasion to give his life for you. Beware. The term of life is designated, but we take into consideration the skill shown in playing the game. Beware for you are now ascending towards the mountain peak."

Translated by Denys Johnson-Davies

Ghada Samman
(b. 1942)
SYRIA

Ghada Samman was born in Syria. She has a degree in English literature and has published several novels and collections of stories. Some of her novels, including her most recent, *The Night of the First Billion*, have been published in English translation. Samman lives and works in Beirut.

A Gypsy without a Haven

Your face speaks to me of vagrancy once again. It brings with it the tang of rainfall on beaches, tender with its sadness and warmth.

Your face. Anguish in the green of your eyes, the lusts of Rome behind your stern features. How long will the beloved curse follow me? When will you no longer appear in the gloom of my room when I put out the light to go to sleep? For it is then that your strange laugh, which smells of your cigarette smoke, comes to me and then I long to dissolve in its scent, disintegrate like a cloud that nobody regrets.

Midnight. The comic programme on TV has just finished, and the innocent, unforced laughter of my grandfather and young brothers and sisters has come to an end. I gaze at him, laughing among the children, the expression on his face as naïve as theirs in spite of the traces left by the slow, forceful gliding of the vipers of Time. I am deeply fond of him: I long to bring back to his lips the smile that was buried with the body of his only daughter, my mother.

He, too, watches me, with contentment in his eyes as I sit there beside my fiancé, Kamal; his glance steals to my hand lying lifeless in that of Kamal. Lying there only so as to bring a smile to that dear face at any cost.

My weary, broken-down grandfather never once complained of me and my brothers and sisters. Not once did he show any sign of irritation from the day my father left to go to a distant country with a woman who was said to be very beautiful; he left my sick mother behind to die soon after.

In spite of his annoyance at my passion for singing, my grandfather never once tried to stand in my way, though he could not conceal his pleasure the day Kamal, a well-to-do engineer, offered me his heart and fortune. Will I have the strength to go through with it? Wearing, for his sake, the mask of an innocent girl? Will I have the strength to go on for the sake of my grandfather's smile?

Your face is a dearly-loved tale of vagrancy; it lures me towards itself, it draws the lost gypsy within me. In your laughter I hear the ring of golden anchor-chains when a vessel strikes landfall. Your arms are my haven, and how can I escape? Night imposes its routine. My grandfather and my brothers and sisters have retired to their rooms; my fiancé has left and every one of my masks has fallen away. I lie in bed and suffer my nightly agony.

I plunge my face under the pillow in search of sleep, for it might be lurking there, but I only find your face—so near . . . yet so far.

I open my eyes and contemplate the curtains. Sleep might be hiding there. My mind searches behind them . . . behind the picture . . . behind the dressing-table, with my eyelashes. I shut out the faint beam of light that steals in through the small window and casts a shadow of bitter reproach over everything—over the image of your face which I see in all things.

It is a procession of faces that I watch in my room—images merging one with the other in my head, thrown up into it by my sleeplessness a score of incidents, a score of scenes your face, adored in spite of everything that has happened . . . yes, in spite of everything; I feel you waking up within my veins as you wake up every night to become one with me, your smile on my lips and the smoke from your cigarette coming out of my mouth.

Those faces, angry vindictive faces, and faces that scream at me, others that have not yet learned how to scream. I curse the hallucinations of insomnia. I curse the city of fears it awakens in my head, this weary life of mine torn into shreds of memories, broken up into scattered whirlpools.

There's nothing left for me but to remember . . . relive.

The sea lay indolent, glistening, naked and bored, heavy with the rays of the sun on her. You were so considerate, so charming that I quite forgot it was our very first meeting: you, the great composer who could make the city laugh and weep, and I, the young girl who longed to be asked to sing one of your songs.

"This is how I love the sea," I said. "Solid and naked, lazy and bored, and not shrouded in the masked veiling of moonlight. Groaning under the weight of the sun on her bosom, the sun that she loves so much."

"Yes, the sea loves the sun when the sun is far away. Have you noticed the sea by night? She has the face of a person in love, all shadows and fears and sighs."

"And when he is near?"

"She loves him all the more, knowing that he will soon leave. That's what true love is: it's longing, it's the search for security; it's the way to an end, not the end in itself. It reaches its climax the instant before the moment of meeting, then, after a few seconds, it is over."

"What a tragedy. To spend one's life reaching out for a cup that will be the death of us if we don't drink from it. And yet once we take it, and sip from it, we die even so. First it's love and longing that kills us, then it's the lack of love. It kills us simply to know ourselves."

"But you're still so young. Do you really believe what you're saying?"

"I'm afraid so."

"Sing me something! Anything!"

And I sang. I sang of the virgin depths that no man has ever penetrated. I sang of the loneliness that no person has ever escaped.

Every one of us lives isolated in a glass case . . . each of us talks but not one of us listens. Our life is spent wandering in woods, on seashores, in and out of islands, without haven or retreat. Even when we sight a harbour in the distance, we realize it is not for us.

"There's a strange agony in your voice; there's a bitterness that is deeply stirring. You'll go far. I can understand you so well."

Happy. Happy with our tale of vagrancy. Why do the faces attack me so? Wretched sleeplessness, peeling away from my eyelids the shreds of the happiness we knew. Faces springing out of my weakness and my cowardice, faces that I love and hate. I know what you are. You're part of me. Just as his face is part of me. And like some fabulous beast with two heads, each facing a different way, I'm torn apart. If only sleep could quieten the whirling city within my head. If I could only forget.

Once, when the night was a shimmering fairy tale flowing from your eyes and jetting itself into the sea in front of us, you stretched out your hand, and your palm held a thousand tales of loss. I didn't hesitate. My hand clutched all those tales of deprivation and for the first time I knew the joy of the clouds that moan out thunder when the ecstasy of their meeting rends them. Lightning sprang from our eyes and I felt the fire moving from my hand to my throat. I found it difficult to breathe. But I would not have needed to do any breathing to stay alive, if only we could have stayed like that. I made as if I wanted to pull my hand out of yours, only so that your grip would hold it tighter, so tight that my fingers would knead themselves together and become one single new finger that could join itself to your hand for ever. The delicious battle continued for a few moments, and like a fish that is delighted at being caught, my hand finally relaxed in yours, and you were gentle with it: you took it tenderly by the fingers and brought it close to the red candle on the table we were sitting at, whose soft light crept up the side of your face. I felt its kindness like a book filled with warm words, rich with the glow of harbours basking in the exciting magic of oriental evenings, and I, a tramp in search of a warm harbour.

You pretended to read my palm. You held my hand in yours and your look sank deep into the wilderness of my eyes. You tried to read the unending misery that you saw in them, to smell the tang of the sad rains that pursued the vagrant tramp and to hear the creak of rusty doors that had remained closed too long and round which thorns and creepers had grown, making the place desolate and unattractive.

"I see a bored gypsy," you said.

"Who loves her boredom."

"Who has no home . . ."

"And who does not wish to have a home because she hates masks. The city is a mask on the face of the wild forest. She is still the daughter of the wilderness."

"There are two men fighting for her. One wants to give her a home."

"And her mask loves the home; and she wears her mask to bring a smile to the faces of those she loves and feels obliged to."

"As for the other man, he has nothing but a new tale of vagrancy to give."

"That is what she wants. Because a home is a transitory thing, while exile and sorrow are the real truth of human existence."

"She is like a child, searching for fame with her sweet singing voice, but no one knows the deep sorrows she has to bear; she goes on living a life of indifference, of vagrancy, of longing for a tenderness she knows she will never find."

"That is why she loves the man who resembles her, who carries in his face a tale of indifference and vagrancy and tenderness. In loving him, she is idolizing her own self."

"It's an admission of her own artistic narcissism."

"What else do you see in my eyes—my palm, I mean?"

"I see a tramp who loves her quest for a haven more than she loves the haven itself. She will hate it if she finds it—if she has to drop anchor among its rocks."

"I'm sorry for this tramp who drags her anchor and her sorrow along, lost and at sea."

"No you're not: you envy her. Because to you she represents the truth of life: she is a naked totem of human reality. You would be miserable if you let her go."

"What else do you see in my eyes?—I mean, my palm?"

Maybe you saw the truth, for you kept silent.

But why do I go on brooding over everything? This sleeplessness opens up old wounds and with its sorcery raises from their graves old tales, revived with the warm blood gushing from their wounds. What a wasted life! How can I forget?

Your face was aglow with hope when you said to me, "Let's go away together—anywhere."

A splendid plan. Not to have to suffer agonies of jealousy every time I think of your wife lying next to you all through the night and robbing my bosom of your breath, sucking it in from the pillow you share. Always together, tramping about together; your breath would belong to me only and your arms would be a haven for me alone. I saw you out walking one evening, you and your wife and children. I watched you from a distance. I walked behind you like a wolf that had made up its mind to snatch the shepherd away from the fold. Quite simply I longed to tear your wife to pieces—to devour her. I did not hide myself from my own eyes behind a mask of false pity and tenderness. I hated her. Then one of your daughters tripped and fell. I heard her crying, as you bent down to pick her up—so tenderly . . . and then it was I who wept . . . cried in the street . . . cried because of the many times I had fallen down and found no one to lift me up, no father to take hold of me, for he had run away with a woman as lost as I am.

That evening, Kamal offered me his life. I would not have to rob someone else in order to have him. That evening I accepted him, not because of your wife, but because of the little girl that I had once been. I consented so that your daughter would not grow up like me and become a tramp without a haven.

But I cannot believe myself—how can I leave you and go away? What about our happy moments spent together, and the people I used to sing to with your voice in my throat, with your melodies in my heart . . . the courage you gave me to face them . . . the sweet taste of conquest, the great success I had when I was able to make strangers respond to the feelings in my breast. I was able, then, to create for myself a huge unknown family with whom I could share my loneliness, my sense of being lost . . . And you, and the little trifles we shared . . . and our laughter. . . .

Once when I was sitting beside you in your car which was littered, as always, with the things you kept strewn there, I looked at the streets, the passers-by and the gay shops, and suddenly cried out, "How marvelous!"

"What?" you asked. "Is it some attractive young man?"

"If it were an attractive young man, I would have stifled the sound in my throat."

"A pretty girl, then?"

"If it were, I would have kept quiet and stolen a glance at your face to see if you too were looking at her."

You burst out laughing. You are mine alright. You will look at all faces and still only see me. You will hug dozens of bodies to you, but it will be my hand only that you will feel in yours. You are mine . . . You were mine. Why do I torture myself so?

What then, you sleepless night that is tearing me to pieces? This bed feels heavy to me, as though I were carrying it on my back. I must escape from this bedroom.

I get up . . . wander through the rooms of the dark house like a murdered ghost that had not been avenged . . . and the shabby ribbons of my life trail behind me on the floor.

I was sitting in a café with a few friends. The discussion grew heated, one of them addressed the visor-face of the stern-looking girl.

"Tell us," he said. "What shall we do? How shall we distribute the leaflets?"

Full of enthusiasm, the silly fool planned and acted . . . like an automaton that is under some ideological hypnosis . . . a city girl with many parts to play and many masks to slip over her face.

But this is my true face, the face of the gypsy who makes fun of other people's idealism. The noise of argument sounds like the buzzing of a gnat in the ears of eternity. Nothing can move the street-woman from her dark, deserted beat as her footsteps stumble along over the rough pavements.

She loves goodness and truth and freedom and the principles that all parties call for; but she does not feel responsible for anything or anyone in this wide world. No one is really interested in anyone else; we are individual grapes that have dropped off an unseen bunch and no legislation or belief or order can put us together again. Why do I contradict myself? How can I explain this overwhelming desire to bring a smile to the lips of my grandfather?

Why is it I care about your daughter and do not wish her to become like me if you were ever to leave her—a gypsy without a haven . . . ? Why do I pretend that no ties bind me to anyone?

But this is no pretence—I really do live the life of a comet that loves its loneliness. Maybe it is only my mask that clings to them, the mask of a well-brought-up girl which has now moulded itself to my face. Who knows what I would find underneath, if I were to pull it off? Has the gypsy's face decayed with time? If I were to fling off my mask would I find I had any face at all?

The image frightens me and I escape from it onto the balcony, with the bubble of feverish faces still pursuing me.

Yesterday morning, the rain washed the windows of Kamal's car as it carried me to view the new house he has prepared for us . . . the rain wept and wept and the streets and the faces appeared through it, strange and far away like the tearful memory of a tale of cherished vagrancy.

"You've made me so happy," whispered Kamal. "I just can't believe that you'll really be mine in a few days."

I did not tell him that I too could not believe it. I felt like a puppet bound with invisible cords to the finger of a madman who delights in moving us whichever way we do not want to go, thrusting us in directions we do not wish to take, snatching from us all the things we love.

Your face dissolved in the rain . . . your face and our tales, your melodies and the gypsy who missed her haven when she lost her face . . . and who lost her face when she realized that the haven was not for her.

"From now on you will sing for me alone," Kamal whispered.

The mask laughed with the joy of a young bride on the threshold of a new life. Your face dissolved in the rain. The day after tomorrow I shall go away with him. When will this night be over? Tired and alone I am, as the gods and the demons are. I go back to my room.

I dress, not knowing what I am doing. I go to the street door . . . I open it to go out . . . where to?

I go back to my room . . . exhausted, I fling myself on the bed. The world of insomnia crumbles over my head . . . the faces leap around, turn, howl, laugh, scream, closer and closer. I fall into a bottomless pit. I give myself up to this indescribable torture—not a pain in one part of the body only, not one that is caused by any one particular idea, but an all-consuming pain, which is tearing at my whole being.

I give way.

With difficulty I open my eyes. The grey dawn comes in at the window. Out of my coma I rise, my pain purified like a rock washed clean by the wind and the rain.

I must go out for a walk, alone; this newly-acquired peace needs to be strengthened. I have to resign myself to the fate I had no hand in preparing.

I softly open the street door; my grandfather and brothers and sisters are still fast asleep.

Alone in the street—in the long sad road, where the darkness creeps into corners while the metallic dawn spreads itself over the pavements and shines down off the windows that stand here and there above me, dispersed and staring.

No one is awake: the city is still deep in slumber, enjoying its limited span of death.

And I, a lost tramp in a brazen city of legends, weep for a lost haven . . . weep for roads I am forced to tread and strangers with whom I have to keep company on the journey through life . . .

pretending I am happy and making believe I enjoy being with them.

I see a man in the distance. He is walking slowly at the end of the road. He comes towards me. Nearer. With a stick he taps the ground. My companion in the deserted street . . . my companion in the brazen city, the companion of my wanderings at dawn . . . in a dawn that will not brighten. He comes nearer. Lost, he wanders towards me, he does not see me . . . He is blind. My companion is a blind man, who taps the ground with his stick, walking along unseen ways. Dawn and dusk are all one to him. I feel a strong link between him and me . . . I walk beside him . . . He does not hear my footsteps. . . .

I walk beside him and feel my way along with my glances as he feels his with his stick. He walks and talks to himself—it does not matter what he is saying. I also mutter and talk to myself. We walk on and on and at a distance we look like two friends.

A fearful satisfaction fills me. Together we represent the closest of human ties. No pretences, no forced conversation. . . .

Beside the blind man I walk, each one of us talking to himself. The sun rises, people pour out onto the street, a stream of bubbles which are faces fizzing up all around me. I lose my blind man in a side-street.

Translated by Azza Kararah

Ibrahim Samouiel
(b. 1951)

SYRIA

Ibrahim Samouiel was born in Damascus. He has a degree in philosophy and psychology and has worked as a social worker with disabled people and young delinquents. Samouiel is primarily a writer of short stories, of which he has published several volumes. A collection of his stories has appeared in Italian, and individual stories have been translated into English, French, and Chinese.

My Fellow Passenger

Both the gesticulations he made and the reptilian hissing sound that came out of his mouth made me think that the person beside me in the bus was out of his mind. His face, when I snatched a hasty glance at it, was expressionless, as though concealing within it a land mine set to explode in accordance with the number of my seat. I tried to distance myself by looking out of the window at the road whizzing by on the other side of the bus.

"Man, it's enough to make you go crazy!"

I was taken unawares by the quavering voice, not realizing that it was addressing me. It was the voice of the man sitting by me, next to the window. I affected a smile as I looked at him but he merely continued to direct his words at me with intoxicated eyes.

"I swear to you, by God, my mind simply flipped. For ten years we were like lovebirds. Not for a day did I spare any pains or say 'No'—the Devil take it!"

He accentuated what he was saying by slapping his thigh. He then drew his hand along the extent of his leg and back as he leaned forward then sat bolt upright.

In order to check the flow of words I said, "It turned out all right, God willing? It seems . . ."

He turned his face toward the window so that his voice was reflected back to me, muffled by the glass. "Yes, we've come to accept that life's become costly. As you yourself say, my dear woman, one just can't believe the cost of things. Fine, what I mean, Fadwa, is that . . ." He turned toward me and the troubled look on his face scared me. "What I mean, man, is if life's all that expensive—the Devil take it! It's a disaster! By God, don't you think it's a disaster?"

I nodded my head, having it in mind to jump in and say something, but he rushed on. "As if we didn't have enough to cope with! Isn't it enough that we're leading this lousy life? The first birth, then the second, and the third time she had twins—four children need-ing a sackful of money spent on them. What with their mother and me, it makes six of us. Then there's the rent for the house. You wouldn't be far wrong if you called it a chicken coop. No, sir. Reckon it at twelve hundred liras from the company and eight hun-dred for working after office hours at Abu Majid's shop. What shall I do? Cut myself into little pieces?"

Seizing the chance to answer him, I said, "Sir, that's how things are, but . . ."

He didn't make room for me to continue, most likely didn't even hear me.

"So the house is leaking—shall we put patches on it? The kids are naked and no better off than their father. We're in need of a thousand and one things. That's a fact. But, as the proverb has it, we go on trimming away at the squab's feathers till we get ourselves a fully-fledged pigeon. Yes, we go on making do with what we've got, but what else can we do? What, indeed! Hassan—now he's with me at the company, a hard worker just like me. He really is. But Has-san smuggles things in addition to the job he does after his regular work. Man, God be my witness, I wouldn't know how to smuggle a day-old chick! No, sir—nor how to flog watches and jeans. Brother, they cleaned me out. I tried, and they took me to the cleaners. I don't deny it. That's what happened. What's the point of lying? We've landed up completely broke. But what did she think she was going to do . . . ?"

His voice broke and he buried his face against the glass as though attempting to penetrate it. I was at a loss to understand what he was saying. I found myself intrigued by his irrational chatter. I tried to guess what it was all about and became even more lost. I leaned my head against the back of the seat, then took out my cigarettes and offered him one. "It can't be all that bad, man. Have a smoke and blow it away."

"By God," he stated, as though crushed, "no one can make it go away except the Lord Almighty Himself, man. I gave up drinking to save money, and after that I gave up smoking as well. What else is there for me to give up? My very life? No, I don't blame her. The poor creature's a real thrifty housewife. God is my witness that she's a better person than I am. The fact is that if it weren't for her the street dogs would have had us. But it's the children . . ."

I dived in so as not to seem like the proverbial deaf man at a wedding. "Certainly it seems the children are . . ."

"You can say that again, may He have mercy on your dear departed. The trouble is there's no milk in her breasts, nor yet in the market. What d'you think would happen if the children were to fall ill? If there aren't any medicines in the government hospitals how am I expected to lay my hands on any? So that's how things are with us. Tell me what to do. Give me some solution."

At that moment all appearance of calm drained from his face and his features took on a look of stark alarm. "Imagine it! She said that was a solution. Good folk, she suggested it as a solution! For sure, either she's gone crazy or I have."

He began slapping at his thighs, which further increased my astonishment and brought the inevitable question to my lips. Then, quite unexpectedly, he gave a tiny nervous laugh which convinced me the man was indeed off his head. "Believe me, there's nothing worse than bottling up one's troubles, man. Keeping silent and cooping it all up has really done for me. For a couple of months I've been living in another world, keeping quiet about what she told me. I'd mull it over this way and that, while I felt like a chicken being roasted over Hell's fire. I was sitting doing my sums for the household expenses, with no clue of what was coming, when she came to me and said, 'Radwan, how's it all going to end?' I said to her, 'God willing, it will turn out all right, Fadwa. I know no more than you do.' She said, 'Radwan, our whole life is one of beggary, and the children are growing up between life and death. The cost of living is killing us—what I mean is, in a word, I want to work.'"

He leaned toward me and there was a strange forlorn look in his eyes. As though he wasn't seeing me, he said, "How should I know? In the beginning I said to her, 'And what about the children, Fadwa?' 'The Provider will look after that,' she said. In order to humor her I said, 'Certainly, He'll look after it, my dear, but what will you work at with that elementary certificate of yours?' 'I'll not

work with my certificate,' she said. 'That's all very well,' I told her,
'—then with what? Your wits?' Then, more downcast than I'd ever
seen her, she said, 'No, Radwan, I'll work. I'll work all right.'"

A yellow pallor clouded his face. I gave up in bewilderment. I uttered not a word, did not even make an attempt to speak. He went
on as though in a trance. "To begin with, I didn't want to take it in.
If I'd understood what she meant I'd have gone out of my mind.
But she left me no escape. She said, 'Radwan, I know it comes as a
surprise, and it's tough for you, but it's a fact that our children are
hungry and our life is hard. I wanted to tell you just so you wouldn't
say I was betraying you. It's been a terrible thing for me, man. Believe me when I tell you that it would be easier for me to lose my
four children.' But I said to myself, 'Keep patient, Radwan. Give
and take with her a bit—talk it over.' In fact, I started to talk to her,
and she talked back. All night long we didn't stop talking and crying. You'd think something awful had happened to us! Some ghastly
calamity! By God, I simply don't know! When morning came she
was hugging me and crying and I was hugging her and crying.
However, to cut a long story short, there was nothing to be done.
After that, to tell you the truth, I gave the matter a lot of thought.
I told myself that I should inform her family. But her family didn't
recognize her at all because she'd fallen in love with me and we'd
eloped. And what should I tell my friends? What would they do but
spread the story? Even to divorce her didn't make any sense. Where
would I park the four children? And where would I find the money
for the price of a second wife? And who's to know what she'd be
like? I won't hide it from you—I thought of killing her. Just for a
second I thought of it, then I laughed at my madness. What wrong
had the children done for me to cast myself into prison and them
into the street? Yes, unjustly, because—God is my witness—all the
years we were together she was like a golden lira. If she hadn't been,
she wouldn't have told me about it at all."

He wiped the saliva from his mouth with the back of his hand. I
was silently engrossed in what he was saying.

"I kept quiet about it, telling myself that, like a summer cloud,
it would pass, and I went back to trying to talk to her about it.

'Would you be unfaithful to me, Fadwa?' 'No, Radwan,' she told me. 'Don't make a mistake. If I'd fallen for someone else and gone with him without your knowing, then I'd really have been unfaithful. But I've got nobody but you in the whole world, Radwan, and you know it. I want to work just so we can eat, Radwan.' Imagine it, she said to me, 'And what do we lose, Radwan? I'd close my eyes and imagine it was you with me. It would be just a moment and afterward we'd live like decent folk.' Brother, her idea drove me out of my wits. I was shattered. God curse poverty and the life it brings!"

His voice was choked with tears as his words spattered against the window. I tried to say something, but my tongue stuck inside my mouth as the mud houses of al-Qastal slipped past the glass of the window.

"D'you know what happened after that?" he asked a moment later in a quaking voice.

"What happened?" I asked eagerly.

The driver's assistant called out, "Come on, lads, and hurry up, anyone who's getting off here. It's not a regular stop."

Radwan and some of the passengers rose to their feet. He was interrupted by the question in my eyes and he muttered something amid the din that I did not catch as he hurried to get off. I moved toward the window and saw him making his way toward another passenger, his hand gesticulating from side to side and thumping his chest, then gesturing toward his head, as an expression of bemusement settled on the other passenger's face.

Translated by Denys Johnson-Davies

Habib Selmi
(b. 1951)
TUNISIA

Habib Selmi was born in a Tunisian village. He earned a degree in Arabic literature from the University of Tunis and then taught for five years in secondary schools. He now lives in Paris, where he is a writer and a journalist. In 1978 he received a Tunisian state prize for one of his novels. Several of his works have appeared in French translation.

Distant Seas

Because we dreamed of distant seas, there were the three of us, Majid, Yassin and I.

We would go down the sandy track when the glare of the sun rose in the vast expanse, and there would come to us the smell of rank water as we approached the well.

We would hear weak and faint the lowing of the calves that had lost their way in the river beds.

Climbing the large olive trees, we would be able to see the river as it dipped down to the south. Always we would stop to view the smoke ascending from the piles of straw that had been collected into large stacks, and we could see frightening forms in that smoke.

Yassin got to know Maryam and he fell in love with her and she with him. She would waylay him every evening in front of the graveyard to give him some almonds, and Majid and I would be pained and would envy Yassin. We decided to steal the almonds from Maryam's field and we began going there every evening stealthily, but Maryam would always be there guarding the trees and chopping off leaves for the cattle. One day, having dressed up in old black clothing and blackened our faces with charcoal and smeared our hands and feet with mud, we went off to the field. As we reached it we saw Maryam; she was sitting on the ground with an olive twig in her hand. We began making weird noises and Maryam became frightened and ran out of the field, at which we went in and filled our pockets with almonds and oranges. When we came out Yassin blocked our way and discovered our theft. He wanted to catch hold of us but we threw him to the ground and kicked him till he was streaming in blood, then we fled. When we had gone very far away, we decided to hide so that his father wouldn't find us and we went to the ravine near the *wadi* and hid ourselves amongst the boulders.

"We'll sleep over there," he said to me as we went.

I was afraid he'd despise me or hit me or seize my almonds from me if I were to tell him I was frightened of the darkness, so I agreed. We walked along a path that was full of thorns and rocks. When we reached the ravine, we started to cut grass and to remove the straw that was piled up on the ground. The sun had not yet set; the colour of the clouds had changed and the earth behind us looked red.

When night descended we stretched out on the ground and talked about Maryam and Yassin. A short while passed and then we heard a howling from afar.

In order to put my mind at rest Majid said:

"The wolves don't come here because of the many fishermen."

For a long time we remained silent. Night filled up the ravine and outside the darkness thickened on the ground. I felt that something was moving alongside me and I drew my legs up to my stomach and made myself smaller. Majid was motionless. I punched him but he didn't move. I imagined that he had been bitten by a snake and had died. I crept out of the ravine and fled.

When we met up again I was afraid. I believed that he would hit me but he didn't do so. He shook me by the hand warmly and gave me some of the almonds he still had in his pocket. After that we talked about Maryam and the ravine in which we had hidden, about the night and darkness and about Yassin, and we decided, after a long discussion, to pay him a visit.

We went to him at noon. His mother met us and made much of us; doubtless she didn't know it was we who had beaten him. She led us to his room and sat us down on beautiful wooden chairs. When he saw us Yassin too was delighted and asked his mother to get us something to drink, then he led us to the garden where he showed us the pigeons, rabbits and chickens.

We reached the sixth form. Yassin, having passed the examination, journeyed to the city and we ceased to have any news of him. Majid became a secretary in a leading trading company, then was promoted and became rich. As for Maryam, she married a large landowner, gave birth to several children, then died. I meanwhile remained close to the land, to the trees and birds, and became a hunter. From the city I bought a gun and cartridges and leather boots to protect me from the thorns and rocks.

I shot a pigeon and I shot a fox and I shot a wolf.

All that has passed away and nothing of it remains but faint pictures that gather in the memory like a strong pulse-beat. This happens when I shoot some large bird or stand in front of an almond tree to gaze at its white flowers.

Translated by Denys Johnson-Davies

Khairy Shalaby
(b. 1938)
EGYPT

Khairy Shalaby is one of Egypt's most prolific fiction writers. His highly regarded novel *The Lodging House* was awarded the Naguib Mahfouz Medal for Literature in 2003, and was recently translated into English. Several of his works have been adapted for television and film.

The Clock

I was walking along a dazzling, crowded street—I think it was Soliman Pasha or one like it. I was pushing aside great multitudes of humanity at every step in order to make my way. All the women of Cairo were naked and gave out a smell of kerosene. There were men who looked like gas cylinders licking the backs of the women and placing money between their breasts and their thighs. Suddenly I saw my younger brother in his peasant's *gallabiya* and white skullcap. Shoulders, thighs, and breasts separated me from him. Delighted to see him, I began stretching out my neck so that he might see me.

He too was stretching out his neck. As we drew closer, it seemed as though we would both be going our own ways. However, each of us prepared to greet the other. When I stretched out my hand he did the same by reaching out between the many obstructions. Our hands met in a quick touch that earned us many rebukes and curses.

Then I don't know where he went. I immediately recollected that I hadn't seen him for years. I remembered that I had wanted to ask him about all sorts of things. My question presented itself: Do you know anything yet about our younger brother who didn't come back from the war? But the question did not come out.

All at once I found myself in a funeral procession. I asked who the dead man was and was told it was the husband of my eldest sister, that he had died in the war, and that there had been news of this. I thought those around me walking in the funeral would blame me if they found themselves alone with me, but I didn't know exactly what I was to be blamed for. Then we arrived at a place that I thought was the cemetery. One thing convinced me that I was right—this was the ancient sycamore tree that was in the center of our village cemetery.

While I was standing far off from those who were making their prayers over the body, I saw my younger brother who hadn't yet come back from the war and about whom we had been unable to gather any information, though we had asked everywhere. His long face with its fair complexion was just as I had known it, ever smiling. He was wearing a *gallabiya*, over which he had put on an army belt. I hugged him and wept.

When I told him we'd had a terrible time trying to find out what had happened to him, he laughed as usual and said that we shouldn't have bothered. Then the procession went off again to enter into the cemetery. There was a certain air of reverence enveloping the mourners, although we come from a family scarcely deserving of acts of courtesy. I said to myself, "Such are the funeral processions of righteous martyrs"—and I had a feeling of jealousy for the deceased.

But suddenly I discovered that Dr. Henry Kissinger, President Nixon, and President Ford were walking at the front of the procession and that they were also receiving condolences. The folk from my village had turned out in gallant fashion and were greeting them and smiling just like them. All of a sudden there was no one there at all. I saw nothing in front of me except for a vast expanse of desert that gave off scorching heat and the smell of kerosene. From somewhere came the voice of a reciter chanting the Quran, while the sun, suspended in the sky, was sinking down into the far horizon like a clock without hands or dial.

Translated by Denys Johnson-Davies

Hanan al-Shaykh
(b. 1945)
LEBANON

Hanan al-Shaykh was born in southern Lebanon but lived most of her early life in Beirut. She attended the American College for Girls in Cairo, and then returned to Beirut, where she worked on a women's magazine and for the literary supplement of *al-Nahar*, the leading daily newspaper. Upon marrying, she moved to Saudi Arabia with her husband, an engineering contractor to the oil industry. In 1980 her third novel, *The Story of Zahra*, was published. A technically sophisticated story of an ill-starred young woman and her suffering at the hands of an uncaring society, it deals explicitly with sexual oppression and the hypocritical attitude of a patriarchal society toward sexuality. It was translated into English and established her as one of the few Arab novelists with a worldwide reputation. In fact, sales of her novels in translation greatly outnumber their sales in the Arab world. Her other novels available in translation include *Only in London*, *Women of Sand and Myrrh*, and *Beirut Blues*, from which the second extract below is taken. Her story collections include *Desert Roads* and *I Sweep the Sun off Rooftops*. For the past several years Hanan al-Shaykh has lived in London.

The Persian Carpet

When Maryam had finished plaiting my hair into two pigtails, she put her finger to her mouth and licked it, then passed it over my eyebrows, moaning: "Ah, what eyebrows you have—they're all over the place!" She turned quickly to my sister and said: "Go and see if your father's still praying." Before I knew it my sister had returned and was whispering "He's still at it," and she stretched out her hands and raised them skywards in imitation of him. I didn't laugh as usual, nor did Maryam; instead, she took up the scarf from the chair, put it over her hair and tied it hurriedly at the neck. Then, opening the wardrobe carefully, she took out her handbag, placed it under her arm and stretched out her hands to us. I grasped one and my sister the other. We understood that we should, like her, proceed on tiptoe, holding our breath as we made our way out through the open front door. As we went down the steps, we turned back towards the door, then towards the window. Reaching the last step, we began to run, only stopping when the lane had disappeared out of sight and we had crossed the road and Maryam had stopped a taxi.

Our behaviour was induced by fear, for today we would be seeing my mother for the first time since her separation by divorce from my father. He had sworn he would not let her see us, for, only hours after the divorce, the news had spread that she was going to marry a man she had been in love with before her family had forced her into marrying my father.

My heart was pounding. This was not from fear or from running but was due to anxiety and a feeling of embarrassment about the meeting that lay ahead. Though in control of myself and my shyness, I knew that I would be incapable—however much I tried—of showing my emotions, even to my mother; I would be unable to throw myself into her arms and smother her with kisses and clasp her head as my sister would do with such spontaneity. I had thought long and hard about this ever since Maryam had whispered in my ear—and in my sister's—that my mother had come from the south and that we were to visit her secretly the following day. I began to imagine that I would make myself act exactly as my sister did, that I would stand behind her and imitate her blindly. Yet I know myself: I have committed myself to myself by heart. However much I tried to force myself, however much I thought in advance about what I should and shouldn't do, once I was actually faced by the situation and was standing looking down at the floor, my forehead puckered into an even deeper frown, I would find I had forgotten what I had resolved to do. Even then, though, I would not give up hope but would implore my mouth to break into a smile; it would none the less be to no avail.

When the taxi came to a stop at the entrance to a house, where two lions stood on columns of red sandstone, I was filled with delight and immediately forgot my apprehension. I was overcome with happiness at the thought that my mother was living in a house where two lions stood at the entrance. I heard my sister imitate the roar of a lion and I turned to her in envy. I saw her stretching up her hands in an attempt to clutch the lions. I thought to myself: She's always uncomplicated and jolly, her gaiety never leaves her, even at the most critical moments—and here she was, not a bit worried about this meeting.

But when my mother opened the door and I saw her, I found myself unable to wait and rushed forward in front of my sister and threw myself into her arms. I had closed my eyes and all the joints of my body had grown numb after having been unable to be at rest for so long. I took in the unchanged smell of her hair, and I discovered for the first time how much I had missed her and wished that she would come back and live with us, despite the tender care shown to us by my father and Maryam. I couldn't rid my mind of that smile of hers when my father agreed to divorce her, after the religious sheikh had intervened following her threats to pour kerosene over her body and set fire to herself if my father wouldn't divorce her. All my senses were numbed by that smell of her, so well preserved in my memory. I realized how much I had missed her, despite the fact that after she'd hurried off behind her brother to get into the car, having kissed us and started to cry, we had continued with the games we were playing in the lane outside our house. As night came, and for the first time in a long while we did not hear her squabbling with my father, peace and quiet descended upon the house—except that is for the weeping of Maryam, who was related to my father and had been living with us in the house ever since I was born.

Smiling, my mother moved me away from her so that she could hug and kiss my sister, and hug Maryam again, who had begun to cry. I heard my mother, who was in tears, say to her "Thank you," and she wiped her tears with her sleeve and looked me and my sister up and down, saying: "God keep them safe, how they've sprung up!" She put both arms round me, while my sister buried her head in my mother's waist, and we all began to laugh when we found that it was difficult for us to walk like that. Reaching the inner room, I was convinced her new husband was inside because my mother said, smiling: "Mahmoud loves you very much and he would like it if your father would give you to me so that you can live with us and become his children too." My sister laughed and answered: "Like that we'd have two fathers." I was still in a benumbed state, my hand placed over my mother's arm, proud at the way I was behaving, at having been able without any effort to be liberated from myself, from my shackled hands, from the prison of my shyness, as I recalled to mind the picture of my meeting with my mother, how I had spontaneously thrown myself at her, something I had thought wholly impossible, and my kissing her so hard I had closed my eyes.

Her husband was not there. As I stared down at the floor I froze. In confusion I looked at the Persian carpet spread on the floor, then gave my mother a long look. Not understanding the significance of my look, she turned and opened a cupboard from which she threw me an embroidered blouse, and moving across to a drawer in the dressing-table, she took out an ivory comb with red hearts painted on it and gave it to my sister. I stared down at the Persian carpet, trembling with burning rage. Again I looked at my mother and she interpreted my gaze as being one of tender longing, so she put her arms round me, saying: "You must come every other day, you must spend the whole of Friday at my place." I remained motionless, wishing that I could remove her arms from around me and sink my teeth into that white forearm. I wished that the moment of meeting could be undone and re-enacted, that she could again open the door and I could stand there—as I should have done—with my eyes staring down at the floor and my forehead in a frown.

The lines and colours of the Persian carpet were imprinted on my memory. I used to lie on it as I did my lessons; I'd be so close to it that I'd gaze at its pattern and find it looking like slices of red water-melon repeated over and over again. But when I sat down on the couch, I would see that each slice of melon had changed into a comb with thin teeth. The clusters of flowers surrounding its four sides were purple-coloured. At the beginning of summer my mother would put mothballs on it and on the other ordinary carpets and would roll them up and place them on top of the cupboard. The room would look stark and depressing until autumn came, when she would take them up to the roof and spread them out. She would gather up the mothballs, most of which had dissolved from the summer's heat and humidity, then, having brushed them with a small broom, she'd leave them there. In the evening she'd bring them down and lay them out where they belonged. I would be filled with happiness as their bright colours once again brought the room back to life. This particular carpet, though, had disappeared several months before my mother was divorced. It had been spread out on the roof in the sun and in the afternoon my mother had gone up to get it and hadn't found it. She had called my father and for the first time I had seen his face flushed with anger. When they came down from the roof, my mother was in a state of fury and bewilderment. She got in touch with the neighbours, all of whom swore they hadn't seen it. Suddenly my mother exclaimed: "Ilya!" Everyone stood speechless: not a word from my father or from my sister or from our neighbours Umm Fouad and Abu Salman. I found myself crying out: "Ilya? Don't say such a thing, it's not possible."

Ilya was an almost blind man who used to go round the houses of the quarter repairing cane chairs. When it came to our turn, I would see him, on my arrival back from school, seated on the stone bench outside the house with piles of straw in front of him and his red hair glinting in the sunlight. He would deftly take up the strands of straw and, like fishes, they'd slip through the mesh. I would watch him as he coiled them round with great dexterity, then bring them out again until he had formed a circle of straw for the seat of the chair, just like the one that had been there before. Everything was so even and precise: it was as though his hands were a machine and I would be amazed at the speed and nimbleness of his fingers. Sitting as he did with his head lowered, it looked as though he were using his eyes. I once doubted that he could see more than vague shapes in front of him, so I squatted down and looked into his rosy-red face and was able to see his half-closed eyes behind his glasses. They had in them a white line that pricked at my heart and sent me hurrying off to the kitchen where I found a bag of dates on the table, and I heaped some on a plate and gave them to Ilya.

I continued to stare at the carpet as the picture of Ilya, red of face and hair, appeared to me. I was made aware of his hand as he walked up the stairs on his own; of him sitting on his chair, of his bargaining over the price for his work, of how he ate and knew that he had finished everything on the plate, of his drinking from the pitcher, with the water flowing easily down his throat. Once at midday, having been taught by my father that before entering a Muslim house he should say "Allah" before knocking at the door and entering, as a warning to my mother in case she were unveiled, my mother rushed at him and asked him about the carpet. He made no reply, merely making a sort of sobbing noise. As he walked off, he almost bumped into the table and, for the first time, tripped. I went up to him and took him by the hand. He knew me by the touch of my hand, because he said to me in a half-whisper: "Never mind, child." Then he turned round to leave. As he bent over to put on his shoes, I thought I saw tears on his cheeks. My father didn't let him leave before saying to him: "Ilya, God will forgive you if you tell the truth." But Ilya walked off, steadying himself against the railings.

He took an unusually long time as he felt his way down the stairs. Then he disappeared from sight and we never saw him again.

She made not a sound. Her eyes were closed as she breathed in the freshness of a light breeze that stroked her gaunt forehead; she couldn't help but give herself up to it.

She heard the sound of the sheet of paper being torn from the pad.

When she looked up she saw that it alone was in his hands and that the pad was resting under a corner of the mat.

"Now read it out to me," she said in a quavering voice as she drew slightly closer to him.

Translated by Denys Johnson-Davies

FROM *Beirut Blues*

We stand by the garden pond breathing in the diesel fumes from the generators. He asks me why we've filled up the pond with stones. I remember how I never used to be able to get to sleep unless I could hear the sound of the water running from its little tap. I can picture what the tap looked like; the neighbours' son Bahij who was about twelve broke it off; metal was his obsession and he took away anything movable made out of metal and sold it; he was known as Bahij the Metal. Jawad puts his arm round me as I tell him about the pond and Bahij the Metal, and presses my shoulder. I seem to have been expecting it. I want to throw myself on him, I don't care where, just throw myself on top of him with all my weight. But I remain frozen, even though I haven't felt like this since my first dance with an adolescent boy.

He is going in two days. Why do relationships require a physical contact to develop? Why can't this continue when we are far apart? I picture myself writing letters, waiting for his. When I try to imagine what I would write I can hardly think of anything. For he has already preserved his days here: the plains reaching to the horizon, the vine trellises, the blackened landscapes, the rocky hilltops. He found out about the contradictions when he called his girlfriend in France from the post office in the neighbouring village. He didn't believe that on a hillside in this devastated land a post office had been built, fully equipped and staffed. Up above it was a beehive where the bees still returned to swarm. Nobody dared to go there but Hashim who launched a surprise attack on the hive, roping himself to the rocks above and swinging down the rock-face to reach the honeycomb.

I drew my lip from between his, and went into my room without a word. I threw myself down on the bed, picking up the mirror which I left there before dinner, when I was trying to see what he saw in my face. But it didn't bother me any more; the electricity was off and I wasn't going to switch on the generator because I couldn't stand the thought of the noise. What's more, I was trying to be like a mole, and pick up every movement Jawad made. The neighbourhood generators had gone quiet because of the lateness of the hour, although the noise of the nightclub was still loud in my ears. I chased away the images and tried to make myself indifferent, saying out loud, "People have to live a little."

I didn't think about the nightclub for long, because I was wondering whether my body was alerted by love or wine. Why didn't he knock on my door? Why couldn't I hear him in the kitchen or the living room? I jumped up suddenly as if I was supposed to be meeting him and had forgotten about it. When I opened my bedroom door, I heard his voice from the living room asking me how to make the electricity come on. The thought that Ruhiyya must be coming back any moment flew out of my head the moment he came near me, so that the darkness entered us both and we vanished like the things around us, of which only the vaguest outlines were visible, or perhaps we just knew they were there, but couldn't really see them. I was losing my self suddenly, losing the thread which tied me down to life and flying like a bird. Our conversation became bolder as if it didn't really count, because we were in the dark. My body took me by surprise as usual and I felt it begin to throb, and I smiled because Jawad couldn't see what was happening to me. We both became bolder and our breathing was like the light suddenly being switched on to reveal everything. His fingers reached out to touch my face, and I knew they were what I'd been waiting for all those years; they blotted out the music and noise, the faces with too much make-up, the mouths full of food and the gyrating stomachs; this tenderness was all that was left. As we moved in close together and I felt his breath on my face where his fingers had been, he asked me in a whisper if he could go on, and how I was feeling. I liked this hesitation, which I had never encountered in the others, this circumspection, this strength of will. The war here and his life in Europe hadn't given him the feeling that everything was permissible, all the barriers down. The fact that I was lying here like this had no connection with the war and the lack of permanence. I had moved far away from the living-room floor, my grandmother's house, the western sector. The desire to hold on to him wasn't like a drug, or because life went on and there was always someone somewhere being born or dying or having sex. I was lying on the carpet where I used to play as a child, and which I used to race across to go to school or meet a friend in my adolescence. For the first time I wasn't shutting off my feelings of love and desire as I entered the house, or transforming them into daydreams.

I discover that making love isn't as easy as it used to be. I'm far away despite my desire for him, expecting far more than this kissing and touching and holding. I take hold of my mass of thoughts and it's like picking up a heavy bird which has begun to walk rapidly along a piano keyboard sounding a jumble of different notes. This closeness has put a bubble in my veins and started to shift the sluggish blood along and make me breathe more deeply, restoring some spontaneity where before was only grim determination. I crave his lips, my hands grip his shoulders, his chest crushes me and his face is immersed in mine, but more than sex this is a way to great calm, as if existence had been poised on one foot and has at last regained its balance. Jawad's eyes look into the distance then focus on me. I pull him to me and call out aloud, "I love you. I love you."

He must be wondering why I'm not trembling with pleasure, what's stopping me even responding to him if I love him as I cry out that I do. Is everything in me blocked and sterile like my work, my future, my car engine which cuts out as soon as I turn the key in the ignition? Do I breathe like a spinster? Have I got the body of a dried-up old maid, although I feel as slippery as if I've oiled myself inside? Of course I was talking to him as I chased the bird which hopped over the piano keys, shifting from black to white; I talk to him in my head as he continues to crouch over me, embracing me, marveling that despite all the heat I'm giving off, I'm not in time with him. I wish I could tell him that I can really feel him, not only inside me but to the very ends of my body and all around it, but I want more than this cohesion of muscle, tendon, bone joint. "More, more, more," I mumble and he gets up and walks about the room.

After a long silence I put on a shocked voice and say, "Imagine if the electricity came back on now and Ruhiyya saw you."

"I wish I could understand what's the matter with you," he says.

I used to be certain that I would be all over Jawad like ink on a white sheet, spreading out and running in every direction until I was part of the fabric, so what is happening to me? Has seeing life diminished by the terrible dancing creatures in the nightclub made me wither like a flower snapped off a bush?

We couldn't begin a discussion: it was difficult if I didn't know what was wrong with me; but he took my face tenderly in his hands again and asked if I wanted him to carry me to my bed.

I clung to his neck as he picked me up and almost dropped me again. I remembered Naser's back pains then quickly drove the thought from my mind as I usually did when it concerned Naser. I smiled to hear Jawad saying, "Good heavens. How heavy you are. Like a lump of concrete."

"Is she as heavy as me?" I tease.

He says nothing.

"Soon you'll be carrying her around."

He throws me onto the bed. The metal springs bounce me back towards him. A wave of happiness rushes over me. My bed is different, laughing as it receives me with the one I love. We are in the house which thinks it's there for everything but lovemaking. It witnesses births, marriages, deaths, people moving in and moving out but not love. It's not used to lovers joining in the room of child-hood and adolescence; they go far away so that they can let their bodies do as they please.

As I think these thoughts, I feel the house embracing me sud-denly, giving out its warmth to me. The furniture watches and greets the union with gladness, breathing softly around us. I have not felt this relaxed with any man before. My roving encounters with Naser hardly made our relationship secure; there was no bed which we used habitually, no sofa whose colours stuck in my mind, no room which brought back certain words. Terror lurked con-stantly at the back of my mind and in the corners of my lips at the thought that his enemies might choose these intimate moments to attack.

Jawad touches my lips again, my arms, and releases me from the throng of thoughts and images and makes them lie dormant.

I followed him seconds after he had left for his own bed, and he was waiting for me; he made a space for me when he heard my foot-steps, put his arm round me and asked me, "Do girls here leave things to nature or do they use something?"

I just laughed, and then he began to breathe regularly so that I knew he was asleep. I studied his face; I was a little girl and this was my grandfather breathing reassuringly beside me, and everything was all right: the top window had been broken by local boys with a sling, not by sniper fire. Then I hear Jawad's voice as if in a dream, telling me that I'm just like my mother and that's how he recog-nized me after all these years.

He was a child when my mother visited them, in a long brown split skirt with a fox fur round her shoulders and dark red lipstick. She smoked a cigarette which she hid each time she heard footsteps, sang songs and laughed loudly. This image of her stayed in his mind for a long time afterwards.

He puts his arms round me. "It's incredible," he whispers. "Here I am with her daughter. It must be fate."

I lay without moving. I wanted to turn over as usual but I was afraid of disturbing him. I must have fallen asleep in the end, be-cause I woke up and the light was streaming into the room and I heard Ruhiyya moving about in the kitchen. A feeling of sadness overwhelmed me when I saw his suitcase. I tried to extricate myself from the embrace of his arms and thighs but he held me tighter. "You can't go," he muttered, his eyes tightly shut.

"Ruhiyya," I said, pretending to be flustered.

"Let her see us together. She can make up a song about us."

As I try to get up I want to ask him if he loves me, but I can't bring myself to, then the sight of our limbs entwined under the cover gives me courage and I wonder how I could have felt shy.

Translated by Catherine Cobham

Miral al-Tahawy
(b. 1968)
EGYPT

Miral al-Tahawy was born in Sharqiya in the Nile Delta and studied at Cairo University. Her first novel, *The Tent*, was published in 1996 to much critical acclaim; the English translation appeared in 1998. Told through the eyes of a young, emotionally scarred Bedouin girl, it provides intimate insight into a primitive and unfamiliar world. Al-Tahawy's second novel, *Blue Aubergine*, has also been translated into English.

FROM *The Tent*

The soft swells and winding curves of the desert's body shift and change. The sands creep and the floods trace furrows of sadness across the lonely desert tracks. Those raging sandstorms always carried something away. The wind would whistle and howl and then snatch up a filly or a mule, and sometimes whole tents and pastures. Musallam disappeared, even though he knew the desert like the back of his hand. He knew its night sky and its changing moods, where to set up his tent, and when the clouds would be heavy with rain. He had roamed far to the east and west, and spent days and nights alone there. He knew all the wells. Sometimes he would stretch out his wizened old legs, take off his *igaal*, and stories would flow from his lips. He would talk about the tribes, their origins, their territories, and their latest news. No one knew the desert like Musallam.

People often wondered about his tribe and lineage. Some said he was a peasant who longed to live the life of the Arabs but had been despised by them. But then when they heard him reciting the poems of al-Mutanabbi and Ibn al-Roumi, and others whom he had memorized and recited at their gatherings, they were amazed. Some maintained that they spotted in his accent the traces of an Azhar education, of someone who had been to the *kuttab* and spent time as a student at the Azhar. Any doubts about his origins also disappeared when they saw how he pruned and grafted his palm trees, and how strong young trees sprouted up from the shoots. He also knew much more about horses than they did, and was more familiar with the different pedigrees than they were. Stubborn young fillies were his specialty. They would leave the horse with him, and he would tame it and fatten it up and then lead it back meekly to its owner. Then there was his deep knowledge of desert plants, which he would gather and pound and blend and use to cure ailments. So, although they were unable to determine his exact lineage, they could not help but revere him, for besides the wrinkles of age on his cheeks and forehead, his bearing was solemn and dignified, and he was generous. His tent was open to all who passed through. Coffeepots bubbled on his fire, and his food was in every mouth. Moreover, he never crossed anyone, nor envied others for anything they had. If anything, he was more generous than any of them. Take wells, for example. They attract shepherds from miles around and are the subject of their quarrels and arguments. Musallam would dig a well and plant his palm trees. Then, if the shepherds came and set up their tents by his, he would set off into the open desert and disappear for two or three days. Then he would return, load up his tent on his camel and move on to set up a new home. He would tap the ground with the sole of his foot, dig his well, and plant his trees. It was as if he had known the new place all his life, or it had known him.

When asked about it, he would laugh and say: "Wells are like udders. They fill up and they dry up, each one at its own time." Their mouths gaped in astonishment. Had he really explored the whole desert and knew which wells were full and which were empty? Had he lived long enough to learn all this?

When Musallam went off this time, he didn't come back. The sandstorm was a swirl of dust. He disappeared from in front of his tent. They searched everywhere and asked every traveler they saw. Accounts of his disappearance varied, as did accounts of his life. They asked Abou Shreek, who guided the pilgrimage caravans, about him, and stayed up long into the night as he told them the following story:

Musallam had been a prosperous and wealthy man. He owned large tracts of fertile agricultural land by the Nile. He married a Turkish woman called Zata or Laza. Abou Shreek wasn't sure of the exact name. She was very fair-skinned and very well built. When she moved, her body wobbled like a sack of ginned cotton. One day he was passing the house of the local governor, and he saw her combing her hair in the courtyard. Her hair was long and luxuriously soft. He was on his gray mare and he stopped right in front of her. He was so overcome by her white skin and her prettiness that he raised his eyebrows. When she stood up to throw stones and sand at him, she looked like a young girl, though she was full of fury. He married her, and it's said that he gave all he owned for her bride price. After that the woman grew even rounder and more corpulent, and maybe she was a bit tyrannical and boasted to him about her Turkish roots. No one knows exactly what happened between them, but he started to loathe living with her and would love to go off on his own with his tent and his racing camel. He hunted more and made many journeys to the east and west of the desert. But he was by his nature inclined to do this, for he had had no children, neither by her nor by any other woman, and he was not fond of the noise and commotion of household life. Abou Shreek believed that the Turkish woman was still alive, and that she was now old and ugly, still white and plumper than the first sack had been; congested veins stuck out of her white skin like blue lines drawn by age.

Translated by Anthony Calderbank

Bahaa Taher
(b. 1935)
EGYPT

Bahaa Taher was born in Cairo. He took a degree in history from Cairo University and began working on the cultural programs of Cairo radio, where he produced the work of playwrights ranging from the Greek dramatists to Samuel Beckett. In 1981 he left Cairo to work in Geneva as a translator in the Arabic section of the United Nations. He is now back in Cairo, where he devotes himself full-time to writing. For his novel *Aunt Safiyya and the Monastery* he received the 1998 State Award of Merit in literature and, from Italy, the 2000 Giuseppe Acerbi Prize. His novel *Love in Exile* is about an Egyptian journalist in self-imposed exile in Europe, where he has to come to terms with the Israeli occupation of Lebanon and his love affair with a younger Austrian woman.

FROM Love in Exile

I was sitting at the café that morning in June, hunched over the newspapers I had bought, the Arabic, English, and French papers, trying to extract something from between the lines, to predict the change that would finally take place in Lebanon and in Egypt and everywhere in the homeland. I was agitated and enthusiastic when Brigitte came in and I didn't notice until she stood in front of me. I greeted her quickly as I gathered the newspapers to clear the table. As soon as she sat down I began to tell her of what I'd read and heard on the radio. I told her, "Israel has launched a comprehensive war on the Arabs on the strange pretext that a person or persons unknown shot its ambassador in London."

But Brigitte kept listening to me without emotion and finally as I was going full steam relating details, she interrupted me with a sullen face, "Enough already! Haven't I told you before? I don't read any newspapers and I have neither radio nor television in my house. I don't want to know anything about this world that I don't understand. Wasn't it you who told me the first time we met that this life is a lie?"

I said to her angrily, pounding the papers piled in front of me, "But this blood is very real!"

She replied calmly, "It was not we who shed this blood nor we who can stop it."

I got up, quite beside myself, and said, "This is the quintessence of callousness!"

It was the first time that I had quarreled with her. I told her, as I gathered my newspapers piled on the table, that she used her personal story as an excuse for her selfishness, to live totally indifferent to everything like all the others. I told her she at least should have appreciated what war meant to me even if it did not mean anything to her.

As I was leaving, she grabbed my hand and said in a beseeching tone, "So be it. I am as you say and worse, but please don't go. Let's stay friends just as we are. I don't want to lose you too!"

However, I jerked my hand away angrily and left. In those days I stayed away from her, living at a feverish pace, cutting newspaper clippings in all languages and watching all news programs on television and writing every day a lengthy report to my newspaper in Cairo about reactions in Europe to this massacre. I translated the angry commentaries and described the demonstrations that leftist parties organized. I turned the radio dial from Morocco to Cairo to Baghdad waiting at every moment for something to happen, something other than these pictures with which television and the papers assaulted my eyes every minute. I was waiting for anything to change this humiliation.

But nothing happened.

Nothing but tanks and bombs, flying and leveling, and planes shelling, and Israel's healthy soldiers smiling at my face on the screen, raising their machine guns in victory salutes. In the refugee camps naked children and mothers wearing plastic slippers ran, slapping their own faces in the midst of huts whose roofs had slid down on their walls to create jagged piles of rubble, of dust and bricks and twisted iron rods amid black and white smoke. And Egypt expresses regret and the economics committee holds a meeting to discuss the five-year plan. And Tyre falls and Sidon falls and the Ain el-Helweh refugee camp is razed and Rashidiyyeh and Miyya-Miyya refugee camps fall and are burned down. Saudi Arabia expresses regret and announces that the new crescent moon has been verified and sends messages to the kings and presidents. Algeria denounces the war, and announces extending new incentives to foreign investors. And the planes are all over Beirut: 200 dead, 400 wounded, 90 dead, 180 wounded. Just figures reported in the news. A whole street burns down and all its buildings lose their facades after it is hit with fuel air explosives. The pictures show the remnants of life in the bare rooms: overturned tables, children's toys stained with blood, photographs, and small statues of the Virgin Mary smashed on the floor in the midst of fires and corpses lying on their backs and others doubled on their sides. A paralyzed old woman in a shelter is sitting in a wheelchair, trying to push it forward or backward in the middle of a ward that has lost its walls but the stones scattered on the floor impede her movement in any direction. She lifts the white shawl off her head and cries.

The image of that woman keeps haunting me at night as I struggle with sleep. I am haunted by the image of a terrified man running in the street amidst the din of guns, carrying a severed human arm wrapped in a newspaper dripping blood. Why is he carrying that arm? I am haunted by the image of Israeli soldiers driving before them, with rifle butts, blindfolded young men whose hands are tied behind their backs. But I tell myself that tomorrow, in the morning, everything will change. This cannot go on if Israel has done this because an ambassador, one person, was injured—a volcano of anger will erupt in us as we see and hear of hundreds dying every day. Our sense of honor could not have been lost forever; after all it is blood and not ice that runs in our veins. Anger will erupt in the morning!

But in the morning comes the second ceasefire, the third, the fifth, and the American envoy comes and the American envoy goes, the seventh ceasefire, an ambulance speeding in the burning streets, its loud siren wailing, Israel cuts off water and electricity to Beirut, a little barefoot girl with disheveled hair is using a mug to fill a jerry can with sewage water. In places other than Beirut nothing happens. The Norwegian nurse tells me that all I've seen on television and all I've read in the papers is something other than the truth.

Translated by Farouk Abdel Wahab

Fuad al-Takarli
(b. 1927)
IRAQ

Fuad al-Takarli was born in Baghdad. He graduated from Law College and was appointed a judge in 1956, rising to be head of the court of appeal in Baghdad. He has lived also in Paris and Tunis and has now settled in Damascus. He published his first collection of stories in 1960. His novel *The Long Way Back* was published in Beirut in 1980 and has been translated into French and English. *The Long Way Back* is a very readable novel about a family inhabiting a house in an old quarter of Baghdad in the early 1960s. The short scene below describes one of the characters pursuing his self-destructive life.

FROM *The Long Way Back*

Husayn began searching through his pockets for cigarettes and did not find any. "What a mess I'm in today. I'm hopeless!"

Midhat offered him a cigarette. He accepted, lit it, and took a long drag. He felt he was about to reach his accustomed peak, when the world was full of joy, life was amazing, truth and fantasy were indistinguishable, and the walls came tumbling down. He didn't want to lie to Midhat: "I don't know. Maybe. One day I went out and didn't go home. I was working at the Rafidayn Bank at the time, and I'd been married three or four years. I don't remember exactly. We were all right financially, and I was on the fringes of some progressive political and literary groups. So, I went out, but I don't know where I was planning on going. There was one thing on my mind—I didn't want to go on living the life I was living."

His friend Faruq had persuaded him to join the famous poker game held in a whorehouse which some of them frequented. Drink, gambling, and most likely women too. They'd left work together with their salaries in their pockets and gone to the place in Karrada. He hadn't even phoned Madiha to tell her he wouldn't be coming home. They had been given a warm welcome and were soon playing cards in a group that grew over the course of the evening as more people arrived and joined in.

"I didn't have specific plans to take a room in a hotel. I just wanted to be by myself, to feel I didn't have any ties or responsibilities. I was obsessed by the idea of finding out what I'd be without my job, my family, children, home, friends."

It had been a wonderful night. Amazing cards. Money piling up in front of him. Whisky flowing. And Marie. She had squeezed in next to him, her breast pressing against his shoulder, her buttock resting on his chair, whispering flirtatiously to him every now and then, and the hours had passed like minutes.

"What would I be, I used to ask myself, if I was dropped naked as the day I was born on an island or out in the wilds somewhere? What would I be without my language and my past? And to tell you the truth, it was as if I was imprisoned by these thoughts the whole time, as if thinking had become a disease with me. I went without food or drink the whole night."

The cards had been extraordinary all night long, and sweet Marie had stayed at his side pouring him drinks and flirting with him. The hours had gone by, and when dawn broke they had only paused briefly for a light meal, and he had caressed Marie's breasts and kissed her in a dark corner. When they went back to the table his head had been empty, beating like a drum.

"I fell asleep and didn't wake till the afternoon. I stayed in bed without eating or shaving. I saw no one that day. I wanted this solitude."

It had got to past one in the afternoon. He had no longer been able to see the cards properly and asked if he could have a rest. He had simply wanted to sleep. It hadn't occurred to him to go home to his family, or even to make contact with them. He had been winning a large sum of money—how much he couldn't remember any more—and wanted to screw Marie. She'd asked him for however many dinars, which he'd given her without hesitation, and taken him off to a room at the back of the house.

"I paced up and down the room. I can remember it so clearly. It was as if I was chasing a shadow—something I couldn't quite grasp. And I came to one conclusion: I couldn't, being the person I was, in that situation and mental state, come to any conclusion, because I couldn't be certain of anything, and I didn't know where to start."

What a fiasco! For him and coquettish Marie. The soft bed had been like a drug. His body had been unable to keep fighting the exhaustion. As soon as he'd put his head on the pillow, intending to relax for a moment, he'd plunged into a profound sleep, which had taken him away from Marie and her warm body.

"But these hours of reflection made me feel a kind of peace of mind I hadn't felt before. It was nighttime. I left the hotel and went to the nearest bar. I drank and drank, as if I was drinking the spirit of life itself. I was terribly drunk, but I went on drinking till midnight and I still hadn't had enough, so I bought a bottle of whisky to take back to the room, and went on drinking till dawn."

They had woken him up in the late afternoon, and Marie hadn't been there. She had gone without leaving anything behind, not even her smell. He had sat at the table feeling, for no obvious reason, that a part of him was missing. He could still remember those few moments before the other players arrived. Through the window the sky had looked clear and blue, full of light and joy, a pure distant world that had suddenly terrified him. When he started playing again, all his luck had deserted him. He had fought back vehemently and hung on to his last bit of cash, but it was pointless: he felt that some stern judgment had been passed on him when he was looking at the sky. The game broke up at dawn, and he left the house empty and drained.

Translated by Catherine Cobham

Zakaria Tamer
(b. 1929)
SYRIA

Zakaria Tamer was born in Damascus. Though he received little formal education, he immediately established himself as a new voice in the Arabic short story with the publication in the 1960s of his first collection, *The Neighing of the White Steed*. In Damascus he held various government posts before going to work on an Arabic newspaper published in London, where he still lives. A selection of his stories in English translation was published in 1985 under the title *Tigers on the Tenth Day*.

A Summary of What Happened to Mohammed al-Mahmoudi

Mohammed al-Mahmoudi was an elderly man who lived alone in a small house. He had neither wife nor children and, being retired, had nothing to do. First thing in the morning he would leave the house and walk leisurely through the streets, stopping for a few moments to buy his favourite newspaper and then continuing his slow promenade in the direction of a café separated from the noisy street by a glass wall. On arrival he would go inside and make for a particular table which afforded him the opportunity of observing the street; there he would sit waiting, without saying anything, for the *narghile* and cup of sugarless coffee. Then taking from his pocket a pair of spectacles, he would put them on and would become engrossed in reading the newspaper, smoking his *narghile* and look-ing out from time to time with bemused eyes at the street.

When he felt hungry, he would rise with sluggish reluctance and leave the café for a nearby restaurant. He would eat listlessly, then quickly return to the café to carry on reading the newspaper, smok-ing his *narghile*, sipping tea and coffee and watching the street until nightfall, at which time he would leave the café, go home, take off his clothes, lie down on his wide bed and at once fall into a deep sleep.

Sometimes he would see his mother in his sleep. She would up-braid him severely for not having married and bewailingly demand a child who would say to her: "Granny, buy me a balloon."

So he would arise from sleep, dejected and embarrassed at his de-sire to weep loud and long.

One day he was sitting as usual at the café reading the newspaper and smoking his *narghile* when the newspaper suddenly slipped from his fingers and, with a moan, he collapsed to the ground. The doctor was immediately called and confidently pronounced that he was dead. Then, in fulfillment of his will, pickaxes and spades were brought and a hole was dug under the table at which he had been accustomed to sit, and he was gently taken up and laid to rest in the bottom of the hole and a lot of earth was heaped on top of him. He didn't grumble or get annoyed but smiled happily at being released from having to walk the streets and go to the house and the restau-rant, and he listened ardently to the conversations of the café's clientele, the gurgling of the *narghiles* and the shouts of the waiters. At night, though, he would feel bored, lonely and frightened, for the café would be empty and its doors closed.

The day came when the café was raided by a number of police-men. They extracted Mohammed al-Mahmoudi from his hole and led him off to a police station. There the police superintendent said to him in a stern voice: "It has come to our knowledge that you crit-icize the acts of the government, make fun of it, curse it and claim that all its laws serve only the owners of properties, cars and large stomachs."

In terrified remonstration Mohammed al-Mahmoudi called out:

"I curse the government? God forbid! I am not one of those who drink from a well and then spit into it. Ask about me. I was an exemplary official and I used to obey orders and laws and would carry them out meticulously. Ask about me. I never once got drunk, never made a pass at a woman, never harmed anyone, and I was . . ."

The superintendent interrupted him: "But the reports that have come in to us about you don't lie and the people who made them are wholly trustworthy."

Mohammed al-Mahmoudi shuddered and said in a quaking voice: "I swear by God that I have lived my whole life without ever talking about politics, and never ever have I insulted the government or those in power."

"Ha ha," said the superintendent, "I condemn you out of your own mouth. You say you haven't insulted the government, but you don't say that you have praised it. Does it not in your opinion deserve praise?"

Mohammed al-Mahmoudi tried to speak, but the superintendent continued talking: "And even if what you say is true, it sounds most strange, for everyone else has become twisted, spiteful and embittered. People insult the government and those in power, oblivious of the necessity to obey authority. They don't realize that it isn't everyone who understands politics."

Mohammed al-Mahmoudi said in a faint voice: "That's so. Everyone is talking about politics and ascribing the most disgraceful attributes to every single responsible person in the state. As for me . . ."

Interrupting him with a meek questioning voice, the superintendent said: "And of course in the café you hear what they say and know the names of those speaking?"

Mohammed al-Mahmoudi nodded his head. The superintendent smiled and said: "It would appear you are a good man and an upright citizen, and I would really like to help you in order that you may escape from the accusation leveled at you, but you too must help me."

Mohammed al-Mahmoudi said in astonishment: "And how am I to help you when I'm dead?"

The superintendent gave a cheerful laugh, then said: "It's very simple and interesting. Listen . . ."

Mohammed al-Mahmoudi listened to what the superintendent had to say, then after a while returned to his hole in the café in a very joyful state, for now he had something to do. No longer would he feel lonely, bored and frightened when the café closed its doors at midnight: it was then that he would hasten to write down, lest he forget, the conversations of the café clientele.

Translated by Denys Johnson-Davies

May Telmissany
(b. 1965)
EGYPT

May Telmissany was born in Cairo. She took a degree in French literature from Cairo University and continued her studies at the University of Montreal. Her novel *Dunyazad*, which appeared in 1997, was chosen for translation into nine European languages under a program assisted by the European Cultural Foundation. It starts with the stillborn death of the title character. In his postscript, Roger Allen, the novel's translator, calls the beginning "also a beginning for a transformed and potentially traumatic future that slowly emerges. The mother narrator tells of the stages of slow and emotionally fraught recovery in a series of narratives, impressions, and dreams." The excerpt below centers on the four-year-old boy who is already a member of the family.

FROM *Dunyazad*

We were sitting at either end of the dining table. He was at the far left drawing, and I was writing at the other end.

Suddenly he looked up, a bit shy, but with a crafty smile as well. "Mama," he said softly, "I saw a pretty girl today."

Shehab? Four years old? I let my pen drop. "What's her name?" I asked, beams of sheer joy radiating from my eyes.

He didn't reply. I went back to my writing, but was totally distracted. He carried on colouring, doing a drawing of himself: one big circle, with smaller ones in the middle for mouth and eyes, then an even bigger one for a fat body with two circular legs hanging down from it.

"Her name's Salma," he tells me after a pause.

A smile from me and one back from him, a smile as tender as the memory of Salma's face that loomed in the space between us.

"Salma?" (I have a friend of that name.)

"Yes, I've just remembered." (Perhaps he never forgot either.)

"Have you talked to her?"

"No!" he replies with obvious exasperation. This time he's drawing a prehistoric lizard, then a dinosaur . . .

I suppress the urge to ask more questions and decide to wait till he tells me more. Is she in the same class? When did he first notice her? What was she wearing? Is her hair black like mine? Why hasn't he spoken to her? Is she a nice girl or is she bad?

"When I woke up, I saw her standing there in front of me" (so he saw her during nap time).

Love at first sight. He must have seen her in a dream, or else imagined that her face was a dream. Shehab al-Din is in love with Salma without even realizing it.

"Mama, I love Salma."

So he does realize. I rush from one end of the table to the other and give him a hug. I decide to play the game through to the end. His little boy's heart is tired; he has to wait two more days before seeing her again.

He tries to wriggle his way out of my hug, but I hold him even tighter, as if in one final craving to possess him. Finally he struggles free. Four years old, and his heart is burdened by the lovely image of Salma.

Finally out of my clutches he seems surprised that I'm laughing happily and thinks I'm making fun of him. He looks a bit embarrassed too.

"I'm going to marry you, Mama."

Not a bad way of dealing with very precocious guilt-feelings. He's not going to leave me for another woman just yet.

"I'm already married to Daddy, my love."

Joyous relief envelops his expression. The whole atmosphere clears, imbued with the scent of clouds that roll away after a heavy seasonal downpour.

I've decided: next Sunday I'm going to pick him up at kindergarten and ask him to point her out to me.

"There are two Salmas in the class," he says, as though reading my very thoughts.

"Two Salmas?"

"Yes, there's pretty Salma and ugly Salma!"

"Which one do you love?"

"Pretty Salma."

"You should talk to her."

He's embarrassed. "I don't know . . . !"

This boy's just like his father. I remembered I had to wait six months before he would admit he was in love with me and then another six months before he made up his mind to visit our house. I remembered too that the first present he gave me was a toy— typical of the romantic ideas of nineties lovers with their addiction to cartoons!

"You should choose a toy to give her."

He stopped colouring. The idea obviously appealed to him. Jumping up from his chair he grabbed my hand and hurried me to his room. His toys were all over the floor, on his bed and on top of the cupboard. First he chose an expensive toy, a piano. This child's a romantic . . . not like his father, but then he doesn't really like the piano in any case.

"That's a big toy, Buba!"

He threw it on his bed. I was taken aback.

"What am I going to choose?"

I had forgotten that Shehab is a Gemini and chided myself. It was too late now; we were firmly into the possible and impossible choice phase. Rejected toys were all thrown on the bed; this one's big, this one's small; I like this one; this one's a present from Uncle K.; girls won't like this one . . .

"Mama, what do girls like to play with?"

An obvious question, one I'd never asked myself. Since Dunyazad I've never even thought I'd have another girl, or that I would buy her cotton dolls of the most expensive kinds made of plastic with proper skin colour.

"Dolls, small animals, musical toys."

To make it easier for him to choose, I went through all the toys in his room. But it wasn't easy. At first he decided on a small doll called Karim, then he changed his mind and decided to give her a big doll in green clothes that looked like an Eskimo; then a wooden soldier, then a train, then a police car, then a box of blocks, and finally nothing at all.

"Talk to her first. If she's nice, you can buy her a present."

"Do you mean she's not nice, mama?" and he starts crying.

Bad move on my part. "I didn't say that, darling," I respond.

"You did!"

Not a bad way of bringing this procession of gift possibilities to an end and moving on to others yet more complex.

"I'm just going to play with boys."

A third possibility, one that provided a radical solution to the entire issue but still made me feel guilty. Now I've given the boy a complex, I thought, as I gave him a hug and he tried angrily to get away.

I spent half the night looking for the right toy for Salma and the other half trying to get her lovely apparition out of my son's mind. He paces round and round the house, while I make valiant but useless efforts to divert his attention. Sometimes she's pretty and not nice, then she's pretty and nice, sometimes he's going to buy her a cookie, then he's turning his back on her in class as though she's his sworn enemy.

By now Salma must be asleep in her own little bed. When she smiles, her teeth probably aren't straight; when Shehab sees her smile, he'll change his mind and stop thinking she's the prettiest girl in the class. A nice hot bath will calm him down, and then I'll tell him the story of Jamil the elephant and Abdel Fattah the crocodile. Just as he's closing his eyes on the image of Salma, I must remind him of where we're going tomorrow; to the zoo, with the pony doing the rounds of the elephant, camel and horses. But tomorrow's trip doesn't erase the image completely. In the middle of the night I'm aware of him fidgeting as he remembers the tiny piano. I shake him a bit, and he gives me a hug. There, in a heady trance, are implanted between us images of first love.

Translated by Roger Allen

Mahmoud Teymour
(1894–1974)
EGYPT

Mahmoud Teymour was born into an Egyptian family of Turkish origin. Several of his relatives made names for themselves in the field of literature; Teymour himself is regarded as the pioneer of the Arabic short story. A collection of his stories, *Tales from Egyptian Life*, was published in Cairo in 1946, and it is possibly the first volume of Arabic short stories to have appeared in English translation.

The Comedy of Death

The doctor entered the room of the sick servant, Mustafa Hasan, accompanied by the eunuch of the women's apartments. It was a dirty room with one narrow aperture, through which streamed thin threads of the sun's hot, scintillating rays; its furniture was old and broken, the most prominent pieces being the rush bed with its filthy, tattered bedclothes, and the wardrobe, whose mean exterior gave no clue to the valuable objects it held.

Mustafa Hasan had been extremely stingy with himself, so that he had been able, in the course of his life, to save two hundred pounds in gold, to which he clung more tenaciously than to life itself.

The doctor felt the patient's pulse, bared his chest, and examined his lungs. He told the eunuch in a low voice that the man could not live more than a couple of hours.

Hardly had the doctor left when the sick man opened his eyes. He was at once attacked by an incessant cough which left him exhausted.

Mustafa Hasan had been a slave of the late owner of the mansion, a pasha, by whom he had been bought at the age of eight. The boy had shown signs of intelligence and energy, which so pleased the pasha that he had him trained in agriculture and estate-management. But before long Mustafa Hasan proved himself unworthy of his master's favor, and his education did him no good. So the pasha took away the high positions he had given him, and neglected him rather disgracefully. In the end, when Amm Murgan, the old doorkeeper, died, Mustafa Hasan was entrusted with the vacant post.

And doorkeeper he remained till his master died, after which his mistress, the new head of the mansion, took pity on him and pensioned him off. A year ago he had been taken ill with lung trouble, so severe that all hope of his recovery was given up. And now he was breathing his last.

After the eunuch had escorted the doctor to the entrance, he went in search of his mistress to her private room on the top floor. He found her sitting on the prayer carpet, reading Ya-Sin, a chapter in the Koran, while the old woman Koran-reciter sat and listened. Hearing the eunuch enter, his mistress raised her gold spectacles and looked up inquiringly.

"What did the doctor say, Bashir Agha?" she asked.

The eunuch, a portly man like a sack of suet, did not reply at once, as he was puffing badly after having climbed the stairs. His mistress agitatedly repeated her question. Bashir Agha brushed his hand over his eyes with a show of deep sorrow.

"Is Mustafa Hasan dead?" the lady shouted.

By this time the eunuch had recovered somewhat and was breathing normally once more.

"Not yet, madam; but I'm afraid he's almost at his last gasp," he hastened to reply.

Two tears rolled down the lady's cheeks.

"Verily we belong to God, and to Him we return," she murmured in a resigned tone.

"The Fatihah be read over your soul, Mustafa Hasan!" the Koran-reader said in her rasping voice.

All three began reciting the opening chapter of the Koran. Bashir Agha saw by his watch that it was ten o'clock.

"Mustafa Hasan will die at twelve . . . exactly as the midday gun goes off," he said to himself.

He went out and made for the sick man's room, to guard the door; for he had appointed himself Mustafa Hasan's official heir, that he might take all he pleased of what the man left.

As soon as the news got about that Mustafa Hasan was dying, the servants flocked from all sides toward his room. They found, however, that Bashir Agha had locked the door and was sitting in front of it, vigorously flourishing a thick stick to scare away anyone who might think of storming the room.

"Has Mustafa Hasan died?" they eagerly asked.

"He's breathing his last," Bashir Agha replied haughtily.

When it was plain that there was no way of gaining admittance to the room, the group dispersed, though a few of its members lingered around the eunuch, talking.

The children crowded outside the window of the room to see Mustafa Hasan dying. One, vigorously defending the position he had secured in front of the window, exclaimed: "Goodness! His belly's so swollen it's almost touching the ceiling."

Cursing the speaker for blocking the best view, another boy cried: "Sparks are flying out of his eyes! His mouth is spitting blood! Fire, blood, fire, blood . . . !"

He took to his heels, repeating the words in a frightened wail. The other tore after him, terror-stricken, into the street, where they gave highly colored accounts of the deathbed scene.

The eunuch's watch marked eleven.

"Only one hour more till death comes to you, Mustafa Hasan," he murmured. "You will journey to the other world, and I shall seize what I please from your rich estate."

He turned to Amm Madbuli, the foreman, an aged man of pious appearance, and whispered in his ear: "In an hour's time Mustafa Hasan will be dead. What shall we do with his estate? Wouldn't it be best to divide it among the servants?"

The old man shook with joy, but feigned indifference.

"Do what you think fit," he replied.

"I shall give you some shoes, three galabias, and a blanket."

"God grant you long life! But won't you choose something for yourself?"

"No. Nothing at all . . . I shall hand over the purse of money to my mistress."

The cleaner heard them and drew near.

"I trust you won't forget me, master," he besought the eunuch.

"I shall not forget you, Othman. I shall give you a lot of slippers. The dead man has stock of expensive red ones."

Delighted at this promise, Othman replied: "God prosper and bless you, sir! But won't the cashmere shawl also fall to my share?"

"Of course."

Othman kissed the eunuch's hands in thanks. Abd el-Qawwi, the water carrier, approached, for he had heard something of what they had been saying. He loudly protested against their secret plotting.

"I have done the dead man many services. Shall I receive nothing from his estate?"

"Did you think I'd forgotten you, you saucy fellow?" roared the eunuch.

Abd el-Qawwi was delighted.

"God keep you always with us! I want very little," he said, in an ingratiating tone. "First, the thick black shoes that used to belong to the pasha. Secondly, the new tarboosh that Mustafa Hasan bought last year and hasn't used. Thirdly, the shawl he got for the Feast, which, to this day, he's never worn. Fourthly . . ."

But here Amm Madbuli, the foreman, interrupted the water carrier, shouting:

"You won't leave anything for anybody else. We want to distribute the estate fairly. There are many servants here. What will be left for Sheikh Abd el-Hayy, the Koran-reader, and Ali, the cook, and his lad, and Sayyid Mutwalli, the dustman, and . . ."

They heard a faint wail issuing with difficulty from the room; it sounded like a voice from the grave. They listened, it was the sick man calling. The eunuch stiffened, and cold sweat poured down his forehead.

"The hour has come," he told them. "Friends, Mustafa Hasan is breathing his last. Let us go in."

Opening the door, he entered; the servants surged in after him. They drew near the sick man, gathering around his bed. Mustafa Hasan raised his head a little, caught hold of Bashir Agha's hand, and asked him urgently, in a shaky voice:

"What did the doctor say? . . . I heard you discussing my estate . . . Is it all over with me?"

Bashir Agha lowered his head and did not reply. The sick man's face paled, and a violent trembling seized him. He had a bad fit of coughing, after which he lost consciousness. They all thought that he had passed away; and there was an awestruck silence. Then they turned their eyes toward the eunuch. He realized what was in their minds, and drawing near to Amm Madbuli, the foreman, whispered a few words in his ear. The man nodded and, approaching the sick man's head, groped under the pillow for the cupboard key. At that moment the supposed dead man opened his eyes; Amm Madbuli withdrew his hand, pretending that he was arranging the bedclothes; but he leaned toward the sick man, and said gently:

"Give me the key, Mustafa, so that I can get you out a woolen galabia and a thick coverlet. I see that you're shivering with cold."

"It's not necessary, Amm Madbuli," the sick man muttered. "I want to keep my galabias and coverlet for use later."

He took the other's hand and began shaking it nervously, his face contracted like a weeping child's.

"I shan't die, Amm Madbuli," he mumbled, in a voice choked with tears. "I shan't die, shall I? I feel a bit better already."

He opened his eyes and tried to sit up in bed.

"I want to get up . . . I feel new strength coming into my

body . . . Leave me alone, Amm Madbuli; I am not as weak as you imagine."

But he had difficulty in breathing. His head dropped to the pillow, and his chest heaved convulsively. His eyes started from their sockets and his mouth opened and shut in its wild search for air. His whole body shook violently. In the end blood flowed from his mouth, and he lay quite still.

Amm Madbuli approached and covered up the body; then, quite openly, he put his hand under the pillow and took the key, which he handed to Bashir Agha. The eunuch immediately told the men to move the cupboard outside. They came forward and heaved at it. After some difficulty they managed to carry it to the door, but it slipped from their hands and broke open. Some of them saw their chance for surreptitious plunder. Others openly pushed aside the broken boards and snatched what they could. A battle of pillage raged, and the whole crowd became embroiled.

The eunuch, anxious about the purse of money—his share, which he had put aside exclusively for himself—kept on shouting in his aristocratic voice, telling them to stop their plundering. But nobody paid any attention. Innate greed burned in their hearts, deafening and blinding them; they became like hungry wolves fighting over their prey. The eunuch saw that action was needed—the time was one for deeds, not words. He came forward, rolling up his sleeves, and, with furious roars, joined in the battle. He pushed this one, kicked that one, butted some and bit others.

At last he reached the shattered cupboard. He threw his enormous body at it, shielding it from sight, and stretched out his hand to where the purse lay—he knew its exact position—and extracted it without difficulty. Then he rose, leaving the others to secure their share of the estate, each according to his strength.

The eunuch went off to his mistress and tactfully informed her of the slave's death, asking her to be so good as to give him the expenses for the funeral. She handed him a large sum, which he took straight to his room. After he had made the door fast, he opened the purse—his booty—and emptied its contents into his lap. Then he counted out, avidly and in great excitement, the two hundred pounds. When he had finished, he rubbed his hands with joy, and carefully put the money away in his cupboard.

"The best thing you ever did, Mustafa Hasan. The best thing . . ." he muttered. "You were stingy with yourself that others might enjoy your money after . . ."

By this time the servants had finished their plundering. They carried away what they had stolen, leaving the dead man no company except the shattered and empty cupboard.

At four o'clock on the same afternoon, the funeral procession of the slave Mustafa Hasan set out. It was led by a group of blind sheikhs, chanting stridently: "There is no God but God . . ." Behind the coffin walked the crowd of servants, headed by Bashir Agha. All of them, except the eunuch, were wearing the new clothes and shoes they had stolen from the dead man. Everyone was satisfied with his gains, save Abd el-Qawwi, the water carrier, who grumbled to his companion:

"Is it right, after all I did for him, that I should get nothing worth mentioning out of it? Look at that black fellow, Othman, wearing the new shawl and cashmere sash. Look at his new tarboosh and his red slippers. There's Amm Madbuli; do you see that beautiful woolen galabia?—not to mention the new blanket and the dozen pair of socks . . . As for me, what have I got?"

Bayumi, the school usher, looked at him.

"What did you get, Abd el-Qawwi?"

"Nothing but these clumping shoes. The departed bought them for ten piasters in the secondhand market," the water carrier shouted.

The eunuch turned around to him, and spat on the ground, bellowing:

"Shut up, you damned fool! . . . You idiot!"

Translated by Denys Johnson-Davies

Abdel Salam al-Ujaili
(b. 1918)

SYRIA

Abdel Salam al-Ujaili was born in Rakka, Syria. By profession a doctor, he has also made a reputation as one of Syria's leading men of letters and has occupied various ministerial posts, including that of minister of culture. He was recently awarded one of the highest Syrian decorations in recognition of his services to his country. He is known chiefly as a writer of short stories, of which he has published nearly twenty volumes. He has also written two novels.

The Dream

In his dream Mohamed Weess saw himself praying. There was nothing extraordinary in this for in his waking hours he was continually praying and never put off performing one of the obligatory prayers. He saw himself reciting out loud, during his first prostration, the *Sura* of *al-Nasr* from the Koran and on coming to the end of it he had woken up in a state of terror.

"God's word is the truth!" he had said, sitting up in bed and wiping his eyes.

Mohamed Weess could not remember why it was that this of all his dreams should have fixed itself in his mind. However, when morning came he set off in search of Sheikh Mohamed Sa'id, the village elder. Around noon he ran him to ground and told him of his dream. The Sheikh, head lowered and with knotted brows, kept silent for a long time before asking:

"Are you sure that you were reciting the *Sura* of *al-Nasr*?"

"Absolutely," replied Mohamed Weess. "I recited it right through in full: 'When there comes God's help and victory, and thou shalt see men enter into God's religion by troops, then celebrate the praises of thy Lord, and ask forgiveness of Him, verily He is relentant!'"

"God's word is the truth!" said Sheikh Mohamed Sa'id. "Celebrate the praises of thy Lord, O Mohamed Weess, and ask forgiveness of Him, verily He is relentant."

"O Sheikh, I trust that this bodes well for me. What do you make of my dream?"

Sheikh Mohamed Sa'id grasped hold of his thick, broad beard and ran his fingers through it. He appeared hesitant about bestowing his great learning on the mere interpretation of dreams.

"O Mohamed Weess," he said eventually, "ask forgiveness of thy Lord, verily He is relentant. The reciting of this sura in one's dream is a sign that one's end is near."

Of a nervous disposition at the best of times, Mohamed Weess felt a shudder of dread course through his entire body.

"What are you saying, O Sheikh?"

"It pains me to face you with this," replied the Sheikh. "However, your consolation is that God's mercy will soon be yours and that death must come to us. No one who has this dream, Mohamed Weess, lives for more than another forty days."

Having delivered himself of this pronouncement, the Sheikh hurried off to make his ablutions for the midday prayer, leaving Mohamed Weess seated on the ground in a daze, his legs completely incapable of bearing the weight of his body.

"Forty days," he muttered through a parched throat. "God give me strength!"

The village in which Mohamed Weess and Mohamed Sa'id lived was a small one and by evening everyone knew of Mohamed Weess's dream and of Sheikh Mohamed Sa'id's interpretation of it. The village was one whose people believed in the interpretation of dreams and so by the following evening everyone was firmly convinced that Mohamed Weess would be dead within forty days. Singly, then in groups, the men paid visits to Mohamed Weess; he was thus forced to keep to his house to receive those who came, in anticipation of his death, to enquire into his health, and to condole with him during his lifetime, on this death. The womenfolk of Mohamed Weess's household came in search of news, casting telling glances at him. They found him in perfect health but with his features set in an abstracted air; mourning and wailing they beseeched God to intervene with the Angel of Death who was seeking to snatch him away while still as fit as ever. Though Mohamed Weess felt no pain or discomfort, the many precautions taken on his behalf, and the many tender enquiries made of him, induced in him an expectancy of pain and discomfort. He stuck it out for the first ten days and continued going and coming between his house and the cattle market. Soon, however, he was unable to hold out any longer; his nerves gave way and people began paying their visits to him during the daytime, whereas previously they had only found him at home in the evening. Twenty days from the date of his dream Mohamed Weess's family found that it was easier not to take up and remake his bed each night for the simple reason that he now remained in it night and day. When thirty days of the allotted period had passed, the various plates of his favourite foods, prepared specially for him by his family, accumulated at his bedside untouched. Dressed in an all-white garment and having let his beard grow, he spent his time in prayer. He wept, not from fear of death or in regret for life, but out of terror for the punishment that lay beyond the grave, and in dread lest God should not forgive him the many times he had taken His name in vain at the cattle market or had cheated the peasants from neighbouring villages. As the days melted away, drawing nearer to the fateful fortieth, so the store of fat which surrounded Mohamed Weess's stomach, empty with hunger, melted away and, in turn, through repentance, his past sins. People—those of his own village and those from round about—talked of the spiritual glow that emanated from his face and of the mystical and mysterious phrases which fell from his lips as he prostrated himself in prayer. Thirty-nine of the forty days passed, and on the evening of the thirty-ninth I made my appearance.

And who, you may well ask, am I?

I am the schoolmaster of the village in which Mohamed Weess works as broker at the cattle market and in which Sheikh Mohamed

Sa'id is regarded as the holy man. I used to spend my summer vacations in Damascus and my return to the school coincided with the thirty-ninth day of the period granted to Mohamed Weess by Mohamed Sa'id. I was acquainted with Mohamed Weess in the same way as I knew all the inhabitants of the village and when Mohamed Atallah, the elderly school porter, informed me about him I was at a loss to know whether to laugh or feel sorry for him. I therefore set off with Mohamed Atallah to comfort him—or to condole with him on his impending death. The courtyard, usually filled with the livestock which Mohamed Weess bought from the market, was now crowded with people who had come to witness the slow creeping of death into his soul. In one corner were the men, in another the women, while in the third stood the sheep and goats which Mohamed Weess's friends had brought during his lifetime that they might be slaughtered on the morrow for the departure of his soul. On entering the room in which Mohamed Weess awaited the Angel of Death, I found him—Mohamed Weess, not the Angel—seated on his bed in a corner praying, while Mohamed Sa'id sat in another corner reciting the Koran in rolling tones. I was struck by the change that had come over the face of the Mohamed Weess I had known: his rounded, ruddy face had become long and pallid, the appearance of length being further increased by his beard, while his pallor was accentuated by his loose-fitting white garment. As he prayed he protracted his prostrations as though wishing that death might take him during one of them. There was no similarity between this saint of God whose whole face exuded a spiritual glow and that other Mohamed Weess whom I used to hear each morning under the school window swearing by all that was holy that if he hadn't lost three liras on the sheep he'd just bought he'd divorce his wife. I had visited Mohamed Weess in a mood of skepticism and curiosity, but the extreme change that had come over him brought me up with a start and persuaded me that he would in fact die on the morrow as fate had decreed. I was filled with anger as I listened to Sheikh Mohamed Sa'id loudly reciting the Koran and glancing sideways at me.

Between myself and this Sheikh, whose nature was compounded

of simplicity, stupidity, and cunning, there existed an age-long enmity. I fought against the charlatanism and trickery with which he gained control of the souls of the ignorant villagers while he never missed an opportunity to set them against me, accusing me of teaching blasphemy to my students and filling their minds with disobedience against God and His Prophet. His zeal in his attacks against me was no wit lessened on learning from people that I came of a family which traced back its ancestry to Zain al-Abidin, the grandson of the Prophet's son-in-law. On the contrary he made this a justification for being hostile to me and used to say, "Look at this man, descended from Zain al-Abidin, who claims that the world turns round-itself; yet," he would say, "I put it to you, has ever any one of you seen the door of his house which was facing east suddenly turn to the west?"

I was, as I said, filled with anger on seeing Sheikh Mohamed Sa'id. I almost shouted out that he was a murderer, that he was killing Mohamed Weess with his poison, the poison of implanting in his mind the thought that he would die within forty days. I recollected, however, that I had never succeeded in getting the better of Mohamed Sa'id by being annoyed or angry, for he was always able to win over the village folk by producing that perennial argument which in his view showed that the earth did not turn. Had it ever happened that a villager had seen the door of his house facing towards the west after it had faced eastwards? And so, *ipso facto*, the earth did not turn. God have mercy on him for his rancour against me, and God, too, have mercy on Mohamed Weess should he remain under the crazy power of Sheikh Mohamed Sa'id till tomorrow morning. Heavy of heart with sorrow and anger, I went off to my room in the school building.

Mohamed Atallah, the school porter, woke me at dawn as I had asked. I had placed three prickly pears, brought with me from Damascus, under the water-jar which stood in the path of the cooling breeze. I took one of these and hurried off to Mohamed Weess's house. The courtyard was empty except for the sheep and goats awaiting their owner's death and so, in turn, their own. The women's quarters were lit up and a low sound of wailing issued forth. The door of Mohamed Weess's room was shut, so I glanced in through the closed window and saw that he was asleep, no doubt exhausted after his long night of praying in readiness for death. I knocked loudly several times, then pushed open the door shouting:

"Give praise to God, Mohamed Weess."

He started up from sleep in alarm. "What is it?" he cried.

"I'm Naji the teacher. Don't be afraid, Mohamed Weess, and listen to me."

I saw the tears trickling down Mohamed Weess's cheeks as he sat there tongue-tied with terror. Fearful that he would die of fright before hearing me out, I said:

"I have come to you because I have just been awakened by my ancestor Zain al-Abidin, God bless him, who said to me: 'Go to Mohamed Weess and tell him that God has tested him and found that he is a repentant servant of His. Give him this, one of the fruits of Paradise, and order him to pray with you and make two prostrations before the rising of the sun; in the first of the prostrations he should recite the *Sura* of *al-Nasr* and God will so extend his days that he shall live to see his children and his children's children.'"

Mohamed Weess swallowed his spittle. It seemed to me that his brain had not taken in all I had said to him as he gazed at the prickly pear I held in my hand. (I was sure that no one in the village had ever seen a prickly pear before.) I peeled it and stuffed it in his mouth, inviting him to swallow it, seeds and all. I then dragged him to a corner of the room.

"Prepare for prayers, Mohamed Weess, before daybreak."

"But I haven't performed my ablutions, Mr. Naji."

I recollected that I too had not performed my ablutions, but fearing that the effect of my suggestion would be lost, I exclaimed:

"Make a symbolical washing, O Mohamed Weess, as the Koran allows. Strike your hands upon the ground."

I prayed standing behind Mohamed Weess. We made two prostrations, during the first of which he recited the whole of the *Sura* of *al-Nasr*. Then I went back to the school to await daybreak.

Within an hour the whole village had heard the new story about Mohamed Weess. All those people who had filled the courtyard of

Mohamed Weess's house yesterday were now crowding the school-yard, all tumbling over themselves to learn how it was that my ancestor, Zain al-Abidin, had come to me bearing God's pardon for Mohamed Weess. At that moment I felt that here at last I had scored a decisive victory over Sheikh Mohamed Sa'id, for neither had Mohamed Weess died nor had the sheep and goats in his courtyard been slaughtered—they had been turned over to me, a present from Mohamed Weess's friends to that saint of God, schoolteacher Naji, the direct descendant of Zain al-Abidin!

But was it in fact a victory? In truth I am not sure. My doubts as to the value of this victory are increased by the fact that I have been unable to reduce by one single person the number of those who take part in communal prayers behind Sheikh Mohamed Sa'id; on the contrary, I have increased his congregation by one: the village teacher, which is to say myself! To preserve the honour of my fore-father, about whom I had fabricated my dream, I am obliged to attend in person behind Sheikh Mohamed Sa'id at all prayers—with ablutions performed, not symbolically but in full!

Translated by Denys Johnson-Davies

Mahmoud Al-Wardani

(b. 1950)

EGYPT

Mahmoud Al-Wardani was born in Cairo. He has published several collections of stories and six novels. He is a senior editor on Cairo's weekly literary magazine *Akhbar al-adab*.

The Day Grandpa Came

At the cool, shady entrance to the house, Mustafa stood leaning his shoulder against the rough wall next to his balcony on the first floor and watched them as they played football in the small lane.

The lane was cut off on the south by a low house whose windows were closed against the blazing heat of a cruel sun, in whose rays the boys seemed to float as they leapt about. Mustafa was wishing that these older boys would finish their game so that those of his own age could rush down right away and occupy the ground. In front of each house were a number of boys watching the game from the cool darkness of the entrances to their homes.

To the left of him the lane was open to Kitchener Street, the wide street that led to the one with all the crazy trucks traveling northward, while the trains, on the other side of the fence, never stopped their whistling and clattering.

He spotted the horse-drawn carriage as it approached, swaying slightly, from the direction of the hospital and stopped right in front of the lane. The ash-gray horse was restless under the burning sun and shook its neck up and down continuously in short movements.

With his back to Mustafa, the old man got down from the carriage and began to collect himself together before turning around to face him, with his white beard the color of milk and his red tarbush that shimmered inside the folds of the snow-white shawl wound around it. He moved slowly, his dark-colored stick dangling from his wrist. Adjusting the position of the three bags he was holding, he stomped along in his loose-fitting overcoat.

He looked all around him, appearing apprehensive as he almost collided with the players in the lane, which he had to cross in order to reach the other side. He tried to keep hold of the bags in his arms, while the stick jerked up and down just above the ground.

Mustafa had straightened up and moved a few steps away from the entrance, then stopped. —It's my grandpa, Sheikh Hashem, Mustafa said to himself, as he made an effort to bring him vaguely to mind. —It's him, it's Grandpa! A long time ago we left Grandpa's house in Mansoura and came back to Cairo. Then we lived in many different houses before settling down here close to the railway. Do you remember me, Grandpa? I remember when I would laugh at you when I saw your rosy face smiling at me. My mother will be happy. I can see her bursting into tears when she meets you.

Reaching the end of the lane, the old man turned in the direction of the children gathered behind the two stones set apart to indicate the goal. He bent down to one of the boys in the blazing sun, moving his head and his mouth. The boy made a sign toward the house, so he rearranged the three bags in his arms and went on his way. Passing close by Mustafa, he went into the dark stairway. He coughed as his stick gave the ground several short taps.

—So, how did you know we lived here, Grandpa? Yes, you're my grandpa, even though you passed right by me as you entered, and I was looking at you and you didn't recognize me. I saw your rosy face and that white beard of yours that I love encircling your face, and your loose clothes that are slightly damp at the neck. I remember all right. Two years have passed while I've been at school since you last came from Mansoura. You came once when I was in the third year and now I'm in the fifth.

Mustafa took the stairs at a run. At the door of the darkened flat he veered off to the hall, from the half-opened doors of which people were calling out to one another. He looked into the door of his family's room and saw his mother crying and muttering in a choked voice, with her face all twitching. His grandfather was laughing and saying in his hoarse, raucous voice, "How are you, my girl Kareema? How are you, girl?"

Before making a place for himself on the sofa, which was covered with a faded blue sheet and rested against the wall close to the open door, he removed his turban and chose a clean place for it alongside him. Then he spotted Mustafa and his face beamed with joy, and he opened his arms as he guffawed. "Come here, Sheikh Mustafa—in the name of God, who would believe it!"

Shy to begin with, the boy stepped toward him before rushing forward into his embrace. He breathed in the clean, dark-colored overcoat his grandfather was wearing. His head turned as he gave himself up to the arms encircling his shoulders. The old man patted his head and kissed him on the forehead.

"Where's Muna, Sheikh Mustafa? By God, you've grown!" he exclaimed.

The boy was trapped in the narrow space between the bed and

the sofa. He could hear the voices of the boys at play through the open balcony. The room seemed to him cramped, with his mother sitting on the floor beside the door, after taking the serving tray out from under the bed. She was wearing a light *gallabiya* of pale mauve with short sleeves and had a white kerchief tied around her head. There was only a very tiny space between the bed and the cupboard that stood next to the door, where she had lit the spirit stove and placed the kettle on it. Crying and trembling, she had propped herself against the cupboard and heard it give a sudden cracking noise. She allowed her gaze to rest on the two of them as she smiled.

"How are you, Grandpa?" said Mustafa. "I've missed you—and my aunts, and my uncle, too."

"By God, you've grown, Sheikh Mustafa," said his grandfather with a laugh. "And the girl Muna, has she grown as much as you?"

"I'll bring her to you right away, Grandpa," Mustafa answered.

He slipped away from him and was almost running when his grandfather called out, "Wait, man, . . . wait."

Putting his hand into a bag beside him, he brought out a fine yellow banana, whose aroma filled the room. Mustafa turned back again, seizing hold of the banana, but his grandfather continued to call out, "Steady, Sheikh Mustafa . . . Steady . . . Take it easy."

Undoing the buttons of the overcoat, he plunged his hand inside and took out a dark, creased leather wallet. He opened it up and produced a new ten-piaster note and pressed it into Mustafa's hand.

Mustafa turned around again, clutching the banana and the ten-piaster note.

Entering the hallway, he was surrounded by darkness. He made his way to the room of Umm Fatima, the mute woman; he found the door ajar and the room empty.

—But how did you get here, Grandpa? After my father died, my grandfather and my uncle came with the big van that looked like an elephant, and the porters filled it up with the many things that were in the house: the contents of a living room, a dining room, and a bedroom. They took us to Mansoura. We lived with them and they piled up our things in the small flat downstairs.

He retraced his steps and walked to Sayyid's room, Umm Nagat's son. Umm Nagat, who was squatting on the mattress plucking the *mulukhiya* leaves off their stalks, said, "There are devils up above at Umm Mohamed's."

She drew her legs together, pulled down her *gallabiya*, which had ridden up slightly, and smiled. "Who have you got with you, Mustafa?"

Leaning his shoulder against the door, he answered, "My grandfather . . . I was looking for Muna."

Before waiting for her answer he stepped back and went out. He jumped down the stairs, then came to a stop at the front door with the boys who were watching the game. Mustafa remembered how the first year after his father's death had passed. —My mother didn't know a moment's peace: my grandfather's dark-skinned wife used to scream at us—at me and Muna, my sister—whenever she saw us.

His heart was beating; he was breathless and could scarcely make out the players in front of him, nor yet the other boys who were around him. He did, however, see a boy close by gesturing to him.

"Mustafa," yelled the boy, "there was an old man who was asking about your mother."

"Yes, it's my grandfather," said Mustafa with a nod of his head.

He found himself darting through the lane, then crossing Kitchener Street to the main street with the crazy traffic going northward while the trains were whistling and making a din and creaking as they slowed down at the gates close to Cairo's main station.

—We used to eat with my mother in our room alone. I wasn't able to talk to my grandfather and laugh with him as I wanted. In fact, when my aunts had come back from school, my grandfather's wife would make me keep to our tiny, over-crowded flat, which I didn't like, until they had finished doing their homework. As for Muna, she was frightened of my grandfather's wife and would stay the whole time with my mother.

Mustafa reminded himself that he had to look for his sister Muna. The flaming sun, mixed with the sticky smell of exhaust fumes and heavy dust, stung him.

He turned back and started running again.

He told himself, "It was in the year when we had returned to Cairo that you dropped in on us, Grandpa—I don't know how. How did you know where our house was? We lived in so many, many houses before we settled in this room in Abdurrahman Khalil Alley."

He found himself going up the stairs and approaching the door of the flat. In the hallway he could hear the raucous voice of his grandfather gently saying to his mother, "Listen to what I'm saying—I know what's best for you."

His mother's voice was choked, so he brought his head closer in order to make out exactly what was going on. He was frightened.

"And the children?" he heard his mother replying.

"The man agrees to take both you and the children," he said slowly.

The mother ended the conversation by suddenly standing up, as she shouted, "Right from the beginning if I'd wanted . . . A man who's a stranger to my children—no, not a man who's a stranger to my children."

He heard his grandfather mumbling and shaking his head, but his mother interrupted him by answering, "I didn't ask a thing of you, nor from anyone else . . ."

He saw his grandfather immersed in the confined light of the balcony, squatting on the sofa in his cotton caftan with its pale stripes, with his overcoat beside him, clean and buttoned up and his bright red turban on top of it with the white shawl wound around it, lying near the three paper bags. His grandfather was not looking at his mother as he spoke to her. She sat with her back against the bed at a distance from him.

Mustafa's eyes met his mother's and he saw that they were bathed in tears and that her face was flushed. He turned to her, without looking at his grandfather, and said, "Muna's upstairs at Umm Mohamed's . . . I'm going up to see her."

Then he went out.

Translated by Denys Johnson-Davies

Tahir Wattar

(b. 1936)

ALGERIA

Tahir Wattar was one of the earliest Algerian writers to employ the Arabic language in his fiction. More than in Morocco and Tunisia, the long French colonial presence in Algeria extended to the work of creative writers. The scene selected here from Wattar's novel *The Earthquake* describes part of the central character's afternoon in Constantine, where he has arrived from Algiers in an attempt to prevent the government from nationalizing his land.

FROM *The Earthquake*

Shaykh Abdelmajid Boularwah turned in their direction and gave them a dirty look. When they saw him they moved away. He found himself staring at a sign on a wall opposite him that led up a flight of stairs onto a main road. The sign read: *Grammont Bill 1850: It is unlawful to abuse animals.* He looked in the direction of the mosque. He smiled, then resumed his walk downward as he looked at other signs on the walls: *Chantilly Brothers: Travel Agency: Constantine, Ain Baida, Khanshia, Tebessa, Sedrata and Township of Constantine: Department of Water and Public Utilities.*

I'll take a shortcut here on the left, he decided, but then suddenly stopped.

"Police, police!" yelled someone from the crowd.

Gangs of young boys shot out from all directions, running away and carrying utensils, spools of cloth, packages of meat, cleavers and knives. A police car whizzed by without stopping as the young boys kept on running, racing each other to get to a secure place. The screaming grew louder as the crowd of boys thickened. There were even grown-ups running along in the confusion. In the midst of it all a young boy fell to the ground with a knife in his stomach and blood flowing in the street.

"He fell on his knife."

"Someone pushed him."

"He's going to die."

"That's for sure."

"Stop a car and get him to a hospital."

"Ammar tripped him."

"No, it was Boujum'a."

"No, he fell on his own."

"I've got seven sheep's heads. Do you want to buy some?"

"Not me. I've got twenty tripes I've got to get rid of."

"Look, he's dead."

The boys disappeared with their stolen meat and only the boy lying on the ground with the knife in his stomach dripping with blood was left behind. A crowd of old men and women gathered around him. Shaykh Boularwah spat in disgust. Deep down he felt glad. He continued on his way, walking down the stone pavement taking wide steps.

As he walked, he was assaulted by a strong, putrid odour. He looked to see where it was coming from. On the grounds of a municipal building there was a pool of stale, brackish water. On the left was a barbed-wire fence that surrounded a huge military barracks. Half of it was being used by the army while the other half had been made into a warehouse for storing food.

Even here there is a warehouse!

The street extends on the right-hand side. There are houses of mud brick covered with sheets of corrugated tin and corrugated tin houses covered with mud. There are several residential units in the area. Scraps of paper, blocks of wood and sheets of tin pollute the streets and sidewalks. Rusty water gushes out from all sides, forming little streams that all seem to come together at the top of the street.

When Sidi Rashid chooses the second solution and shakes this rock free of all these people and their wicked, sinful ways, he won't have to exert much effort. All it will take will be for one of the

Kudiya buildings to topple over these shacks and smash them. Then these streams of water will flush them all into the Rhumel Valley.

Three unveiled women suddenly came out of an alley. They walked down the street, looking as though they had a long way yet to go. He stared at them from the corner of his eye.

Still in their prime, but they look so gaunt, with dark complexions and puffy eyes. One of them was wearing trousers, another a loose flowing dress and the third a skirt above her thighs.

"He said we're going to Oran. We'll stay there a week and then come back."

"I'm not going anywhere!"

"What's holding you here in this cemetery? One beer costs more than water from the Zemzem well in Mecca."

"But we have no idea who his two friends are."

"So why should that bother you. Why do you care?"

"I'm not going anywhere out of Constantine, especially during the wedding season."

"So you dance all night long for a measly ten bucks that'll only end up in your pimp's pocket. Come with us to Oran for a few days. It'll do you good to get away and relax."

Just at the moment that the three women were about to pass Shaykh Boularwah, one of them started to sing in a loud voice:

"O, good neighbour, Hammoud, come and do with me as you please!"

A whiff of expensive perfume filled his lungs and he lowered his eyes as they passed him. The scent of the perfume started to fade away and a nauseating stench replaced it. He looked up and right in front of him were black spots that covered part of the dirt road and the two sides of the street. He looked more closely and made out that they were goat skins. He recalled the scene of the boy lying on the street with the knife in his stomach and the other boys waving their hands with the meat, knives and cleavers. He spat and continued on his way.

Translated by William Granara

Latifa al-Zayyat
(1923–96)
EGYPT

Latifa al-Zayyat took her doctorate in England and was a professor of English at Ain Shams University, Cairo. Two of her novels, *The Owner of the House* and *The Open Door*, are available in English translation. The events of *The Open Door*, published in 1960, begin in 1946 and end a decade later with the attack by Israeli, British, and French forces on Suez. The novel was strikingly modern for its time, not only in its depiction of the central character's political and sexual development, but also in its use of the colloquial language, a stylistic choice that is still considered politically, culturally, and religiously divisive. The novel was made into a popular Egyptian movie.

FROM *The Open Door*

From behind the tombs, heads rose, and hands settled in wary readiness onto rifles and machine guns. But the signal had not yet come. The airplanes released more parachutists behind the wall of the airport, and the parachutes ballooned, one after another, white, like abscesses full of pus.

In their defense positions at al-Gabbana, the forces fidgeted, hands shaking with impatient rage on the guns. But still the signal did not come. Hundreds of anxious eyes moved between the commander and the opening parachutes spread across the air. The commander sensed the heavy anxiety around him; he could almost hear the mute question that choked the air—the question asked over and over by the individuals of the popular resistance, and even by the trained army personnel who were accustomed to obeying orders without question.

What are we waiting for?

The commander went on waiting. Not a muscle in his face moved. Layla wiped the sweat off her brow and whispered to Isam, "What are we waiting for?" Isam put out a shaking hand and patted hers, smiling at her in his shy, half-smiling way. They felt close, as if the waiting that trembled in each one's depths had erased the chasm between them, when Layla had insisted on following Isam to his post and, in front of his commander, had embarrassed him into acquiescing. She fidgeted anxiously now, fear creeping through her. It was not death that frightened her, no longer. What was she? A drop in an ocean, and the ocean would surge whether or not she was there. If she were to die, she would be one of thousands who had died; if she lived, she would still be one of millions whose right to live had been plundered. No, it was not death that frightened her, nor the enemy who was hidden there behind the airport wall. Her major enemy crouched here, deep inside, waiting to attack. She closed her eyes against that weakness and pressed her lips together tightly so that no tremble could penetrate. Once again she was experiencing that overpowering desire to look out for those around her and to feel that she was one with them, part of a larger whole. She straightened a bit behind the grave that shielded her and raised her head cautiously. Before her eyes stretched rows of heads, some covered by helmets, others bare, some were black mingled with white, others very young. Her body grew slack again as she watched this huge mass of heads. When she turned to look behind, again she saw face after face, some tense, others calm, row after row of massed faces. When her eyes came to one face she sucked in her breath and held it, seeing in her mind's eye Adil digging the grave of his beloved, throwing his head back, in his eyes that look she would never forget. For it was the same expression—the same blend of love, fierce loathing, challenge, determination, and assured readiness—she now saw in the eyes of this man. Adil? She took a deep breath and swept her eyes across the faces. Every face was different but now she saw something that had escaped her notice before, the same look she had seen in Adil's eyes. She turned to gaze forward again, exhilarated. She felt strong. She was no longer alone.

She was with them now. With them, and the love that pounded in their hearts was in hers, too, and so was the loathing, and something of the calm, assured preparedness. Before Layla appeared her own image, bending to snatch the oar as it sank into the Nile. Yes, at the right moment that stronger person hidden inside would push open the door, would go out calmly and coolly, would act wisely, exactly as she must. Yes, when the moment came the miracle would happen. Her eyes swam with a vision too lovely to bear.

Noticing her tears, Isam attributed them to fear. "Go back, Layla. The door, the gate—it's just over there. Crawl over to the gate." His voice became softer. "You're a woman, no one will blame you, this isn't your place, after all."

Layla felt dizzy, as if she were looking down from a high tower. Deep inside she felt that trembling helplessness again. Could she? Could she do it? Could she stay, could she keep going? When she was a woman? A woman, and that was all. Where would the strength come from? Where?

The enemy airplanes were releasing a new wave of parachutists into the airport grounds, within range of the fire of the armed defense forces in al-Gabbana. At the same time, the wind began to howl. Strong, angry gusts hurled into the air a yellow curtain of sand, as the airplanes dropped load after load inside the airport. The wind carried some of them far, in the direction of the neighboring area, toward civilian homes.

The commander gave the signal.

"Hit him! Give it to him!" It was the quavering voice of an old woman, hunched on the ground, staring straight ahead; the child she held in her arms wailed. A heavy rock in the hand of a young woman sailed at the head of a parachutist as he tried to get his balance. He fell to the ground, his skull shattered. The young woman stood straight, putting up her left hand to wipe away the sweat. But before her hand could touch her forehead she dashed forward, screaming. She had noticed more parachutists falling, a swarm of bats. Her shout reached other women, inside their huts preparing food for their children, for husbands and sons who would return—or would not. The scream told them that the danger their sons and husbands had gone to meet was knocking at their doors. The wooden slats were flung wide open and women came out armed with the weapons they had ready. Necks of broken bottles, kitchen knives, heavier blades, pestles. The high-pitched screaming reached the children standing in awe and curiosity before a hut that sat alone far to the right. They scattered, terrified. Inside the hut a woman tried to get up, fear on her face. She bent double as the pain that had gnawed at her since the morning came again. The hands of the midwife, gripping the rim of a pan of boiling water that she had been trying to lift from the burner, stopped. She straightened, ran to the door, paused to glance around. The woman inside moaned, sweat pouring from her forehead onto her eyes.

"What is it?" her voice was choked. The midwife went back inside, her face grim, snatched two rags from the floor, and raised the boiling water. She strode to the door as the young woman screamed in despair and pain. She crawled after the midwife, the sweat almost blinding her, her body convulsing in rapid contractions. At the threshold she clutched the midwife's ankle, muttering, "Don't leave me, don't leave me alone." But she could not go on, for the pain attacked her again, sharper this time, unbearable. She felt something round and hard almost pulling from her body and muttered, "I can't, I'm done for." Still at the threshold, the midwife turned to look at the young woman flat on the dirt floor behind her. Their eyes met. In the midwife's eyes the young woman saw reflected what was happening outside, she saw the death that threatened her, that endangered the life pulsing in her belly. Her grip on the midwife's leg relaxed; she curled up and broke out in sobs. The midwife left the hut, steam rising from the boiling water. The woman raised her head, tears standing in her eyes, and began to slither across the floor to her mattress. Carefully she lay down, pulled up a white sheet, and covered her body.

It was her first baby. She had never done this before, but she would do it. She would give birth, by herself, no matter what was happening around her. The child was there inside of her and wanted to come out. All she had to do was to help. She must relax, but that seemed impossible. A scream of fear from outside jolted her body; the wail of a child, a whispered "there is no god but God," a wait. Steps thrusting forward, calls, a clattering on tin rooftops as if horses galloped there, the voice of the bent old woman trembling in the air. "Hit him! Give it to him!" A moan, the howl of a dog, black smoke curling into the hut. Drops of water hissing on the fire, screams of pain, a silence harsher than the noise. A group pushing, colliding with the wooden walls, shots, the voice of the old woman ringing out, a huge explosion that shook the hut until she thought it would collapse over her. And then a wait, harsher than the explosion.

The face of the young woman, lying on the bed, her body convulsing. She bit on the hem of the white sheet, balled up in her mouth. She must . . . she must . . . relax . . . or the child would die in her belly. She ripped the sheet from her mouth and wiped the sweat off her face. She tried, with the endurance only a birthing mother knows, to concentrate all her attention on the child threatened with death inside her body.

Little by little the wailing, the fire, all of the moaning and smoke and frightened steps and long groans and suppressed sounds of victory disappeared. The outside world disappeared. There was no longer anything in her consciousness but this child, this child who wanted to come out, into life. As the children slipped from their hiding places, as the older ones gathered the butcher's knives, the kitchen knives, and the ropes used to hunt down the parachuting soldiers, as the women dried their sweat, their heads still dizzy, as if they had awakened suddenly after a frightening dream, before counting their losses and gains, before realizing exactly what they had just done, the air carried a thin, broken wail that soon became an unbroken cry, stronger, clear, a ululation of joy, the scream of life.

Layla screamed, a ululation of joy. The human masses pushed her forward toward the airport. The second wave of parachutists had been mowed down on the airport grounds and the remnants of the first wave were in retreat before the Egyptian forces. British airplanes hovered over the spot where the two forces engaged but could get no nearer and withdrew, powerless. A battery of explosions in quick succession erupted in scattered parts of the city, and fires broke out in the petrol depots, in homes, along the city streets. The English forces tried to slip the encirclement, tried to return to their hiding places behind the walls of the airport. The Egyptian forces pressed on to block their escape. The ground was exploding—storms of sand, fire flaming from the guns, a flood of shots leaving big circles in the sand, white smoke, green spots gleaming, reflected in people's eyes. Bodies falling, the dead, the wounded crawling behind the lines, people pushing forward to take their places.

Among the dead lay Isam; among the wounded, Layla. The circle tightened around the English soldiers and the circle of fire tightened on the city. The sun was setting, and darkness settled on the scene. A flame, a flickering light, kept the darkness at bay, and revealed from afar the enemy in bedraggled retreat.

Translated by Marilyn Booth

Mohamed Zefzaf
(1945–2001)
MOROCCO

Mohamed Zefzaf lived his early life in the poor quarter of Qunaytira and studied at the Rabat College of Humanities. He later became a schoolteacher in Casablanca and was one of Morocco's leading novelists and short story writers. His complete works have been issued by the Moroccan Ministry of Culture. Several of his novels have appeared in French, Spanish, and Russian translations. As with most writers from North Africa, little of his work is available in English.

Snake Hunting

"I'm only an old woman, a widow," she said. "I've no children, no one in this world but God. If I don't defend myself, who will?"

"I'm frightened that one day one of the snakes will do for you," said a woman.

"If God means for a person to die, be it by the sting of a piece of rope, there's no one can stand against Him. And anyway, even though I kill so many snakes each year, the place still isn't rid of them."

She was well known for killing snakes. She had a special way of seeking them out under a pile of straw or a stone. She had bracelets made of snake skin, as well as belts, of various colors. The snakes' heads she would sell to itinerant druggists in exchange for sugar, tea, oil, or soap; she was told they were used in magic and sometimes for treating children, though she herself had never thought of employing magic, even for the sake of the person most close to her, her late husband. She knew that every sorceress came to a bad end: a broken leg, or blindness in both eyes, or the loss of a child or of livestock.

A woman carrying a basket filled with mud on her head looked at her. "Sister, I don't know how God gave you this courage and strength to attack snakes and vipers in their lairs."

"Why should I be afraid? As a child I saw my grandfather mount a horse in the middle of the night, as naked as God created Adam. Then he gave chase to a band of robbers who had come to steal our cows. He feared neither the cold nor the robbers' guns. At the end of that night I saw him firing down into the plain at the robbers. He returned home only when he'd got the cows back. My grandmother went and covered him up lest we see his nakedness. How can a woman like me with such a grandfather be afraid of snakes?"

The woman went off and left the old widow. Several parts of her body were wound round with variously colored snake skins. She was scattering seed to her chickens and calling to two cockerels that had strayed away from the rest. She dug her fingers into the ground and threw a clod of earth at the cockerels, which immediately joined up with the others. Their brilliant colors glistened under the sun's rays.

She would count her hens every two hours in case some snake or other animal—or even a human being—had passed by. More than forty years ago there had been foxes and wolves, but these had now completely disappeared. Perhaps they had been exterminated by the people who had built these scattered houses that were visited only at night in order to do things with the women there. The number of her hens had not grown less, nor would it do so, for she took care of them. She would sell one only when it had become plump. She was proud of the fact that her chickens were the plumpest and their eggs the biggest; the eggs of other people's hens were as small as pigeons' eggs or goat droppings.

She made her way toward the house built of mud and straw. Seeing Azzouz coming in her direction and getting down from his cart, she smiled to herself: she had thought of something to say to him that was likely to enrage him—though in fact he never got angry with her. Still several paces away from her, she heard him say, "And how are you, you old mouse? Still hunting snakes?"

"Men aren't capable of it. Do you remember when there were eight of you and just one snake was able to get the better of you and you were only able to kill it by drowning it? What sort of manliness was that? You became the laughingstock of your wives and daughters."

"Our mothers didn't suckle us on poison as yours did."

"What sort of manliness was that? The best of men, the best of all of you died and I wouldn't marry after he died. There's no man worth a nail paring of his."

"May God have mercy upon him! Why talk of those who have died, you old mouse?"

"Your wife's situation is no better than mine."

The two of them began to laugh. Then she threw down the dried-up branch she was carrying, brushed the dirt from her hands, and wiped them on her gown.

"Have you been to Ain Diab?"

"Yes, but I left the cart on the track by the seashore and carried the two sacks of fodder on my back right up to the cart. I avoided the main road because you know what the police could do to me if they caught me."

"I do."

"We also needed a sack of sugar. We'll split it among us all— that's why I've come to you."

"Leave me a kilogram or two, though I don't have any money."

"Ever since the death of your husband you've been one of us. When have we ever asked you for money? You can pay with a chicken. We can see about it later on when I've had a word with the gang."

Turning in the direction of the cart, he said, "If you need any fodder, we have some. You can come and take it or I'll send it to you with the girl Mannana."

At that moment she felt she wasn't really on her own. On the other hand, she would feel all alone when she thought about those accursed snakes that threatened her chickens the whole year round. When her chickens were attacked by some disease, that was God's decree and had nothing to do with anyone. But when she told herself that she was still capable of killing a snake, she felt assured that God would not one day let her die of hunger.

She had her own special way of hunting snakes. She would lie in wait for the snake whenever she heard her chickens cackling. Having discovered its hiding-place, she would quickly grab it by the tail and whirl it around and around in the air until it became dizzy, then bang it time and time again against a sharp piece of rock. When the rock was bespattered with blood and she felt the snake's body had lost all power of resistance, she would throw it to one side—but keep an eye on it from a distance. Seldom, though, did the snake's body make any movement, for she threw it aside only when she was certain it was dead. Sometimes a snake would make its escape and hide among the stones of the wall, though the old widow was quite capable of spending the whole day waiting for it to emerge.

She entered the house. Hearing someone outside calling "Auntie!" she immediately recognized the voice. She went out into the courtyard.

"Mannana!" called the old woman. "Come along, come nearer. Do you want an egg to boil?"

"My father sent you this nosebag," said the young girl. "It is full of fodder."

"Come along, come nearer."

The girl was barefoot, her head done up in a tattered kerchief. From her hand there dangled a nosebag made of doum-palm leaves, trailing along the ground. She rid herself of the nosebag and began scratching her backside, then her hair. The old woman noticed this and told her, "You're all dirty. You most likely don't let your mother wash you when she wants to. Your hair will get full of lice—and having a lot of lice shortens one's life. You've got to live a long time so you can marry and have some sons for your mother."

She approached the girl and took up the nosebag, hanging it on a wooden peg sticking out from the wall. Then she went into the house and came out with an egg in her hand, which she gave to the girl.

"Careful you don't break it."

"Do you still hunt snakes, Auntie?" Mannana said to her.

"They've disappeared these days. If I didn't do it, I wouldn't have a single live chicken."

"I'm frightened you'll be bitten one day by a snake."

"Don't be frightened—your auntie's still strong enough to kill all the snakes of Ouled Jerrar. Do you want me to boil the egg for you?"

"No, I'll boil it at home."

"Boil it and eat it on your own—and don't offer any of it to anyone."

"All right."

The young girl disappeared behind the trees that acted as a hedge around the old woman's house to the west. There was a mud oven over near the front door. Some hours ago she had put some dry charcoal in it and was now waiting for the pieces to catch fire. It was hard going, though, despite feeding it with kerosene. At first the flames had flared up, but this had had no effect on the dry charcoal. From time to time she would hear the crackling of flames coming from the mud oven and would go out and have a look at the pieces of charcoal in the hope they would have reddened, and several times she fanned the oven with a piece of tin and then blew on it. She put a pot on top of the oven, containing some sardines, carrots, and flour. She did not know who would be sharing the meal with her that day. Sitting on the hot sands, she heard the chickens cackling as they scattered, and she told herself that there must be a snake about. She got to her feet ready for action and went off in search of it. Her eyes bulged as she looked for it among the grasses. Behind her she heard Mannana's voice, "Auntie, is it a snake?"

She turned to her. "Haven't you gone home yet?"

"No, the egg broke."

"I told you so. Stay where you are so the snake doesn't bite you. I'll boil you another egg."

The chickens scattered in terror, jumping up onto the short reeds that grew around about. The old woman looked for some sign of the snake but could not find it. There was only a frog, its head tucked into its body, slowly hopping along.

"There's no snake," said the old woman, "—only a frog."

"Kill it like you kill the snakes," said the little girl.

"No, I don't kill frogs," said the old woman. "Come and kill it yourself. Come and learn how to kill frogs before killing snakes."

The little girl approached, looking at the fat frog.

"Pounce on it quickly," said the old woman, "and seize it by its legs and swing it around in the air till it's dizzy, then bang it against this sharp rock."

Mannana was timid, frightened, but some strong urge spurred her on to pounce down and seize the frog by the leg. Then she began swinging it around and around like some rag toy, while the woman egged her on. "Go on, go on, it's not dizzy yet." Then Mannana banged the frog against the sharp piece of rock and its intestines spurted out, though its body still stirred in its death throes. The old woman went up close and looked down at the body, then pulled the child away by her hand.

"That's what I do with snakes. Now you'll wash your hands and I'll boil you an egg. Next time I'll teach you how to kill a snake."

Translated by Denys Johnson-Davies

Acknowledgments

Thanks are due to a number of friends in Cairo and other parts of the Arab world for suggestions about writers who might be included in the anthology, as well as useful snippets of information about when a certain writer was born or the exact title of another writer's first novel. Such friends include three experts on the subject of modern Arabic literature—Ferial Ghazoul and Samia Mehrez of the American University in Cairo (AUC), and Mona Anis of the *Al-Ahram Weekly* newspaper—and two fellow translators, Peter Clark and Humphrey Davies. Additionally, at the AUC Press, Jacinthe Assaad, Shaymaa Abdou, and Sigrún Valsdóttir all valiantly searched the shelves of the AUC Library for copies of books that I wished to consult. I owe a special word of thanks to Mark Linz, director of the AUC Press, for making it possible for me to undertake this project. I am grateful to Neil Hewison, who once again was my editor, not only for doing the job of an editor with his usual tact but also for being available to discuss with me basic questions about the shape the book should take.

Sources of Stories and Excerpts

Ibrahim Abdel Meguid. Translated by Farouk Abdel Wahab. *No One Sleeps in Alexandria*. Cairo: The American University in Cairo Press, 1999. Translation copyright © 1999 by the American University in Cairo Press.

Mohammed Abdul-Wali. Translated by Abubaker Bagader and Deborah Akers. "Ya Khabiir." *They Die Strangers*. Austin: Center for Middle Eastern Studies at the University of Texas at Austin, 2001. Translation copyright © 2001 by the Center for Middle Eastern Studies at the University of Texas at Austin.

Yahya Taher Abdullah. Translated by Denys Johnson-Davies. "Rhythms in Slow Time." *The Mountain of Green Tea*. Cairo: The American University in Cairo Press, 1983. Translation copyright © 1983 by Denys Johnson-Davies.

Leila Abouzeid. Translated by Barbara Parmenter. "The Discontented." *The Year of the Elephant: A Moroccan Woman's Journey Toward Independence*. Cairo: The American University in Cairo Press, 1992. Translation copyright © 1989 by the Center for Middle Eastern Studies at the University of Texas at Austin.

Yusuf Abu Rayya. Translated by Denys Johnson-Davies. "Dreams Seen by a Blind Boy." *Arabic Short Stories*. London: Quartet Books, 1983. Translation copyright © 1983 by Denys Johnson-Davies.

Idris Ali. Translated by Peter Theroux. *Dongola: A Novel of Nubia*. Fayetteville: The University of Arkansas Press, 1998. Translation copyright © 1998 by the Board of Trustees of the University of Arkansas. Reprinted by permission of the University of Arkansas Press.

Daisy Al-Amir. Translated by Barbara Parmenter. "The Doctor's Prescription." *The Waiting List: An Iraqi Woman's Tales of Alienation*. Austin:

Center for Middle Eastern Studies at the University of Texas at Austin, 1994. Translation copyright © 1994 by the Center for Middle Eastern Studies at the University of Texas at Austin.

Radwa Ashour. Translated by Marilyn Booth. "I Saw the Date-Palms." *My Grandmother's Cactus: Stories by Egyptian Women.* London: Quartet Books, 1991. Translation copyright © 1991 by Marilyn Booth.

Ibrahim Aslan. Translated by Denys Johnson-Davies. "The Little Girl in Green." *Arabic Short Stories.* London: Quartet Books, 1983. Translation copyright © 1983 by Denys Johnson-Davies.

————. Translated by Mona El-Ghobashy. *Nile Sparrows.* Cairo: The American University in Cairo Press, 2004. Translation copyright © 2004 by the American University in Cairo Press.

Alaa Al Aswany. Translated by Humphrey Davies. *The Yacoubian Building.* Cairo: The American University in Cairo Press, 2004. Translation copyright © 2004 by the American University in Cairo Press.

Liana Badr. Translated by Sahar Hamouda. "Extracts from *A Land of Stone and Thyme.*" Edited by Nur and Abdelwahab Elmessiri. *A Land of Stone and Thyme: An Anthology of Palestinian Short Stories.* London: Quartet Books, 1996.

Hala El Badry. Translated by Farouk Abdel Wahab. *A Certain Woman.* Cairo: The American University in Cairo Press, 2003. Translation copyright © 2003 by the American University in Cairo Press.

Salwa Bakr. Translated by Denys Johnson-Davies. "Dotty Noona." *The Wiles of Men and Other Stories.* Cairo: The American University in Cairo Press, 1992. Translation copyright © 1992 by Denys Johnson-Davies.

————. Translated by Dinah Manisty. *The Golden Chariot.* Reading: Garnet Publishing Ltd., 1995. Translation copyright © 1995 by Dinah Manisty.

Hoda Barakat. Translated by Marilyn Booth. *The Tiller of Waters.* Cairo: The American University in Cairo Press, 2001. Translation copyright © 2001 by the American University in Cairo Press.

Mohammed Barrada. Translated by Denys Johnson-Davies. "Life by Installments." *Arabic Short Stories.* London: Quartet Books, 1983. Translation copyright © 1983 by Denys Johnson-Davies.

Mohamed El-Bisatie. Translated by Denys Johnson-Davies. "Drought." *A Last Glass of Tea and Other Stories.* Cairo: The American University in Cairo Press, 1994. Translation copyright © 1994 by Denys Johnson-Davies.

————. Translated by Hala Halim. *Clamor of the Lake.* Cairo: The American University in Cairo Press, 2004. Translation copyright © 2004 by the American University in Cairo Press.

Mohamed Choukri. Translated by Denys Johnson-Davies. "Flower Crazy." *Arabic Short Stories.* London: Quartet Books, 1983. Translation copyright © 1983 by Denys Johnson-Davies.

Rashid al-Daif. Translated by Paul Starkey. *Dear Mr. Kawabata.* London: Quartet Books, 1999. Translation copyright © 1999 by Paul Starkey.

Zayd Mutee' Dammaj. Translated by May Jayyusi and Christopher Tingley. *The Hostage.* New York: Interlink Books, an imprint of Interlink Publishing Group, Inc., copyright © 1984 by Zayd Mutee' Dammaj. Translation copyright © 1994 by Salma Khadra Jayyusi (PROTA). Reprinted by permission.

Brahim Dargouthi. Translated by Denys Johnson-Davies. "Apples of Paradise." *Under the Naked Sky.* Cairo: The American University in Cairo Press, 2000. Translation copyright © 2000 by the American University in Cairo Press.

Ahmad Faqih. Translated by Russell Harris, Amin al-'Ayouti, and Suraya 'Allam. *Gardens of the Night: A Trilogy.* London: Quartet Books, 1995. Translation copyright © 1995 by Quartet Books.

Fathy Ghanem. Translated by Denys Johnson-Davies. "Sunset." *Azure: The Review of Arabic Literature, Arts and Culture*, n.d. Translation copyright © *Azure*.

Gamal al-Ghitani. Translated by Farouk Abdel Wahab. *Zayni Barakat.* Cairo: The American University in Cairo Press, 2004. Translation copyright © 1988 by Farouk Abdel Wahab.

Nabil Gorgy. Translated by Denys Johnson-Davies. "Cairo Is a Small City." *Arabic Short Stories.* London: Quartet Books, 1983. Translation copyright © 1983 by Denys Johnson-Davies.

Abdou Gubeir. Translated by Denys Johnson-Davies. "Have You Seen Alexandria Station?" *Under the Naked Sky.* Cairo: The American University in Cairo Press, 2000. Translation copyright © 2000 by the American University in Cairo Press.

Emile Habiby. Translated by Anthony Calderbank. "At Last the Almond Blossomed." Edited by Nur and Abdelwahab Elmessiri. *A Land of Stone and Thyme.* London: Quartet Books, 1996. Translation copyright © 1996 by Nur and Abdelwahab Elmessiri.

Tawfik al-Hakim. Translated by Abba Eban. *Diary of a Country Prosecutor.* London: Saqi Books, 2005. Translation copyright © 1989 by Zeinab al-Hakim.

Yahya Hakki. Translated by Denys Johnson-Davies. "The Lamp of Umm Hashim." *The Lamp of Umm Hashim and Other Stories.* Cairo: The American University in Cairo Press, 2004. Translation copyright © 2004 by the American University in Cairo Press.

————. Translated by Denys Johnson-Davies. "A Story from Prison." *The Lamp of Umm Hashim and Other Stories.* Cairo: The American University in Cairo Press, 2004. Translation copyright © 2004 by the American University in Cairo Press.

Sherif Hetata. Translated by Sherif Hetata. *The Net.* London: Zed Books Ltd., 1986. Translation copyright © 1986 by Sherif Hetata.

Bensalem Himmich. Translated by Roger Allen. *The Polymath.* Cairo: The American University in Cairo Press, 2004. Translation copyright © 2004 by the American University in Cairo Press.

Taha Hussein. Translated by Mona El-Zayyat. *A Man of Letters.* Cairo: The American University in Cairo Press, 1994. Translation copyright © 1994 by the American University in Cairo Press.

Gamil Atia Ibrahim. Translated by Denys Johnson-Davies. "The Old Man." *Arabic Short Stories.* London: Quartet Books, 1983. Translation copyright © 1983 by Denys Johnson-Davies.

Sonallah Ibrahim. Translated by Anthony Calderbank. *Zaat.* Syracuse, NY: Syracuse University Press, 2001. Translation copyright © 2004 by the American University in Cairo Press.

————. Translated by Mary St. Germain and Charlene Constable. *The Committee*. Cairo: The American University in Cairo Press, 2002. Translation copyright © 2001 by Syracuse University Press.

Ulfat Idlibi. Translated by Peter Clark. *Sabriya: Damascus Bitter Sweet*. New York: Interlink Books, 1997. Translation copyright © 1997 by Peter Clark.

Yusuf Idris. Translated by Denys Johnson-Davies. "House of Flesh." *Egyptian Short Stories*. Colorado Springs: Three Continents Press, 1978. Translation copyright © 1978 by Denys Johnson-Davies.

————. Translated by R. Neil Hewison. *City of Love and Ashes*. Cairo: The American University in Cairo Press, 1998. Translation copyright © 1998 by the American University in Cairo Press.

Walid Ikhlassi. Translated by Denys Johnson-Davies. "The Dead Afternoon." *Modern Arabic Short Stories*. Cairo: The American University in Cairo Press, 1993. Translation copyright © 1967 by Denys Johnson-Davies.

Jabra Ibrahim Jabra. Translated by Roger Allen and Adnan Haydar. *In Search of Walid Masoud*. Syracuse: Syracuse University Press, 2000. Translation copyright © 2000 by Syracuse University Press.

Said al-Kafrawi. Translated by Denys Johnson-Davies. "The Hill of Gypsies." *The Hill of Gypsies and Other Stories*. Cairo: The American University in Cairo Press, 1998. Translation copyright © 1998 by the American University in Cairo Press.

Ghassan Kanafani. Translated by Denys Johnson-Davies. "The Slave Fort." *Arabic Short Stories*. London: Quartet Books, 1983. Translation copyright © 1983 by Denys Johnson-Davies.

————. Translated by Hilary Kilpatrick. *Men in the Sun*. Boulder: Lynne Reinner Publishers, 1999. Translation copyright © 1978 by Lynne Reinner.

Sahar Khalifeh. Translated by Trevor Le Gassick and Elizabeth Fernea. *Wild Thorns*. New York: Olive Branch Press, 1989. Translation copyright © 1989 by PROTA.

Edwar al-Kharrat. Translated by Ferial Ghazoul and John Verlenden. *Rama and the Dragon*. Cairo: The American University in Cairo Press, 2002. Translation copyright © 2002 by the American University in Cairo Press.

Betool Khedairi. Translated by Muhayman Jamil. *A Sky So Close.* New York: Anchor Books, 2001. Translation copyright © 2001 by Betool Khedairi. Reprinted by permission of Anchor Books, a division of Random House, Inc.

Elias Khoury. Translated by Paula Haydar. *The Journey of Little Gandhi.* Minneapolis: University of Minnesota Press, 1994. Translation copyright © 1994 by the University of Minnesota Press.

Mohamed Khudayir. Translated by Denys Johnson-Davies. "Clocks Like Horses." *Arabic Short Stories.* London: Quartet Books, 1983. Translation copyright © 1983 by Denys Johnson-Davies.

Ibrahim al-Koni. Translated by May Jayyusi and Christopher Tingley. *The Bleeding of the Stone.* New York: Interlink Books, an imprint of Interlink Publishing Group, Inc., 2002, copyright © 2002 by Ibrahim al-Koni. Translation copyright © 2002 by Salma Khadra Jayyusi (PROTA). Reprinted by permission.

―――. Translated by Denys Johnson-Davies. "The Ill-Omened Golden Bird." *Under the Naked Sky.* Cairo: The American University in Cairo Press, 2000. Translation copyright © 2000 by the American University in Cairo Press.

Naguib Mahfouz. Translated by Denys Johnson-Davies. "The Conjurer Made Off with the Dish." *The Time and the Place and Other Stories.* Cairo: The American University in Cairo Press, 1991. Translation copyright © 1978 by Denys Johnson-Davies.

―――. Translated by Denys Johnson-Davies. *Arabian Nights and Days.* Cairo: The American University in Cairo Press, 1996. Translation copyright © 1996 by the American University in Cairo Press.

―――. Translated by William Maynard Hutchins and Olive E. Kenny. *Palace Walk.* Cairo: The American University in Cairo Press, 1989. Translation copyright © 1989 by the American University in Cairo Press.

Mohamed Makhzangi. Translated by Denys Johnson-Davies. "The Pilot." *Under the Naked Sky.* Cairo: The American University in Cairo Press, 2000. Translation copyright © 2000 by the American University in Cairo Press.

Alia Mamdouh. Translated by Denys Johnson-Davies. "Presence of the Absent Man." *Under the Naked Sky.* Cairo: The American University in

Cairo Press, 2000. Translation copyright © 2000 by the American University in Cairo Press.

Hanna Mina. Translated by Olive E. Kenny and Lorne Kenny. *Fragments of Memory: A Story of a Syrian Family.* New York: Interlink Books, an imprint of Interlink Publishing Group, Inc., 1993. Copyright © 1975 by Hanna Mina. Translation copyright © 1993 by Salma Khadra Jayyusi (PROTA). Reprinted by permission.

Ahlam Mosteghanemi. Translated by Baria Ahmar Sreih and revised by Peter Clark. *Memory in the Flesh.* Cairo: The American University in Cairo Press, 2003. Translation copyright © 2003 by the American University in Cairo Press.

Sabri Moussa. Translated by Elizabeth Bloeger and Vivien Abadeer. Edited by William Hutchins. "Benevolence." *Egyptian Tales and Short Stories of the 1970s and 1980s.* Cairo: The American University in Cairo Press, 1987. Translation copyright © 1987 by the American University in Cairo Press.

'Abd al-Rahman Munif. Translated by Roger Allen. *Endings.* London: Quartets Books, 1988. Translation copyright © 1988 by Roger Allen.

Muhammad al Murr. Translated by Peter Clark. "Your Uncle Was a Poet." *Dubai Tales.* London: Forrest Books, 1991. Translation copyright © 1991 by Peter Clark.

Buthaina Al Nasiri. Translated by Denys Johnson-Davies. "I've Been Here Before." *Final Night: Short Stories.* Cairo: The American University in Cairo Press, 2002. Translation copyright © 2002 by the American University in Cairo Press.

Emily Nasrallah. Translated by Thuraya Khalil-Khouri. "A House Not Her Own." *A House Not Her Own: Stories from Beirut.* Charlottetown: Gynergy Books, 1992. Translation copyright © 1992 by Thuraya Khalil-Khouri.

Ibrahim Nasrallah. Translated by May Jayyusi and Jeremy Reed. *Prairies of Fever.* New York: Interlink Books, an imprint of Interlink Publishing Group, Inc., 1993. Copyright © 1985 by Ibrahim Nasrallah. Translation copyright © 1993 by Salma Khadra Jayyusi (PROTA). Reprinted by permission.

Haggag Hassan Oddoul. Translated by Anthony Calderbank. "Nights of Musk." *Nights of Musk: Stories from Old Nubia.* Cairo: The American

University in Cairo Press, 2005. Translation copyright © 2005 by the American University in Cairo Press.

Yusuf al-Qa'id. Translated by William Hutchins. "Three Meaningless Tales." *Egyptian Tales and Short Stories of the 1970s and 1980s.* Cairo: The American University in Cairo Press, 1987. Translation copyright © 1987 by the American University in Cairo Press.

Abd al-Hakim Qasim. Translated by Denys Johnson-Davies. "The Whistle." *Egyptian Short Stories.* Colorado Springs: Three Continents Press, 1978. Translation copyright © 1978 by Denys Johnson-Davies.

Somaya Ramadan. Translated by Marilyn Booth. *Leaves of Narcissus.* Cairo: The American University in Cairo Press, 2002. Translation copyright © 2002 by the American University in Cairo Press.

Alifa Rifaat. Translated by Denys Johnson-Davies. "An Incident in the Ghobashi Household." *Distant View of a Minaret and Other Stories.* London: Quartet Books, 1983. Translation copyright © 1983 by Denys Johnson-Davies.

Nawal El Saadawi. Translated by Shirley Eber. "She Has No Place in Paradise." Selected and edited by Ben Bennani. *Paintbrush: A Journal of Poetry and Translation.* Vol. 28, 2001/2002. Translation copyright © 2001 by Truman State University.

———. Translated by Sherif Hetata. *Woman at Point Zero.* London: Zed Books, 1975. Translation copyright © 1975 by Zed Books.

Tayeb Salih. Translated by Denys Johnson-Davies. *Season of Migration to the North.* London: Heinemann, 1969. Translation copyright © 1969 by Denys Johnson-Davies. Permission granted by Peters Fraser and Dunlop on behalf of Tayeb Salih.

———. Translated by Denys Johnson-Davies. *Bandarshah.* London and New York: Kegan Paul International/Paris: UNESCO Publishing, 1996. Translation copyright © 1996 by UNESCO. Permission to use this extract is granted by Peters Fraser and Dunlop on behalf of Tayeb Salih.

———. Translated by Denys Johnson-Davies. "The Cypriot Man." *Arabic Short Stories.* London: Quartet Books, 1983. Translation copyright © 1983 by Denys Johnson-Davies.

Ghada Samman. Translated by Azza Kararah. "A Gypsy without a Haven." Selected and edited by Ben Bennani. *Paintbrush: A Journal of*

Poetry and Translation. Vol. 28, 2001/2002. Originally published as "A Street Walker" in *Arabic Short Stories 1945–1965*, edited by Mahmoud Manzalaoui. Cairo: The American University in Cairo Press, 1985. Translation copyright © 1985 by the American University in Cairo Press.

Ibrahim Samouiel. Translated by Denys Johnson-Davies. "My Fellow Passenger." *Under the Naked Sky*. Cairo: The American University in Cairo Press, 2000. Translation copyright © 2000 by the American University in Cairo Press.

Habib Selmi. Translated by Denys Johnson-Davies. "Distant Seas." *Arabic Short Stories*. London: Quartet Books, 1983. Translation copyright © 1983 by Denys Johnson-Davies.

Khairy Shalaby. Translated by Denys Johnson-Davies. "The Clock." *Under the Naked Sky*. Cairo: The American University in Cairo Press, 2000. Translation copyright © 2000 by the American University in Cairo Press.

Hanan al-Shaykh. Translated by Denys Johnson-Davies. "The Persian Carpet." *Arabic Short Stories*. London: Quartet Books, 1983. Translation copyright © 1983 by Denys Johnson-Davies.

———. Translated by Catherine Cobham. *Beirut Blues*. London: Chatto and Windus, 1995. Translation copyright © 1995 by Chatto and Windus.

Miral al-Tahawy. Translated by Anthony Calderbank. *The Tent*. Cairo: The American University in Cairo Press, 1998. Translation copyright © 1998 by the American University in Cairo Press.

Bahaa Taher. Translated by Farouk Abdel Wahab. *Love in Exile*. Cairo: The American University in Cairo Press, 2002. Translation copyright © 2002 by the American University in Cairo Press.

Fuad al-Takarli. Translated by Catherine Cobham. *The Long Way Back*. Cairo: The American University in Cairo Press, 2001. Translation copyright © 2001 by the American University in Cairo Press.

Zakaria Tamer. Translated by Denys Johnson-Davies. "A Summary of What Happened to Mohammed al-Mahmoudi." *Tigers on the Tenth Day*. London: Quartet Books, 1985. Translation copyright © 1985 by Denys Johnson-Davies.

May Telmissany. Translated by Roger Allen. *Dunyazad*. London: Saqi Books, 2000. Translation copyright © 2000 by Roger Allen.

Mahmoud Teymour. Translated by Denys Johnson-Davies. "The Comedy of Death." *Atlantic Monthly Supplement*, 1956. Translation copyright © 1956 by Denys Johnson-Davies.

Abdel Salam al-Ujaili. Translated by Denys Johnson-Davies. "The Dream." *Modern Arabic Short Stories*. Cairo: The American University in Cairo Press, 1993. Translation copyright © 1967 by Denys Johnson-Davies.

Mahmoud Al-Wardani. Translated by Denys Johnson-Davies. "The Day Grandpa Came." *Under the Naked Sky*. Cairo: The American University in Cairo Press, 2000. Translation copyright © 2000 by the American University in Cairo Press.

Tahir Wattar. Translated by William Granara. *The Earthquake*. London: Saqi Books, 2000. Translation copyright © 2000 by Saqi Books.

Latifa al-Zayyat. Translated by Marilyn Booth. *The Open Door*. Cairo: The American University in Cairo Press, 2002. Translation copyright © 2002 by the American University in Cairo Press.

Mohamed Zefzaf. Translated by Denys Johnson-Davies. "Snake Hunting." *Under the Naked Sky*. Cairo: The American University in Cairo Press, 2000. Translation copyright © 2000 by the American University in Cairo Press.